I0588751

And the
Women Watch
and
Wait

And the Women Watch and Wait

A novel of
the Great War in Australia

CATHERINE MEYRICK

Courante Publishing

Copyright ©2025 Catherine Meyrick
The moral right of the author has been asserted.

All rights reserved. No part of this book may be reproduced, stored in a retrieval system, communicated or transmitted, in any form or by any means (electronic, mechanical, photocopying, recording or otherwise), without prior written permission of the copyright holder, except in the case of brief quotations embodied in critical articles and reviews.

No AI Training. Without in any way limiting the author's exclusive rights under copyright, any use of this publication to 'train' generative artificial intelligence (AI) technologies to generate text is expressly prohibited. The author reserves all rights to license uses of this work for generative AI training and development of machine learning language models.

This is a work of fiction. References to historical events, real people or places are used fictitiously. Other names, characters, places and incidents are the product of the author's imagination and any resemblance to actual persons, living or dead, events or locales is entirely coincidental.

Published by Courante Publishing, Melbourne, Australia.
courantepublishing@gmail.com

Cover Design by Dee Dee Book Covers
Images courtesy of the State Library Victoria
– Mary Gertrude Cooney by Vincent W. Kelly c.1917-1924
– Horse & cart, Mallee tree by Wilf Henty c.1901
Shutterstock Images
– Scene just before the evacuation at Anzac. Australian troops charging near a Turkish trench. 1915. Photographer unknown.
– Australian landscape walking trail by Mastersky

A catalogue record for this book is available from the National Library of Australia.

ISBN-13: 978-0-648250876
ISBN: 0648250873

This book is written in Australian English, both formal and vernacular, and uses Australian grammar, spelling and publishing conventions.

There are those at home, with cheerful smiles
Yet whose hearts are like to break,
For a woman's lot is to watch and wait
And stifle the grief that stirs,
While the man strides forth in careless strength,
A-swagger in boots and spurs.

from **A Soliloquy**
by Lance Corporal William O'Brien
1st Light Horse Brigade

Map of Coburg

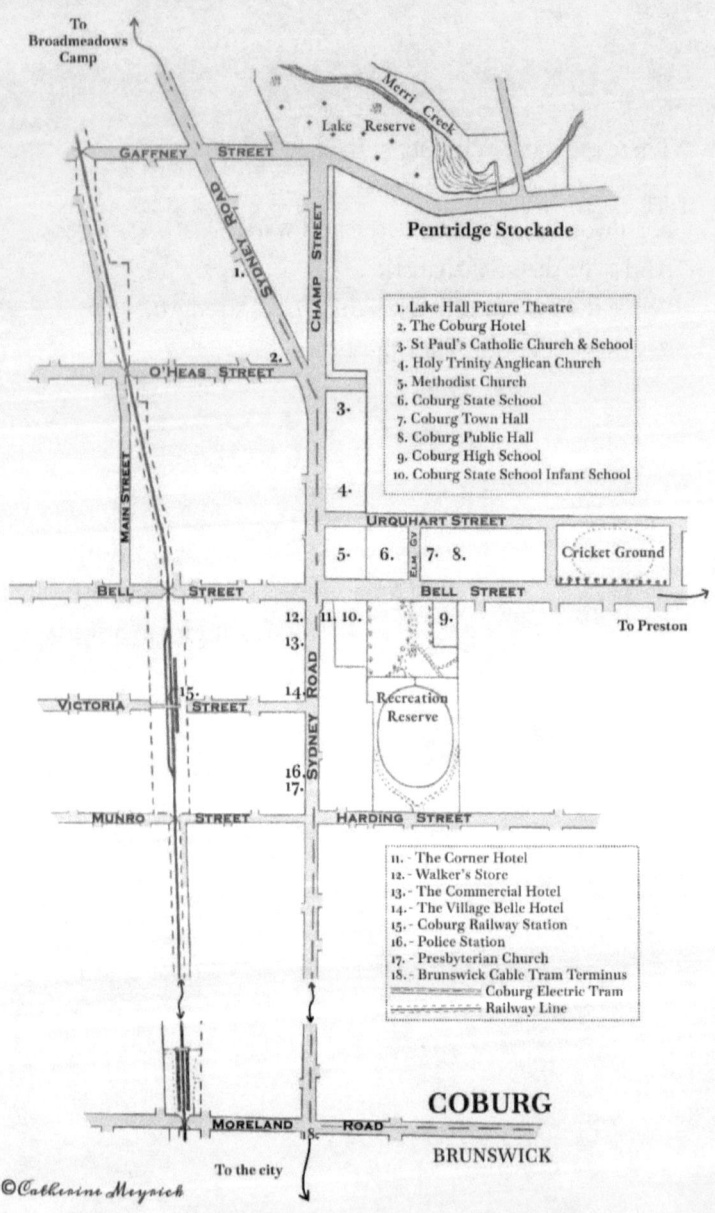

To
Broadmeadows
Camp

Merri Creek

Lake Reserve

GAFFNEY STREET

SYDNEY ROAD

CHAMP STREET

Pentridge Stockade

1.

O'HEAS STREET

2.

1. Lake Hall Picture Theatre
2. The Coburg Hotel
3. St Paul's Catholic Church & School
4. Holy Trinity Anglican Church
5. Methodist Church
6. Coburg State School
7. Coburg Town Hall
8. Coburg Public Hall
9. Coburg High School
10. Coburg State School Infant School

3.

MAIN STREET

4.

URQUHART STREET

5. 6. ELM. GV 7. 8.

Cricket Ground

BELL STREET

BELL STREET

To Preston

12. 11. 10.

13.

9.

VICTORIA STREET

15.

14.

SYDNEY ROAD

Recreation
Reserve

16.
17.

MUNRO STREET

HARDING STREET

11. - The Corner Hotel
12. - Walker's Store
13. - The Commercial Hotel
14. - The Village Belle Hotel
15. - Coburg Railway Station
16. - Police Station
17. - Presbyterian Church
18. - Brunswick Cable Tram Terminus
        Coburg Electric Tram
        Railway Line

MORELAND ROAD

COBURG

BRUNSWICK

To the city

©Catherine Meyrick

1914

The paper ribbons bridging the water between the staying and departing stretched to their utmost as the singing excited crowd followed the slowly moving steamer right to the pier head. Then the slender links broke one by one and the flagship, finally released, was on her way to war.

Departure of HMAT *Ulysses* from Port Melbourne
on 22 December 1914
The Argus 3 February 1915 p.9

1

November 1914

Light streamed through the glorious stained-glass windows making a dappled mosaic of colour across the white altar cloth. Kate stepped forward and knelt at the altar rail. Peace washed through her as she stared up into the placid marble face of the statue of the Mother of God set in the blue and gold painted niche above the altar.

But it was only for a moment—thoughts of Jack flooded back. He said, they all said, it would be over in six months. They were anxious to be off, afraid they would miss out on being part of this great adventure. She prayed they were right and by this time next year they would be home and she and Jack would be married.

She closed her eyes and recited St Patrick's Breastplate, changed so she could say it for Jack.

Christ be with him, Christ within him...

Her prayer finished, Kate rose and gazed around the Lady Chapel. It was a jewel box of colour, the walls and ceiling painted in rich yellows, greens and reds; decorated with swirls, white lilies and, in the shadows of the vaulted ceiling, angels.

She went to the bank of votive candles flickering on the brass stand near the archway to the nave of the church. Taking a thruppenny bit from her handbag, she dropped it in the collection box and picked three candles from the tray beneath the stand. She lit the candles and placed them in a row—each flame carrying a murmured prayer.

Glancing back to the statue, she whispered, 'Holy Mother, watch over them all.'

The church was hushed despite the number of people coming and going—to confession, to kneel and pray, or simply to sit for a moment of peace apart from the world.

Kate slipped into the pew beside Aunty Mary, who was kneeling, her head bowed as the beads of her rosary slipped through her fingers. She knew her aunt was praying for her cousins, Brendan and Vince, already sailing towards the war in Europe.

Kate gazed towards the comforting red glow of the sanctuary lamp suspended from the arched ceiling near the altar. She knew she should slide to her knees and pray but she couldn't help but stare around. The church was more richly decorated than the churches she was used to at Briagolong and at Maffra, from the ornate stencilling on the walls of the Lady Chapel to the large Stations of the Cross with their golden background. Statues stood in niches: St Francis in whose honour the church was named, the Sacred Heart, a crowned Madonna in a gilded blue robe. A vast painting of the crucifixion hung high behind the marble altar where the golden-doored tabernacle stood beneath a small dome held up by pillars of red marble. This church was every bit as beautiful as her father had said.

Her prayers finished, Aunty Mary slipped her rosary beads into her handbag and nodded at Kate. They moved into the main aisle and, facing the altar, genuflected.

Their foreheads still damp from the holy water they had blessed themselves with as they left, they walked through the church gate and out into the hurry and rush of the city of Melbourne.

Kate craned her neck, staring up at the buildings, barely noticing as they turned into Elizabeth Street. The clock in the Post Office tower ahead of them chimed the half-hour.

'Stop it, Katie, everyone will be thinking you're just down from the country.'

'Well, I am.' Kate laughed. 'The city's so big. And there are so many people.'

The streets were busy—carts, drays and horse-drawn vans; traps and buggies; cable trams and more motor cars than Kate had seen in her whole life. People crowded the footpaths but it was the fashionable women among them, the bright colours of their outfits that caught Kate's eye: deep blues and dark rose, burnt orange, magenta and jade green. And the hats! Not only the usual broad or narrow brimmed hats trimmed with flowers, feathers, or satin and velvet ribbon, but asymmetrical almost brimless creations with large stiff bows sweeping skyward. And although Kate felt nondescript in her dark skirt, pale blue blouse and modest hat, she knew she was going to love living in Melbourne.

There were soldiers in the streets too. Surely, they were all meant to be in camp training at this time of day. Her heart gave a little leap. Perhaps Jack was somewhere here. Perhaps she would run into him.

'Just along here,' Aunty Mary said.

They turned into a narrow street and, a few shops on, Aunty led Kate into a tea room.

A waitress in a smart black gown with a white apron and cap seated them at a table by the window. Once she had taken their order for a pot of tea and cake, Aunty removed her dark gloves and bent forward, sniffing the carnation in the specimen vase at the centre of the table.

'Ah, they don't have the scent like those at home.'

'Do you miss Ireland?' Kate asked.

'I did when I first arrived, but rarely now. I've spent more than half my life here and it is here those who mean most to me are.'

The pot of tea and the sugar-sprinkled cake arrived promptly and Aunty poured. She took a small bite of the teacake. 'Hmmm, not as good as mine.'

Kate laughed softly. 'Nor Mum's.'

'Still, 'tis a pleasure to be waited on now and again.' Aunty reached across the table and squeezed Kate's hand. 'I am so glad you're here, my treasure. The house has been empty without the boys.'

She picked up her teacup and sipped.

'While you are here, would you fancy serving in the shop too?'

'Ooh yes. I'd love to.'

Kate thrilled at the idea. This last week had been a whirl of so many new things. For the first time in her life, she had travelled alone. But could it really be counted as alone when her mother had arranged it all? At the Maffra railway station, Mum had seated Kate in a carriage with an older couple, almost telling them Kate's life story, how she was going to Melbourne to stay with her aunt whose two sons had left with the first contingent of the Australian Imperial Force to go and fight the Germans. The woman had talked, almost without drawing breath, as the countryside flew by, giving Kate advice on everything from how to make over an old hat to putting forward young men in their place. She took Kate under her wing, making sure when they arrived at Flinders Street Station that it truly was Aunty Mary she was leaving Kate with.

'God love them,' Aunty had said with a laugh when Kate later explained who they were.

'Will you look at that?' Aunty Mary nodded out the window as a soldier strolled by, a young woman walking close, her arm through his. 'Poor lass, she'll not be leaving hold of him until the boat sails. Just married too, by the glitter of her ring.' She looked across at Kate. 'Vincent wanted to marry young Reenie Casey, though to be honest, I think it was more the other way around. You met her Sunday last, after Mass—the girl in the red velvet hat. I told him there was time enough for that when he came back. He gave her a pretty brooch which, despite her smiles, disappointed her. When you marry you need time together, not a few days here and there followed by who knows how many months apart.'

Kate was barely listening caught by the thought that she and Jack could marry before he left.

Hemmed in by the crowd, Kate watched as the long column of recruits marched up Sydney Road. Fit looking men from all walks of life. The bulk of them were in their twenties but there were many who were older and some, too, who were smooth-faced and looked barely old enough to wield a razor. Most were dressed in their civilian clothes—office workers in suits and good hats, among them one or two straw boaters. Many more were in their working clothes, not their Sunday best, wearing battered hats, a few with caps, most carrying small suitcases, haversacks, or even swags slung across their shoulders. A handful were already in uniform. Some marched smartly, backs straight and heads erect, others doggedly as if the ten miles from the recruiting office in the city to the training camp at Broadmeadows was a test of endurance. For yet others it was as if they were off to a picnic, ambling along, gazing at the shops and houses on the roadside, waving to the crowds cheering them on. Among the knots of young women watching, one or two blew kisses. One cheeky fellow broke ranks and helped himself to as many kisses as he could before he was hauled back by his mates. A swarm of boys, and a few younger girls, ran beside the marching recruits. There was a thrill in the warm afternoon air, an atmosphere of excitement. This was the greatest adventure of their lives.

A boy rushed past Kate to get onto the road, dragging her string bag along her arm as he went. She pulled it back, thinking she should get back to Aunty's and get the corned beef and chops she had bought into the ice box before they spoiled in the heat.

She pushed her way through the crowd to Aunty's shop.

The door was wide open and Aunty's voice carried out to the street. 'You're far too young.'

Gus, the delivery boy, was loading parcels into his basket. He stopped and stood to his full height. 'Look at me, I'd pass for eighteen.'

'But you are only sixteen.'

Kate glanced at him as she passed through. He was already well on his way to six foot and, no doubt, if a recruiting officer wanted to believe he was eighteen, he would be. Running the deliveries for Aunty Mary was one of the various jobs Gus had been doing since he was fourteen. Some of them, Aunty suspected, were not quite legal. He had a job on Saturday afternoons he never quite explained with one of the local barbers who was reputed to be an unregistered bookie. Aunty had said to Kate that, with the way Gus had sprung up, she was surprised he hadn't already found himself a man's job.

'Even if you say you are eighteen, you will still need your parents' permission,' Aunty finished with the air of someone closing her argument.

Kate walked through to the kitchen. She put the meat in the ice-box, washed her hands and, tying on a large blue apron, went back into the shop.

She breathed in, savouring the mixture of scents—spices, pepper, mustard, nutmeg and cinnamon, coffee and cocoa, cured sausages, soaps. It was an Aladdin's cave of groceries. Cakes and biscuits in square tins; cans of jams and fruit; tins of ham, and fish, and condensed milk filled the shelves that stretched to the ceiling, along with the boxes of soap and starch, packets of matches and of tea, as well as bottles of vinegar and sauces. A basket of eggs sat on the counter alongside the jars of confectionery. Already Kate knew the items' places on the neat shelves and their prices too.

She took her place beside Aunty Mary at the counter, a smile ready for the next person to walk in, a smile she had no need to force.

Gus was standing by the door. 'He shot through weeks ago. We don't know whether he's enlisted or has gone bush.' There was a bitterness in his voice. 'No loss—he was only good for boozing and battering us around.' He adjusted the basket of deliveries on his hip. 'Mum will sign the papers. It's better pay than I get with my delivery rounds, and she'll get my allotment regular so there'll be nothing for her to worry about.'

Aunty groaned. 'Ah, Gus, it is dreadful it has come to this. I'll keep you in my prayers.'

'When I come back,' Gus grinned broadly, 'I'll share a glass of porter with you, Mrs Burke. Celebrate my return.'

'Away with you, Fergus Aloysius Kelly. And you who took the pledge not to drink alcohol only two years ago when you were Confirmed.'

With a wink at Kate, Gus left the shop whistling. He had a swagger beyond his years.

Aunty turned to Kate. 'Old Bridie Johnson was in earlier and had me get down one of every tin of fruit on the shelf. And the questions! *This pineapple, can I make a pie with it? Now, will it give me dyspepsia? I'm a martyr to the dyspepsia.* And, of course, all she left with was a small bag of lemon drops.'

Kate grinned. Aunty's imitation had Mrs Johnson to a T.

Aunty pointed to the bare spaces on the shelf, halfway up the wall. 'Would you mind putting them back for me?'

She watched as Kate climbed the ladder. 'Brendan used to do the climbing for me. I'm getting too old for it all.' She turned away. 'Ah, Mr McGregor. Do you have a fine bundle of letters for me today?'

'Only two, I'm afraid Mrs Burke. One for you and one for a Miss Catherine Burke, care of you.'

Kate now stood beside her aunt.

'And this would be Miss Catherine Burke?' The postman, a short red-faced man who fitted his uniform a little too well, cast his eye over Kate. 'And isn't she the picture of what you must have been in your youth?'

'Now, is that very likely,' Aunty said without smiling, 'with Kate being the daughter of my Michael's brother? She is staying with me for a few months, until the boys come home.'

'And the sooner that is the better.' He gave Aunty her letter but kept hold of Kate's. 'This one has a Broadmeadows postmark.' He raised an eyebrow. 'A letter from your sweetheart?'

Kate's face blazed red. She blinked fast, not wanting to answer.

'That's enough, Mr McGregor.' Aunty, already a tall woman, stood erect and seemed to tower over the postman. 'Give Kate her letter, she has work to do in the house.'

'It was only a bit of teasing, Mrs Burke.' He handed the letter to Kate.

'Kate's a young lady from the country, not used to rough city ways.'

'My apologies. I'd best be on my rounds.' He tipped his cap and scurried out the door.

'There's no harm in him, Aunty said, once he was out of sight. 'He tries to be the charmer—knows the pretty words but lacks the charm himself.' She turned to face Kate. 'Now go out the back and read your letter.'

~

The backyard was quiet except for the buzzing of a solitary bee in the pot of lavender outside the washhouse. Kate sat on the wooden bench on the verandah and carefully ran her finger beneath the flap of the envelope. Inside was a single sheet of thin blue paper.

My darling Kate,

It was grand to get your letter. Coburg is only 4 miles away, close enough for me to visit you easily. Knowing you are waiting at the end, I bet I could run it in not much more than 20 minutes.

They are working us hard at marching and drill and all sorts of manoeuvres. I am as tired at the end of the day as when we are reaping at home. They are a good group of blokes here. The tucker is not bad but nowhere near as good as Mum's. Not sure when we will be going, not too long, I hope.

I managed to get a leave pass for Sunday after Church Parade. Thank your Aunty for the invitation. Would she mind if I brought a mate? He has no family to visit him.

I can barely wait to see you.

With all my love,

Jack.

Scrawled across the bottom of the page were three big Xes.

Kate closed her eyes and put her lips on each of them. How she wished Jack was here with her. To sit beside him holding hands, to rest her head against his shoulder, and those quick kisses... She sighed. This war, she hoped it finished soon so they could get on with living the life they were meant to have.

She read the letter three more times, folded it carefully and placed it in the pocket of her apron.

Back in the shop, she said, 'Aunty Mary, Jack said to thank you for the invitation, he will be coming on Sunday. He wants to know if he could bring a friend, someone with no family here.'

'Of course, the young man can come. There is always room for one more at my table.' Aunty stared at Kate, the hint of a frown on her face. 'You didn't say Jack Sheehan was your sweetheart, simply a friend from home. There's been no mention of him in your mother's letters.'

'His family's farm is next to ours and we've known each other all our lives but I'm the only one he dances with these days.'

'In that case,' Aunty laughed, 'you are practically married.'

If only that were true.

3

Kate and Aunty Mary had been to early Mass at St Paul's, a brisk ten minutes' walk up Sydney Road, and were back in good time to get to work on the Sunday dinner. Kate had prepared the vegetables, now roasting with the leg of lamb. The aroma filled the kitchen, and leaked beyond the closed kitchen door to the rest of the house. The dining table was set and Aunty was sitting calmly in the kitchen having a cup of tea.

Kate was a bundle of nerves, starting at every noise in the street.

'Stop your pacing, Kate.' Aunty put her teacup down. 'You will have me as restless too. Go and change into whatever finery you want to impress this boy.'

Kate went to her room and put on her best blouse. Mum had helped her sew it last summer. It was made of pale blue voile with three quarter-sleeves, pintucks at the shoulders, a row of buttons down the back. Embroidered daisies were sprinkled across the front. Beneath it she wore an opaque high-necked camisole. The blouse had been Kate's favourite, until now. She wished she had a new dress in a striking colour like those worn by the fashionable women she had seen in the city.

She stood in front of the tall chest of drawers, angled the oval mirror on top, and tidied her hair. The sun shining through the window glistened golden on her light brown hair. Kate wished it always looked like that. She wished her grey-blue eyes were a deeper blue or a pretty green like her mother's and her sister Hannah's. And she wished this room, her cousins' bedroom, had a dressing table where she could sit and arrange her hair, or a long mirror that would give her a good view of herself. She heard her mother's voice, *Stop it Kate—be glad for what you do have.*

Finally, satisfied with her hair, she took Jack's letter from the drawer of the bedside table and sat on the edge of the bed rereading it. She had it off by heart.

She started, her heart lurching at the loud rap on the house door.

'Will you get that, Kate?' Aunty Mary called from the kitchen.

Kate looked into the mirror and pinched her cheeks, pressing her lips tight together. She settled her shoulders as she walked to the door which opened onto the side street.

She gave up trying to control her smile as she threw it open.

And there he was—a soldier in his khaki uniform. He seemed taller and broader and, impossibly, so much more handsome than Kate's memories. Beneath his peaked cap were those laughing blue eyes.

A joy that mirrored hers lit up his face.

He stepped into the house and caught her tight around the waist, swinging her off her feet. As he lowered her down, he kissed her.

It was no more than a brush of his lips, but the scent of him, the pressure of his arms around her and she could barely breathe, her legs almost not strong enough to hold her upright. She wanted to laugh, to cry at the delight of him.

Jack moved away from her but kept tight hold of her hand.

Another young soldier had come into the hallway behind Jack— as tall, darker hair, perhaps younger, perhaps not.

'Kate, this is Bert Wilson, a mate of mine.'

Bert took off his cap. 'A pleasure to meet you at last, Miss Burke. Jack talks about you all the time.'

'Pleased to meet you, Bert,' Kate said, smiling happily. 'And do call me Kate.'

'Kate, bring your young man inside,' Aunty Mary called as she came along the passage. 'You can't be doing your courting on the doorstep for all to see.'

Kate blushed and glanced up at Jack who seemed untroubled by the attention.

'Now, you must be Jack Sheehan by the grip you have on our Katie's hand.'

'I am.' Jack grinned at her. 'It is a pleasure to meet you, Mrs Burke.'

'The pleasure is mine entirely, Jack.' She looked towards Bert who was staring up at the framed picture of the Sacred Heart that hung opposite the door—the first thing a visitor saw when he or she entered the house.

Bert held out his hand. 'Albert Wilson, Mrs Burke. Friends call me Bert. Thank you for inviting me.'

'You are indeed welcome, Bert. Now come into the dining room and sit yourselves down. Kate will get you a drink. I have a couple of bottles of beer in. My boys like a beer with their Sunday dinner.'

'Water will be fine for me,' Bert said. 'I don't drink alcohol.'

'Would you like a splash of raspberry vinegar in it? It is the last of the vinegar I bottled earlier in the year.'

'Thank you, but I wouldn't want to take the last of it.'

'Now, don't worry about that—there will be plenty more early next year. And you can call in and have another drop when you get back.'

~

Seated at the head of the table, Aunty Mary said, 'I don't know if Kate has told you but my two, Brendan and Vincent, left three weeks ago. Perhaps when you get over there, you will meet them.'

Both Jack and Bert murmured in answer, intent on their meal, shovelling away as if they hadn't eaten for a week.

Aunty laughed. 'Aren't they feeding you properly at the camp?'

Jack swallowed his mouthful. 'We get enough to eat, but it's nothing like this.'

Bert nodded furiously as he helped himself to more potatoes from the serving dish on the table.

When Bert had cleaned his plate, Aunty and Kate took the plates and serving dishes away and brought out the bread and butter pudding.

Kate noticed Aunty had given Bert a larger serving than the rest of them.

'Help yourselves to the cream.' Aunty nodded toward the jug Kate had placed in the centre of the table.

Bert needed no encouragement.

Kate thought, if left alone, he might have licked his bowl clean. His manners at the table were of the sort that her mother sharply reprimanded her brothers for—he had eaten from his knife and rested his elbows on the table.

Bert placed his spoon in the empty bowl and sat back in his chair. 'That was the best meal I've ever eaten.'

Aunty raised her eyebrows. 'But not as good as your mother's cooking.'

Bert said nothing in reply.

'Where are you from, Bert?' she asked.

'Hobart. But I've been working in Victoria for a few years.'

'And your family?'

'All gone, bar an older sister,' he said without a touch of regret.

Aunty Mary sighed, as if feeling the loss for him. And in that moment Kate could see Aunty Mary had taken another boy under her care.

'I am so sad to hear that. You are welcome to come here any time.'

'That is kind of you, Mrs Burke.'

Aunty got up from the table. 'A cup of tea, boys?'

Jack shook his head, 'I don't think I could fit it in.'

'Me neither,' Bert said. 'The way I am at the moment, Jack will need to borrow a wheelbarrow to get me back to the camp.'

'You've no one to blame but yourself,' Jack laughed. 'Didn't I say Kate's aunt would give you a proper taste of Irish hospitality?'

'You did.' He stood and pushed his chair under the table. 'I'll help with the dishes.'

Aunty's eyes widened in surprise. 'You will do no such thing Albert Wilson—you are my guest.' She smiled at him. 'But thank you for the offer.'

'Leave that, Kate.' Aunty Mary took the stack of bowls from her. 'You should show these young men the sights of Coburg.'

'I will but I'll help with the dishes first.'

Aunty shook her head. 'Off with you now and get your coat and hat.'

'The least we can do is carry the dishes out.' Bert looked across at Jack. 'Get up off your behind and help you lazy ... fellow.'

As Kate walked towards her room, she heard Aunty say, 'The municipal band is playing at the cricket ground. You should go and listen to that. And keep together, it is easy enough to get lost when you don't know a place well.'

Kate thought there was little chance of them getting lost— Coburg's streets were mostly straight lines and right angles.

They strolled along Sydney Road towards Bell Street, the footpaths still shining from a light shower earlier in the afternoon, Kate arm in arm with Jack, Bert at the other side of him.

Coburg was nowhere near as busy as the city but it bustled in its own way. A town on the northern edge of Melbourne, the streets away from the main road and the railway line were slowly filling up with newly built houses. A horse tram ran down to Brunswick where a much faster cable tram went into the city. The road was lined with buildings of all descriptions, some decades old, including several hotels, the police station, the Presbyterian church and the Post Office, and shops of all sorts. Grand buildings with ornate mouldings and parapets atop the upper storey, some with recessed balconies and verandas trimmed with wrought-iron lacework, stood alongside more modest single-storied houses and shops like Aunty Mary's. These shops provided everything a person could want from confectionery and ladies draperies to pots and pans and sewerage pipes. Yet, even in Sydney Road, there were still vacant blocks. It was a growing place, a place of new opportunities, and it thrilled Kate to be here and to be part of it.

'Looks like you're the chaperone, Bert,' Jack grinned. 'Here to keep me out of mischief.'

Bert rolled his eyes. 'Given some of your antics, I'll have my work cut out.'

Kate glanced across at Bert. 'What sort of antics?'

'Well, for example, he...' Bert jerked his head towards Jack, '...decided the blokes in our tent needed to prepare themselves for life in France, so he got hold of several bottles of wine from an old feller selling from a cart in Camp Road. If that wasn't enough warning, this wine was in lemonade bottles. They guzzled it down and the next day had a fine dose of the Jimmy Britts.' Bert stopped, his eyes wide. 'Oh, sorry Kate, excuse my French.'

Jack laughed. 'I doubt that sort of French will get you far with the Mam'selles when we get to France.'

'Your French is no better, more likely to get you on a charge.'

This was a Jack Kate had never seen before—more high-spirited, at ease away from the watching eyes of home.

With the sun shining now, there were plenty of others out for a Sunday stroll, families with children, couples, girls in twos and threes, a number of soldiers. Some of the young women gave Jack and Bert the glad-eye. Jack seemed not to notice. Kate was aware, too, of some of the soldiers doing the same to her. It was as if the uniform made them bolder. One or two greeted Jack and Bert and stopped to be introduced.

They decided not to go looking for the band.

'We wake up to a band playing every morning,' Bert said.

'And if we are truly lucky, it's a Scottish pipe band,' Jack added.

Bert groaned.

They crossed Bell Street and walked on past the churches: the modest Methodist set behind a paling fence lined with pines trees; Holy Trinity, the Anglican church, with its tall spire; and then St Paul's Catholic church with its presbytery and its school run by the Sisters of Mercy.

The high bluestone wall of Pentridge Prison ran behind both the Anglican and the Catholic churches. Once past St Paul's, the prison jutted out towards the street, a fence of iron pickets keeping the public away from the prison wall. Sentry boxes stood at the top of the towers built at intervals along the wall, warders on guard within them. The heavy entrance gate was set into an arch beneath the central clocktower.

At the end of the prison, they crossed the road to Merri Creek. Beside it, a reserve had been fenced off, shrubs planted and paths laid. Near the bridge behind the prison, excavation of the creek bed was underway. Aunty Mary had said there were plans to erect a weir there to create an ornamental lake. It would make this a delightful place to stroll on Sunday afternoons.

Jack and Kate left Bert at the road and slowly made their way down to the creek bank.

On the opposite shore, an ibis flew down and landed in a tree.

Bert walked the distance to the stone bridge. He stopped when he reached it, lit a cigarette, leant his elbows on the parapet and gazed out at the creek.

Jack looked towards him. 'He's a bit far away to keep his eye on us from there.'

'So, if we were to step beneath that willow along the bank, he wouldn't notice or rush down with a big stick?' Kate laughed.

'Katie,' Jack's grin lit his eyes, 'what are you suggesting?'

'Nothing,' Kate gasped. 'That wasn't what I meant at all.' She blushed, realising it did sound that way. She wasn't naturally so forward.

Jack bent towards her, smiling.

She closed her eyes waiting for his kiss, but nothing came.

She opened them and followed Jack's gaze.

A small family group were standing at the water's edge not far from them. The creek was not a private place.

Waterfowl floated serenely on the water, an unseen flurry of activity beneath—the way Kate felt at this moment.

'Are you enjoying yourself out at the camp?'

'Overall. They work us hard pretty much from sunrise to sunset. I'm learning things I never thought I'd need to know. They're a good bunch of blokes but there are one or two who would shake the socks off you while you slept. The sort you wouldn't want to introduce to your mother, much less your sweetheart.'

He turned to Kate and took both her hands in his. 'I've missed you so much, Kate. The first thing I'll do when I get back is marry you.' He paused, his brow wrinkled. 'If that's what you want.'

'You know it's what I want.' She laughed. It was all she had ever dreamt of.

It wasn't ladylike, and she knew her mother would have a fit if she knew, but she had to say it. 'Why can't we marry now? It will be weeks before you go.'

There was longing in Jack's sigh. 'I'd need not only your father's permission but my Commanding Officer's too. I doubt I'd get it as I reckon we will be gone by Christmas. And we'd have barely any time together—I'd have to stay living in camp. And it would be hard for you if you ended up with a child.'

'I can't think of anything better.' She blinked back sudden tears. 'And I would go home to Mum and Dad, or to your parents if that was what they wanted.'

He put his fingers against her lips. 'I want to be around when our first child is born, I want to watch him grow. I don't want another man raising my child.'

Kate gasped. 'Don't say that!' A shiver ran along her spine. 'You *are* coming back.' As long as she said it, it was true.

'Yes. I am coming back to you.' He squeezed her hand. 'And we will have the biggest wedding the district has ever seen.'

Kate forced a smile. Her mother had no good word to say about her own stepfather but, at least, as Mum had been twelve when her father died, she did have memories of him. Something their child would not if she and Jack were to rush into marrying. Kate shook her head to clear it of the ridiculous thought—Jack *was* coming back.

He turned at the sound of a shrill whistle. Bert was on the path above them, making a mime of pointing to his watch.

'Bert wants to be back by teatime. He's keen on his meals though you can't tell. He's as lean as a whippet.'

'Aunty wouldn't mind if you stayed for tea.'

'I'd love to but I don't want to impose on our first visit.'

They walked slowly back up the slope, hand in hand, stretching out their time together.

Bert was now talking to another soldier. A dark-haired young woman wearing a plush velvet hat was on the soldier's arm—Vince's sweetheart, Reenie.

Reenie smiled brightly. 'It's lovely to see you, Kate.' She looked around. 'Is Mrs Burke here too?'

'Aunty Mary's at home, resting after dinner.'

'Kate, this is my brother Pat,' Reenie said.

Kate quickly put aside the barely formed suspicion she had entertained at the sight of the young man on Reenie's arm.

Not as tall as Jack and Bert, Pat Casey was dark-haired and good-looking like his sister. Even when he wasn't smiling, he looked as if he saw humour in the world around him.

They went back together, past the prison. Reenie had wound her arm through Kate's, the men walking behind them.

'You should come to our next Children of Mary meeting.'

'The young women's group? I'm not a member. The closest one was in Sale, nearly thirty miles from our farm.'

'Ours is a very friendly group—there are over a hundred of us. We meet once a week in the schoolroom for prayers and talks on faith and life. There's a monthly Communion when we wear our veils and blue capes. And we do have a lot of fun too. We run a stall at the church fetes and occasionally a concert or a euchre night and a dance to raise funds for the parish, sometimes together with the Catholic Young Men's Society.' Reenie barely drew breath. 'The Preston group held a ball last June. Vince took me. The girls wore the loveliest dresses. Mine was blue crepe de chine with a white ninon overdress sprinkled with silver bugles.'

'That sounds beautiful,' Kate said. 'I thought the Children of Mary was only for girls who had just left school.'

'Most stay until they marry. We have some single ladies who are in their thirties and forties.' She looked at Kate, her brow furrowed. 'How old are you?'

'I'm twenty.' Was adding four months to her age really a lie?

'And I suppose you'll get married as soon as Jack gets back.' She turned towards Kate, her eyes sparkling. 'He is handsome.'

Kate smiled but didn't reply. She didn't want to talk of her dreams with someone she barely knew.

Reenie pressed on. 'A few of us get together once a week to knit socks for the soldiers. You should join us.'

Kate could see the eagerness in Reenie's pretty face. She seemed so keen to make Kate a friend. And, Kate supposed, Reenie saw her as another connection to Vince.

'I'd like that.'

Reenie and her brother left them at Bell Street. Bert and Jack walked Kate back to her aunt's.

'We'll be off now, Mrs Burke,' Jack said. 'Thank you for dinner.'

'Yes, thank you,' Bert added. 'It was a feast.'

'Next Sunday, Kate and I could come out to the camp and bring a picnic lunch.' Aunty Mary looked from one to the other. 'I went out one Sunday to see my boys. We had a wonderful day.'

Jack's eyes lit up. 'And, Kate, I can show you around.'

Kate smiled. She would happily let him show her the latrines if it meant spending more time with him.

After saying goodbye to Aunty Mary, they left by the garden gate. Bert led the way, Kate hand in hand with Jack, behind him.

'I'll see if I can get leave to visit again.' Jack stopped at the corner of the shop. 'They ration it out, otherwise the camp would be deserted on Sundays and in the evening.'

His goodbye was no more than the touch of his lips as his fingers slid from Kate's grasp.

She watched as he and Bert started off up Sydney Road.

Jack turned and, walking backwards, blew kisses to her. He was still the handsome silly boy she had loved since she was eight and he had bloodied the nose of a boy who had pulled her hair. Jack was the boy she would love always.

5

Much as Kate enjoyed working in Aunty's shop, she could barely wait for the week to pass. When Sunday finally arrived, it brought a perfect day—sunny with not a cloud in the sky. Aunty had arranged a ride out in Mr O'Meara's van. He sold fruit and confectionery from a small shop not far from hers. He had been going out each Sunday to sell fruit to the soldiers and their visitors on the roadside, along from the entrance to the camp.

Kate, squeezed in between Aunty and Mr O'Meara, gazed at the countryside as the horse trotted up Sydney Road. The houses spread out soon after they passed the Coburg Hotel, becoming golden paddocks broken by stately gum trees. The road was busy with all manner of buggies and carts, charabancs both horse-drawn and motorised, kicking up great clouds of dust.

They turned into Camp Road, the Campbellfield Hotel marking the corner. It was the place where many soldiers went to drink since they had closed the wet canteen at the camp. Aunty had said she didn't understand why they made it hard for the soldiers to have a well-earned drink or two after a long day's work.

The camp was on slightly higher ground than the road. As they approached, the white tents were bright in the sunshine. Mr O'Meara stopped the van at the side of the road and got out to set up his stall. There were others already there selling everything from peanuts to ice-cream and buns, as well as lemonade and ginger beer. Not far from the camp, a farmer had opened up a paddock to allow visitors to park their buggies and motor cars.

People were arriving in both directions—from Sydney Road and from Broadmeadows where they had travelled from the city by train. They streamed through the gate, past the sentry standing tall and alert, a bayonet fixed to his rifle. Family and friends passed him in twos and threes or larger groups, carrying parcels and baskets as

Kate and Aunty were. Some visitors had no connection to any of the soldiers and came to look around, taking pride in Australia's army of volunteer soldiers and the part they would soon play in defending the British Empire. Others, knowing there were soldiers without family to visit them, came to offer fruit, cake and a few friendly words to ease the loneliness of those men who were already far from home.

Soldiers lined the roadway beyond the entrance, searching for familiar faces; the visitors scanned their faces as intently.

Kate saw Jack as soon as she and Aunty went through the gate. It was too far away to see his features, but she instantly knew it was him. He pushed through the crowd towards her. She lowered her basket and was in his arms. He lifted her up and she gazed into those vivid blue eyes. For two breathless moments his lips were on hers, then she was back on solid earth. She did not dare look at Aunty Mary.

Jack picked up Kate's basket. 'G'day, Mrs Burke. Let me carry your basket.' He walked between them. 'Should we have lunch first, or will I show you around?'

'Good day, Jack.' Aunty said, the hint of a smile on her lips. 'Lunch might be best. We don't want to be carrying the baskets with us all day.'

'I could put them in the tent but one of the other blokes might help himself.'

'There is plenty to go around.'

They made their way to the edge of the camp, to the rows of pine trees along the boundary where they could sit in the shade. There were others there already with the same idea—family groups of wife and children, the father in uniform; others with a brother or cousin who had enlisted; a few couples not long married or with an infant in arms; and some, like Kate, there with their sweethearts.

'Will Bert be coming?' Aunty asked.

'I told him to head over this way when he was ready. As soon as you open the baskets, he'll be here like a shot.'

Kate laid the checked blanket she had been carrying on the ground. Jack put the baskets down and stretched out at one side, resting on his elbows. Kate sat beside him, her legs neatly arranged beneath her skirt, as Aunty busied herself setting out the feast.

Jack watched her. 'You have enough in there to feed a small army.'

'Better too much than not enough. I'll be leaving anything not eaten for you to have later.'

Looking at the well-stocked baskets, no matter how hungry they were, it would be impossible to even eat half of what Aunty had brought—cold chicken, boiled eggs, ham and mustard sandwiches, fruit scones and jam tarts, an entire butter cake, apples and a bag of plump cherries. She had included a thermos flask of hot sweet tea.

'You must have been baking the whole week,' Jack said.

'Only the last couple of days. Kate helped me.'

'What did you make, Kate?'

'The easy things: the boiled eggs, the ham sandwiches and the fruit scones.'

He helped himself to a ham sandwich.

'Good afternoon, Mrs Burke.' Bert stood in front of them.

'Bert, 'tis a pleasure to see you. Sit yourself down and eat up.'

Jack swallowed his mouthful and tilted his head towards Kate, still looking at Bert. 'Didn't I tell you, he'd be here as soon as the basket was opened.'

'You can talk, lying there, already stuffing your face.'

'Is the food here very bad?' Kate asked.

'No.' Bert helped himself to a chicken leg. 'It's the sameness of it all. Though, we have probably got fussy. There have been times in the past when I would have thought I was in heaven if I'd had what they serve us here.'

Kate sat in the shade, close to Jack, watching the other soldiers and their visitors. She had never been among so many people before. The camp looked neat and orderly despite the crowds. The tents, Bell tents Jack had called them, stood like rows of pristine napkins twirled into conical shapes. In one area, great heavy guns with large wheels were lined up. So big, Kate thought, they would need a team of horses, or even bullocks, to move them.

Jack followed her gaze. 'That's the heavy artillery over there, 18 pounders. The wagons beside them are for the ammunition.'

Further on the horses were assembled.

She turned to Jack. 'You didn't think to join the Light Horse?'

'I probably should have,' he shrugged, 'but I enlisted with Len and Dick Simmonds. Dick may be a crack shot but, as we know, anything faster than a trot and Dick ends up flat on his back. I wanted to stick with my mates.'

In the distance a brass band played *The Wearing of the Green*.

Aunty frowned. 'Strange for them to be playing a song about the English hanging Irishmen when a good number of the soldiers here are sons of Irishmen.'

Bert stared at her. 'I don't understand, Mrs Burke.'

'Take no mind of me. I'm just being a cranky old woman.'

'It's only the tune not the words,' Jack said evenly. 'My father says all that is the past. Here in Australia, we should look to the future we can build without the old hatreds.'

'And he is right, but some things are difficult to forget. And there are people here who would still like to see us ground under.'

The band music changed to the cheerful *Ta-ra-ra Boom-de-ay*. Aunty sipped her tea and stared towards the horizon.

Bert finished eating and lay back on the blanket, his arms folded behind his head. 'I could nod off here, sleep the afternoon away.'

Jack stood up. 'Or you could stay awake and talk to Mrs Burke while I show Kate around and see if that photographer is here.'

Kate stood beside Jack. Aunty looked up at them, her brow wrinkled.

'Have you had your photo taken, Bert?' She didn't give him time to answer. 'I'd like one of you, if you don't mind. We should go together.'

They packed the remains of their meal into the baskets, both still more than half full, and strolled towards the tents. The lower parts of the tents were rolled up, and everything within looked tidy. Neat piles of folded blankets were lined up outside, rifles stacked beside them.

As they moved through the rows of tents, Kate was aware of sentries standing at regular intervals, alert to all that was happening around them. The number of visitors had grown vastly since they arrived. The band was now playing the *Hallelujah Chorus*.

'This is it,' Jack said.

The tent flap was pinned open. A soldier rested against a stack of blankets outside, smoking. He scrambled to his feet as Kate and Aunty Mary approached.

'Kate, this is Peter Jennings, another poor bloke who shares this tent. Pete, this is my girl, Kate.'

Pete ground his cigarette underfoot and held out his hand. 'Pleased to meet you, Kate.'

'Look.' Jack raised the baskets. 'Supplies. Don't touch them until we get back.'

'I wouldn't dare,' Pete laughed.

Kate poked her head inside the tent. Possessions were set in neat piles around the edge. She glanced back at Jack. 'How many of you sleep here?'

'Nine of us.'

Kate gasped. 'How do you all fit?'

'Feet to the central pole, heads at the edge. It's not bad when it's cold, with blankets and a greatcoat over you. But it's thoroughly unpleasant on warm nights. I prefer the stars for company then.' He placed the baskets at the rear of the tent. 'We should go and find the photographer. There's sure to be a queue.'

Jack was right, so they waited patiently. Aunty and Bert chatted happily. Kate and Jack stood close together, silent, holding hands. She caught the eye of another girl—only for a moment—then both looked away, recognising the fear and the longing already present beneath their happiness.

The photographer was businesslike. They each had a photograph taken alone, one together.

Kate was about to move away but Jack said to the photographer, 'One more photo, mate?'

'Quick, Kate, swap hats.'

Kate pulled her hat off, forgetting to remove the hatpin, and her hair half tumbled down.

Jack plonked his slouch hat on her head and set her beribboned hat on his. They stood still as the photographer caught a moment of timeless happiness.

The heat of the sun was fading as they finished their stroll around the camp.

'We should find Mr O'Meara,' Aunty said. 'If he's sold his produce, he'll be wanting to get home.'

Jack's goodbye was a chaste kiss in front of Aunty Mary.

As they drove home, Kate stared out across the paddocks, not seeing the passing countryside. It had been a pleasant day but it felt like the start of goodbye.

6

Jack and Bert came for dinner the following Sunday under the guise of visiting grandmothers sick in hospital. They spent the afternoon lounging on the bench on the back veranda, Jack slowly finishing the bottle of beer Aunty had provided, Bert beside him, smoking.

Kate sat, content, listening as Jack and Bert joked and told tales of life in the camp, of the drills and the marching, the manoeuvres and mock battles, the tents, the erratic showers, the mud and the dust. And the food—plenty of it, with meat at both breakfast and dinner, but not home cooking, and the disappointment of only bread and jam for their evening meal.

'Or, if you want variety,' Jack said, 'you can have jam and bread.'

They guessed at when they would finally leave, wondered what the trip by sea to England would be like.

'When I first came over from Hobart, the steamer trip was pretty rough.' Bert drew on his cigarette and exhaled. 'Left and right of me people were throwing up. Didn't affect me a bit.'

'It was bad on the way here from Ireland,' Aunty said. 'The seas so rough that I and my cousin were on our knees praying the ship would sink and put us out of our misery.' She paused, perhaps thinking this was not the best story for soldiers about to sail into seas where German boats might be patrolling. 'Ah, but these days the boats are much better.'

Bert butted out his cigarette in the ashtray beside him and went to the edge of the veranda. 'Your pile of split wood is getting low, Mrs Burke.'

'It is,' she nodded, frowning. 'Gus usually does that on Saturday mornings, after his deliveries, but he didn't turn up yesterday. Kate had to do the deliveries for me.'

'I'll split a few logs before I go.' Bert pushed the sleeves of his flannel shirt up as he strolled down the yard to the woodshed.

Aunty got up from her wicker chair. 'I'll put the kettle on. Bert will be thirsty when he's finished there.'

Kate went to follow her. It didn't seem right to be sitting idly, watching a man hard at work.

Jack caught her hand as she moved past him. 'Don't go inside. I doubt Aunty Mary needs your help.'

'Aunty Mary?' She arched an eyebrow.

'I'm practising. She will be soon enough.'

Kate glanced down the yard to where Bert was busy with the axe, and bent forward and kissed Jack lightly.

'Kate,' Aunty called from inside. 'Will you get that little table from the sitting room? We'll have our tea on the verandah.'

'I'll get it.' Jack got up and went through the door.

The sounds of the afternoon washed around Kate—the murmur of conversation between Aunty Mary and Jack, the crack as the axe split through the wood, further off the clop of horses and the jingle of harness in the street, the muted squeals and laughter of children playing. A blackbird alighted on the fence, calling to its mate. A perfect Sunday afternoon as spring turned towards early summer. And although the world was not as she wished, Kate was happy.

Bert walked back towards the house and ducked into the wash-house to clean up. Jack brought out the table and Aunty placed the tea tray on it. She poured the tea and handed around the plates with slices of golden butter cake.

Finally, she sat and sipped her tea. 'I read the camp is filling up—troops coming from all over the place.'

'Tasmania, Queensland and South Australia—plenty expected in the next couple of weeks.' Bert rolled down his sleeves and picked up his cup of tea. 'Won't be long now.'

'You'll be getting leave soon to see your families.'

Jack nodded. 'Saturday after next probably. A few of us are hoping to get leave together. Some of the mothers are organising a do at the school to send us off.'

Kate stared at him. He hadn't said anything of it to her.

'And will you be going back to Hobart, Bert?' Aunty Mary asked.

'No. I'm supposed to be going with Jack. I put Smith's Creek as my address when I enlisted. If I get the leave, I might hang around the city.'

'You are welcome to stay here—you can sleep in the boys' room. Kate will come in with me.'

'I wouldn't want to impose.'

'Go on, Bert,' Jack said. 'Mrs Burke wouldn't be asking if she didn't want you.'

'We would love to have you stay. I miss having boys to cook for.'

Bert looked across at Aunty Mary, genuine pleasure on his face. 'I'd be honoured.'

Bert left not long after but Jack lingered and had tea with Kate and Aunty Mary.

The dishes done, Kate and Jack sat on the bench on the verandah, a distance between them.

'So, you're going home.' Kate tried to hide her disappointment.

'If the leave is approved.' Jack shrugged. 'It isn't always. But if it is, why don't you come too?'

Kate thought for a moment. The reason she was here was to help Aunty Mary and Saturdays were busy.

'Mum would not be happy with me travelling over a hundred and fifty miles with a group of soldiers.'

'Not even with me there?'

Kate opened her eyes wide. 'Especially not with you there.'

He grinned. 'A wise woman, your mother. I will try to catch the early train back so we can spend the last afternoon of my leave together.'

Kate tried to smile. It was better than nothing.

'This means it won't be long before we are off. It'll be good to be on the move at last.'

A lump settled in her throat. 'You will write to me?'

'Of course, I will. And I'll tell you all about the places we sail through and what England is like. Might even get a chance to visit Ireland when it's over.'

She could feel the loss of him already, the weight of the empty months until he came back.

Jack stood up and stepped off the verandah. He turned to Kate and held his hand out. 'Come here.'

She went to him, resting her back against him as he closed his arms tight around her. They stared up into an inky sky strewn with glittering pinpricks of light. Kate was entranced as Jack showed her stars and constellations, giving them names that sounded like magical incantations.

She gasped, 'Look, a shooting star.'

Kate closed her eyes and wished for Jack's safe return and for all the years following when she would never be apart from him again.

He eased his embrace and drew away from her. 'I have to go. I don't want a blot on my record if I'm caught sneaking in late.'

Jack went and said goodbye to Aunty Mary and came out with a package under his arm—fruit and cake and biscuits to see him through the week, just as Bert had left with earlier.

They walked out into the street. At the side door, Jack stepped into the doorway and pulled Kate with him. He put his package down and wrapped his arms around her. This time his kiss was far more than the light touch of his lips.

'Oh Katie,' he groaned, his nose pressed against her hair. 'We've got to finish this war quickly so I can come home to you.'

'I love you, Jack.' So much that it hurt.

She clung to him, lost in their kisses. All she was aware of was the closeness of his firm body and the sharp longing that spread through her.

Jack let go of Kate, his hands brushing down her back as he

stepped away.

She was trembling. She didn't want him to leave. Ever.

'I'd better get going.' He picked up his parcel.

At the corner, Jack caught sight of a charabanc loaded with soldiers trundling up Sydney Road. He raised his arm and shouted.

Kate watched as he ran across the road. He turned and waved back to her and clambered on board.

She forced herself to stand there, waving, until the charabanc was lost among the other vehicles heading towards the camp. She hated these goodbyes, knowing that one day it would be the last.

~

Kate hurried along the passage to the shop when she heard the bell jingle.

A stocky boy of twelve, thirteen at most, had just come up to the counter. 'Mrs Burke?'

'Indeed, I am,' Aunty said.

'Gus said to give you this.' He handed over a piece of paper, folded several times.

'He's not coming in today?'

'Nah, he's enlisted.'

Aunty gasped. 'But he's only sixteen.'

'Mum signed the papers. He said if she didn't, he'd go to Sydney and enlist under a new name and say he had no family.'

'Oh, your poor mother.' Aunty unfolded the note and read it.

'What's your name?'

'Joe, Missus.'

'Well, Joe, when you see Gus, pass on my best wishes to him. And tell him to call in if he has time.' She looked the boy over. 'You're not looking for a job?'

'I got one closer to home keeping nit for a bookie on Saturdays. S'posed to be at school the rest of the week.'

Aunty raised her eyebrows. 'But not today?'

'Nah, got to see a man about a dog.'

Kate pressed her lips tight to stop herself laughing. Aunty was trying not to grin. Joe was every bit as cocky as Gus, though half his size.

'One moment, Joe.' Aunty shovelled a few boiled lollies into a paper bag. 'Here you are.'

'Thanks Missus.' Joe took the bag, his eyes alight. 'Gus said you were a bonzer old sheila.'

Aunty was lost for words and Kate could barely hold back her laughter as Joe swaggered towards the door, calling 'Hooroo' over his shoulder as he left.

'Well, I've never been called *a bonzer old sheila* before.'

'It certainly is a compliment,' Kate laughed.

'With Gus gone, it looks like Joe believes he is the man of the house. And he might very well be.' She glanced across at the small pile of parcels on the end of the counter. 'I'll have to find another boy to do the deliveries. And get someone to chop the wood.'

'I'm happy to do the deliveries,' Kate said.

'That would be a great help. I'll draw you a map. Luckily none are far away today.' She pulled out a sheet of paper from the drawer and sketched some lines on it. She looked up and said, 'Poor Mrs Kelly, what choice did she have but to let Gus go?'

Kate started packing the deliveries into the basket. 'It's a good thing that one is so short, or I imagine he would be off too.'

She heard Aunty's sigh and in it the worries that no one dared speak of, worries that Kate did not allow herself to imagine.

7

December 1914

Aunty unlocked the shop door just as Bert arrived.
'You're bright and early, Bert.'

He glanced out to the sunshine-bathed street. 'Not a moment to waste on a beautiful day like this.' He turned back to Aunty. 'Mrs Burke, this is kind of you.'

'Think nothing of it. And you come and go as you please—you are one of the family while you are here.'

To Kate it seemed that Bert was not only grateful but astounded by Aunty's generosity.

She packed her deliveries while Aunty took Bert to the boys' bedroom to drop his haversack. He followed Aunty Mary back into the shop. 'While I'm here I can chop some wood for you.'

'Ah, thank you, Bert. I don't have anyone to do it at present. Gus has enlisted although he's only sixteen.'

'If you're a decent specimen, it's easy enough.'

Kate looked up. He spoke with what sounded like the certainty of experience.

'I'll build up your wood stack and do any odd jobs. Weed the garden too, if you want. I can tell a weed from a vegetable. If you'll show me where the tools are, I'll get to it straight away.'

Kate waited until Aunty came back to the shop then went off on her deliveries. Aunty Mary had bought a ladies bicycle for Kate to do the deliveries and Kate was thoroughly enjoying her outings around Coburg's streets.

They sat down to eat just after one o'clock, the shop now closed for the day. Between baking and the shop, Aunty Mary's morning had been busy. There had been no time for cooking a hot dinner but the table was laden with dishes—plates with sliced ham, cheese; bowls of hard-boiled eggs, salad, and potato salad; as well as bread and butter.

Bert took his seat at the table, his face shining from his quick scrub in the washhouse after spending the morning weeding and hoeing. He picked up his knife and fork the moment Aunty Mary finished saying grace.

'Do you have any plans for tonight, Bert?' she asked.

'At the moment an early night in a soft bed sounds better than a night on the town.' He turned his attention to the meal.

'There's sure to be a dance on somewhere nearby. You and Kate could go.' She looked towards Kate. 'Ask Reenie, she will know of somewhere.'

'I don't know...' Kate's voice trailed off.

Bert glanced at Kate, clearly as uncomfortable as she was. 'Jack mightn't be too pleased.'

'Away with you, I'm suggesting you go to a dance together not that you run off and get married.'

'It's a nice yard you have here, Mrs Burke,' he said quickly. 'I wouldn't mind something like it one day—a good sized vegetable garden, fruit trees, a few chooks. There's not much more you'd need to buy to feed yourself.'

'Indeed, it provides us with more than enough. I make jam from the stone fruit and pickles from the tomatoes and sell them in the shop.'

Bert nodded, a far-away look in his eyes, perhaps imagining the life he wanted when he came back.

After lunch Kate stood at the sink, washing the dishes. Aunty was in the dining room, the table covered with account books, invoices and receipts, as she added up the week's takings and expenditure and made lists of items to be reordered—tasks that had previously been Brendan's responsibility. Bert sat outside having an after-dinner smoke.

The boards creaked as he stood up and stepped off the verandah. He walked along the brick-paved path at the centre of the yard to the woodshed which was set between the vegetable garden and the chookyard. A few minutes later, Kate heard the steady rhythm of the axe as he split the logs.

The gentle cooing of a pigeon carried on the still, warm air. It could be a perfect afternoon but Kate felt empty. Was this what she would feel every single day until Jack came home?

Late in the afternoon, under orders from Aunty Mary, Bert wallowed in the bath in the washhouse for a good half hour. He came out wearing a shirt and trousers of Vince's as Aunty had told him she would be washing his shirts and underthings tomorrow, no matter that it was Sunday, and there was to be no argument.

Bert took them to the pictures in the evening, Aunty taking the middle seat. The Pathé Gazette before the main feature showed images of Belgium: blighted trees, buildings no more than rubble, shuffling refugees carrying their belongings, the marching armies. Kate had read of the German atrocities—bayonetting children, and worse to the women, even the nuns. It was suddenly real. This was what Jack and Bert and her cousins were heading towards, a place of cruelty and ruin, a place of danger, a place that needed them. Kate prayed the war would end quickly.

~

Kate and Aunty Mary went to early Mass. Images from the newsreel filled Kate's mind as they said the now regular prayers for peace. They were formal and long and, in Kate's opinion, offered little protection to the soldiers who were in danger. She murmured to herself the latter part of St Patrick's Breastplate, as she now did every day.

Against the death wound and the burning.
The choking wave, the poisoned shaft,
Protect him Christ, till Thy returning.

They came home to breakfast already prepared—porridge made, toast browning in front of the open firebox. Bert poured water into the teapot as they came through the door.

'Bert, you are a marvel,' Aunty said.

'It's the least I can do.'

'Tomorrow, before you leave, I'll make you a breakfast to set you up for the day—steak, eggs, sausages, bacon.'

'Thank you, Mrs Burke. I'm sure, if I lived here, I'd be rolling rather than walking down the street by the year's end.'

After breakfast, Aunty busied herself in the washhouse with Bert's laundry. He pottered around the yard, pulling the odd weed he had missed, adding a few logs to the already substantial pile of split wood, even helping Aunty Mary hang the washing out on the line stretching from the house to near the gate of the chookyard.

After dinner, when Kate came back from feeding the scraps to the hens, Aunty Mary said, 'Bert's gone out for the day but says he won't be in late.' She gave a light laugh. 'We shall see, I know what young men are like.'

They spent the afternoon on the verandah sewing, putting the finishing touches to the flannel shirts they had made for Jack and Bert. The Red Cross had asked for volunteers to sew shirts and pyjamas and to knit face washers and socks for the soldiers as the army didn't supply everything. Kate had been keen but Aunty had said to wait, they would make what Jack and Bert needed and once they had gone, then they would help the Red Cross.

As she sewed, Kate thought of Jack, imagining him in those familiar surroundings, hoping he was taking no notice of the girls who would have turned their fluttering eyes on her handsome soldier. Beside her, Aunty told stories of neighbours and family far away, not seeming to notice that Kate wasn't listening.

That night Kate lay awake, Aunty snoring gently beside her. The niggling unease she had felt when Jack first enlisted was growing. There were moments of sheer panic. She tried to breathe slowly, tried to keep calm. Jack would be here tomorrow and she would think only of the present moment when she was with him. The future would take care of itself.

~

Bert had come in well before midnight, whistling softly, and was up early, bright-eyed and clean shaven. He clearly had not lived up, or was it down, to Aunty's expectations of young men.

He ate a breakfast he described as fit for a king and thanked Aunty. 'If I can have my washing, I'll get dressed and be on my way.'

'You will not,' Aunty replied. 'I have to iron your shirt and press your uniform. And you will have dinner with us. You can't be getting back to camp sooner than the men you were supposed to be with all weekend. Wait until Jack arrives.'

She handed him a newspaper. 'Go out the back and have a read. You are on holiday.'

Kate was left alone in the shop. She concentrated on measuring, counting out change and sensibly answering customers' questions. But in the quiet moments, always, her mind wandered back to Jack. She knew, at the earliest, he would not be back until the afternoon, still she jumped with every jingle of the shop door.

They didn't have dinner until two o'clock. Kate wasn't sure if Aunty had delayed the meal to give Jack time to arrive or to force Bert to stay a little longer.

The aroma of Aunty's braised steak and onions had been making Kate's stomach rumble for what seemed like hours. Served with mashed potatoes, carrots and crisp green beans, the meat almost melted in the mouth.

Bert sat back when he had finished and sighed. 'I reckon this is the sort of food they serve in heaven.'

Aunty beamed at him.

Kate tried to appear cheerful. 'You won't be leaving this week, will you?' She couldn't bear it if she didn't see Jack before they embarked.

Before Bert could answer, Aunty said, 'They won't be going for a couple of weeks yet.' They both stared at her. 'The Coburg Patriotic Committee has arranged a send-off for local boys on the nineteenth—it can't be before then.'

'But that's almost Christmas,' Kate said. 'They can't send you away so close to Christmas.'

Bert rolled his eyes. 'As if those at the top ever take the concerns of the ordinary man into account.'

He got up from the table. 'Mrs Burke, thank you for everything. I'll be dreaming of these meals, and that soft bed, the whole time I'm away.'

'It has been a pleasure having you here, Albert Wilson. And when you come back, there will be a warm welcome here for you.'

He went to the bedroom to change and came back with his haversack over his shoulder, now loaded not only with Aunty's sewing but a tin of homemade biscuits and cake.

He put his bag down and gave her a box of chocolates tied with a bright red ribbon. 'I doubt we'll be getting any more leave. I've had the grandest time.'

She kissed him on the cheek. 'I'll write to you.' There were tears in her eyes as she folded him in her arms. 'And keep you in my prayers the whole time you are away.'

Kate could have sworn Bert's eyes were glistening too.

As he left, he said to Kate, 'He'll be here today. I've never known Jack not to keep his word.'

Kate wanted to believe him.

Aunty sniffed as the door closed behind Bert.

'He's one of nature's gentlemen. He won't admit to it but I'd say he's closer to eighteen or nineteen than the twenty-two he claims.' She rummaged in her pocket and pulled out her handkerchief. 'His mother died when he was four and his father was a good-for-nothing so he ended up with the Department of Neglected Children. He spent most of his childhood boarded out with different families. He said most treated him well, but one or two beat him black and blue.' She sniffed again. 'Yet he is always cheerful, grateful for everything he has.' She blew her nose loudly. 'We must count our blessings.'

As she turned away, she murmured, 'And pray without ceasing for all of those boys.'

8

Kate carried the cutlery and plates into the dining room and began setting the table for two. Jack hadn't arrived. He must have caught the later train and would get back to Melbourne so late he would need to go straight to the camp. And Kate would not see him until next Sunday, if she could find a way to get herself out to Broadmeadows.

Aunty came and stood at the doorway.

Kate didn't look up. She kept her head down as she placed the knives and forks on the tablecloth, struggling to control her face.

She caught a faint whiff of beer and her heart leapt.

She spun around.

Jack was standing there, grinning like a small boy caught with his hand in the biscuit tin.

'Katie, I'm sorry.'

All her worries fled—he was here now. It was all that mattered.

Jack stepped towards her. His arms were around her, his head on her shoulder, his lips against her neck, on her ear lobe, her lips. She held tight to him, lost in the kiss.

She heard the faint creak of floorboards in the passage. Aunty was coming.

Kate managed to force herself away from Jack by the time Aunty was at the door. She was certain she looked as mindlessly happy as Jack did.

'I've kept some of the braised steak we had for lunch. Kate can warm that up for you.'

'Thank you, Mrs Burke. I forgot to have a proper dinner.'

She nodded her head, her eyebrows raised. 'I can see that.'

'What happened?' Kate asked. 'Was the train late?'

'I ran into a couple of mates when I arrived at Flinders Street station and they took me to Young & Jackson's and shouted me a drink.'

'That was generous of them.' It was clearly more than one drink. He smiled at her, a smile that made her forget everything else.

'I'll explain it to you later.' Jack turned to Aunty Mary. 'If you don't mind, Mrs Burke, I'd like to stay here tonight.'

'You're welcome, Jack, but won't you be in trouble if you're not back there tonight?'

'I'll leave before first light and be there in time for roll call. I won't give them the chance to consider me AWL.'

He didn't seem as drunk as Kate had first thought, keeping up a conversation with Aunty as they ate.

'I read in Saturday's newspaper that you will be going to Egypt, not England,' Aunty Mary said.

'I'd rather be in Egypt than England at this time of year. Better heat and sand than shivering in a bloody freezing English winter.' Jack grimaced. 'Sorry, Aunty Mary, I forgot myself.'

'Aunty Mary, indeed!' Aunty attempted to frown but seemed pleased all the same. 'I suppose I will be one day.'

Grinning, he said, 'Just as soon as this war is over.' He turned to Kate. 'I'll have plenty to write and tell you about—I might even get to ride a camel or a—' He stopped mid-sentence. 'I forgot, Billy gave me a message for you. *Daisy has had a calf. Cow and calf both doing well.*' Jack laughed. 'What is he? Ten years old and he talks like an old man who's been on the land for fifty years.'

Kate smiled, thinking of her little brother beside Dad, both standing with their legs apart, their fists planted on their hips as they watched the cows file into the shed.

Jack unbuttoned his top pocket and pulled out a folded piece of paper. 'Jessie drew you a picture of the calf.'

Kate unfolded and flattened the paper with its crayon drawing of a small black cow with spindly legs, green scribble along the bottom for the grass and a great yellow sun in the blue sky. She felt a sudden longing for her brothers and sisters. 'They will have grown while I've been away.'

'Not that I noticed. You've been away barely two months.'

'It seems much longer.' She gazed at Jack. Time seemed to have stretched out. She had seen him less often than she would have at home, yet the time together had been longer and without the constant presence of younger brothers and sisters.

Aunty sent Kate and Jack to the sitting room while she did the dishes. 'You give him a talking to, Kate, leaving you waiting all afternoon.'

They sat close together on the sofa, Kate's arm through Jack's.

'The do was on Saturday night at the school. The children had decorated the room and after the speeches, they sang a few songs. And each of us was given a pipe, a tobacco pouch and a pound of tobacco. I've got Bert's share safe in my haversack.'

'And that was all?' Kate said.

'Oh no, there was dancing and a decent supper.'

Kate raised her eyebrows. 'And who did you dance with?'

He grinned at her. 'Don't know if I'm game to say with the way you are glaring at me.'

'You didn't!' Kate gasped and pulled away from him. 'Not that Molly Blackwood.' She was a real Miss with her dark curls and her pretty face and her eyelashes fluttering at the best-looking boy in the room.

'No.' Jack laughed softly. 'Molly quickly attached herself to Len Simmonds. I danced with my mother and yours, and your sisters Hannah and Elsie. Then I slipped outside with Dick and we shared a bottle of beer he had hidden in the hedge.'

Kate rolled her eyes. 'I bet it was more than one bottle and by the end of the night half the men were out there.'

'You might be right.' He took her hands in his. 'Yesterday Mum had every relative and friend she could lay claim to for twenty miles around come. Your family were there and I got the chance to have a talk with your father.' He stared deep into her eyes. 'He is happy for us to get married as soon as I get back. So...' He slid off the sofa and onto his knees. 'Catherine Burke, will you marry me?'

She laughed with the pure joy of it. 'I will, John Sheehan.' She bent forward and kissed him, the gentlest of kisses holding a world of promise.

He scrabbled in his pocket and pulled out a small box. He opened it and offered it to Kate. A worked gold band with three diamonds, the middle one larger, glimmered in the gaslight.

She breathed, 'It is beautiful.'

He slid it along her fourth finger. It fitted perfectly.

'How did you know the right size?'

'You didn't seem to notice but I have been comparing our hands a lot lately. Your ring finger is the same size as the middle section of my little finger.'

Jack moved back onto the sofa and drew Kate close.

His kisses wiped the world away, longing and desire flooding through her. All she wanted was Jack. All of him as he was. Now. Forever.

A plate crashed to the floor in the kitchen.

'Botheration!' Aunty swore loudly.

Kate jolted back, away from Jack, her breath shortened.

She sat still, staring ahead.

'Kate.'

She stood and fled towards the door.

'Kate.' His voice was urgent.

She turned back, tears welling in her eyes.

'You need to tidy yourself.'

She looked down. Her blouse had come loose from her skirt, some of the buttons were undone.

Jack slowly got up from the sofa and straightened his own clothing.

Kate tucked in her blouse, settled her shoulders and walked away, her eyes wide, trying to force back the tears.

Aunty was on her knees in the kitchen, sweeping the shards of china into the dustpan.

'Can I help, Aunty Mary?'

'I dropped the dish as I was drying it.' She looked up at Kate. 'Oh, Katie, my treasure.' She put the dustpan by the hearth and went to Kate, wrapping her in her arms. 'He's not going forever. They will all be back soon enough.' She brushed her thumb across Kate's cheek, wiping away a tear. 'You go back in there and talk to him of all the happy things that will happen when he comes home.'

Kate forced back a sob. Aunty Mary trusted her when she wasn't worth it. And Jack? What would he think of her now? Letting him put his hand beneath her blouse—even now she could feel the weight of his hand on her breast. She was no better than those young women the papers wrote about who hung around the camp at all hours.

She stood in the doorway of the sitting room. 'Aunty dropped a serving dish.'

'Come and sit down.' Jack placed his hand on the cushion beside him.

She came over and sat apart from him, staring at her hands clasped tight in her lap. She was afraid to look at him, afraid of what she would read in his face.

'You must think me as bad as those women out at the camp.'

'Don't be ridiculous.'

She looked up, stunned by the harshness in his voice.

'Tell me, how many boys have you kissed?'

'What sort of question is that?' She snapped back. He must think the worst of her.

'No, tell me.' He waited but Kate said nothing. 'It's one, isn't it? Me! Don't you ever compare yourself. You are nothing like them. They have been with dozens of men. And, with them, it's more than kissing.'

'I've never cared for anyone but you,' she said quietly.

He gave a sly grin. 'What about Bertie Hobson?'

'I was eight! He tried to kiss me but I pushed him away. Then he pulled my hair.'

'I remember and I gave him a bloody nose for his trouble.'

'You did.' She could hear Aunty moving around in the kitchen. 'How could I have let that happen?'

'Let what happen? We kissed. Nothing else happened.'

'But if Aunty hadn't dropped the dish.' Embarrassment flooded through her. 'If she had come in and found us.' She hid her face in her hands.

'One of us would have come to our senses and realised where we were.' He reached towards her. 'Now come here.'

Kate moved closer and he placed his arm around her.

'When I come back,' he lowered his voice, 'we'll have our own place and no one will walk in on us and we will be able to kiss all we like.' He grinned, raising an eyebrow. 'And more.'

Kate looked up at him from beneath her lashes, blushing. Her heart was racing, she loved him so much and, if she wasn't careful, it would start again.

She rested her head against him and they began to talk, softly, of their future together, the life they would have, the children they would love, how they would sit like this in the evenings for the rest of their days.

In the quiet and comfort, they drifted towards sleep.

'Time for bed.' Aunty Mary stood at the door. 'Both of you.'

'A few more minutes. Please, Aunty.'

She tried to look stern. 'If you are not in bed in ten minutes, I'll come and drag you both by the ear.'

They rose, reluctant, and Jack went outside to the lavatory. Kate filled a glass of water and, sipping it, stood at the door. Jack was in the middle of the patch of lawn between the path and the fruit trees, his boots and socks off.

'Come out here and take your shoes off.'

She sat on the veranda and undid her shoes, slipping off her stockings under cover of her skirt.

She walked across the cool grass to him.

Jack bowed to Kate. She curtsied. He slid his arm around her waist, took her hand in his, and they danced, Jack humming *When Irish Eyes are Smiling*.

'My mother's parents were English, you know.'

'But she must have had an Irish heart to fall in love with your father.'

He sang softly as the moon bathed them in silver light. His voice grew in strength, ringing out through the night.

...And when Irish eyes are smiling,
Sure, they steal your heart away.

~

Kate blinked in the bright light as Aunty dragged the curtains open.

'How late is it?'

'Eight o'clock. You looked so peaceful, it would have been cruel to wake you.'

Kate pushed herself up on the pillows and picked up the cup of steaming tea Aunty had set on the bedside table. She took a sip and said, 'Has Jack gone?'

'He was gone before I woke. And that room, you wouldn't know he had been there. The bed is so neatly made.'

'I hope he got back in time.' Kate put the teacup back on its saucer. 'Aunty,' she said, holding out her left hand.

Aunty came over, a smile slowly spreading over her face. 'Ah, it is beautiful.' She looked up, her eyes shining. 'My treasure, I wish you both every happiness life can bring.'

'You don't think we are being silly? You said you were set against Vince and Reenie getting engaged before he left.'

'If I am honest, Reenie is flighty. It is to be expected—she's only seventeen, far too young to be marrying. She needs time to grow up and see it is more than a pretty ring on her finger and a fancy wedding dress. And time to realise what a fine young man she has in Vincent himself.' She grasped Kate's hands. 'But with you and Jack, it shines from your faces—you were made for each other.'

'I wish we could marry now but he said we should wait.'

Aunty nodded.

'We will be married as soon as he is back and you will have to shut the shop for a week so you can come and help me.'

'And I will with the greatest of happiness.' She smiled at Kate, but there was more in her eyes. Kate would not try to read what was there.

9

Every evening for the rest of the week, a soldier on his way into town dropped by to deliver a note from Jack. After the first, Kate had one ready to send back. They were brief, often no more than snippets of news and declarations of love, always ending with big Xes at the bottom that Kate kissed back. It was agony to know Jack was only just over four miles away but she had no chance to see him.

Aunty started, nearly dropping her serving spoon, at the sharp rap on the back door late Saturday afternoon.

Jack pushed the door open and came in. 'I hoped I might take you both to the pictures tonight.'

'That's kind of you, Jack,' Aunty said before Kate had a chance to greet him. 'We would love to come.' She moved away from the kitchen table and took a plate from the dresser. 'You'll join us for tea?'

'I grabbed something before I left.'

'Bread and jam no doubt. That's no meal for a man at the end of a long day. You'll find room for a spot of Kate's stew.'

Jack grinned. 'I'm sure I can force myself.'

He followed them into the dining room as Kate set him a place and Aunty put the serving dish on the table.

As they began their meal, Aunty asked, 'How did you manage to get leave?'

'I am in disguise—sitting before you is Private George Smithers from Ballarat. Poor Private Smithers, a recent recruit, has a bad case of the trots and daren't wander far from the latrines. He kindly gave me his pass and, to my good fortune, there was a new guard on sentry duty who has never seen either of us before.'

'That was a grand stroke of luck.'

'Were you in any trouble getting back on Tuesday?' Kate asked.

'No, I slipped past the sentry and the patrols without a problem. All the sergeant said when he saw me was, *You're up bright and early*. I won't be doing it again—that sort of luck runs out.'

'Ah, Jack,' Aunty laughed. 'Yet here you are now, tempting Fate again.'

Once the meal was over and the dishes done, Kate and Aunty Mary put on their hats and coats and they all walked smartly up Sydney Road to Lake Hall.

Kate, sitting between Jack and Aunty Mary, thrilled as the lights dimmed—she had been to the pictures only once before she arrived in Melbourne and the novelty hadn't worn off. Aware of Aunty beside her, she kept her hands in her lap and was soon laughing along at the antics of the Keystone Cops and of Charlie Chaplin. The feature, *The Fatal Three*, was mesmerising. Kate gasped and, at times, sat open-mouthed as a gripping tale played out on the screen of life behind the footlights and fatal visions, climaxing in a life and death struggle on the cliff tops, the excitement and tragedy heightened by the music of a small orchestra. Towards the end she found she was gripping Jack's hand. She eased her hold but did not let go.

Jack leant close and whispered, 'As soon as it finishes, I have to go. I want to be back well before midnight.'

Kate squeezed his hand and forced herself to be grateful for this time beside him, not to yearn for more than was possible.

As the final scene played out, he leant close and kissed her. Kate lost all thought of the activities on the screen, of the people around her, as she kissed him back. She was rudely brought back to the here and now by a sharp shove of her seat accompanied by the angry throat clearing of an old man behind them.

She could see Jack grinning in the flickering light from the screen. He turned to her again, his kiss hard and quick, then he stood and pushed past the knees of those in the seats beside him.

Kate stared towards the screen where 'The End' appeared. She didn't care about the old man but she hoped Aunty hadn't noticed.

'Oh, that was an exciting film,' Aunty said as the lights came up. She glanced along the row. 'Has Jack gone?'

'Yes, he said he has to be back before midnight.'

'He wouldn't want to be late and have them looking closely at that leave pass.'

They walked home down Sydney Road with the departing crowd, past the Coburg Hotel. Through the windows they could see a few soldiers, unlike Jack, in no hurry to be back at the camp.

'I saw the scariest picture show a couple of years ago,' Aunty said as they crossed Bell Street, the crowd of picturegoers thinning out. 'It was before Mick died, God rest him. It was about a man who brought a body back to life, made a monster of the poor creature. I was terrified by it. When we got home, I told Mick to wait at the back door when I went to the lavatory. I didn't want to be out there in the dark by myself. And do you know what he did? He tiptoed up and banged on the wall. I was out of there and halfway up the yard, my skirts still hoisted and himself doubled over with laughter.' She sighed, a faraway look on her face. 'Aaah, how I miss him. He was a grand man.'

'Oh, Aunty.' Kate didn't know what to say. She rubbed her hand against her aunt's shoulder.

''Tis the way life is. I'm grateful for the years I had with him. He was here to raise the boys and fine men they are, just like Mick. He's there upstairs now, with our little ones on his knee, waiting for me.'

Kate remembered her mother saying that, in the year before Brendan was born, Aunty had lost two babies to diphtheria: three-year-old James and nine-month-old Honora. Yet Aunty rarely spoke of her sorrows.

She looked across at Kate, smiling gently. 'But I won't be joining them for a while yet as I have work to do here. I need to see the boys married and a grandchild or six.' She gave Kate a gentle elbow in the ribs. 'And some grandnieces and nephews too.'

'I'll see what I can do.'

As they crossed Sydney Road, near Harding Street, a cold wind gusted along the road.

Aunty shivered. 'The sooner this war is over the better.'

Kate shivered too. Six months everyone had said at the start but it had been going over four months now and it had not truly begun for Australia.

~

The newspapers had announced that the parade of the 4th Infantry Brigade would leave the Broadmeadows camp at seven o'clock on the morning of the seventeenth of December. People began lining Sydney Road well before seven although it would probably take the parade over an hour to get to Coburg. Kate went out before eight and stood at the edge of the road. Aunty stayed in the shop as her customers kept coming but she said she would stand on the doorstep when the men marched by, on tiptoes if need be so she could see over the heads of those crowding the footpath.

Aunty, like many shopkeepers, had decorated her verandah with strings of pennants; others had bunting and both the Union Jack and the Australian flag on display. The crowd was packed with schoolchildren. Many adults, having decided that work could wait an hour or two, stood waving small flags. Some climbed on ladders; boys even shinned up the lamp posts. As soon as the faint sound of the brass bands was heard, cheers and shouts of 'Here they come' went up. The onlookers cheered themselves hoarse in the thirty minutes it took the three-mile-long column to pass. 'Good luck, lads! You're the right sort!'

The brigade commander, Colonel Monash, accompanied by his staff, rode at the head of the column, followed by headquarters staff. Accompanied by their bands, the battalions marched in order. The commanding officers led their units, eight companies of infantry in each. They were followed by machine gun sections, transport wagons and pack-horses and, in the case of the 14th Battalion, its massive travelling kitchen.

First was the 13th Battalion from New South Wales then, from Victoria, the 14th Battalion marched by. Try as she might, Kate could not see Jack. In files of four, the soldiers held themselves straight and tall, all in khaki, slouch hats on their heads, rifles on their shoulders, fixed bayonets flashing in the bright morning light. They marched with a steady rhythm, their tanned faces grim, no longer individual men but a single solid mass moving as one. After the 14th came the 15th from Queensland and Tasmania and the 16th from South and Western Australia. The 4th Field Ambulance marched at the rear with seven Red Cross ambulance wagons, each with a white flag bearing a scarlet cross. Kate did not allow herself to think too deeply about the need for their presence. She waited until they all had passed, standing there for those who, like Bert, had no family or friends here to cheer them on, for those who already were far from home.

They would march on to the city, up Collins Street and along Spring Street to arrive at the Federal Parliament House at noon where the dignitaries, including the Governor-General, the Prime Minister and the Minister for Defence, would be waiting. At the order of *Eyes right*, each soldier was to turn his head to the right in salute as they passed them. The parade would continue down Bourke Street to the General Post Office, along Elizabeth Street and on to Royal Park where they were to break for lunch.

Aunty Mary had told Kate this was the same route as the parade Brendan and Vincent had taken part in before they left in October. That day had been dull and grey with rain slick over everything— today was beautiful with blue skies and sunshine, and not too much heat.

Up until the last minute, there was a constant stream of customers. But, finally, Aunty locked the shop door and they put on their hats, picked up their well-stocked baskets, and walked down to Moreland Road to catch the Brunswick cable tram. The tram quickly filled up until they were packed in tighter than sardines in a tin. All had come with the same intention, carrying baskets and bags of food to share what was likely their last meal with their loved one before he sailed away.

The southern end of Royal Park was a sea of khaki. The men stood or sat around on the ground, some stretched out, rifles stacked, their haversacks opened. They had been provided with sandwiches and tea by the camp cooks who had been hard at work while they marched. Fruit and pie vendors were doing a roaring trade, their vans parked on the street. And family and friends had brought delicacies not on the army's menu.

Kate had wondered how they would ever find Jack but he was on the lookout for them. He guided them to where he had been sitting with the Simmonds boys from home. They jumped up, pleased to see Kate, wishing her every happiness on her engagement. Jack introduced Aunty who immediately warmed herself to them by sharing the contents of her basket.

Aunty looked around. 'Where's Bert?'

'Not sure.' Jack shrugged. 'Probably had to see a man about a dog.'

'What does that mean?' Kate asked.

'It can mean whatever you want it to mean.' Jack grinned. 'If we were at home, I'd have said he had gone to water the lemon tree.'

'Oh.' Kate blushed.

The young men around her burst out laughing.

Aunty shook her head, trying not to smile. 'Boys!'

Bert strolled over, greeting Aunty Mary with a wide grin.

'Sit down Bert and help yourself.'

'Thank you, Mrs Burke.' He reached into the basket and took the last jam tart. 'I should have got here sooner.'

'There's plenty of sandwiches left. Biscuits too,' Aunty said.

They sat quietly in the sunshine. Kate storing up the moments,

Jack sitting close beside her.

'Pretty,' she said, running her finger across the single stripe sewn on the sleeve of his tunic. She looked up into his eyes and smiled. 'Lance Corporal Sheehan. It has a ring to it.'

'It has,' he said, gazing back into her eyes.

'I love you.' She mouthed the words.

Her heart thumped as he said them back. She could feel fear rising, feel the prick of tears. She would not look ahead.

'If I behave myself...'

Her fear ebbed as he spoke.

'...I should get another stripe and that comes with an extra shilling a day. It'll be useful to have a bit put by when we get married.'

Kate looked at her hand, held tight in Jack's, the sunlight sparkling on the diamonds of her ring. She prayed that Jack would be home and they would be married long before this time next year.

Too soon the men were called to attention. They stood and went off to form their lines without hesitation.

Jack put his arms around Kate. 'Any chance you can visit on Sunday? I expect we will be leaving next week.'

Kate whimpered, fighting a rush of panic. For months she had known the day was steadily marching closer. Why were the words a shock?

'I'll do my best but it depends on Aunty—she won't let me go by myself.'

'I don't want that either.' He gave her the briefest of kisses and was gone.

Aunty picked up the empty basket. 'If we hurry, we can catch the tram before they march off and you can wave to him as they go through Coburg.'

They got back to Coburg in good time. Kate stood across the street from the shop, the footpath far less crowded than the morning. She could hear the faint sound of an approaching brass band.

The soldiers still marched in silence, in rhythmic step, but they were marching at ease, their rifles carried more comfortably, slung on their shoulders. Small groups of young children marched, or skipped, down the middle of the road beside them.

Kate searched the men's faces as they passed, telling herself that if she saw him, all would be well.

And there he was.

A smile hinting at his lips, he winked as he marched by.

10

Kate sat in the back of the Caseys' buggy beside Reenie and her mother, Mrs Casey holding her youngest daughter, four-year-old Teresa, on her lap. Reenie's younger brother, Nick, and sister, Cecilia, were at the front with their father.

Aunty Mary had arranged for Kate to travel with the Caseys, as she was going to the monthly meeting of the Sacred Heart sodality, a devotional group for the adult women of the parish.

The sky was grim and overcast, threatening rain, but Mrs Casey kept up a bright chatter. Kate thought, perhaps, it was more to keep her own sadness at bay—Pat Casey was leaving too.

'I believe you are now engaged, Kate. You have our very best wishes for the future,' Mrs Casey said. 'Have you known your young man long?'

'All my life, Mrs Casey. Jack's father's farm is beside ours.'

'I've known Vince all my life,' Reenie muttered beside her.

Her mother gave her a warning stare. 'Your aunt says you are going home to Gippsland for Christmas.'

'Yes, and Aunty Mary is coming too.'

'It would be a lonely Christmas for her by herself.' Mrs Casey said and lapsed into silence

Kate stared out at the sodden paddocks and tried to keep her mind empty.

They parked the buggy in the farmer's paddock along from the camp and walked through the gates.

Jack was waiting with Pat Casey near the guard post. They came straight over and Jack introduced himself to Mr and Mrs Casey.

'I'm sorry, we won't be staying long today, Jack. We will meet back here at four o'clock.'

'I'll make sure Kate is on time,' Jack said.

They walked away together, Kate's arm through Jack's. He

56

hadn't kissed her.

'I've brought some cake and scones and a thermos of tea.' Kate tried to sound cheerful.

They wandered through the camp and ended up sitting outside the YMCA hut in a burst of sunshine.

'Did you get your photos?'

'Yes, Aunty collected them.'

'I've got mine here.' He patted his breast pocket. 'I sent the one of me to Mum.'

'I put you in a frame on my bedside table. You are the first thing I see when I wake and the last thing at night.'

'I kiss mine goodnight.'

'Don't the others in your tent make fun of you?'

He grinned at her. 'They wouldn't dare.'

It was enough to sit in silence, their arms touching. They shared the tea and a scone but the time ticked by.

It was nearing four o'clock when they walked slowly towards the gate. Jack stopped and drew Kate close. She closed her eyes, burying her face against his chest. 'I don't want you to go.'

'I'd like nothing more than to be at home with you.' Jack gave a long drawn-out sigh. 'But I have to do my duty.'

Kate thought of the Pathé Gazettes showing the devastation of Belgium. Someone had to put an end to it. Still, she prayed it would be over by the time Jack reached Egypt.

She blinked away her threatening tears. 'This really is goodbye.'

He nodded. 'I'm not meant to say, but I'm sailing on the *Ulysses*.' He kissed her, a gentle public kiss.

Mrs Casey stood beside them, her eyes red and swollen. 'We need to get going, I'm afraid.' Her smile was half-hearted. 'Nice to have met you, Jack. When we hear you are on your way to the port, we'll bring Kate with us to wave you off.'

'Thank you.' He squeezed Kate's hand.

She reached up, brushed her lips against his, and walked with Mrs

Casey through the gate and along Camp Road.

She glanced back.

Jack was standing by the guard post.

She turned and ran to him, throwing herself into his arms. She pressed her lips to his, putting all her love, her longing, and her hope into that one deep kiss, not caring that the whole world was watching.

Then she walked away, tears streaming down her face.

~

The bell on the door jangled furiously as Reenie burst into the shop.

'They're on their way to Port Melbourne,' she gasped. 'Come on, Kate.'

'Quick Kate, go and get your hat,' Aunty said.

Kate ran into the house, pinned on her hat, shoved her gloves into her handbag and raced with Reenie to the railway station where Mrs Casey was waiting.

They were swept into the train by the crowd of people, all with the same thing in mind—to get to Port Melbourne.

Kate caught snatches of the conversation around them.

'...special trains from Broadmeadows...' '... supposed to be secret ...' '... they were cheering and singing ...' '... *Waltzing Matilda* and *Tipperary* ...' '... and *Australia will be There* ...'

Some boys further along the carriage started singing *Australia Will Be There* and the rest of the carriage joined in.

Outside Flinders Street station Mrs Casey managed to hail a cab, but it was slow travelling; everyone else on the road seemed to be heading in the same direction. Kate's heart pounded, fearful the troopships would leave before they got there.

Thousands were standing in the sun outside the gates to the pier which were guarded by police and sentries. The mass of women, mainly, pressed close, waiting as the soldiers slowly filed up the gangways into the towering steamships. Kate stood on tiptoes, near to tears, trying to see over the heads and hats of those in front of her. She needed to see Jack—just a glimpse of him. She told herself that if she saw him, everything would be right, he would come back to her.

Finally, the men were on board and the gates opened. Reenie caught Kate's hand as the crowd surged forward. She led the way, pushing through the press of people until they were standing alongside the *Ulysses*.

Slowly, through the afternoon, to the cheering of both those on the pier and the men on the ships, the transports moved one by one toward the heads of the bay until, by three o'clock, only the *Ulysses* remained. Kate stared up at the men crowding the decks, some sitting precariously on the rails. She had not once caught sight of Jack.

Reenie squealed, jumping and waving to Pat who was leaning over the rail two levels up. Beside her, Mrs Casey stood rigid, her eyes wet, fighting to keep control. She blew Pat a kiss. He clearly saw his mother as he blew one back to her.

The sun beat down from a clear sky. The air was humid. Perspiration trickled from Kate's damp hatband down her neck. She had the beginning of a headache. She was sick with the waiting, the thought that she would not see him.

Reenie pushed a thermos cup of cold sweet tea into her hands. Her mother had come well prepared.

The headache faded as she sipped the tea. She continued her search for Jack.

She glimpsed Bert and waved to him but she doubted he saw her.

Those on the pier called to the men on board and they answered back, but in the uproar who could understand what was said or who was saying it?

She heard her name called—*Kate, Kate*—as clear as if the world was silent.

She looked up.

There he was. She could make out every feature despite the distance, even the beautiful blue of his eyes.

He was smiling at her, waving.

I love you.

She heard his voice as if he were beside her and called the words back.

She had seen him. He *would* come home to her.

Another soldier moved to the front blocking Kate's view. She kept calling Jack's name and waving furiously even though she had lost sight of him. He might still be able to see her. As long as he could see her, they were together in this place.

Streamers of paper ribbon—mainly red, white and blue—fluttered between the ship and the shore. With the slowly setting sun, a lone voice began to sing *Auld Lang Syne*. One by one those on the pier and the men on the deck joined in until the whole world was singing its goodbye, its promises never to forget.

In a brief moment of silence, the troopship pulled away from the shore.

Ribbons snapped, a band played, and those watching from the pier sang beneath their tears as they followed the movement of the steamer.

The Last Post sounded.

The HMAT *Ulysses* sailed off carrying her men to war.

1915

Australia's infantry forces have been heavily engaged, and although the full story of the courage and determination they showed in effecting a landing, which was strongly resisted, and of their gallant bayonet charges at the heights has not yet been told, sufficient evidence of the fierce fire they had to face is to be found in the lists of names. The reality of war is striking home, and the crowds who wait around The Age office for the lists are notably grave-faced and ominously quiet of speech.

The Age 8 May 1915 p.15

11

Jack had been gone four months, Kate's cousins six, and news of them was slow in coming. Aunty Mary now had a newspaper delivered each day and she and Kate pored through it for any news they could find of the Australian forces overseas. Letters sent by soldiers to family and friends were sometimes published and told of the sea journey and gave a glimpse of life in the camps as well as the sights of Egypt.

Vince's first letter had arrived late in January and was full of the trip to Egypt, their activities on the ship and what they had seen and done—whales and flying fish; the locals at Colombo in their little boats, surrounding the troopships, selling everything from cigars and cigarettes to coconuts and vivid silks and glittering stones; their reactions to the sights and pungent smells of Cairo. He had ended the letter—

> This soldiering is a fine lark. When you run into any of my mates who have not stirred themselves to enlist, tell them I said to hurry up & get over here or they will miss out on the fun.
> Brendan is in fine fettle & sends his love. He will write next time.

Aunty had laughed, 'You would think they could each find a few minutes to write to their mother.' She clearly wasn't troubled and happily shared the news of her boys to anyone who came into the shop that afternoon.

Kate had to wait until March and then all she received from Jack was a postcard of two pyramids and a palm tree.

> My dearest Kate,
> It was a grand trip over, except for the food. Bert was laid low with seasickness despite his boasting. We have

seen the pyramids & the sphinx & had a ride on a camel—
I will take a horse any day. Sand everywhere, even in the
food. Missing you, my darling.
With all my love,
Jack.

And three big Xes across the bottom.

These scraps made the waiting almost bearable. She knew Jack
was safe when he had written to her. But was he now? She pushed
down her fears, and tried not to think too far ahead. And prayed.
It was all any of them could do to keep them safe. Each evening
after the day's work was done Kate and Aunty Mary said the rosary
together.

The rosary finished, they would sit by the fire in the sitting room
now the autumn days were drawing in, Aunty knitting socks to be
passed on to the local Red Cross committee. Kate finished by hand
the flannel shirts and pyjamas she had sewn on Aunty's sewing
machine in quiet moments during the day. They didn't have time
to attend the Red Cross's sewing meetings, instead Kate went each
Tuesday afternoon to the room set aside for Red Cross use at the
Coburg Town Hall. She took back what they had finished, and
collected wool and new items to be sewn.

The season of Lent, with its forty days of fast and abstinence,
drew to a close and Holy Week arrived. Kate accompanied Aunty
Mary to the sequence of services held from Holy Thursday to
Easter Sunday, from the stripped altar, the empty tabernacle, and
the overnight vigil of Holy Thursday to the covered statues, the
doleful chant and the reading of Christ's passion and death on
Good Friday. The lights were put out, the flame in the sanctuary
lamp extinguished. The parishioners left the darkened church in
silence. Kate walked away with a sense of desolation deeper than
anything she had ever felt.

Holy Saturday was a normal working day, unlike Good Friday
which had been a public holiday. While the baptismal font and

holy water were blessed and the new Paschal candle lit in the church, Kate and Aunty Mary were busy with customers catching up on the shopping they had missed the day before. Easter Sunday was fine and cloudless, the altar decorated with flowers, the church packed with people—even those erratic in their attendance— dressed in their Sunday very best, and Fr Hayes and Fr Devine in bright vestments. High Mass was sung by the choir in full throat, the altar bells jingled brightly and incense floated on the air. The faithful lingered in the churchyard afterwards, exchanging Easter greetings, then strolled home to their Sunday dinners. Kate and Aunty Mary's Easter dinner of roast chicken had the usual trimmings but it lacked festivity as it was only the two of them. Next year would be different. Next year the boys would be home. Next year would be a real Easter celebration.

~

Tuesday brought two letters, one for Aunty Mary and one for Kate. Kate slipped hers into her apron pocket to read when she was alone.

'Ah, Brendan's turn to write.' Aunty quickly scanned her letter and muttered, 'Holy Mother of God', as she blessed herself.

'What is it?' Kate asked, forcing down the sickening rush of panic.

Aunty read—

> We were sent to the Suez Canal, to have a go at the Turks who were hoping to get across to Egypt without any trouble. Unfortunately, we did not manage to get a shot at them as the Indian troops got there first and saw them off with their tails between their legs. We expect to be in the thick of the fighting by the spring.

Her brow was furrowed. 'It would be spring over there now.' She blinked. 'Oh, he is a good boy. He has visited an ancient tree that the Holy Family rested under on the flight into Egypt. He says there is a beautiful church there.' She tried to smile brightly as she read on.

> We ran into Kate's sweetheart and took him out for a drink. He is a bonzer bloke. Vince will write next time. He is busy at present writing sweet nothings to Reenie and refuses to let me look over his shoulder.
> From your loving son Brendan.

She looked up as the door jingled and old Mrs Johnson came in. She was a tiny sharp-eyed woman, dressed in black, in the style of twenty years earlier.

'You go and read your letter, Kate. I know it's burning a hole in your pocket. I'll call if things get any busier.'

Kate went out to the back verandah, her panic disappearing as she read Jack's letter.

> Hoping all is well with you, my love. We are fighting fit here. Our officers are decent men & treat us well, cannot say as much for some of the British officers who behave like little tin gods. And, as you would expect, the average Australian does his best to take them down a peg.
> We thought we were drilled hard at Broadmeadows, but it has nothing on this. Marching across miles of sand carrying a full kit of 80 pounds certainly toughens a man up. Sometimes it feels like we are more camels than men. We are in camp near the town of Heliopolis, a place with some fine buildings & even a botanical gardens & a zoo. Otherwise, there is sand & sand & sand as far as the eye can see.
> They have turned a large hotel here into a hospital for the troops. I visited there the other day to see poor Dick Simmonds who is crook. He collapsed on one of the marches. He has heart strain & debility & they say he will be shipped home when he is well enough. Sad for a bloke to come all this way then miss out on the action.
> The train ride from Alexandria took us through some real countryside. There are irrigation channels everywhere. The

soil is rich & dark & they grow all sorts of crops but use old fashioned wooden ploughs & oxen for ploughing. The sheep here are bigger than ours & there are goats galore as well as camels, mules & donkeys.

Kate smiled. Jack truly was a farmer at heart.

I am glad I volunteered. It is a great experience. There are rumors running wild at the moment. It seems we

Frowning, Kate stared at the letter. Almost the whole paragraph had been blacked out. All that was left was the final line.

I can come home to you, my love.

She had heard that letters were censored. Jack must have written something about where they were going. She hoped it was over quickly and he could come home to her.

I look at your photograph every night & go to sleep remembering your arms around me & your kisses.

Kate closed her eyes, reliving the memory of Jack's arms around her and his kisses. She blushed—the censor would have read this too. If Jack didn't care, she should try not to either

She pressed her lips to the Xes he had written across the bottom of the page. She laid the sheet of paper on the bench beside her, pressing her hand over it. He had touched this paper, as she was now—it was almost as if they were touching hands.

She read the letter a second time, then took it to her room and slid it into the handkerchief case she kept in the drawer of the bedside table. Made of pale green satin, Kate had embroidered it with small pink roses, and daisies in an array of colours. It was a perfect place to keep her mementoes of the weeks before Jack had left: his postcard and the notes he had sent when he could not get leave, the tickets from their visit to the picture theatre, the photos of him. She drew out the photograph of the two of them together, caught in that moment of pure happiness. Jack was smiling, there was light in her own eyes. Yet she remembered how she had felt in the minutes they had waited for the photographer, anticipating the longing that was now threaded through every moment of the day.

~

Mrs Johnson, seated on the chair provided for customers on the other side of the counter, was in full flight.

Aunty Mary was sorting the tins of ham and corned beef that had been delivered earlier in the day. Occasionally, she murmured, 'Is that so?' 'Fancy that!'

Aunty glanced over her shoulder as Kate came in. 'Would you mind doing the biscuits?'

Mrs Johnson, not noticing the interruption, kept on with her tale of minor scandal.

Kate, standing on the lowest rung of the ladder, moved the four nearly empty biscuit tins from the shelf onto the counter. She scooped out the remaining biscuits, mostly broken, and put them all into the last of the tins.

'Oh, I'll have a ha'penny worth of broken biscuits,' Mrs Johnson said.

Kate put two scoops into a paper bag and handed it to Aunty who rang up the price on the cash register, taking Mrs Johnson's halfpenny before she gave her the bag.

Mrs Johnson turned in her chair as the bell on the door jingled. At the sight of Mrs Miles, a sturdy woman with a firm opinion on everything, Mrs Johnson said a quick goodbye and scurried out the door.

Kate unsealed the new biscuit tins and placed them on the shelf as Aunty served Mrs Miles. She climbed further up the ladder and pushed the tinned meat along, dusting the shelf as she went.

Mrs Miles paid for her pound of tea and stayed on chatting about her daughters' tally of socks knitted for the Red Cross.

The bell jingled again.

'Good afternoon, Tom.'

'And good afternoon to you Mrs Burke. Mrs Miles.' It was not an old man's voice.

Kate didn't turn to see who it was but continued dusting and tidying the shelves.

'And what can I do for you today?'

'I have a list of a few things Mother wants.'

'How is your mother? I haven't seen her since before Easter.'

'She's well. Only just back from Ballarat—she's been staying with my sister Johanna and her tribe.'

'Aah, that would be lovely for—'

'I'm surprised you haven't enlisted, Mr Ryan.' Mrs Miles spoke over Aunty Mary. 'A fit young man with no responsibilities.'

'And why would I do that?' His reply was harsh.

'It's what every decent young man is doing.'

'It's not my fight, Mrs Miles.'

'You won't fight to defend Australia?'

'Australia is not under attack.'

'Hmmph! Disgraceful!'

Kate turned on the ladder at the outrage in Mrs Miles's voice.

Mrs Miles glared at the young man and marched out of the shop.

'You want to be careful, Tom,' Aunty said. 'She's just the one to go reporting you for making disloyal statements.'

Kate came down and stood beside her aunt who was now ringing up Tom's purchases on the cash register.

Tom Ryan was lean and tanned. Although he was serious at the moment, his face was pleasant. The crinkled skin at the corners of his hazel eyes gave him the look of someone who laughed easily.

'But what about defending those who cannot do it for themselves, like the people of Belgium—the women and children.' Kate paused. 'You have read what the Germans have done to the nuns there?'

He passed Aunty his money and gazed at Kate, frowning slightly before he answered.

'There are others closer to Belgium better able to help. And I'm afraid England is more interested in having a go at Germany for its own ends, than defending the innocents of Belgium. And, I have no wish to fight the English king's battles.'

'Whisht, Tom,' Aunty hissed. 'Now that sort of talk *will* get you into trouble.' She handed him the string bag with his mother's purchases. 'Not everyone feels the way you do. My boys, Kate's fiancé, every bit as Irish as you and they were glad to go.'

'I know, Mrs Burke, and I pray they come home safe. But I don't see any need to go myself nor do I need to justify my reasons to anyone. But I will heed your advice.' He nodded to Kate and left the shop whistling.

Aunty stared after him. 'I never know with that one when he is being serious or simply stirring people up for the pure devilment of it.' She shook her head. 'Devilment can get you into trouble in times like these.

12

The early morning rush over, Kate opened the newspaper and flicked through pages of advertisements until she came to the news reports. Her interest was caught by a headline about the Dardanelles Expeditionary Force which said, 'Colonial troops form the backbone'.

Kate looked over to Aunty Mary who was rearranging the display in the front window. She had placed two large vases of gum leaves at each side of the window and was now draping an Australian flag and a Union Jack behind the goods on display.

'Colonial troops would be Australian, wouldn't they?'

Aunty nodded. 'They would, among others.'

'The Dardanelles are part of Turkey and not far from Egypt,' Kate murmured. Her grasp of geography had increased since the start of the war.

All through April there had been frequent mention of the Dardanelles and of the actions of the British Navy there, bombarding Turkish forts and sinking Turkish ships. An article earlier in the month had said the Australian forces would not be going to Belgium or France but to the Dardanelles. That information had originally been copied from a German paper, so who knew if it could be trusted?

Everyone who came into the shop had a theory about what was happening but no one knew anything for sure. Most, like Kate and Aunty Mary, only knew what was reported in the newspapers. There were others who said they knew for a fact, that they had information from a letter sent from a family member in Egypt, or from a friend of a friend, or an aunt's cousin's husband who worked at Victoria Barracks, the army headquarters in Melbourne. But no one truly knew, rumours swirled, and a growing disquiet gripped those with men overseas.

There were moments when Kate could barely breathe. She was certain something was happening, but they were not being told. She knelt in church on Sunday, knelt in the sitting room for the rosary, knelt by her bed at night, woke in the darkest hours but the prayers would not come. All she could do was say, over and over, *Lord keep him safe, please keep him safe, bring him home to me safe*. Life became one long cry for Jack's life.

The news broke on Monday morning, colonial troops had seen action at the Dardanelles. Nearly every person who came in to the shop was full of the news—this had to mean Australian troops. Some were glorying in it. Others were unsure, preferring instead to wait anxiously for firm news. A few, women mainly, were still and quiet.

Aunty didn't open the newspaper.

Kate spread it on the counter and turned the pages slowly. And there it was, seven pages in.

DARDANELLES ATTACK

TROOPS LAND AT THREE POINTS

WAR SHIPS RESUME BOMBARDMENT

Colonial troops had landed on the Gallipoli Peninsula. But it was only an unofficial report and not from Britain but from Athens.

Kate groaned.

'What's wrong?' Aunty's voice was sharp, panicked. She came and read over Kate's shoulder.

'Unofficial?' Tears welled in her eyes. 'Why are we not being told anything officially?' Her voice cracked as she said what Kate had not dared let herself think. 'Has it all gone wrong?'

The newspapers made it no clearer over the next couple of days. The same thing was said, over and over, in slightly different ways. British and French troops were mentioned. Did British include those from other parts of the British Empire who had been in Egypt: Australian, New Zealand and Indian troops? Wednesday's *Age* offered a little more—enough to allow them to imagine. The landing of troops had begun before sunrise last Sunday and continued all day with serious opposition from the enemy.

Kate stared at the page—that could only mean one thing but the paper said the landing was successful. Did it truly mean that none of their soldiers had come to any harm?

Aunty closed her eyes and blessed herself.

Kate tried to swallow the pain swelling in her throat.

Confirmation finally came on Thursday afternoon when the Prime Minister, Andrew Fisher, announced in Parliament that the Australian Expeditionary Forces had been transferred from Egypt to the Gallipoli Peninsula where the action was proceeding satisfactorily. By nightfall the news was across Melbourne, spread as much by word of mouth as by the evening newspaper. It was said that while the members of the House of Representatives had cheered when Mr Fisher had read his prepared statement to the House, the Senate had received the news in almost complete silence. Mr Fisher had then read a cable received from the Secretary of State for the Colonies in London which spoke of the 'splendid gallantry and magnificent achievement' of the Australian soldiers.

Kate dreamt of Jack that night, a swirl of memories: his arms around her as they danced in the church hall; the first time he kissed her properly in the shadows in his mother's sitting room on New Year's Eve sixteen months ago; his joy when he saw her after six weeks in camp; the beauty of his voice as he sang to her in the moonlight. Clearer still, she dreamt he was with her, feeling the dip of his weight as he sat on the side of her bed. She could see his face—the line of his cheek, the curve of his lips, the laughter and light in his eyes. She reached up, her fingers skimming the light stubble along his jaw as he kissed her.

She woke the next morning to the rattle of a cart in the street, the dream fading but for the memory of his lips on hers, the prickle of his skin beneath her fingers, and a longing so painful it took her breath away.

All Friday no one spoke of anything but the Australian soldiers' bravery, revelling in the news of their 'magnificent achievement'. Aunty was quiet, unsmiling, little more than murmuring in answer to her customers' comments.

When the shop was empty, early in the afternoon, she opened the newspaper and pointed to the editorial. 'Have you read this?'

Kate nodded. It was an angry piece of writing and she agreed with every word.

'Why aren't they telling us which battalions are there? I doubt every single Australian soldier left Egypt.' Aunty stabbed her finger at the page. 'This is right.' She read aloud—

> It was neither kind nor fair in Britain to keep the people of Australia waiting even for a moment for their casualty lists. If the Imperial authorities temporarily lacked or were unable to supply the information, they should have kept back alike their praise and their meagre battle news until they could tell us all we wish and have a right to learn at once.

She glanced down the column of print and read further.

> It irritates when it is applied to the suppression of news that is impersonal to us; but when it keeps us ignorant—without reason—of what is happening to our sons and brothers at the front, it is intolerable.

'When have those that run the British Empire ever had a care for the ordinary people, even those in their own country?' She was fighting back tears. 'It seems the papers knew but were forbidden to publish it. No wonder many of the rumours have turned out to be true.'

Mrs Miles pushed the door open and swept in. She looked across at Aunty, her head tilted to the side. 'Oh, Mrs Burke, what is the matter?'

'This news from the Dardanelles,' Aunty said.

'Isn't it wonderful?' Mrs Miles's eyes lit up. 'Those brave young men, such a credit to Australia.'

'We don't know if anyone has been injured...' Kate forced herself to say it '...or killed.'

Aunty gave a whimper. Her lips pressed tight, her jaw rigid, she turned away and walked back into the house.

This was more than worry—it was as if Aunty was convinced the worst had happened.

'No one has been killed,' Mrs Miles waved her hand dismissively. 'The Minister of Defence said no one was lost on the ships on the way to the Dardanelles and there are no casualties. Besides, the paper said the family is told before names are printed and I haven't heard of anyone getting news like that.'

'I read the paper too.' Kate exhaled through her nose. 'The Defence Minister actually said that the government *had not been informed* of any casualties.' She said the words slowly. 'The British government is as likely to be holding them back as they did the news that our men had gone to the Dardanelles. It has taken them five days to tell us.'

Mrs Miles sniffed. 'No doubt they had their reasons.'

'Stupid reasons if you ask me. Now what would you like, Mrs Miles?'

Mrs Miles jerked her head, her lips pressed tight as if holding back a sharp reply.

She gave Kate a list of baking ingredients—sugar, flour, baking soda, ginger, mixed peel—and started up a conversation with an elderly man who had just come in, talking with assurance of the progress of the war.

Kate wished she would close her mouth and go away.

~

On Saturday morning, six days after the landing at Gallipoli, *The Argus* published the first casualty list in a special war edition.

Aunty managed to get a copy. It listed the names of twenty-two officers, six of them Victorian, who had been wounded.

Aunty gasped. 'Lieutenant-Colonel Elliott has been wounded. He is in charge of the 7th Battalion. A good man and a fine soldier, Brendan says, tough but fair.' She blessed herself and placed the newspaper on the counter. She walked back into the house, her lips moving in whispered prayer.

Kate glanced through the list. The first paragraph included the ominous statement that no list of privates had yet been received, nor information on whether any Australians had been killed. *The Age*, the paper they usually read, reported on the progress of the war in Europe, of the German's use of poison gas, as well as praise for the gallant heroism of the forces in the Dardanelles. There were also claims of massive numbers of Turkish casualties and prisoners. Nothing to ease Kate's mind. Nothing to tell her that those she cared for were safe.

Aunty Mary didn't come back into the shop and Kate didn't hear the usual clatter in the kitchen as Aunty did her Saturday morning baking. Later, when the shop was quiet, Kate found her sitting on the back verandah, her rosary beads in her hands.

Kate sat beside her and placed her hand over her aunt's.

Aunty stared down the yard, her eyes glistening. 'I feel dreadful, Kate. It is as if my heart is squeezed in a vice. I can scarcely breathe.'

'You don't need the doctor?'

Aunty shook her head. ''Tis a pain no doctor can heal.'

The shop door jingled and Kate stood up.

'If you don't mind, my treasure, I'll stay out here. I can't face the prating of the likes of Bridie Johnson or *Queen* Victoria Miles this morning.'

Nor can I, Kate thought.

13

Monday brought a casualty list with the names of four officers and fourteen men who had been killed in action, most of them from Victoria. The list of the wounded had grown with the addition of fifteen more names, all officers—not a single private. Kate's unease grew as she read an article describing the men who had been killed and their lives before they enlisted. It said what was in every person's mind, 'It is to be feared that fresh casualty lists are now on their way from the front'.

Aunty Mary was back in the shop but was not her usual talkative self. She often left Kate to serve the customers while she unpacked deliveries, tidied the shelves, or went out the back to weigh and packaged dry goods like flour and sugar into the amounts people usually bought.

Kate did her best to act as if life were normal, that heavy clouds were not massing above them.

On Tuesday evening she went to Reenie's house in Main Street. She had joined the knitting circle Reenie had organised—most of the others were friends of Reenie's from the Children of Mary. Once a week, they sat together knitting khaki or grey socks and face washers. Tonight, all that could be heard was the click of knitting needles, the soft crackle of the fire and the hiss of the gaslight.

'Those socks are a bit big, aren't they, Kate?' Reenie's voice was startlingly loud in the quiet room. 'You're not knitting them too loosely?'

'I am not. The pattern you gave me was much too small—more suitable for boys' feet.' Kate held the half-finished sock up. 'These are a much better size for a man's foot.'

Reenie giggled. 'I don't know much about men's feet.'

Kate glared at her and Reenie, seeming to realise her joke had fallen flat, asked, 'How is Mrs Burke? I've been meaning to call in and see her.'

'She's worried like the rest of us.'

A couple of the other young women murmured agreement.

'Tell her not to worry,' Reenie said brightly. 'I made Vince a medal wallet before he left. Pat too. Fr Hayes blessed the medals for me—a Miraculous medal, a St Christopher and a St Michael. They will be safe.'

Kate wondered why she hadn't thought to do that. She would make one for Jack and send it to him.

Reenie was still talking. 'I would know if anything had happened to Vince.'

'And Brendan? Would you know about him too?' Kate asked. 'Aunty Mary worries about both her sons.'

'Oops.' Reenie grimaced. 'I'd forgotten Brendan.'

Kate clenched her hands and said nothing more. How could anyone be certain?

Annie Watkins, the young woman sitting beside Kate on the sofa, placed her hand on top of Kate's. Kate glanced at her and saw understanding in her eyes. Her brother was in the same battalion as Brendan and Vince.

Annie lived with her parents in Harding Street, not too far from Aunty's shop. Since her brother had enlisted, she had taken to driving his car and had offered to take Kate to and from Caseys so she would not be walking home alone in the dark.

Later, as she stopped the car across from the shop, Annie said, 'Don't mind Reenie—she rarely thinks before she speaks.'

Kate gave a laugh. 'I am learning that.'

'Reenie is as worried as the rest of us. I wish there was more news but they have good reason for not telling us everything.'

'But if someone is injured or killed, it's cruel not to let their loved ones know.'

'It is.' Annie sighed loudly. 'I find the Children of Mary a great help in unsettled times like this. The prayers and devotions at our weekly meetings bring me comfort. The companionship as well. There are several other young women with brothers overseas. You should consider joining.'

'I'm not sure,' Kate said slowly. 'I really do not want to leave Aunty Mary on her own another night each a week.'

'I'm sure Mrs Burke wouldn't mind.'

'I'll think about it.' But she had already thought about it and had no intention of spending an extra evening at the church. Her mind would drift away from the prayers to what might or might not be happening to Jack. It was better to sit listening to Aunty Mary's stories or hum along with the gramophone. Though, if Annie had suggested a weekly visit to the pictures, Kate doubted she would have thought twice about leaving Aunty on her own. She might even have asked if Aunty could come too.

'With all that's happening, I wish I could do more than knitting socks. I've thought of volunteering as a nurse but, of course, they want volunteers who are trained and experienced, and over twenty-five. If I trained, I would be old enough by the time I finished, but still not experienced. And, I pray it will be over by then.'

'It must be,' Kate said quietly.

'The Matron from Pentridge is running a First Aid course for women at the Town Hall. I am going to enrol in it. If I have that, I might be able to find something useful I can do here.' She turned to Kate. 'Would you be interested?'

Kate hadn't thought beyond sewing and knitting. She was filled with admiration for Annie. She was a teacher in a Catholic girls school, but found time to be involved in several of the parish groups as well as now knitting for the Red Cross. She was the most prolific of Reenie's knitters.

'Yes, I would,' Kate said. Being of use to others might help ease the pain and longing.

~

By the middle of May, fifteen casualty lists had been published.

While most of those listed as killed in action were officers, there were hundreds and hundreds of names of ordinary soldiers who had been wounded. An officer from Coburg had been killed, the Anglican Minister's son, and a number of men from both Coburg and Brunswick were wounded. The war was no longer *over there*; it was here, sliding its cruel cold fingers into the hearts of those around them.

Kate forced herself to read the lists suspecting, dreading, that it was here she would first learn of any harm come to Jack, praying each day as she slowly turned the pages of the newspaper that his name would not be there.

~

Aunty Mary smiled as Fr Hayes, the elderly Irish Parish Priest, came into the shop. ''Tis a delight to see you, Father.'

Father did not smile back. He took off his hat and said, 'Might I have a word, Mrs Burke?'

The colour drained from Aunty's face. 'Of course.' She walked ahead of the priest into the house.

As he passed Kate, he said quietly. 'It would be best to shut the shop, Miss Burke.'

Kate locked the door. She stood, desolate, as her Aunt's bitter cry of lamentation pierced through her.

Her eyes stinging, she hurried to the sitting room.

Fr Hayes was sitting at the edge of an armchair. Aunty was on the sofa, bent over, her arms tight around her middle, tears running down her cheeks, her mouth clamped shut. A pink telegram lay on the cushion beside her.

Kate brushed it to one side and sat beside her, winding her arm around her aunt.

Aunty pressed her face against Kate's shoulder, her body quaking as she sobbed.

Kate looked towards Fr Hayes.

'It is your cousin, Vincent. He has been killed at the Dardanelles.'

It was like the slice of a knife. 'When?' Her voice creaked.

'Between the twenty-fifth and Thursday last. The telegram gives no more detail.'

'Why do they keep us waiting so long, then tell us very little?'

Father shook his head slowly.

Kate went to ask, *And what of Brendan?* She stopped herself. It was tempting Fate.

Father looked at Aunty. 'Mrs Burke, would you like me to pray with you?'

Aunty Mary nodded and drew her rosary beads from her apron pocket and knelt on the floor. Kate slipped to her knees beside her. Fr Hayes led the prayers, Aunty murmuring the responses, so Kate answered clearly. Said by rote with a gentle rise and fall, it was almost a chant, meditative and calming. Kate's thoughts drifted to her cousin and her memories of him: a boy, then a young man, full of laughter and practical jokes, and clever too—he had a position in the accounts office of one of the department stores in the city, and was studying bookkeeping and accounting at night school.

Pain gripped her throat, her eyes prickled. She had to keep herself in check, Aunty needed her. She forced herself to concentrate on the words Father was saying.

'Eternal rest grant unto him, O Lord.'

Kate and Aunty Mary answered, 'And let perpetual light shine upon him.'

'May he rest in peace.'

'Amen.'

Father raised his hand in blessing. *'In nomine Patris, et Filii et Spiritus Sancti.'*

'Amen.'

Kate got up and stood beside her aunt, now sitting back on the sofa.

'I'll call again on Monday, Mrs Burke. We can arrange a special Requiem Mass for Vincent.'

'Even without...?' Aunty looked at him, her eyes dull.

'We can. It is his soul and our prayers that matter now.'

Aunty bowed her head, her lips moving as she silently prayed.

Fr Hayes turned to Kate. 'Perhaps you could get a strong cup of tea for your aunt.'

'Would you like one too, Father?'

'It is kind of you but I have another call to make.'

Kate saw the sorrow in him, the burden of carrying such news to those who at this moment believed their loved one to be alive.

She walked him to the side door.

Father stopped in the doorway. 'Your cousin was a fine young man. Please tell your aunt that Vincent will be mentioned during the Mass tomorrow. His name will be in the newspapers early next week.' He rested his hand on Kate's for a moment. 'It is good you are here with Mrs Burke.'

Once he had left, Kate went to the kitchen and set about making a pot of tea.

Kate carried Aunty's cup of tea into the sitting room and placed it on the side table.

Aunty Mary paused her prayers and picked up the cup. She took a couple of sips. 'Someone will have to tell Reenie.'

'I'll do that later.' Much as she didn't want to, Reenie needed to be told before Vince's death became common knowledge.

Aunty placed her cup back on the saucer. 'I'm going to lie down.'

Kate followed her out and saw her go not to her own room but to Kate's, the room Vince and Brendan had shared.

The side gate creaked, footsteps pattered along the verandah. Kate went to the door and came face to face with Mrs Johnson.

'I saw Fr Hayes leaving earlier. Is anything wrong?'

Kate stared down the yard away from her. There was nothing else she could do; she would have to tell the old stickybeak.

Mrs Johnson watched Kate, her eyes glittering with interest.

'My cousin Vincent has been killed.'

'Ooh. At the Dardanelles?'

'Yes.'

She went to step around Kate. 'I'll come in and pay my respects.'

Kate stepped back, blocking her way. 'Another day. My aunt is indisposed.'

'Ah, 'tis to be expected. I'll sit with her, offer her some comfort.'

'She is not ready to see visitors. Come back in a day or two.'

Mrs Johnson's face flushed. 'You are a heartless young woman, to be sure. You cannot leave your aunt alone, without comfort, at this time.'

'My aunt is not alone or without people to comfort her.' She stepped back into the house and pulled the wire door shut. 'Come back tomorrow afternoon.'

The old woman glared at her. 'I have never, in all my life, met such a rude young article as yourself.' Her lips tight, she jerked her head and marched away.

'And I have never met such a rude old bat as you,' Kate muttered as she shut the door.

She closed her eyes, pressed her shoulders back and stretched her neck. She didn't want to, but she needed to go and tell Reenie before she heard an embellished story from a nasty old busybody like Mrs Johnson.

14

Kate put a notice on the door saying the shop was closed but would reopen next week. Then she went to see Reenie.

Mrs Johnson stood up as Kate came into the kitchen with Mrs Casey. An empty teacup and a plate scattered with biscuit crumbs sat on the table in front of her. She must have run all the way from the shop.

'Miss Burke.' She gave Kate a terse nod of the head. 'I'll be on my way, Ellen. Tell young Irene I will keep her in my prayers. Poor, poor girl. I'll see myself out.'

Kate and Mrs Casey waited, silent, until they heard the click of the side gate.

'I thought she would be here until teatime.' Mrs Casey's face crumpled. 'Oh Kate. I don't want to believe it.'

Her eyes wet, Kate shook her head, words were too hard.

She forced herself to ask, 'How is Reenie?'

'She's at the church helping with the flowers for Mass tomorrow. I'll collect her in a few minutes.' She put her arms around Kate, tears welling in her eyes. 'He was such a lovely boy. Poor Mary... I can't...'

Kate couldn't let herself give in to grief. 'Is there anyone else I should tell?'

'Maggie Ryan. She and Mary are close. I'll send Cecilia round to her with a note so you can go straight home. I'll come and sit with Mary too, bring Reenie if she's up to it.

'I'll pray for Vince, for the repose of his soul.' She clamped her hand over her mouth, her shoulders quaking. 'But we must pray... for the living... my Pat, and for Brendan and your Jack, for all those fine young men.' She drew a sharp breath and held herself erect. 'I want this war to end. I want them back safe. And whole.'

Kate nodded, trying not to sob. 'I'd better go.'

Mrs Casey grasped Kate's hand and kissed her. 'I'm glad Mary has you with her.'

The thought of Aunty Mary alone in her grief was unbearable.

~

Mrs Ryan came and sat with Aunty Mary, weeping quietly with her, and praying. A gentle white-haired woman in her mid-sixties, she had come from the same village in Ireland as Aunty Mary. Mrs Casey called in late in the afternoon but did not stay long. She had to get back to Reenie who was lying curled on her bed having cried herself to sleep.

After Mrs Ryan had left, Kate and Aunty Mary spent the rest of the evening in the sitting room in front of the fire drinking tea and telling stories of Vincent.

'When I pulled back the blankets to get into bed, I screamed.' Kate shuddered, remembering her fright. 'There was an enormous blue-tongue lizard there, slowly blinking as if I'd woken it up. And I could hear them giggling, Vince and Jim, outside the door. They were more like twins than cousins, and as bad as each other.'

Aunty nodded. 'Indeed, imagine the mischief if they'd grown up side by side.' She smiled, staring into the past. 'When Vincent was seven, we spent Christmas with you all, and your father caught him heading off into the scrub with his good Sunday harness and bridle. Bill asked where Vincent was off to with that and Vincent said he had found an old man koala he was going to ride.'

Kate raised her eyebrows. 'I've never seen one that big.'

'To Vincent's mind, he was big enough. Your father gave him a talking to about not helping himself to other people's property and the dangers of old man koalas. But Bill, just like my Mick, couldn't be cross for long, and especially not with Vincent.

'My poor boy.' Her eyes filled with tears. 'I hope they have koalas up there big enough for him to ride.'

'If not a koala, there's sure to be camels.'

When their stories turned to silent remembering, they said the rosary and went to bed.

At Mass the next morning, Fr Hayes asked all present to join him in praying for the repose of the soul of that fine young man, Vincent Burke, recently killed at the Dardanelles. He prayed, too, that peace might soon be restored.

Vince's name was in Tuesday's paper in the seventeenth Casualty List. One of thirty-four men who had died of wounds. The list began with the horrifying statement that 2,102 men had either been killed or wounded. That was two whole battalions. So many men, so many women weeping, so many hearts breaking.

On Wednesday morning a Requiem Mass was said for Vincent. This Kate understood, it was almost normal, not the unreality of a death that was mere words on a slip of pink paper. Throughout the day visitors poured through the house, bringing with them food, drink and condolences, and stories of Vince—it was a wake with the usual tears and fond remembrances but without a body. Aunty sat through it all. Although wrapped in the fog of grief, she smiled at her visitors' kind words, answered their concerned questions, and accepted their solemn kisses.

Just over a week on, she stepped back into the shop. Aunty Mary straightened her shoulders and stiffened her back. 'Brendan will have no time for mourning. If he can bear it, I must too.'

~

Life followed its usual pattern and, sometimes, Kate forgot to be afraid. She daydreamt of Jack's return. She saw a pretty hat, or a dress, in the street and thought of making something similar for herself. She sat with the other young women and knitted, listening to their talk of dances and visits to the moving pictures. At home, she sewed flannel shirts and pyjamas for the Red Cross. She went with Annie to the First Aid classes. When they learnt to apply dressings and bandages, she did not allow herself to imagine the wounds they would cover.

In quiet moments, fear would spring upon her, stabbing through her with the thought that Jack was dead too. It wasn't true. He *was* coming home. He had said he would and he always kept his word.

Most often, fear stood silent at Kate's shoulder, closer than any friend, closer than her guardian angel.

One by one everyone she knew was affected. Annie's brother had been wounded and was in hospital on the Greek island of Lemnos. The newspapers told and retold stories of heroic exploits and brought the war to sickening life. Even as Kate skimmed the paper, trying to avoid these articles, there were words and phrases that leapt into her eyes and compelled her to read on.

> As soon as the boats touched the beach, the Australians thirsting to come to death grips with the enemy, flung off their packs and rushed to the attack. They revelled in the bayonet work. With deafening yells, and not waiting to form a line, they ran on, each man feeling himself a single-handed match for the enemy. At the sight of this wild onslaught, the Turks, in the nearest trenches were seized with panic, and fled to the second line, pursued by the Australians.

But would so many be dead and wounded if the Turks had fled at the sight of them?

She continued her daily search of the casualty lists, her heart in her mouth. She saw Len Simmonds' name. Poor Mrs Simmonds, a small busy woman with a rich unladylike laugh, no doubt silent now. At least Dick had been sent home. Jack would be missing Len, but not as badly as Brendan missing Vince. Wrapped in their own worry and sorrow, was easy to overlook how these deaths would affect the men over there.

Empire Day, the day celebrating the British Empire, came and went with patriotic displays, flags and speeches, more fervent than last year. The children of St Paul's school took their part alongside the children of the State School, marching down Sydney Road from Urquhart to Harding Street and back again. They played games of basketball and football together, donating the usual prizes for the sports to the Red Cross. The day ended with a patriotic moving picture at the Coburg Public Hall. All were united in their support of the men who had gone to fight for the Empire, for Australia, for the freedom of small nations.

~

A postcard arrived from Jack with a snapshot enclosed in the envelope of him and Bert, a pyramid in the distance behind them, arms slung across each other's shoulders, eyes shaded by their slouch hats. All Kate could see was their wide grins.

It was only a few lines on the card but she could hear Jack's excitement.

> This is called the Cheops pyramid at Giza. They say it is the biggest of them all. Bert and I have climbed it. Not long now, my love. Once it is over I will be on the first troopship home to you.

It was a voice from far away, from Egypt, from before they had been sent to the Dardanelles.

15

June 1915

Kate stood behind the counter replenishing the jars of lollies that had been raided on Friday night and Saturday, often by an indulgent father bringing in a child or three with a penny each to spend. Sometimes the father was in a new khaki uniform.

The doorbell jingled and Kate glanced up.

'Mum!' She sped around the counter, throwing herself into her mother's arms.

'My darling girl.' Her mother lifted a whisp of hair away from Kate's face and tucked it behind her ear. 'You look quite the lady grocer.' Although she smiled, Kate saw the sadness in her mother's eyes.

'Aunty is teaching me well.'

Mum's smile faded. 'How is Mary?'

Kate shrugged, her eyes prickling. 'She forces herself to keep going.'

'I'll go and see her.'

'She's in the kitchen, weighing and packaging the flour and rice.'

Mum's forehead was puckered. It was as if she wanted to say more but, instead, she picked up her case and went to Aunty Mary.

Ten minutes later, both Mum and Aunty Mary walked back into the shop.

Kate saw their red eyes, saw the sorrow etched in their faces, the trepidation—and she knew.

'Kate, I need to—' Mum began.

'No. No!'

She wouldn't listen. She pushed past them, walked through the house, out into the yard. She stood, her arms tight across her bosom, staring into the bright uncaring sky. The pain swelling in her throat, stabbing down into her heart. She leant her head back and opened her mouth in a silent scream.

She knew it was true.

He had come to say goodbye.

And now he was gone beyond her reach. Gone where she could not follow.

Had she not prayed enough, loved him enough to keep him safe?

Mum came up behind Kate and placed her hand on her shoulder.

Kate turned and clung to her mother, sobbing, her tears wetting her mother's blouse.

'When?' she whispered.

'They didn't really say—some time between the twenty-fifth of April and last Wednesday when the telegram was sent.'

Kate squeezed her eyes tight shut.

Weeks?

And she hadn't known.

But she had.

She had ignored it, explained it as fear.

She opened her eyes. 'And Mrs Sheehan?'

'Beside herself.' Mum blinked fast, her eyes glistening. 'They all are. The poor woman—she barely got through the Requiem they had for Jack on Saturday. She is thinking of you and sends her love.'

Kate could not bring herself to imagine what Mrs Sheehan was suffering, her own pain was too much. She walked away and sat on the verandah.

Mum followed her. 'Will we say the rosary for him?'

'Maybe later.' She didn't want to pray. She didn't want to think. 'I just want to sit here and be quiet.'

Mum gently squeezed her shoulder. 'I'll go back in to Mary.'

Kate pressed her hands down hard on her thighs, her fingers stretched out. Light flashed on the diamonds in her ring, rainbow flares, beauty barely lasting from moment to moment.

She didn't know how long she sat there. The birds, the whole town was silent. The sun was bright but the wind chilling. She was cold but it didn't matter. Nothing mattered.

She stood up and went back to the shop.

'Kate, there's no need,' Aunty said.

'I need to be busy.'

To have no time to think.

She stood, motionless, behind the counter.

A young soldier in his neat uniform stepped into the shop. Fresh-faced and clear-eyed. Fit and healthy. Well-made. A man who was alive.

Kate walked away, down the passage to her bedroom.

She picked up the photograph on the bedside table and stared into Jack's face. The arched eyebrows, the beautiful eyes full of life and light, the hint of a smile, his perfect lips, lips she would never kiss again. How could there be a world in which Jack did not exist?

She took the handkerchief case from the drawer and began to read his letters, hearing his voice in every line. Her sight blurred by her tears, she curled into herself on the bed. She dreamt of sunshine by the creek, of Jack's eyes—those striking blue eyes. The solid reality of him in her arms. Of laughter and dancing. Of the wonder of him. Of him.

She woke in the darkness, her head tight with pain, loss sitting on her like a great weight. Her arms empty, aching for him. She would never hold him again, never feel his arms around her.

A blanket had been draped over her. Mum must have come in.

She sat up. She needed a drink of water and to go to the lavatory.

Aunty Mary and Mum were sitting in front of the stove, their chairs close together, talking softly.

Kate paused in the doorway. They hadn't heard her come in.

'We have lost him too. He would have been our son.' Mum said, tears in her voice. 'He was a wonderful boy—clever, high-spirited, well mannered, fun to have around.'

'Yes, and he had that touch of mischief too.' Aunty Mary sighed. 'Like Vincent.'

'But despite the moments of mischief, you could see the solid, decent men they would become.' Mum grabbed Aunty's hand. 'And young Des Sheehan is talking of putting his age up so he can go. His mother said she'll tie him to the bed if he tries anything like that. And his father has threatened to brand him on the shoulder with the date of his birth.'

Aunty groaned and laid her head against Mum's. 'Could we have stopped them? Vincent was only twenty. I could have refused to sign the papers but he was keen to go with Brendan. I thought they'd be safer together.' She clamped her hand over her mouth as a loud sob escaped.

Kate walked to the sink.

Aunty looked up, her face streaked with tears.

Aunty Mary had loved him too.

Kate heard Jack's voice. *Aunty Mary. She will be soon enough. She would never be his aunty now.*

'Kate, I've kept you some tea.'

Kate shook her head. 'I'm not hungry. I just want a drink of water, then I'll go to bed.'

~

Kate lay staring into the darkness.

Mum had come in and whispered her name but Kate had pretended to sleep. She had pressed a kiss on Kate's forehead before getting into the other bed.

Kate wanted no comfort.

A horsedrawn cart clattered by. Mum murmured and rolled onto her side. Kate waited, listening to her mother's even breaths. She slid out of bed and dressed quietly.

Following her usual routine, she lit the fire in the stove and filled the kettle, her mind empty of all but the tasks she needed to do, one by one.

She sat on the verandah and watched as the sky lightened on a grey gusty day.

Through the closed door, she could hear Mum and Aunty Mary

in the kitchen, preparing breakfast. No one came out to get her, and she was glad. She did not want to talk. Did not want to explain.

The town stirred to life, the traffic rumbled in the street—carts, trams and motor cars—children squealing and singing out as they ran to school, a lone hawker called his wares.

She sat, aware of nothing but the effort of breathing and the pain leaking into every corner of her existence.

The clouds slowly broke apart.

The kitchen was silent now.

Kate went in and picked up the newspaper Aunty had left lying on the dresser.

She opened it, spreading it over the plate and cup set out on the table for her breakfast, turning the pages until she came to the columns of names.

One line to mark a life.

L.Cpl. Sheehan, J. 14th Batt. Smith's Creek.

So many lines. So much slaughter: 761 men killed, 69 missing, 4,519 wounded, and some of them would die too.

She pulled out the chair and sat, her elbows on the table, her head in her hands. She wouldn't go into the shop today. She would stay out here and sew, put off facing those who would offer her an appearance of sympathy while thinking, if they had not lost someone already, *Thank God it's not me.*

Sorrow set like a rock. She would go to early Mass tomorrow, for all the good it would do.

~

Mum only stayed until the end of the week. It wasn't until she had gone that Kate realised the comfort her presence had brought. She had helped in the shop, chatting brightly with the customers and charming even Mrs Miles. She sat beside Kate when visitors came, answering when Kate's silences drew out. Most often these visitors were Aunty's friends, kind and well-intentioned. None had known

Jack, not even Reenie or Mrs Casey. There was no one who she could talk of him to other than Mum and Aunty Mary, no one to truly share the lost laughter and the tears.

As she was packing her case, Mum had asked Kate if she wanted to come home with her. Kate's sister, Hannah, could take her place here. But Kate couldn't leave Aunty Mary. It would be desertion. They had been through the worry and the misery together. And, strangely, it was here that her strongest memories of Jack were— here he had formally proposed to her, here she had danced barefoot in the moonlight with him, here they had shared their dreams of the future. She feared her memories of him would fade if she left.

Everywhere Kate looked there were new recruits in uniform. When she walked along the street, turned into a shop, even at Mass, a man's gait, the set of his shoulders, the colour of his hair, and she thought she glimpsed Jack. Each time her heart lurched at the impossibility of it. It was imagination. Jack would never hide from her, or tease and haunt her like this.

He would come like he had, just days after the landing, and sit beside her. She was certain that was the moment he had died. He had come back to her, as he said he would, and kissed her goodbye. She knew that he had exchanged the pain of earth for the joy of heaven—Fr Hayes had said that of Vince at his Requiem and it was as true of Jack too. But the knowledge brought no easing of her pain.

Aunty had three letters in the space of a week. The first was from Vince's Commanding Officer, who wrote of Vince's diligence and his bravery, the esteem he was held in by the other men and their sorrow at his loss. He mentioned Brendan in his letter, knowing they were brothers. It was a letter from someone who knew and cared about his men. There was a letter, too, from the chaplain, Fr Hearn, who had been with Vince when he died on the hospital ship *Galeka*. He had given him the Last Rites and had prayed at his burial at sea. Aunty Mary folded the letter and closed her eyes, her lips moving, soundless, as she prayed.

The last letter to arrive was from Brendan. Aunty wept as she read it and kept the contents to herself. The letter seemed to bring her comfort. She set her shoulders and faced the world as if there was not a great ragged tear in her heart.

16

July 1915

Australia Day was set for the end of the month, a day to raise money for sick and wounded soldiers.

Annie called in one evening with a pile of two dozen fine linen handkerchiefs.

'I'm hoping to get these done in time for the Mayoress's Australia Day stall at the corner of Sydney and Moreland Roads.' She placed them on the sideboard along with a box of bright embroidery silk. 'Do you think you could help me, Kate?'

Embroidering flowers into the corner of handkerchiefs was the last thing Kate wanted to do but she didn't feel she could refuse. Annie was kind—she called in at least twice a week, encouraging Kate to go on brisk walks on Sunday afternoons to Merri Creek and back, or to the cricket ground if a brass band was playing. She convinced Kate to return to the First Aid classes and, in the end, Kate had been glad of it. She had to concentrate, not let her mind wander and, as she knew few of the other women well, no one asked prying questions.

'Of course, I'll help.'

Annie sat at the other end of the sofa, the lamp on the table beside her. 'I'm going to embroider a sprig of wattle in the corner. I found some beautiful yellow thread.'

Kate nodded. 'I'll do the same.' She couldn't think of anything else.

She went to the sideboard and sorted through the box of thread. Annie had thought of everything—needles and small scissors, even a couple of threaders. There was an assortment of bright coloured thread in the box including a skein of sky blue. 'Or perhaps some forget-me-nots.'

Aunty Mary came into the room and picked up a handkerchief. 'I could crochet a small lace border around the edge of these.'

'Oh yes, Mrs Burke. That would be wonderful.'

Kate stared from one to the other, certain they had plotted this between them.

She took a pencil from the box and lightly drew a small sprig of flowers onto the handkerchief.

Back in her armchair, Kate set to work embroidering the leaves and stems in green.

Aunty and Annie chatted but Kate concentrated on her stitches.

'Have you heard any more of Harry?' Aunty asked.

'We had a letter on Monday from him. He's in Egypt now, in hospital at Heliopolis. He has lost his leg below the knee, so he will be sent home when he's well enough.' Annie's eyelashes fluttered in an effort to hold back tears. 'They'll give him a false leg. Mother says it could have been worse, and I know she's right, but it will be hard for him.' She drew a long shuddering breath. 'At least he has a position seated at a desk and they said they would hold it for him.'

Aunty murmured, 'Those poor boys who make their living by labouring, how will they ever manage?'

Kate placed her sewing on the arm of her chair and moved over beside Annie. She grasped her hand and Annie laid her head on Kate's shoulder as tears slid down her cheeks. Kate thought of those strong healthy young men who had left, their bodies now broken. Life would never be the same.

~

There was no straight path away from the sorrow and the loss. Just when Kate felt that she could finally bear it, something else would happen that ripped away the scab and lay the wound bare.

Letters were printed in the newspapers from men who had been at Gallipoli. Kate stopped reading them after the letter on the front page of *The Brunswick & Coburg Star* from a soldier writing from his hospital bed in Heliopolis. He talked not of glory and brave deeds but of 'a terrible landing' with narrow escapes as shells landed in the water near their boats, the Turks shooting down at them from the hills above the beach as they landed—'if they could shoot straight not a man of us would have landed'—shells bursting around them sending dirt and stones twenty feet in the air, hitting men and 'taking half their body or their head clean off'. Kate rushed to the sink, gasping for air. Was this how Jack died?

The image would not leave her.

She thought of it when she next saw soldiers in the street, so many rushing to enlist, rushing to share the glory of Gallipoli, rushing to their deaths. Were they fools? Even the young assistant priest at St Paul's, Fr Devine, had volunteered. He had a brother there already, a surgeon. And the local doctor too, Dr Dyring, a man in his fifties, had joined the Medical Corps. His wife was leaving with him to nurse the soldiers in Egypt. They received enthusiastic send-offs complete with speeches and songs, patriotic bunting and gifts. Parishioners packed into St Paul's schoolroom to farewell Fr Devine, Aunty Mary included. Kate refused to go— never again would she cheer any man sailing off to his death.

Then there was *The Hero of the Dardanelles*, a moving picture everyone was flocking to see. Reenie asked Kate if she would come with her. She said she wanted to understand what happened last April. The picture was advertised as 'the story of a man who fell fighting for the cause of civilisation'. Kate had heard that the hero didn't die but was wounded so, perhaps, it was a story she could bear.

Aunty Mary and Mrs Casey came with them to the Alhambra in Brunswick, a vast modern picture theatre with seating for over fifteen hundred people. They took their seats in the stalls and relaxed as the serial played, the final episode of *Tillie's Punctured Romance* with Charlie Chaplin. Then the film started. Kate was drawn into the story, the story of so many men who, like the hero Will Brown, after some hesitation did their duty and enlisted. The scenes of the camp in Australia, the marching and the drill with rifles and bayonets, and of the soldier's life in Egypt were just as

Jack and her cousins had described them, even the camel rides.

The music changed and Reenie grabbed Kate's hand. 'Big Lizzie', the massive gun on one of the British warships, pounded the Turkish positions as the troops came ashore in small boats. Under a hail of bullets and shrapnel from the high ridges, wave after wave of Australians raced up the beach towards the Turkish lines. Kate gasped as the smoke cleared—so many men lying on the beach, their rifles beside them. Dead and wounded. She didn't know what she was watching. Was this real? Were men dying in front of her? Beside her, Reenie turned and buried her face against Kate's shoulder. Kate closed her eyes. She sat there for the long minutes, rigid, waiting until the music became calm. Will Brown was now in hospital in Cairo. Finally, he was sent home and married his sweetheart.

Of course, he did.

The hero had to live or the call to enlist at the end of the film might fail.

Many in the crowd seemed to have enjoyed the film but Kate and Reenie, Aunty Mary and Mrs Casey walked home in silence.

As they made their way to bed, Kate said, 'I kept my eyes shut for most of it.'

Aunty grasped her hand, her eyes damp. 'Oh Katie, I tried not to but, in the end, I did too. We try to be brave but it is nothing compared to what those men do every single day.'

17

The following night, Kate went to Reenie's knitting circle. The young women were unusually silent, concentrating on their knitting.

'Are you going to tell us about the last picture you saw, Reenie?' Rita asked. A thin pale girl who had just left school, she looked on Reenie with eyes of adoration, seeing her as the most glamourous young woman she knew.

'I haven't been to the pictures this week,' Reenie answered, her voice flat and expressionless.

Kate looked across and saw in Reenie's eyes the deadening ache of loss.

Grief had felled Reenie for several weeks after the news of Vince's death. Kate thought she had recovered quickly—and had judged her for it. She was clearly a better actress than many of those she watched at the pictures. Beneath her cheerful performance, her heart was breaking as surely as Kate's.

Annie had not come tonight as she had a concert to attend at her school so Kate walked home alone. It was not much more than fifteen minutes along Bell Street then Sydney Road, both lit by street lamps.

When she reached the corner of Bell Street, desolation swept through her. Without Jack, she had no future. She ached with the loss of him. She crossed the road, weeping as she walked past the churches, towards the creek. They had stood there together beside the creek, in the dappled light near a willow tree. Here, perhaps, she would sense him with her again.

Across the road from the corner of the prison, light fell from the windows of the Coburg Hotel, shining on the footpath, now slick with light rain. The door opened, a burst of loud conversation and laughter escaping. A man came out and stood beneath the street lamp, staring across the road at her.

Kate hurried on past the dark bulk of the prison. Dim light shone in the watchtowers, but the shadows were deep along the walls. She heard footsteps behind her. She turned and stood still. The footsteps had stopped but they started again as she walked on. When she sped up, so did they. Was it the man from outside the hotel? If he lived here, in Champ Street, surely he would be on the other side of the street where the houses were.

She came to the end of the prison and crossed the road to the creek. The moon broke through the clouds for a moment. It was not the pretty place she had visited in the daylight. Down towards the bridge, construction was underway of the weir needed to create the new lake. In the darkness, the grounds were desolate, the bushes nothing but black mounds. It was meant to be a pleasant reserve, somewhere you could wander with your sweetheart.

If you had one.

Kate's sweetheart was gone, gone where there was no reaching him.

She longed to be swallowed by the darkness.

The moon slid out again.

Two men were down by the water. They turned and stood watching her.

She glanced over her shoulder and saw the shape of another man in the shadows beside the prison. The man who had followed her up Champ Street?

Her heart thumped.

The two men began walking up the rise, not directly to the road but towards Kate.

The fine hair on the back of her neck rose. She gulped down her fear and hurried along the path beside the reserve.

Feet thudded behind her. They were running.

She didn't want to die, or worse. Especially not worse.

She ran, pounding up the middle of the road towards the dim

glimmering of light on Sydney Road.

One of them shouted after her.

She tried to run faster.

He shouted again. 'Miss Burke.'

He knew who she was!

She half-turned. Stumbled. Managed to right herself.

'Kate.'

He was getting closer.

'Kate! It's Tom Ryan.'

She looked back. Yes, it was.

She stopped, bent over, her breath ragged, near to sobbing.

He caught up with her.

'I'm sorry, I didn't mean to frighten you.'

'Well, you did.' Anger surged through her. 'What did you expect, following me in the dark?'

'I was concerned. It's not safe for a woman wandering around in the dark, especially not down here.'

'I wasn't wandering. I knew where I was going.' She glared at him. 'You should have shown yourself earlier.'

'You looked like you wanted to be alone. I was trying to keep an eye on you from a distance.' He frowned, as if thinking fast. 'I'll walk you home.'

'I can manage myself. I'll be safe on Sydney Road.'

'You have to go past four pubs. I *will* walk you home.'

Kate said nothing. If he hadn't been there, what might the other men have done?

They turned into Sydney Road.

He didn't take her arm but walked beside her on the gutter side of the footpath.

'You're from Gippsland, I hear.'

'Yes.' She didn't want to talk. She was cold now, her face damp from the light rain. All she wanted was to get home.

Kate stopped listening but Tom continued talking despite her silence.

As they neared Harding Street, he said, 'Father worked on the railways. They went to live in Maffra once he retired.'

She almost spoke. Maffra was a pretty town.

'I was born at Longwarry. Most of my brothers and sisters were born somewhere along that railway line.'

She couldn't help herself. 'Are your parents from Gippsland?'

'No, Mother came from Kilkenny when she was eighteen and Father arrived with his family from Cashel in Tipperary when he was six, in the aftermath of the Great Hunger.' He paused and said quietly, '*An Gorta Mór.*'

She turned her head and stared at him.

Fine droplets of rain glistened on the shoulders of his jacket and on his hat.

He had a pleasant face. Kind.

'What language is that?'

'Irish.'

'You can speak it?'

'I learnt as a child but I have forgotten most of it.' He paused, frowning. '*Le do thoil* and *go raibh maith agat* and, of course, *Éirinn go Brách.*'

'What do they mean?'

'Please and thank you, and Ireland forever.'

They walked on in silence. It was awkward but Kate felt as if she had forgotten how to make conversation. She doubted she would ever want to again.

'Your parents are Irish, aren't they?'

Kate fought back a sigh. 'They were both born here. In Australia. Mum's parents were English but Dad's were from Tralee.'

Tom started humming.

She had heard the tune before but couldn't think what it was. It would niggle her for days if she didn't ask.

'What is that?'

'*The Rose of Tralee*, a beautiful song except for the last verse—I always leave that one out.'

She supposed, having started, she should keep talking to him. 'Are you on the railways too?'

'I am but I'm a fitter and turner, not a line repairer like my father and a couple of my brothers.'

'You didn't want to follow in their footsteps?'

'That is a long story and perhaps better left for another time.'

They had arrived at Aunty Mary's shop.

'Well, here we are.'

'Thank you, Mr Ryan.'

'My pleasure, Miss Burke.' He tipped his hat to her. 'Good night to you.'

He took a couple steps but turned back. 'Promise me one thing. Promise you won't go walking by yourself in the dark again.'

'I promise.' She nodded her head slowly. 'My lesson is learnt.'

He smiled at her and walked away into the darkness.

Yes. She had learnt her lesson. As painful as life was, in that moment of terror, she had discovered that although Jack was gone, she wanted to live.

18

August 1915

Aunty was washing up the breakfast dishes when Kate opened the shop. There were no early shoppers, so she got to work on the grocery orders she would deliver later in the morning.

The door jingled open and Annie burst in, dancing across the floor. 'He's home!'

Jack is never coming home.

Kate shook her head to clear it and forced a wide smile. 'That is wonderful, Annie. Is he here in Coburg?'

'Yes!' She laughed.

Aunty came in, a tea towel in her hands.

'He is back, Mrs Burke.'

'You saw him at Port Melbourne?'

'I did. I saw him helped into a car and I pushed my way through to him. I jumped on the footboard and kissed him on the cheek. He grinned and said, 'Sis, it's great to be home'. Mother said I was a disgrace making a show of myself like that, but I don't care.' Happiness shone in her face. 'And the best part—when we got back from Port Melbourne, there he was, sitting on the verandah waiting for us. They drove them to the hospital but those who were well enough were allowed to come home for the night. He's on crutches but a stranger carried his kitbag until he could hail a cab for him.'

She spun on the spot, her skirt flaring out. Kate had never seen quiet, serious Annie so full of life.

She stopped and said, more soberly, 'He has to go back to the hospital but he's safe from harm now.'

Mrs Johnson pushed the door open and looked around. 'Oh, Miss Watkins,' she said, as if surprised to see Annie there.

Kate was certain the surprise was feigned, that the old woman had followed Annie up the street.

'I hear your brother is back.'

'He is indeed, Mrs Johnson.'

'Did you go to Port Melbourne to welcome him?'

'We did. Both Father and I were able to take the afternoon off work. There were thousands of people there, most with a sprig of golden wattle on their jackets or in their hatbands but all utterly happy. It was like the parades before they left. Flags, bunting and streamers were everywhere. There was an arch covered with wattle at the entrance to the pier with a kangaroo on the top and a sign, *Welcome to Our Brave Heroes*.'

A couple of other women had come in and stood listening.

'They looked well and so glad to be home. Everyone was cheering and one fellow climbed on the rail and sat there—'

'Was that the one with a missing leg?' Mrs Johnson spoke over Annie.

'Yes,' Annie said warily. 'Were you...?'

'It was in the paper this morning. My daughter reads me the war news every morning.'

Annie went on. 'This soldier shouted at the top of his voice, *Are we downhearted?* And the rest of them roared back, *No!*'

'And ladies from the Wounded Soldiers Welcome Committee, I think it's called, handed a gift to every soldier who came through the gate, cigarettes, and fruit, and other things. The people in the street were too—flowers and lollies, cigars even. They were driven in very fancy motor cars to the base hospital in St Kilda Road.'

'Some of the soldiers had nasty injuries.' Mrs Johnson looked at the two other women who were listening intently. 'Four were carried off on stretchers and put in ambulances. And there were men with scars all over their faces. One even had an eye shot out and was blind in the other and—'

'That's enough!' Aunty Mary interrupted. 'Kate, why don't you take Annie out the back and have a cup of tea.'

Annie raised her eyebrows at Kate as she walked towards her, a look of relief on her face.

Aunty's voice carried along the passage behind them. 'Now ladies, how can I help you?' She sounded as she had when Kate first arrived, strong and in charge.

Annie sat at the kitchen table while Kate made the tea.

'Mrs Johnson was right, there were some men who were badly wounded, but they all seemed pleased to be back, happy despite everything.'

'She might be right but that old...' Kate pressed her lips together looking for the strongest word to describe Mrs Johnson, *...bat* enjoys talking about other people's problems far too much.' She sat opposite Annie and held her hands. 'And Harry really is well?'

'Yes, apart from his leg. He says, once he has a false one properly fitted, he will be able to manage with a stick rather than crutches.' She smiled, blinking back tears. 'And he plans to be playing cricket again next year. He says even if he were hopping, he would be faster than some of the boys he used to play against.'

Annie took a sip of tea and placed the cup back on its saucer. 'There is a function at the Melbourne Town Hall next Tuesday afternoon. Harry can only have two guests so Mother and Father will go—they get to watch from the balcony. I can watch the soldiers arrive from a reserved area close to the front of the Town Hall. Reverend Mother has already said I can have time off school for that too.' She laughed lightly. 'I'm certain she has some plan to have me make up twice the time I have taken off. Will you come with me?'

'Of course.' Among them would be men who had known Jack, men she had met. She should wave them welcome at least.

That night Aunty Mary sat by the fire knitting a balaclava to send to Brendan. She had read that winter could be bitterly cold in the Dardanelles, even snow. She wanted to make sure it reached him before winter set in. Kate was busy finishing the latest lot of flannel shirts she had sewn.

'Sometimes, I would like to give Bridie Johnson a good hard slap. She never thinks before she opens her mouth.'

Kate nodded. 'I had noticed that.'

'I am glad Harry and all the others are home.' Aunty paused and blinked. 'But I can't help thinking of those who will never come home.'

Kate murmured. 'Nor can I.' Not a day passed that she didn't think of them.

~

Kate stood beside Annie not far from the entrance to the Town Hall. They each held a small posy of violets.

The day was cool and bright with high clouds. Thousands lined the streets, all waving small flags or carrying posies—golden wattle, narcissus or violets—that they threw into the passing motor cars. Flags and bunting, and banners proclaiming *Welcome Home* flew from the buildings everywhere.

Kate and Annie, together, leant across the barrier as they heard the sound of the approaching band. It was almost drowned out by the cheering. At Collins Street, the procession turned westward to make a circuit of the city and pass the Parliament and, finally, travel down Collins Street to the Town Hall.

The sleek, shining cars drew slowly underneath the Town Hall portico, stopping at the stairs for the soldiers to get out. Many of the men looked well, though some had livid scars on their faces, a few with bandages or patches on injured eyes. With others, their injuries were not immediately obvious. Some were pale and drawn, strained perhaps by the noise and the attention.

Around them, women called out when they caught sight of their soldier, handkerchiefs crumpled in their fists. Annie saw Harry and called to him, tossing her bouquet into his car. Kate leant forward and watched as, car by car, the men alighted. A number had to be assisted from the cars and up the stairs, limping and leaning on a fellow soldier or an usher; others struggled up on crutches.

Kate still held her posy, so she tossed it out. A soldier, in the car rolling slowly past them, stood up and caught it one handed. He grinned at Kate and winked. His height and build were a match for Jack although his hair was darker. An empty sleeve was pinned to his right shoulder. As the car moved on, Kate clamped her hand over her mouth, her shoulders shaking as she forced back a sob.

Had the great adventure been worth the cost?

19

October 1915

Aunty Mary concentrated on the living but in unguarded moments when she paused, lost in memory, Kate saw the weight of sorrow she carried. She was polite to her customers, offering kind words to those who needed it. She smiled but her easy laughter was gone and the light had dulled in her soft grey eyes. She wrote each week both to Brendan and to Bert. She had an ongoing correspondence with some of the bereaved wives and mothers of men in Brendan's battalion and others she knew who had lost their sons and husbands. As well, she wrote to some of Vince's mates who had written to her after his death. She delivered a Christmas billycan to the Coburg Red Cross to be sent to an Australian soldier overseas. Packed inside were items she thought would be of use and bring some comfort: tobacco, cigarette papers, socks, dried raisins, chocolate, butterscotch, small tins of pressed ham and of condensed milk, playing cards, shoelaces, and a cheerful Christmas card. She made smaller parcels for Brendan and Bert and included a Christmas card signed by both Aunty Mary and Kate, a letter, and a cigar to smoke on Christmas Day. She hoped her two boxes would arrive on time.

As they were doing the dishes one evening, she announced, 'At Christmas, I'll invite a boy or two from the camp for dinner, someone who's already far from home. I'll ask Fr Hayes to arrange it—he will know the chaplain out there.'

Aunty Mary, though grieving as Kate was, had turned her grief into care for others. And beside her, Kate felt shame. Habit alone forced Kate out of bed each morning, and the knowledge that Aunty Mary needed her. She did not know how to set her grief aside. She was not sure she wanted to.

~

The postman arrived with his morning delivery—a single letter for

Kate. It was in a light green envelope, the sort the army now used for personal letters that would only be read by a censor at the base, not an officer in the soldier's unit.

Kate's hand shook as she took it.

Last week she had received a bundle of her own letters, letters that had not reached Jack—letters written when he was alive, when there was a future. She had hidden them at the back of the drawer in her room and tried not to think of them.

She stared at the envelope, a lump in her throat, barely breathing.

A letter from Jack? A letter that had lost its way?

Her sight blurred by her tears, she couldn't read the writing on the front.

She swallowed hard.

The shop was busy but Aunty said, 'Go and read your letter.'

Kate sat on the verandah and wiped her eyes. Her racing heart slowed as she realised the enveloped was not addressed in Jack's firm handwriting but a shaky scrawl. The declaration on the front, saying that the sender had written only of personal matters, had been signed by Bert Wilson.

> Dear Kate,
>
> Sorry I did not rite before. I am in hospital. A bullet went in my arm but nothing to worry about. I am on the mend and I will go back to the ~~figt~~ fight in a few weeks. I will be rite as rain for shooting & using the baynet. I am sorry Jack died. He was the best mate a man could have. True as steel. I miss him & wont ever forget him. He was a good soldier good enuf for a medal. A real hero. He was beside me & we was charging the Turks when he copped it. A bullet in the throat & he was gone. It was quick & clean. No time to feel pain. I hope it helps you to know that.

Kate gasped and clamped her hand over her mouth, breathing through sobs.

She stared down the yard, unseeing. *I hope it helps you to know that.* It did.

> He talked about you all the time. How he was going to marry you when he got home. The first thing he would do. I wish with all my heart it turned out diffrent.
> I know my mate has gone to a better place.
> Your friend Albert Wilson.
> P.S. I will rite again. I know Jack would want me to. Let me know if I can help you with any thing.

Kate folded the letter. One reading was enough.
Oh, my love.
She heard Jack's voice, singing as they danced.
> *...when Irish eyes are smiling,*
> *Sure, they steal your heart away.*

But he hadn't stolen her heart away with him. It was still here, aching endlessly for him.

~

Most weeks there were marches through the city of new recruits and departing soldiers, soldiers of the Light Horse, soldiers from the Officers' Training School, the Scouts. For some life went on in a whirl of dances and socials, euchre parties, bazaars, concerts and theatrical performances organised by the Red Cross, the Lady Mayoress's Patriotic Fund, the local churches and schools. All were raising funds for comforts for the soldiers both overseas and in the training camps, for the Belgian Relief Fund, the Patriotic Relief Fund, the Serbian Relief Fund, among others. Recruiting meetings and farewells, both private and public, were held for those about to embark overseas. Civil concerns were not forgotten either with the sports clubs raising money for the unemployed, the Ladies Benevolent Society for those in poverty and for the hospitals. The local churches had parish activities to help repay debts incurred in the building of their places of worship and their schools.

And, now, Coburg had a new recreation reserve on Bell Street. It was set between the newly built, but as yet unopened, Higher

112

Elementary School and Coburg State School's Infant School. The area of the reserve facing Bell Street was planted with trees and shrubs; paths wound through them edged with rockwork. A large football ground was laid out to the rear of the gardens, fenced off, with a raised embankment for spectators. A metalled road led from the football ground to Harding Street.

The carnival opening the reserve was on Saturday afternoon. It hadn't entered Kate's mind to go but Annie arrived to take her, and Aunty Mary as good as pushed her out the door.

Something else they had plotted together.

The dark clouds overhead suited Kate's mood, though it didn't seem to dampen anyone else's enjoyment. Light rain was falling when Kate and Annie arrived just as the Mayor declare the grounds open. It cleared up quickly and the local school children began their displays of physical drill and folk dancing.

Annie slipped her arm through Kate's and they followed the paths around the reserve past the jumble and the refreshment stall, and the extremely popular soft drink and confectionary stall. In the background the Coburg Municipal Band played, adding to the cheerful atmosphere.

They met Mrs Casey and Reenie near the amusements. Reenie was on the arm of a soldier who she introduced as an old school friend of her brother Pat.

'Lovely to see you, Kate,' Mrs Casey said. 'A pity the weather isn't better. I expect it will be bright sunshine tomorrow.'

'Or by half past three,' Annie laughed. 'Any time of year, we can manage four seasons in a single day.'

'Have you heard from Pat?' Kate asked.

'I had a letter last week. He was in good form when he sent it, but these letters take so long to get here.'

Reenie tapped her mother's arm. 'Ben and I are going over to the hoopla. He says he'll win me a budgerigar in a cage.'

Kate watched them walk away, Reenie leaning in close to the

113

young man as she chattered away. She turned back to Mrs Casey. 'Reenie seems well.'

'She puts on a brave face,' Mrs Casey said. 'But there have been times when I am certain she has been weeping in her room.' She looked past Kate to Reenie, laughing with Ben as he tried to throw his hoops. 'She was too young to marry, but she truly loved Vince.' She blinked and tried to smile. 'Why don't you come over one afternoon and we'll have a cup of tea together.'

'Thank you, Mrs Casey, I will,' Kate said politely. She liked Mrs Casey—she was a motherly woman and, despite the worry in her brown eyes, she smiled and did her best to put others at their ease.

A small group were ahead of them. One man was in uniform, a lance corporal's stripe on his sleeves. A silly giggling young woman hung on his arm. Kate was sure she had never made such a display of herself.

Harry was with them, struggling along with his stiff leg and his walking stick. When he stood still, he looked as upright and fit as the men he was with. His face was more relaxed than when he had arrived home. Despite the swing of his leg, he didn't seem to be in pain. But most people were good at hiding their pains.

Annie caught up to them and introduced Kate. The usual pleasantries were exchanged. Kate answered politely but she had no wish to talk to strangers. She was aware of the interest of two of the men. She kept her eyes on Annie and Harry. Perhaps she should become a nun, that would stop them looking at her.

But she didn't want to be a nun. She had not had much to do with nuns, but their lives seemed so quiet and well-ordered, and ruled by others. No doubt they saw it differently. They couldn't wear striking hats or scarlet dresses or twirl about barefoot on the grass. Not that Kate wanted to either but, if she ever changed her mind, she could.

They walked past the long queue of children and women of all ages waiting patiently for the most popular amusement in the whole carnival, 'Beheading the Kaiser'. An effigy of the Kaiser was attached to a stand; his head, an empty tin with his face pasted on it, suspended from a string and resting on his shoulders.

Kate stopped and watched as an elderly woman came forward and was blindfolded and handed a stick. With one vicious swing of the stick, she knocked the Kaiser's head clean off to a roar of approval from those waiting. It was good to see him get his just deserts. He had started this war and it was his fault that the man who had been Kate's future, the love of her life, was dead. Yet Kate couldn't summon the anger to behead him herself.

'Let's go and watch the fancy dress football,' Annie said.

They went to the new oval and watched the end of the football match, and the fierce competitive pillow fights that followed, kapok and feathers flying everywhere. Later, as they walked out onto Harding Street, a bicycle skidded up beside them, the rider calling out, 'G'day Miss Burke.'

Kate hadn't seen Joe Kelly for months. He had grown little more than an inch in the last year but he now had dark down on his upper lip.

'Good day, Joe. How are you today?'

'Fighting fit, Miss.' He grinned at her, a tooth missing at the front which seemed only to add to his charm.

'Have you been at the carnival?'

'Nah, up this way doing business.'

'Same as last time?' she asked, raising her eyebrows. 'Seeing a man about a dog?'

She heard a whisper of Jack's voice. *It can mean whatever you want it to mean.* She could not let herself think of him now.

'A cockatoo this time.' Joe grinned broadly.

She wondered what that meant. 'Have you heard from Gus?'

'He's sent the odd postcard. He has to be careful but with what he hints at, it sounds like he's a sniper.'

She groaned. 'That's dangerous.'

'All of it is.' Joe shrugged. 'I was sorry to hear about your feller. Gus said he was a great bloke.'

'Gus met Jack?'

'Coburg boys always find each other. And almost being Mrs Burke's nephew, he counts as a Coburg boy.'

'You should call in and see Aunty Mary. She'd love to hear your news of Gus.'

'I will.' He looked Kate up and down. 'You know, just because your feller's gone, you shouldn't give up. You're a bit of all right for your age.'

Beside her, Annie snorted in shock.

'If I was a couple of years older, I'd take you out myself.'

All Kate could do was laugh.

With a wave of his hand, Joe was off, dodging cars and racing around the corner into Sydney Road.

'Honestly.' Kate was still laughing. 'With Joe Kelly, I feel like I'm talking to someone twice his age.'

'Who knows three times as much about the world,' Annie added. 'I dread to think what he will be like in five years' time.'

Kate stared into the distance. Five years time—where would they all be then?

~

Memories crowded in on Kate, each one ripping open the wound anew.

This time last year, I arrived in Coburg.

This time last year, Jack visited Aunty Mary's for the first time.

This time last year, we spent the day with Jack at the camp.

This time last year, Jack asked me to marry him.

This time last year, Jack sailed away. Forever.

And on that day the newspapers roared out another great military success.

AUSTRALIANS LEAVE ANZAC
SUVLA BAY EVACUATED

A REMARKABLE ACHIEVEMENT

All troops at Suvla Bay and Anzac, with guns and stores, have been transferred, with insignificant casualties, to another sphere of operations.

Kate wept.

There had to be some purpose to it. All those men. Thousands of Australian men. Dead. And so many more injured and maimed. Their lives and those of their loved ones changed forever.

Yet they had chosen to go. They had proven themselves fierce fighters, indomitable spirits. Kate thought of the man with the missing arm who had caught her posy. He retained the cheerful exuberance he had left with. Young Joe Kelly had the same.

She prayed that the war would be over before Joe was tall enough to trick a willing recruiting sergeant into enlisting him.

1916

For months past recruiting has been dwindling. Voluntaryism has failed, and all efforts to stimulate it have ended in failure ... Reinforcements are the need of all troops. Tragic stories could be told of the handicap of fighting under fatigue, which has at times been caused by the lack of men to relieve the fighters ... Honour calls. It calls for the reinforcement of our own men for further aid to the Empire and to our Allies.

The Argus 22 August 1916 p.7

20

April 1916

Almost a year had passed since the landing at Gallipoli and the certainties of life had unravelled. Many were losing their taste for glory. Marches were not cheered with quite the enthusiasm that they once were. Some stood silent and stared as the men marched past, perhaps wondering who among these would not be coming home.

Recruiting was slowing and those who were fervent in their support for the war pushed harder for more men to go, some adamant that single men of military age should be compelled. At a recruiting rally held in the Coburg Public Hall there had been interjections asking why those recruiting, and eligible politicians, had not joined up when they were urging others to do just that. When the police had tried to remove an interjector, some of the audience had booed the police.

It had come as no surprise to learn that the *other sphere of operations* to which their men were being sent was France. These soldiers had survived the horror and bloodshed of Gallipoli, only to face the blighted landscapes of France and Belgium displayed so clearly in the gazettes shown at picture theatres all over Australia.

Aunty Mary received a brown paper parcel from Thomas Cook & Son, the travel company assisting the army with handling mail. She knew what it contained as she, like other families, had been notified that these parcels were coming. She took it out to the kitchen and left it on the table until the shop was closed. She carefully opened it and spread the contents out: Vincent's identity disc, his rosary beads, a prayer book, a tin box containing badges and buttons and a collection of postcards. Aunty shuffled through them. From where Kate stood, they looked to be scenes of Egypt.

Aunty stopped at one, her eyes widening. 'Oh, dear.'

Colour flooded her face. 'Boys!' She handed Kate the card.

Kate's eyebrows shot up. A dark-haired young woman reclined on a couch, possibly completely naked beneath an artfully draped veil.

'Oh dear, indeed.' She blinked. 'Vince's Egyptian sweetheart?'

'Good heavens. Not at all. It's a postcard. I believe hawkers sell them in the streets in Cairo.' She set the card aside from the rest. 'I can't be showing that to Reenie. I shouldn't have shown you.'

'It doesn't matter. As you say, *Boys*.' But Kate did hope there was nothing like this in whatever might have been sent to Mrs Sheehan.

'I won't worry. The Chaplain was with him at the end. My boy, no matter what his faults on earth, is with the angels now. Vincent's purgatory came before his death, not after.'

A week later an official envelope arrived. The shop was empty so Aunty Mary tore it open as the postman walked out the door.

She read quickly and looked across at Kate. Her eyes were dry but pain was plain in her face.

'Official notification. Vincent died on the twenty-fifth of April.'

'The first day.'

'He was on a hospital ship—the chaplain told me in his letter last year.' She pressed her lips tight, her face crumpling.

Kate thought of *The Hero of the Dardanelles* and the men lying on the beach. How long had Vince lain there in agony before he was moved to the hospital ship? Perhaps Jack had been the lucky one.

~

Easter arrived. They attended the church services as they had last year, following the cycle of betrayal, death, descent into Hell and resurrection.

Beyond the greetings of friends outside the church on Sunday morning, their Easter was a muted celebration, overshadowed by the anniversary of the Gallipoli landing in the week following.

There were services of remembrance with patriotic songs and speeches at schools and in public halls as well as fireworks and marches in the city. The last Friday of April was Anzac button day. Young women, Reenie among them, were everywhere in the city and suburbs with their tins, selling buttons. The funds collected would go to assisting wounded soldiers. Kate refused to take any part. She could not smile pleasantly and make small talk with strangers or, worse, graciously brush aside the light flirtations of young, and not so young, men. Not when all she could think of was the dead.

Memorial services were to be held in the city at the Anglican Cathedral of St Paul and at St Patrick's Catholic Cathedral on the Sunday following Easter, five days after what was now called Anzac Day. The men returned from active service, many of whom were now discharged because of their injuries, were to fall in together. The Catholic troops would then march the short distance up Gisborne Street to St Patrick's and the other denominations down Collins and along Swanston Street to St Paul's.

Harry Watkins was marching, much steadier in his gait now. Annie and her parents were going to watch the march from a spot near St Patrick's. If there was room inside, they would stay for the service. Kate, Aunty Mary and Reenie went together and sat at the back of one of the almost full side aisles. The cathedral filled until there was nothing but standing room at the rear.

St Patrick's was overwhelming with its vast length, arching pillars and vaulted ceiling. Honeyed light fell through the translucent alabaster of the nave windows, bathing the church in a golden glow. Kate had loosely wound a black tulle scarf around the crown of her hat. She now pulled it down, covering most of her face.

Military music carried from outside the church, marking the arrival of the soldiers. They entered through the main doors and took their reserved seats in the nave. From his carved throne at the side of the sanctuary, Dr. Carr, the Archbishop of Melbourne, presided over this Requiem for fallen soldiers. Two chaplains, one in a khaki uniform, sat with him.

The service started when Dean McCarthy, the Vicar General of the archdiocese, entered the pulpit and began the recitation of the Sorrowful Mysteries of the rosary. Each Mystery was a decade of Hail Marys meditating on an event in Christ's Passion and death. The first Mystery, the Agony in the Garden, was said for victory and for peace; the second, the Scourging at the Pillar, for the dead heroes of Gallipoli.

The beads of her rosary running through her fingers, Kate wept, hot silent tears running down her cheeks. For her, this was Jack's funeral, the only service she would attend for him, the only way she could publicly mark his death.

The third Mystery was said for the relatives of those dead heroes, the fourth for the soldiers still defending the country, and the fifth that the nation may turn to God.

The sermon followed the rosary and brought many others to tears. The priest, Fr Lockington, spoke of faith and honour. The words washed over Kate, leaving little impression except for the thought that they were all in a place of peace and light.

The dead men shall live; the slain shall rise again.

But the priest was talking of the final judgement, not here, not now.

Jack was gone from her.

The sermon over, the Archbishop in his black cope and white mitre, the other clergy around him, proceeded to the catafalque, the symbol of the tomb. It stood in front of the sanctuary and was draped in black and covered with the Australian flag and the Union Jack. The Archbishop prayed as it was sprinkled with holy water, incense wafting into the air with the swing of the thurible.

The Archbishop said the final absolution and the choir chanted,

Eternal rest grant unto them, O Lord,
And let perpetual light shine upon them.
May they rest in peace.
Amen.

Four buglers sounded the Last Post and the choir sang *Faith of Our Fathers*, the one hymn they all could sing regardless of ability, a hymn that united them in their shared history of persecution and struggle, of life and death.

The soldiers marched out of the cathedral and on to St Paul's to meet with the soldiers of the other denominations and go on to the King's Domain where politicians and military dignitaries would address them.

Kate, Aunty Mary and Reenie travelled home in silence, lost in their memories.

~

Kate woke long before dawn and stared into the darkness.

Jack was gone. She knew his spirit had not lingered.

She was here.

Alone.

She thought of Aunty Mary with her grief for Vincent and her constant fear for Brendan, yet Aunty spent her time comforting others. And she was the one Kate leant on.

She was not truly alone.

In the years stretching ahead, she had to find a way to live, to be a comfort to those around her, to be of use.

Kate rose and dressed. She sat on the verandah as the night sky slowly faded to the soft pink of a clean new day.

21

June 1916

Kate closed the back door carefully. Above her, the glitter of the stars faded in the morning twilight. She could hear, in the distance, the lowing of cows as Dad and Jim brought them down for the milking. She walked away from the house, towards the creek. Rufus, the elderly family dog, padded at her heels.

She sat on the bench outside the washhouse beside the creek, breathing in the sharp clean air. The scents of home washed over her: gum leaves and leaf litter, rich earth and running water and, as she had passed it, the whiff of the cowshed. This place had been her whole life until twenty months ago. Everywhere held memories of her childhood, of warmth and safety, laughter and games. There had been difficulties too—hard years with not enough rain or too much, the terror of advancing bushfires averted at the last minute. She smiled, remembering that it was not far from here that Dad, a few years earlier, had scooped up great handfuls of the crystal water and drank, saying there was nothing better on this earth, only to discover half an hour later a cow lying dead in the creek upstream. They had tried to hide their amusement as he told Mum of the dead cow, but Billy was too young to hold his laughter in. Once he started, no one else could stop. And Dad was never angry with any of them for long, no matter what the affront to his dignity.

Birds chattered as the sky lightened. In the distance a kookaburra laughed, welcoming the new day.

The backdoor of the house slapped shut—Hannah heading off to the dairy to prepare for the milking.

Kate stood and went into the washhouse. It wasn't washing day so she didn't bother heating the copper. She could have had a warm jug of water in the bedroom she shared with her sisters, but since living with Aunty Mary she had come to enjoy the leisure of privacy. She splashed the cool water on her face, shivering with the sting of the air on her skin, truly awake.

Washed, her hair roughly pinned up, she stood outside, staring out across the creek. She was empty—no pain, no joy. Not even longing.

She had been right to come home.

The protesting squeal of a small child carried on the still air. Kate turned and walked back to the house.

Mum was at the stove, jug in hand, filling the cast iron urn that sat at one end of the range. She looked over her shoulder as Kate came in. 'You're up early.'

'I couldn't sleep.'

A slight line between her brows, Mum said, 'Do you have plans for today?' She pulled the kettle to the front of the stove and topped it up with water.

'I should visit the Sheehans.' She heard Mum's slow breath. She should have visited the day after she arrived, a week ago.

'They will be glad to see you.'

Would they? Or would it be another reminder of their lost son and a future that no longer existed.

Mum went into the pantry and came out with a plate stacked with sausages and the remains of a slab of bacon. She placed it on the table and began slicing the bacon.

Maggie, four years old now, raced in barefoot and giggling and threw herself against Kate's legs. Kate hoisted the child up onto her hip. Maggie put her arms around Kate's neck and snuggled against her.

Maggie had been barely two when Kate left for Coburg. She was wary of Kate at first, but soon made up for that, following her everywhere. Kate pushed away the thought too painful to touch, that she would never hold the children she had dreamt of, Jack's children.

Mum smiled gently and said, 'Perhaps you can get the little ones dressed. And later,' she paused a moment before rushing on, 'we should talk about whether it would be best if you stayed here rather than going back to Coburg.'

'I have to go back, Mum. Aunty Mary is expecting me.'

'Hannah can take your place.'

'She can't.' Kate said it with more force than she intended. 'I doubt she even wants to.'

Mum blinked, surprised at Kate's vehemence. 'We will talk later.' The frying pan rattled as she placed it on the stove.

No matter what Mum and Dad thought, she was going back, she had promised Aunty Mary. And the worst of it was that Aunty Mary had feared this would happen.

When Kate had told her she wanted to go home for a few weeks, Aunty had said, 'Of course you must.' She had forced a bright smile. 'You'll be coming back though?'

'Yes, I will.' Kate had hugged her. 'It's ages since I've seen them all. And I must visit Mr and Mrs Sheehan.'

Annie had arrived then and Aunty had said baldly, 'Kate's going home.'

'For good?' Annie had looked as distressed as Aunty Mary.

'Only for a few weeks.'

She sensed neither Aunty nor Annie had quite believed her.

She *was* going back to Coburg, even if she had to walk the ten miles to the railway station.

~

Kate pulled back on the reins, bringing her horse to a halt on the gravelled drive at the side of the Sheehans' house. It was a large weatherboard house with a verandah running around three sides. A formal garden spread out in front of the house—Mrs Sheehan's pride and joy. The roses had been pruned back but the swelling tips of the massed daffodils would soon burst into flower. The only bright blossoms were the pinks and whites of the camellias at the side of the house.

Kate had a faint memory of this house being built, of balancing on the floor bearers, her arms outstretched, as she followed Jack through the wooden frame. The original house had been like her parents', initially two rooms then added to as the family grew. And while home wasn't elegant, it was comfortable and welcoming.

Mrs Sheehan hurried down the steps as Kate dismounted. She must have been sitting on the verandah.

She threw her arms around Kate. 'Oh, Kate,' she sighed, tears in her eyes, eyes the same vivid blue as Jack's. A slender, beautiful woman, her face had once glowed with happiness. Now it was ashen against the dull black of her gown.

Mr Sheehan came around the corner of the house. 'Ah, Katie, it is wonderful to see you.' He patted her arm and walked over to her horse.

Kate watched as he led the horse along the drive. He looked years older than when she had seen him last, his hair greyer and his shoulders stooped.

'It's hit him hard.' Mrs Sheehan said. 'He never says much.' She turned back to Kate. 'Now, my darling, come inside.'

Kate followed her up the front steps and along the passage to the sitting room.

'I'll get Rosie to bring us some tea. Back in a tick.'

It was a beautiful room and, unlike her mother's sitting room, only used for guests—somewhere children weren't often allowed. It was tastefully furnished with paintings of flowers in carved frames on the walls. Two vases, figurines and a glass domed clock were arranged along the mantelpiece, a brass fire screen and fender stood on the hearth and a tall side-board against the far wall. The window gave a splendid view of the farm down towards the river. Where a mirror had hung above the fireplace, now there was a large dark-framed photograph of Jack, smart in his uniform.

Kate looked away, trying to hold on to her memories of the room as it had been. She had only been in here once before, though she had peered through the door many times when she was younger, wishing she could sit in one of the high-backed armchairs with their pristine lace antimacassars and drink in the scent of the roses in the large bowl that sat on the polished side table. Today the bowl was empty.

It had been dark in this room on New Year's Eve two and a half years ago. A balmy night, the adults sitting on the verandah, the younger children asleep in one of the bedrooms. Jack had been home eighteen months after several failed attempts by his parents with boarding schools in Melbourne, and even agricultural college closer to home. They had ambitions for him but Jack wanted nothing more than to be a farmer. He was adamant he would learn all he needed from his father and the other men of the district. Anything else could be found in the serious books on farming in the library of the Briagolong Mechanics Institute. And it seemed he had no interest, either, in the fashionable girls he had met in the city.

Jack had taken Kate's hand and led her into the empty room. They had stood in the shadows and kissed. Her first proper kiss. Not a mere brush of the lips or a peck on the cheek—a kiss she could drown in. She knew then with a fierce certainty that Jack was all she could ever want.

Kate pulled herself out of her memories with a shake of her head. She unpinned her hat and placed it on a chair.

Mrs Sheehan came in and sat on the sofa. 'Now, sit beside me.' She patted the cushion. 'Ah, Kate. This world we live in.'

'I know.' A single tear trickled down Kate's cheek. She roughly wiped it away.

Rosie carried the tea tray in and set it on the table. Her face pale, expressionless, she looked to be not much older than Kate. She closed the door silently behind her as she left.

'Rosie's a new widow,' Mrs Sheehan said softly. 'Her husband was killed a week before they withdrew from Gallipoli. She needed work and I thought I could do with another woman around the house.'

Just like Aunty Mary—even in her grief, she thinks of others.

Mrs Sheehan poured the tea. 'Milk? Sugar? Or lemon perhaps?'

'A slice of lemon, thank you. Not too strong.'

Mrs Sheehan handed Kate her cup. 'How are you finding life in the city?'

'I like Coburg—it's on the edge of town so open paddocks aren't far away. And often enough, when I am out on my deliveries, I meet ambling cows and sheep, even goats. There are several dairies and a large poultry farm. It's almost like home. I'm busy and have made friends there. And we now have an electric tram. Sydney Road was a mess for a few months while they put the new tracks in.' Kate stopped. Why was she babbling on like this? She took a sip of her tea. 'I'm glad I went to stay, otherwise Aunty Mary would have been by herself.' Perhaps it was easier the more you spoke of it. 'My cousin Vince was killed on the day of the landing.'

'Poor Mrs Burke.' Mrs Sheehan paused for a moment, her eyes closed. 'Your mother told me.'

'Brendan, my other cousin, is in France. We are praying hard for his safe return.'

'From the moment they left we have prayed without ceasing.'

Yet it did not keep them safe.

Mrs Sheehan closed her eyes and rubbed her fingers across her forehead. 'This is not like usual times, even when a death is unexpected. Then you grieve and slowly you learn to live with the absence in your life. But this...' She pressed her lips tight, drawing a shaky breath. 'With this, there is always something to bring the misery back. A month ago, I received a letter telling me of the date of Jack's death. Ten months on! And, two weeks ago, they sent me his belongings.' She glanced at a cardboard box on the side table nearest her.

'What was the date?' Kate held her breath.

'The twenty-ninth of April.'

She waited as a wave of longing washed over her. 'I thought it was that day.'

Kate looked at Mrs Sheehan. 'I had a dream in the night that Jack came and sat on the edge of my bed.' She stopped, not knowing how to explain. 'It... It was... real. I truly felt the prickle of his bristles beneath my fingertips.'

And the weight of his kiss.

'Oh, my love.' Her eyes shining, Mrs Sheehan grasped Kate's hands. 'He came to say goodbye to you.'

Kate nodded.

He had kept his word.

'Do you feel him with you?'

'Never after that.'

'Ah, he has gone to his reward. He was a good son, an honourable man and, I'm told, a brave soldier. I wish...' Her voice trailed off.

'I had a letter from his mate, Bert. He said it was quick and clean.'

'Would that be Albert Wilson? The young fellow who was doing the fencing here before the war broke out.'

'Yes. They were good mates.'

'I had a letter from him too. He told me how it happened. It was a relief to know...' Mrs Sheehan stopped, held herself rigid, fighting for control. 'There are so many horrible stories...'

She shook her head as if forcing the thought away and let go of Kate's hands. She lifted the box from the side table, setting it between them on the sofa. Inside were Jack's disc, a set of rosary beads, a couple of pamphlets, photographs, postcards showing the sights of South Africa and of Egypt, coloured stones.

She ran her fingertips over the stones. 'As a little boy he was a bit of a magpie.' She took out the photo of Jack and Kate wearing each other's hats. 'This is such a happy photo of you two.'

When she looked at it now, all Kate remembered was the fear and longing before it was taken.

She picked up Jack's disc with his name, number, unit and

religion stamped on it. He was wearing this to the very last. She bent her head and pressed it to her lips, sobbing softly.

She looked up.

Mrs Sheehan was watching, her chin quivering.

'Oh Kate. I will always think of you as my daughter. You would have been but for this dreadful war.'

She drew a folded paper from among the cards. 'This is a letter Jack was writing to you.' She passed it to Kate. 'All I read was the greeting.'

Kate's heart shuddered.

She stared at the square of folded paper in her right hand and placed her other hand over it.

The last thing he had written to her.

She felt the slow beat of her heart.

This morning, she thought she had left the pain behind. She had been mistaken.

She could not read the letter here—she needed to be alone.

Kate looked over at Mrs Sheehan. 'I'll read it later.'

Mrs Sheehan nodded. 'Now drink up your tea. It must be getting cold. Hot water?' She picked up the water pot. 'How long are you here for?'

'I'll go back on Saturday week. I don't want to leave Aunty alone for too long.'

'You'll come back though?'

'I'll visit again but I'm staying with Aunty Mary until the war is over.'

Who knows how long that will be?

22

After Kate had unsaddled the horse and led it to the paddock, she walked along the creek, following the same path she had after Jack had told her he was enlisting—not much more than twenty months ago, yet it was a lifetime.

She sat among the ferns on the creek bank and stared out at the water. It was deceptive, deeper and faster than it first appeared, rocks hidden beneath the barely ruffled surface.

The letter was two small pages, ending halfway down the second page. There was no signature, no kisses at the bottom.

> My darling Kate,
> Well, we are on the move finally. This is what we have been training for. By the time you get this, you will know the outcome. Whatever it is, those last months with you were the best and the happiest of my whole life. I look forward to the future we will have when this is over. You know my dreams as well as I do.
> But I must be sensible and say what I know you do not want to hear. The worst may happen and if it does, I do not want you to spend the rest of your life mourning me. I want you to live and, yes, to love again. I want your life to be full of everything we wanted together and if it cannot be with me, then with a decent and kind man who will care for and love you as much as I have. When he appears, you will know. Do not ignore your heart out of loyalty to me. If I do not make it, I want you to remarry.
> Remarry! Look. I think of us as married already, my love. And I will

It ended there. He had been called away and never had the time to finish.

She reread the letter, her face wet with tears, hearing his voice as if he were speaking from another room, not here beside her. He wanted her to have a life without him. But it would feel like she was betraying him. The letter was meant to set her free, but she did not want to be free.

She lay on the ground, the earth and leaves soft beneath her, and closed her eyes against the late afternoon sun.

~

Kate shuddered awake. Rufus nudged her face with his damp nose, whimpering.

She reached out and ruffled his coat. 'You good boy, Rufus. I must have fallen asleep.'

She struggled up, cold and stiff. The sun had set but a purply-red smear touched the horizon, so perhaps not that long ago.

She shook out the back of her skirt and straightened her jacket. 'We'd better get going, boy. They'll be wondering what has become of us.' She clicked her fingers at the dog who fell in step with her. As she walked, she rubbed her hands over her eyes and cheeks, brushing away the dried salt of spent tears.

'Kate!' Her father's voice, far off.

'Dad!' Kate called back. 'Cooo-ee.'

He answered with a kookaburra's laugh, closer now.

She saw the light of his lamp, bobbing along the path at the side of the creek.

Kate knew not to run in the dark, especially beside water, but she picked up her pace.

'We were worried you might have had an accident,' Dad said when they met.

'I'm sorry, I fell asleep among the ferns.' She slid her arm through his. He was always calm and comforting, rarely angry.

'Ah well, no harm done.'

She smelt the woodsmoke on the clear air before she saw the welcoming light from the windows.

'Best you go and explain to your mother. She's been quite

concerned.'

Mum turned from the sink as they came in. Her eyes were red as if she had been crying.

'I'm sorry, Mum. I sat for a moment by the creek and fell asleep. Rufus woke me up.'

'It would be not sleeping well last night and getting up so early.' She wiped her hands on her apron. 'Your dinner's in the oven. Sit down and I'll bring it over.'

'I'll do it.' Kate picked up the pot holder and opened the oven door. The fire had burnt low and the plates were on the lower shelf, a dish of water beneath them to stop the food from drying out. 'I'll finish the dishes if you like.'

Later, when the boys and the younger girls were in bed, they sat in front of the fire in their comfortably crowded sitting room. Mum's attention was on the moss-stitch sleeve of a cardigan she was knitting; beside her, Kate was busy with khaki socks.

Hannah, curled up at the other end of the sofa, stared at the glowing logs in the fireplace, her knitting set aside. She glanced along at Kate. 'Do you knit anything other than socks?'

'No, and I don't knit that much. Aunty Mary is the knitter— socks, mittens, scarves and balaclavas. I usually sew flannel shirts and pyjamas. The Red Cross provides the material.'

'I know they make them, but do the soldiers really wear pyjamas when they are in the trenches?'

'They are used mainly for soldiers in hospital. But some do at the training camps. Jack told me about one soldier at Broadmeadows who used to get up early to have a good wallow in the bath. He would walk through the lines of tents in a satin dressing gown. He was most offended when one other early riser, yelled out to him, 'Hoy, Doris. Want to come out for a dance tonight?'

Over in his armchair beside the fire, Dad took his pipe out of his mouth and chuckled, 'A satin dressing gown—that certainly is asking for the boys' attention.'

'William!' Mum glared across at him.

'Sorry, dear.' He puffed on his pipe.

Kate concentrated on her knitting. She had spoken of Jack without thinking—the first time she had spoken naturally about what life had once been. Rather than the ache that mention of his name usually brought, this time it was a wistful sadness.

'When are you planning to go back, Kate?' Mum asked.

Kate drew in a breath. 'Saturday week.'

'I would prefer you to stay here.'

'Aunty Mary needs me! If I don't go back, she'll be by herself.'

'I understand that but, as I said this morning, Hannah can take a turn at helping her.'

Both Kate and Hannah spoke at the same time.

'It's not the same.' 'I will not.'

Hannah leapt out of her seat. 'I've got better things to do here.' She marched out, slamming the door behind her.

'Please, Mum.' Kate pleaded. 'I've been with Aunty through this last awful year. It would be like I was deserting her. She needs me, I know exactly what to do in the shop. She relies on me. It wouldn't be the same for her with Hannah.'

'When Mary asked for one of you to stay with her, I never expected it would be for this long.' Mum put her knitting down and pressed her hands hard onto the sofa. 'I wouldn't have let you go, if I had known.'

'It's not Aunty Mary's fault the war has gone on so long. No one thought it would be like this, that so many men would die. Aunty never dreamt Vince would be killed. We've been through the very worst together. It would be cruel if I didn't go back. She says I'm like a daughter.'

'But you are *my* daughter and I want you here.'

Making Mum angry wouldn't help. 'But Mum, if the war hadn't started, Jack and I would probably have been married by now.' She forced herself not to think beyond the argument to what she was truly saying. 'I still wouldn't be here with you.'

'She's right, Julia,' Dad said quietly.

Mum bowed her head. 'But Kate would only be a buggy ride away.' Her voice creaked. 'I would see her. She would come and visit. She wouldn't be a stranger.'

Kate breathed out slowly. It hadn't occurred to her that her mother missed her.

'I'm sorry, Mum. I should have written more often,' her voice caught, 'but what could I say in letters? Can you imagine what it would be like if Jim had gone and you were dreading every day the same would happen to Billy?' Mum gasped but Kate went on. 'I couldn't leave Aunty alone at Christmas—her first Christmas with Vince gone, not off somewhere else, but gone forever.' She paused for a moment. If she was not careful, she would cry. 'She invited two country boys from the Broadmeadows camp for Christmas dinner. They were far from home and they did enjoy themselves. Then the anniversary of Anzac, of Vince's death, came hard on Easter. I couldn't leave her alone for that.' Kate glanced at her mother. 'Please Mum.' Her mother's eyelashes glistened in the firelight. 'If I can stay until Brendan is home again, I promise I will come home to visit more and I will write every fortnight. Truly, Aunty Mary needs me.'

Mum's shoulders slumped. 'And, I suppose, you need her too.' She put her arm around Kate and Kate leant against her. 'I want a letter every week.'

'I will. I promise.' She would write every day if that was the price of going back.

~

The following week was busy. On Sunday they all went to Mass in Briagolong. Afterwards, Kate chatted with a girl she had been at school with, now married with a young baby. Her husband had enlisted a month ago. Despite her cheerful smile, Kate saw worry in the young woman's eyes. She said her husband had waited until the child was born to join up. He was going because Britain needed our help. What decent man wouldn't go and give a hand when good people, people we are related to, are suffering at the hands of savages like the Germans, no matter how far away they were? Kate couldn't disagree. All she could say was that she would keep him in her prayers.

Dick Simmonds came over in the middle of the week. He was more serious than Kate remembered, the loss of his brother, only sixteen months older, weighing on him. They shared their stories of Jack and Len. Kate found she could talk easily of Jack to Dick, laughing at their escapades in Egypt. It reminded her of the night with Aunty Mary when they had talked of Vince, laughing and crying. Perhaps having no one who truly knew Jack beside her had made this last year harder.

Mrs Sheehan arrived on Friday afternoon, a bitterly cold day with clouds threatening rain. Mum brought them tea in the sitting room where the fire had already been lit and left them alone.

Mum had barely closed the door when Mrs Sheehan began. 'I wanted to say goodbye, Kate, but, more than that, I want to say to you what no one else will.' She grabbed Kate's hands and stared into her face.

'Do not spend your whole life mourning Jack.'

Her whole life? She couldn't see beyond the next week.

'I can't imagine loving anyone else.'

'Let time take its course but don't lock up your heart forever. Jack would not have wanted it.'

'Now.' Mrs Sheehan placed the brown paper wrapped parcel she had with her in Kate's lap. 'This is some material I bought a while back—it's too young-looking for me.'

Kate unwrapped the paper and brushed her fingertips over the burnt orange silk. 'It's beautiful but—'

Mrs Sheehan cut her off. 'No buts. I want you to have a pretty dress made from it and to wear it when you go dancing.'

'I haven't danced since Jack left.'

'One day your feet will itch to dance. Life is a gift and you must live every single moment of it.'

Kate could not imagine dancing again. She wanted no other man's arms around her.

As she refolded the paper around the material, light flamed in the biggest diamond of her ring. Jack was gone. Forever. Was she even engaged?

She looked across at Mrs Sheehan, her brow puckered. 'What should I do with Jack's ring?'

'That ring was his gift to you. It is yours to do whatever you want with. Wear it for as long as you need to. Then, wear it on your right hand if you wish, or place it with your other memories of Jack. Your heart will tell you what to do.'

She squeezed Kate's hand. 'We must go on and live the life granted to us.'

Mrs Sheehan picked up her teacup, sipped and wrinkled her nose. 'And next time you are up here, we might manage to drink our tea while it's still scalding hot.'

23

Kate sat on the platform at Flinders Street, waiting for the Coburg train. Her mind was miles away from the railway announcements, the whistles, the beat of hurrying feet, and the chatter and laughter of busy people looking towards the pleasures of Saturday evening.

The train had been late leaving Maffra this morning and was held up at every second station along the line. The afternoon was sliding towards evening with what little warmth there had been now fading.

Kate pulled her coat tighter and tugged at her gloves.

It had been a long day. Mum and Dad had come to the station to wave her off. To avoid the long buggy ride in the dark, they had stayed overnight with Mum's elderly aunt in Maffra. It wasn't until the train was finally pulling out of the station and she was waving to them that Kate realised they were worried about her. Mum was trying to smile brightly but Kate could see the strain around her eyes. It was harder to tell with Dad with his hat and his white bushy beard, but she had seen the concern in his grey-blue eyes when he had kissed her goodbye. She would write every week as she had promised; Mum said that she would be happy even if it was only a short letter. All she wanted was to hear from Kate.

'Miss Burke?'

Kate looked up, slowly focusing on the man in front of her.

Tom Ryan raised his hat.

'Mr Ryan.' She forced herself to smile.

'Do you mind if I sit?'

Ingrained courtesy prevented her from saying, *Go away, I want to be by myself.*

'Not at all.' She moved slightly to the side out of politeness, not as a gesture of welcome.

'You've been away?' He nodded towards the small suitcase beside her neatly placed feet.

'I've been visiting my family.'

'A long trip then.'

Kate's silence seemed to confound him. He sat in silence too.

As the train pulled into the station, Tom stood and picked up Kate's suitcase, walking with her towards the second-class carriage. He opened the door for Kate, stepping in behind her, and put her case onto the luggage rack, his haversack beside it.

Outside, the guard checked the doors and blew his whistle and, with a start, the train moved forward.

Tom sat opposite Kate. For the first time, she saw him for what he was—a courteous man, only a few years older than she was, who seemed genuinely concerned rather than feigning it to make her take notice of him. She wondered why. Perhaps he was simply a good man.

She relaxed. She should make some effort, say more than yes or no to his questions. 'You're on your way to see your mother?'

'I am. I try to visit her most weekends. My youngest sister, Agnes, married last year. She and her husband are staying with Mother but they will be moving to Sale soon. He is starting a new job at the butter and cheese factory there.'

'Your mother will miss her.'

'She will. Work has spread us wide—there are nine of us living from Adelaide to Wangaratta. I board in North Melbourne, only a five-minute walk from work but when Agnes leaves, I'll come to Coburg so Mother isn't alone. What about your family?'

'They are all at home except for me. There are seven of us, five girls and two boys. I am the eldest girl and the baby is Margaret— she is four.'

Tom was a talker and his conversation ranged over the places he had lived and the people he had met and their eccentricities and foibles.

It was easy for Kate to listen and to answer his gentle questions. Dusk was falling as the train pulled into Coburg station. He lifted Kate's suitcase down from the luggage rack. 'I'll walk you home.'

There was no point saying she could manage quite well herself, Tom would accompany her anyway.

He carried her case to the back door.

The door was shut, not locked, but there were no lights burning.

'That's strange,' Kate said. She stood in the doorway and called to Aunty Mary but there was no answer. 'She must have gone visiting. I didn't let her know I was coming today.'

Tom placed Kate's case inside the door. 'I'll wait until you have a light on.'

Kate lit the lamp at the centre of the kitchen table. It was quicker than fussing with the gaslight.

'Thank you…' she paused, this Mr and Miss business was starting to sound silly, '…Tom.'

'My pleasure, Kate.' His face lit up and he grinned at her.

She smiled politely at him.

Tom tipped his hat and went on his way.

Kate's smile faded as she closed the door behind him.

She carried her case into her room, set it on her bed and, this time, did fuss with the gaslight. Back at the bed, she flicked open the catches on her case and, setting Mrs Sheehan's material to one side, took out her handkerchief case of letters and photographs. She read through each letter then gazed at Jack's photograph, her eyes damp and stinging. She had cried so much this last year, it was a wonder she had any tears left. As she slid his photo back in with the letters, the light glittered on her ring. She could not imagine not wearing it. Perhaps Mrs Sheehan was right and time would change how she felt but, for now, she would cling to anything that tied her to Jack, that would fill the aching emptiness.

'Kate! Is that you?' Aunty Mary called from the kitchen.

Kate opened the bedroom door. 'Yes. I'm in here.'

The floorboards creaked in the passage. Aunty seemed almost to be running.

The joy in Aunty Mary's face was unmistakable. She held her arms wide. 'Katie, my treasure.'

'Aunty.' Kate sank into the warmth and comfort of her embrace.

Aunty stood back, her hands resting on Kate's shoulders. 'You do look well. Did you sleep for the whole three weeks?'

Kate laughed. 'The little ones did their best to make sure I never slept late.'

Aunty was still smiling. 'I am so happy you are back.'

She went to the bed and touched the material, rubbing the cloth between her thumb and two fingers. 'What's this?'

'Mrs Sheehan gave it to me. She said it was too young for her.'

Aunty Mary nodded. Perhaps she had what had been Kate's first thought—that it would be a long time before Mrs Sheehan would wear anything but black.

'She told me to make a dress from it.' She shrugged. 'I will. One day.'

'You should do it sooner than that. There is a very good dress-maker in Munro Street. I'll pay for her to make it and for whatever trimmings are needed.' She spread the cloth over her outstretched arm. 'You will look beautiful.'

Kate thought of some of the dresses she had seen in the windows of shops in the city, her mind filling with the flick and swirl of hems spinning out, floating on air. The material would make a perfect dress for dancing.

But the only man she wanted to dance with was dead.

24

September 1916

The year advanced with the names of places where battles were raging—the Somme, Fromelles, Moquet Farm, Pozières—becoming as familiar as those earlier names burnt into their hearts: Gaba Tepe, Lone Pine, the Nek, Krithia, Sari Bair. They were a drumbeat that rumbled through their daily lives foreshadowing the minister's knock on the door and the casualty lists with their long columns of names massed together, sometimes in print half the size of the surrounding articles.

On the last day of August, a cold and bitter day, the newspapers had reported that Prime Minister William 'Billy' Hughes had announced, in the way of politicians, that there would be no conscription of men for the war—then came the sting in the tail—until a referendum had been held. If enough Australians wanted it, men would be compelled to fight half the world away.

The government only had the power to conscript men for service within Australia and Hughes, who had been appointed Prime Minister the previous October, was a firm believer in conscription for overseas service. He did not have the support of his own party, the Labor Party, to push the necessary change through Parliament so, certain of public support, he turned to the people. He said voluntary enlistment would continue for a month but if sufficient men did not come forward, single men over twenty-one with no dependents would be required to register and undertake military training. With wily politician's words, he said that they would not be sent away against their will *unless* and *until* the people of the Commonwealth of Australia had declared for conscription for overseas service. This was, Kate thought, simply a way to make sure men were ready to be shipped off the minute the referendum was won.

She trembled with rage. Jack had volunteered and gone willingly and his death had torn her soul in two. How much worse would it be if he had been compelled to fight against his will. Despite what so many said, it was not as if the German army was on Australia's doorstep. These old men should go themselves.

The following day's casualty list showed 264 men dead and 1,304 wounded, only marginally less than the last of August which had been described as 'the most formidable yet released'. What would the next one be? And the one after that? And the injured sent home with missing arms or legs, scarred faces, hacking coughs, haunted eyes. Would any man be left untouched by the time this war was over?

~

Everywhere Kate went as she rode around the streets delivering grocery orders, she saw handbills and posters. They were displayed in shop windows and plastered on fences, arguing both for and against conscription. Some were defaced, others torn down and trampled on the ground in an attempt to obliterate their message. The headlines caught her eye.

She stopped and read some of them, both the Yes and the No.

SHALL AUSTRALIA PAY HER DEBT?

VOTE Yes

~

COMPULSORY DEPORTATION OF OUR MANHOOD OVERSEAS
MEANS RACE SUICIDE.

~

EVERY ELECTOR WHO VOTES 'NO'
CONDONES THE SLAUGHTER OF INNOCENT THOUSANDS

~

WHOLESALE SLAUGHTER
EXTERMINATING AUSTRALIA'S MANHOOD
VOTE NO!!

These arguments meant little to Kate whether they were about honouring promises to Britain, sharing the sacrifice of the war equally, or protecting jobs from the foreign workers some believed would be brought in to replace the men who had left.

At nearly every house, the person who opened the door wanted to talk. Some argued that only those who had freely volunteered should pay such a price as this war demanded. Others held firmly that the cowards and shirkers who had not enlisted should be forced to their duty so the war could be brought to a speedy end. As Kate nodded politely and said little, all assumed Kate agreed with them, no matter what their point of view. Her deliveries now took twice as long.

~

Miss White, a fine-featured elderly woman who kept house for her even older brother, read from a list as Kate collected her groceries together. Kate had to prompt her several times to get to the end of the list. Miss White was more interested in Aunty Mary's quiet discussion with Mrs Davidson at the other end of the counter.

Mrs Davidson, a thin anxious woman, furrowed her brow and said, 'I wish I knew how Hugh was voting, I'd do the same. He has a far better idea of what is needed over there.'

'Ah, Mrs Davidson, I feel the same. I wrote to Brendan as soon as it was announced but I doubt I will hear back from him in time.'

Miss White moved closer to them. 'But Mrs Burke, surely there is only one way we can vote. My brother Alfred says the Germans want us to vote No.'

The women stared at her.

'He says it's obvious. They know how good our men are and what fierce soldiers. The Germans are hoping we vote No because then they won't have to face more of our fine Australian lads.'

'Your brother is absolutely right, Miss White.' A straight-backed elderly gentleman with a fine white walrus moustache had stepped into the shop.

'It is fortunate there are men in Australia like those on the

Brunswick council. Their Mayor, Councillor Phillips, has made sure those anti-conscriptionists will not be allowed to congregate in the streets and hold open-air meetings. It is a pity our Council does not show the same backbone. Councillor Phillips is absolutely right when he says anyone who refuses to back our brave soldiers, who are fighting for us, are aiding our enemies.'

'Oh yes, indeed, Mr Roberts.' Miss White nodded vigorously. 'But our council isn't so bad. Alfred told me that they charge the anti-conscriptionists to use the Public Hall but those supporting conscription get it for free.'

'That is good to hear,' Mr Roberts said. 'If I had my way they would all be locked up.'

Aunty's colour had risen but she said nothing. Mrs Davidson, sitting on the chair at the end of the counter, stared down at her baby, a child her husband had never seen. A warder at Pentridge Prison, he was one of those who had joined up in the surge of enlistments following the Gallipoli landing. Aunty Mary had mentioned the struggle Mrs Davidson now had with four children and little more than her husband's army allotment to live on. She was one of the few Aunty allowed to buy goods on tick.

'Now, Mr Roberts.' Aunty Mary smiled and raised her voice in a forced joviality. 'How can I help you?'

When the door closed behind their customers, Aunty said, 'Well, that is my lesson learnt. No conversations about conscription out here, even quiet ones.' She sighed. 'I do wish I knew what Brendan thinks of all this. It seems wrong to force someone to fight against their will—would they be of any use if they didn't want to be there? But if I knew more men would make it easier for Brendan, if it meant he was less likely to come to harm, I would not hesitate to vote Yes.'

For Kate, this was the heart of the matter. And she still didn't know how she should vote.

~

Conscription and the referendum were all anyone wanted to talk about. The newspapers were full of it—arguments, letters, reports of meetings held across the city and the country by all manner of people and groups. And, as the weeks passed people's opinions hardened.

Kate saw the anger simmering beneath the surface when Mrs Miles came through the door.

Ignoring Aunty Mary's pleasant 'Good afternoon', she asked for a pound of flour and a box of cocoa. Her shopping safely in her basket and her purse tucked away, she looked straight at Aunty and said, a twist to her mouth, 'It's good finally to know where you lot stand.'

Aunty blinked. 'My lot?'

'Yes, you Irish Catholics and your Archbishop Mannix. I hear he gets his orders straight from the Kaiser himself.'

A flush spread up Aunty's face. 'Don't be ridiculous.'

'Ridiculous, is it? Don't tell me you haven't heard what he said at that bazaar at Clifton Hill? *Conscription is a hateful thing.*' She gave a loud harrumph. '*Australia has done more than her full share.* And you lot will blindly do as you're told and vote No and the boys over there will not get reinforcements. Then what will happen? We'll lose the war. How will you feel when we are all forced to speak German?' Her voice was a snarl by the time she had finished.

Kate opened her mouth to contradict Mrs Miles but Aunty Mary was ahead of her.

'That is just the Archbishop's opinion,' she said, her voice even. 'He might want people to vote that way, but we are free to vote how we like. He thinks Australia has done enough considering how small a country we are.'

'Done enough? It won't be enough until the war is won.'

'Archbishop Carr is the head of the church here in Melbourne, not Dr Mannix. And Archbishop Carr has said the church should have no influence in the matter of conscription. So have many other Archbishops. The Archbishop of Perth has even helped the campaign for recruits. They are all loyal to Australia.'

'Loyal? That Carr? He's a traitor if ever there was one, collecting money for those sly Sinn Fein rebels in Ireland, stabbing England in the back last Easter when she is fighting for her life. I suppose you donated to it?'

Aunty Mary ignored the last question. 'That collection was for charity. It was to relieve the distressed people of Dublin, who are homeless, who have lost all they had as a result of the rising last Easter.'

'Typical of your lot,' Mrs Miles sneered. 'Collections for foreigners, or for yourselves—fetes for paying off parish debt—but nothing for our poor brave boys. You should be all locked up like the Germans, traitors every single one of you.'

Kate moved over and stood beside Aunty Mary.

Aunty gripped the edge of the counter. 'You listen, Mrs Miles. I have one son dead—he died at the landing on Gallipoli. I have another son fighting in France. Both are Australian born sons of Irish parents loyal to Australia. And I am certainly not the only one with sons fighting. And, what about Father Fahey, leading a charge at Gallipoli, when the all the officers in his unit had been killed?' Aunty drew breath through her nose. 'And... and... the last Australian soldier to win a Victoria Cross was an Irishman from Kings County. So don't you dare call me a traitor or tell me the Irish are not patriotic.' Her eyes narrowed. 'How many sons of yours are fighting in France?'

'As you well know, Mrs Burke, I have no sons.'

'You have plenty of daughters. Aren't any of them loyal enough to serve as a nurse?'

Mrs Miles gasped.

'Loyalty is easy, isn't it, when you will never have to pay the price?'

Mrs Miles face was almost unrecognisable, contorted with a hate Kate did not understand. She spun on her heel and left, slamming the door behind her.

Aunty's shoulders slumped; her hands gripping the counter were all that was holding her upright.

'Do you want to go out the back and sit down?'

'I'll be fine.' Aunty gave a half-hearted laugh. 'It seems I've lost another customer.'

'*Another* customer?'

'There are a few who seem to have stopped coming in since the conscription referendum was announced. I suppose either because I'm Irish or because I'm Catholic, or both.' She clenched her jaw, her anger holding back tears. 'We are not traitors. Those of us here in Australia are not responsible for what happens in Ireland. When they rose at Easter, I thought them damned fools but the reprisals, trying men by secret-court martials, allowing them no defence, executing them—it is what the English have been doing in Ireland for over seven hundred years.'

Kate had no strong view on Ireland. Her father rarely offered an opinion on politics of any sort. Growing up in a small community, the only difference between Catholic and Protestant she had been aware of was that they visited different churches on Sundays.

She wrapped her arms around her aunt. 'Oh Aunty, the likes of Mrs Miles are nasty, narrow-minded idiots.'

It was foolish to think you knew how another would vote in the privacy of the polling booth. There were plenty of non-Catholics campaigning for the No vote, including many in the Labor Party and the unions. And there were Irish people and Catholics who would vote Yes.

Aunty Mary's face was still flushed. 'Here I have the right to vote which I wouldn't have in England or Ireland, and no one—not a priest nor a bishop, not a politician nor an agitator, nor a stupid arrogant bigot—will tell me how to vote.' She drew herself up to her full height. 'I will do what I think is best for my son.'

How had it come to this? When Kate had arrived in Melbourne two years ago, they had all been united, they had supported the war and the young men marching away. And now, although they all wanted the war to be won, they squabbled viciously over how this was to be done. Yet one thing was certain, their hearts ached for those who had marched away. They all wanted them safe. They all wanted them home.

25

October 1916

Meetings large and small were held everywhere, both for and against conscription. The newspapers listed them with the times, the speakers, or if they were ladies' meetings. Kate had wanted to hear the arguments of both sides and thought she might go to one or two of the smaller local meetings.

Aunty Mary was aghast.

'Absolutely not! Even the ladies' meetings are rowdy. I read the other day of the police removing women from one. What if you got caught up in a brawl and were arrested or hurt or even just had your name in the paper? Your mother would haul you home before either of us could get a word out in your defence.'

Kate sighed. Aunty was right. She might be twenty-one but, despite the occasional lapse, obedience to her elders, parents in particular, was an ingrained habit. She would have to make do with newspaper reports and articles.

The newspapers reported in great detail on many of the bigger meetings such as the massive anti-conscription meeting held at the Exhibition Building in Carlton or the enthusiastic meetings in favour at the Melbourne Town Hall. No matter where they were held, some ended in uproar with opposing parties interjecting and hooting and counting speakers out. Open air meetings were often in danger of descending almost to riot. A procession through the city led by the United Women's No-Conscription Committee was rushed at by a group of men who tried to seize their banners. The procession reached the banks of the Yarra River and women, including leading pacifists Adela Pankhurst and Vida Goldstein, spoke to a gathering of near to sixty thousand people. Then a group of soldiers arrived, some said to break it up, others said merely to listen. Chaos erupted, the soldiers were attacked, police moved in and, it was reported, women were jostled and one woman was hit in the head with a brick. Kate was shocked—it was as if Melbourne was at war with itself.

~

Kate pulled the collar of her jacket closer as she walked along Bell Street towards Sydney Road. It was the middle of spring and the weather its usual changeable self, either a reminder of winter or a foretaste of summer. Today had been a reminder of winter, bitterly cold but, thankfully, no rain.

Reenie's knitting group had broken up early tonight. Even Reenie had been subdued and hadn't given her usual performance of the latest picture she had seen. She said that *Not My Sister* was a horrible film about seduction, betrayal and murder and she would be more careful of what she watched in the future. Reenie had brightened up at her mother's suggestion that the next time they knew a nice cheerful film was on, the young women should make an outing of it, perhaps go down to Brunswick where there was a choice of picture theatres. Kate found herself nodding enthusiastically. It seemed like a pleasant distraction from the ill-will stirred up by the referendum.

Annie was in bed with the flu, so Kate walked home alone. As she neared Sydney Road, she noticed a noisy group of people gathered outside the Public Hall, further on. It was most likely a conscription meeting of some sort.

Surely, there would be no harm if she stood at the edge of a meeting and listened. She walked past the State School to where the group of men, mainly, spilled away from the Public Hall, past the Town Hall and into Elm Grove.

She couldn't hear what was being said on the platform with the noise, though the meeting did seem to be nearly over. She caught a glimpse of the speaker, Frank Keane, a local councillor and staunch Labor Party man—a man Aunty had described as decent with the interests of ordinary people at heart. The people outside the hall must be opposing conscription. As those inside the hall spilled out into the street, they were jeered at and abuse was yelled at them by the anti-conscriptionists.

'Kate.' Tom Ryan pushed through the crowd to her. 'What are you doing here?'

'I was passing and wondered what was going on.'

'It's late to be out wandering.'

Kate felt a twitch of irritation. Why did everyone believe they could tell her what to do? 'You're not my father, Tom.'

'No,' he said.

She was sure there was a twinkle of amusement in his eyes and that annoyed her further.

'I'll walk you home.'

Kate rolled her eyes. 'If you must. But there are electric street lights on Sydney Road. And with the hotels now shutting at six o'clock, there's not much to worry about.'

'I'm not so sure. Men will always find a drink if they want it. And I very much doubt this early closing of the pubs will improve our morals and aid the war effort like the wowsers claim.' He glanced back over his shoulder. 'We'd better move off. Things could get a bit willing here.'

Others had the same idea, many meeting-goers walking smartly away, across Bell Street and towards Sydney Road.

'Was this two meetings at once?'

'Yes, a recruiting meeting inside with that bigoted Orangeman Oswald Snowball railing against Catholic treachery, no doubt. And those against conscription out here in competition.'

A thin fierce-looking woman, dressed entirely in black, stepped into their path and faced Tom. 'Why are you not in uniform young man? A fine strapping fellow like you should be doing his duty.'

Before Tom could answer, she turned to Kate. 'And you, young woman, are a disgrace. Walking out with a coward and shirker like this! A patriotic woman would tell him to go away, that you would not consider him for a dance, much less marriage, until he had come back from the war.' She stabbed her finger at Kate's chest. 'If girls like you spurned these callous brutes there would be far more recruits.'

Kate knocked her hand away, seething at her description of Tom as a callous brute. 'You can't tell by looking if he is fit, or if he is a returned man with an injury that's not obvious, or whether he is the sole support of his mother and sisters.'

'I dare say none of that applies to this one—returned men wear their badges with pride and there are badges, too, for those who tried unsuccessfully to enlist. I have four sons, all have enlisted. They would have been ashamed to look another man in the face if they had not gone. And two of them have paid the ultimate price while cowards like this sit at home.'

'And *you* won't be happy until half the men in Australia pay the same price.'

'You tell her, lass.' A ring of men had formed around them, like schoolboys when there was the chance of a fight.

Beside her, Tom called her name.

'Don't be ridiculous,' the older woman spat. 'Less than fifteen per cent of soldiers die. And, in all, total casualties are no more than one in three.'

'Kate.' Tom said again, louder this time.

'So, which third of these men will you choose? This one dead?' Kate pointed to a man grinning at them. 'This one to lose his leg?' She turned to the other side. 'This one gassed? It's your choice. You're the one who is so keen to send every living man off.'

'You stupid girl. Many of the men at the front have been fighting for eighteen months. If they don't get reinforcements, many more will die.'

Kate saw a flash of pain in the woman's face, but it was quickly swept away by anger.

'If the shirkers did their duty, this war would be over sooner and they could all come home.' She held herself erect, glaring along her nose at Kate. 'And, as the mayor of Brunswick said, *The woman who votes No condemns a brave man to death in order that she may save a coward.*'

Rage surged through Kate. Her head spinning, she raised her hands to push the old battleaxe out of her way but couldn't move.

'Kate, come on.' Tom had caught her wrists and, with his arm tight around her, pushed through the crowd. 'You need to get away from here.'

Halfway across Bell Street, Kate shook him off and marched ahead. Her heart pounding, she turned into Sydney Road, and slumped against the wall of the Corner Hotel, catching her breath.

Tom caught up with her. He drew her arm through his. 'You can't wait here. There were coppers at that meeting. You don't want them questioning you, even if you haven't done anything.'

She started to laugh. The whole thing was ridiculous. 'And Aunty Mary didn't want me going to meetings because of the unruly behaviour of some. Little does she realise I am one of the unruly ones.'

Tom grinned. 'I won't tell her if you don't.'

They walked on, still arm in arm. She felt alive—she wanted to run down the street, to twirl about, to shout out *Vote NO!*

At the next corner, she stopped and stepped away from Tom. She tried to look stern as she said, 'And tell me, young man, why are you not in uniform?'

He blinked, his mouth open in surprise. 'Oh, you mean Billy Hughes's *voluntary* compulsory training.'

'I do. I'm glad you are not wearing a uniform.' Her lighthearted mood faded as she thought of the young men who could soon be forced to enlist if the referendum returned a majority for Yes.

'I did as required and presented myself.' Tom looked as serious as Kate now felt. 'I was too much of a coward to risk gaol by not registering.'

'Not even to avoid fighting for the English king?'

He shrugged. 'It's no longer so simple. Martin, my cousin, has joined up—he's probably in France now. He wanted me to go with him.' He stared into the darkness. 'It wasn't long after we heard about the rising in Ireland at Easter. Talking to him about the British reprisals and centuries of injustice didn't sway him. He said it's about the German threat to Australia if Britain falls—we would be easy pickings for the Germans.' He closed his eyes and rubbed two fingers hard between his dark eyebrows, as if he were in pain. 'There is some sense in his argument but I wasn't convinced so I let my cousin, my best mate, go off by himself.'

It clearly troubled him, but Kate didn't know what to say.

'How did you avoid being sent into camp?'

'I had a bout of bronchitis not long back. When I went for the medical, I was still able to cough and wheeze like an old man taking his first pipe for the day. They sent me on my way, told me to come back in six weeks. I have a scrap of paper to prove it.'

Kate hadn't heard him cough tonight. 'You are well now?'

'Oh no, I think it might be incurable.' He began slowly, building to a hacking cough that became a wheeze.

'That is impressive. And you can do it at will?'

'I can, but I doubt I took the doctor in. It was the end of the day and he couldn't be bothered arguing with me.' His eyes narrowed. 'They fingerprinted us, like criminals. They claim it is so they can identify us properly but they saw no need before this.' He jerked his head. 'Anyway, I'll try for an exemption as I'm the only son at home but they might argue that Mother could go to one of the others. If this referendum succeeds, I doubt I will manage to wriggle my way out of it.'

Kate groaned. She couldn't bear the thought of Tom dying too. She liked him and enjoyed talking to him and, more importantly, he asked nothing of her.

'Until tonight, I didn't know how I would vote.'

He raised his eyebrows. 'You certainly gave that crowd the

impression of being quite firm in your position.'

They stopped outside Aunty's shop. 'Would they have won at Gallipoli if they'd had more men?'

'No.' He paused, his eyes on her face, as if weighing his words. 'The problem wasn't the men—they sent the best, the healthiest—the problem was the plan. If they'd sent twice as many, they too...'

Kate had stopped listening. *The best, the healthiest men*, men like Jack. She felt the sting of tears behind her eyes. All the lives lost over the last eighteen months, men like Jack. She ached with a sadness that was more than her own inconsolable loss.

Tom had stopped and was watching her.

She smiled politely. 'Thank you for getting me safely home.'

'My pleasure.' He lifted his hat and smiled back.

He had a lovely smile.

~

As they were sitting at their evening meal the next day, Aunty said, 'Bridie Johnson said there was a brawl at the anti-conscription meeting outside the Public Hall last night—two women, rolling around on the footpath, screaming and pulling hair.'

Kate stopped eating, her knife and fork frozen in her hands. She forced herself to ask, 'Who were they?'

'Women from outside Coburg, so Bridie says. These meetings attract all sorts of dubious characters. This is why I don't want you going to any.'

If Mrs Johnson didn't know Kate was one of the *brawlers*, it was unlikely anyone else would. Aunty had said she was able to sniff out gossip from a mile away. Kate wanted to laugh at the ridiculous way the story had grown. But, if Tom hadn't hauled her away, she might well have ended up rolling on the ground with the woman. The thought was mortifying.

She kept a straight face and said, 'Thank heavens, it'll be over soon.'

The following Saturday was referendum day. It was a sober day with no heated arguments or disturbances at the polling places—helped by the fact that the government had ordered all the hotels closed.

Kate and Aunty Mary went to vote in the afternoon, passing the posters on fences and in shop windows urging either Yes or No. Overnight large Noes had been daubed in white paint on the footpaths and fences, even over Yes posters. At the polling place at the Coburg Public Hall, Kate had her name struck through on the electoral roll and was handed her ballot paper. In the privacy of one of the booths, she read the question on the paper:

> Are you in favour of the Government having, in this grave emergency, the same compulsory powers over citizens in regard to acquiring their military service, for the term of this war, outside the Commonwealth as it now has with regard to military service within the Commonwealth?

A confusing and complicated way of asking are you in favour of the Government sending conscripted men to fight overseas.

Kate picked up her pencil and with firm strokes placed an X in the box marked NO.

From the start of counting, the vote was close with the No votes marginally ahead. When the absentee votes came in a few days later, the newspapers gleefully reported reductions in the Noes' lead but it was not enough—the final result was a majority of just over seventy-four thousand votes for the Noes. *The Brunswick & Coburg Leader* turned defeat into victory, reporting that Coburg had returned 'a fine affirmative vote' only a few hundred votes behind the Noes.

Kate had no great feeling of victory but rather of a disaster averted. In the aftermath, Billy Hughes was expelled from the Labor Party but managed to remain Prime Minister by forming a government made up of those members of the Labor Party who supported conscription and the pro-conscription Nationalist

Party.

Voluntary recruiting continued. Casualty lists were published, long and unremitting. More women wore black; more scarred and wounded soldiers returned. The coalminers were on strike and with no coal for their furnaces, Hoffman's mill and other factories in Brunswick and Coburg laid men off—they stood in huddles on street corners. For some the only way to support their families was to enlist.

The year staggered to its close yet Christmas was, as ever, a bright point. There was the magic of Midnight Mass followed by a day of good humour and good company—Kate, to her surprise, enjoyed it all. Two recruits from Broadmeadows came for dinner, country boys from New South Wales who had enlisted in Victoria. Aunty watched with pleasure as they devoured their meal. She joined them on the verandah afterwards, drinking her tea as they sat smoking, drinking beer and sharing their store of laughter, jokes and stories. Kate stayed inside and kept herself busy with the dishes and cleaning up. She was afraid, if she sat outside in the sunshine, memories of two other young men would come flooding back.

The recruits left with their haversacks overflowing with cake, biscuits, fruit and a tin of sandwiches made with leftover chicken and ham. Aunty also gave each a scarf, a balaclava, gloves, socks and a flannel shirt. She said she hoped the war would be over by the time they had need for them. They had thanked Aunty profusely, giving her a box containing two linen handkerchiefs embroidered with Whitework and trimmed with Irish lace—a gift that brought tears to her eyes. She made them write down their names, numbers and units and promised to write to them.

They had been polite to Kate, perfect young gentlemen. Perhaps they were aware of her story or simply respectful of the ring on her finger. She wondered if she now wore it not only in memory of Jack but as a way of keeping men at bay.

1917

I have been in the thick of it for the last three weeks, and at present we are resting. We gave Fritz a bad time, and never before have I seen so many German dead. We had suffered severe bombardments, and all we wanted was to get at the enemy. It was quite a relief when we got the news that we were going over. It was like music to our ears when our guns opened. Ye Gods, what a stunt! Over we went. I will never forget driving Fritz out of his pill boxes—concrete 12ft. thick, which no gun can penetrate. But little bombs and the bayonet are very persuading. We took about 500 prisoners in our sector. There was no holding our chaps who all had dear friends and comrades of years who had fallen beside them.

Letter from Corporal W. R. Campbell
'somewhere in Belgium'
The Riverine Herald 20 December 1917 p.3

26

January 1917

Kate watched as the clear water flowed over the pale gold of the sand, the light froth skimming the rock she was standing on. The sun was warm on her back and the bare skin of her forearms. She looked out from beneath her broad brimmed hat, towards the sparkling blue-green water stretching towards the limitless blue of the clear summer sky.

She thought of Jack and of her cousin, Vince. The foreign waters that Jack's grave overlooked, the same waters where Vince lay so far from home, were they as beautiful and as calm as this? Did it matter where they lay? Their souls, their very essence, had gone where they could not be reached. All that remained were fading memories. The living moved on and changed and it was as if those memories belonged to someone else. Kate knew she was not the girl who had come to Melbourne, not the young woman who had lost her sweetheart, not even the one who had dwelt in the darkness of grief for the last eighteen months. It shadowed her still but life was changing and, almost against her will, the past was drifting away, and Jack with it.

Aunty Mary had stood silent, staring out across the water, when they arrived. Kate was sure she was thinking of Vince. She had said that he loved coming to the beach. Did she see him splashing in the water, a happy carefree boy?

She glanced back towards the esplanade where her aunt and Mrs Ryan sat on a blanket beneath their large umbrellas. They were sharing a thermos of tea as they chatted, the remains of their picnic in the baskets beside them.

Williamstown Beach was an easy train ride from the city, making it popular with many from the northern suburbs of Melbourne. Today's summer weather brought the crowds. Women and men sat beneath umbrellas or makeshift awnings near the esplanade;

others strolled along the beach fully dressed, a few men in shirt-sleeves carried their jackets. Children clambered over the rocks and splashed in the shallow water, shoes off, legs bare, boys with their shorts rolled up, young girls with their smocks hoisted high. And far off, a handful of daring young men and women swam in what some considered modest bathing costumes.

She looked down as a small wave splashed up from the edge of the rock wetting the hem of her grey skirt. Other young women were wearing lighter summer frocks, an inch or two shorter. Kate closed her eyes. She was tired of the dark skirts and grey or navy blouses she had been wearing for nearly two years. Even the pale blue blouse Aunty had insisted she wear today seemed drab. She wanted a pretty frock; she wanted to twirl in it, the skirt floating out; she wanted to kick off her shoes and lift her skirts and run through the shallows; to spin around, to dance in a man's arms. She thought again of Jack, the last time she danced with him. Sadness washed through her. And guilt. And that made her angry at herself. She knew the words of his letter by heart. *I want you to live and, yes, to love again. I want your life to be full of everything we wanted together.* The past was fading, but she could not imagine the future.

Tom Ryan stood beside her, his sleeves rolled up to below his elbows, his jacket slung over one shoulder. His hat was pushed back as he squinted towards the horizon. The lines around his eyes were clear in the bright sunlight.

He looked like he laughed often, yet Kate could not remember him laughing properly. Perhaps it was simply there was little to laugh about these days.

Tom stepped off the rock and held out his hand to her.

Kate took hold if it. His hand was firm and calloused. A sure, steady hand.

She let go once she was on the firm sand.

As they walked along, not far from the water's edge, she looked over to the wooden building on a long pier, the water beside it fenced off by thin planks of wood stretching from the pier into the water.

She read the sign on the wall of the building. 'What are hot sea baths?'

'You can bathe there in hot sea water—it's supposed to be good for all sorts of ailments. It runs to a timetable so men and women can swim separately. When the red flag is up, it's the women's turn, and the blue is for the men. Some of the locals here don't much like the idea of mixed bathing.'

Kate watched the children playing in the water. 'It looks like much more fun out in the open.'

'Truly, you have never been to the beach before?'

'Never. I've paddled in the shallows of the creek, but not the sea. We lived too far away.'

'I suppose this isn't truly the sea—it's a large bay. The sea itself can be colder and wilder.'

Tom bent and picked up what looked like a stone and went to the water's edge.

Kate followed him.

Washed clean in the water, he handed it to Kate.

It was a small piece of glass, a beautiful green, its edges smooth and rounded.

'This is so pretty.'

'It's sea glass. It's been worn smooth by the sea. You usually find it among the rocks.'

Kate held it on the palm of her hand, the colour fading as it dried.

'It will brighten if you wet it again,' Tom said.

Kate went to hand it back to him but he said, 'No, keep it as a memento of your first visit to the beach. If you didn't go to the beach, where did you go for your holidays?'

'Sometimes, not often, one or two of us children would stay with Mum's aunt in Maffra or her sister in Sale. But farmers rarely have time for holidays. The cows won't milk themselves because you want a few days away. And there's plenty to do—we all had jobs of some sort.'

'What was yours?'

'When I was younger, it was feeding the chooks and watering Mum's flower garden. But before I came down here, it was mainly helping Mum with everything from the sewing and cooking to minding the little ones.'

'She was happy to let you come down here?'

Kate stopped as a boy turned a cartwheel across their path. 'At first she didn't mind, but now she thinks I have been away too long.'

'Would you like a lemon squash or an ice cream?' Tom nodded towards the row of refreshment rooms on the other side of the road.

'Oh yes, an ice cream please.' She felt like a child being given a special treat.

Tom rolled his sleeves down and put on his jacket.

They crossed the road and walked along the footpath, past the first crowded refreshment room. Tom spied a table inside the door of the second, just vacated, and pounced on it.

He drew out the chair for Kate to sit and ordered for them both. 'You didn't go home for Christmas?'

'I should have, and Mum wanted me to, but I didn't want to leave Aunty Mary. She had arranged Christmas dinner for a couple of young soldiers from the camp, country boys. I worked in the shop while she did all the baking—not just all the Christmas extras but she made biscuits and cake for them to take away. I do think she enjoyed herself.'

The ice creams arrived in bowls, topped with grated chocolate and walnuts. Kate took her first mouthful. 'This is...' a dozen words rushed through her mind but she settled for the ordinary, '... delicious.'

'Don't tell me you have never had ice cream before.'

'Of course I have. I'm not a complete hayseed.'

'I wasn't suggesting that at all.'

Kate leant back in her seat and looked up towards the ceiling. 'I wonder what I have done, that you haven't.'

'I've never milked a cow.'

She screwed up her nose. 'Milking cows isn't anywhere near as glamourous as eating ice cream and promenading at the beach. But, and this isn't glamourous either, I bet you have never raised a poddy calf.'

'I have not.' Tom frowned slightly. 'I've heard the name though.'

'They are hand-raised, usually, because their mother has died. I had one, Gertie, she was lovely, almost like a big friendly puppy. She would follow me everywhere given the chance. One Sunday— I was about twelve—we were waiting for Mum to come out so we could go off to Mass. I wandered off to talk to Gertie. She was so pleased to see me that she slobbered all over my good Sunday dress. Mum was cross and to hide the mess she made me wear the only clean pinafore she had. Hannah's! And it was a bit too small. So there was I, looking like a grubby child when, only ten minutes earlier, I had been a young lady in a pretty dress, nearly old enough to have my hair pinned up.'

Tom threw his head back and laughed. The first real laugh she had heard from him. It was a rumble that came from deep inside him. It lit up his whole face.

Kate looked past him to a severe looking older man with a neatly clipped moustache at the next table who was glaring at them. Was it their noise or the fact that Tom was enjoying himself and not in uniform? She smiled brightly at the man and he looked away.

Tom raised his eyebrows.

'It's the old grump on the table behind you. He's not game to look at me now.' She finished her ice cream, scraping her spoon across the bottom of the bowl. 'That was absolutely scrumptious.'

'Food of the Gods.' He placed his hands on the table. 'I suppose we should get back to the old ones.'

She smiled at him. 'I don't know they would like to hear you calling them that?'

He grinned back. 'Far older than us anyway.'

Later, Kate sat in the train taking them back to North Melbourne where they would catch the Coburg train. Aunty and Mrs Ryan, seated along from her, were talking nineteen to the dozen about the virtues of homemade soda bread over the local bakers' offerings. The afternoon had almost been like a dream—the whole world and its worries had floated away. Kate felt a hope for the future that had been missing for so long. She wanted to be like the other young women, carefree and wearing pretty dresses. She doubted she could be carefree but she could sew a couple of new dresses. That would make Aunty happy. She would ask her where the best place was to buy the material.

The carriage was hot and Kate's gloves damp with perspiration. As she slipped them off, the sun glinted on the stones in her ring. She stared at it. One day she would take it off. But not yet.

She looked up as Tom turned his head to stare out the window. She was sure he had been watching her.

He had a pleasant face. His straight eyebrows and the slight bump in his nose gave him an air of purpose and strength. Since the night of the *brawl*, he had called in most Friday nights to do some of his mother's shopping and stayed for a chat if the shop wasn't busy. And, if Kate was honest with herself, she looked forward to Tom's visits. She knew he was someone who would offer help if ever she needed it. A good friend, that was it. She didn't want to kiss him.

She stared at those firm straight lips.

Tom glanced across at her. Their eyes met. Kate caught her breath and looked away. It was dreadful to be caught staring at someone. Heat rushed up her cheeks. No, no, she didn't want to kiss him. But, perhaps, if they were at a parish social event and he asked her to dance, she would do that. It would only be polite.

She turned her head and watched the passing houses as the train sped on. She hadn't thought of Jack as she had walked along the beach with Tom, or sat in the refreshment room with him, or even sitting here on the train. Until now.

The past was fading like the colour of the sea glass, and she could not stop it.

Kate didn't know that she wanted to.

27

Aunty Mary's eyes lit up. 'You must. There are plenty of shops on Sydney Road where you can buy material. Walker's is a good place to start—they usually have a sale in January. There are several drapers near Moreland Road or you could go to Brunswick. There are plenty of ladies drapers down there. Courtney & Harper too, they have a fine selection.'

Kate realised, now that she had mentioned it, there would be no getting out of buying material and making some new dresses.

'You should take Reenie with you. She has an eye for what is fashionable.'

'If I go with Reenie, she will have me looking like a fashion plate.'

'And why should you not? You are a fine looking young woman, Kate.' She smiled as she sang, 'Lovely and fair as the rose of the summer.'

Blushing, Kate grinned. ''Tis a pure flatterer you are.'

Aunty Mary laughed, a joyful bubbling sound Kate hadn't heard for two years.

'I'll have you speaking like you're Irish born by the time we are finished here.' Her eyes sparkled. 'You have that orange material you brought back with you. I can get it cut and made up for you— a good frock you could wear if you went out in the evening. Miss Cooper in Munro Street does a very good job.'

A dress suitable for social evenings, a dress to dance in—Kate couldn't do that. Not yet. 'Thank you, but I haven't decided what I want to do with that material.'

It took three weeks for Kate to collect together the material she wanted. The first trip out, on a Wednesday afternoon, she did take Reenie with her. As she had resolved not to buy a thing, she didn't mind Reenie's exuberant suggestions. It gave her a good idea of what the latest fashions were like. By the time they had finished,

Kate was certain they had visited every single draper and ladies outfitter along Sydney Road from Bell Street to Brunswick Road. Brunswick was busier than Coburg, many more and grander shops, far more people—almost like the city itself. There were recruiting posters everywhere, in windows of some of the shops and on walls, as there had been since she arrived in Melbourne. Kate no longer took any notice of them.

The shops they entered were treasure houses of silks, linens and lace, voiles, crepes and embroideries, buttons as pretty as gemstones. They finished their shopping with a visit to Mrs Martin's tea rooms near the city end of Sydney Road. Kate pushed aside her memories of her first trip to a tea room with Aunty Mary when Jack was alive and, despite the war, the future was full of hope. She came home with a pattern for a skirt. Her outing with Annie the next week, late on Friday afternoon, was more subdued. Annie had suggestions of ways to get the best value from her purchases, looking amongst the oddments for lengths of cloth suitable for making blouses, buying dress pieces, cut and ready to sew. This time Kate bought pieces for two blouses, material for a skirt, a new pair of gloves and a dress pattern. The picture on the front was almost a dream—a couple of inches shorter and with a fuller skirt than she usually wore, three-quarter sleeves and a higher waistline covered with a sash of the same material. It was perfect for a day trip to the beach and a walk along the esplanade. She showed it to Aunty Mary when she got home.

'I do like that.' Aunty stared at the picture on the cover of the envelope. 'I like the open collar. The hemline is shorter but it is still modest.' She smiled at Kate, pleasure in her face. 'You will look lovely.'

Kate went on her final shopping trip alone and bought exactly the material she wanted for the dress, voile printed with sprigs of flowers, and a pair of shoes with straps, buckles and a louis heel. Her everyday shoes were in good repair and would last quite a while longer; these would be for special occasions.

Aunty Mary paid Kate a small wage and, as she had spent so little of it, she had covered the cost of her purchases with a small amount left over. She had seen a hat she had liked but could not afford. Reenie, who now worked as a sales assistant for a milliner two days a week, had advised her she could buy the basic hat at a much lower price and trim it herself, but even that would have to wait.

Kate looked at her collection of material piled beside the sewing machine under the window in the sitting room. The world had not changed, the war and its horrors dragged on, yet the thought of a pretty new dress made her happy.

~

Kate saw Tom Ryan around Coburg more frequently. As well as his Friday evening visits to the shop, he was often at the same Mass she and Aunty attended, though he was with his mother near the front while Aunty and Kate slipped into the back row at the last minute. And Tom and Mrs Ryan came with them on the way home, going out of their way, and walking down to Munro Street. Mrs Ryan said she didn't like using the bridge over the railway line at Victoria Street where they lived. She never mentioned why she didn't take the shortest route of all, along Bell Street.

Kate was almost certain Aunty was arranging outings with Mrs Ryan. They went to the pictures occasionally on Saturday evening. The seating usually ended up with the two older women sitting side by side, then Kate and, finally, Tom. Kate enjoyed the pictures. She laughed through the comedies like *The Worst of Friends* and Charlie Chaplin in *The Floorwalker*, was fascinated by the Pathé Gazettes, and sniffed back her tears when romantic dramas were shown such as *The Tortured Heart*, a tale inspired by Romeo and Juliet. She sat with her hands folded in her lap, aware of Tom beside her, their arms not quite touching. He never tried to hold her hand. He was simply there. Afterwards they would walk along Sydney Road, the old ones behind them, Tom and Kate in front.

Once or twice, after the Ryans had turned into Munro Street, she was aware that Aunty wanted to say something but held back. Kate didn't want to explain what she felt, she didn't understand herself. All she could say was that she liked Tom's company and when she was with him, she sometimes forgot there was a war.

~

An Irish concert was held in the Coburg Public Hall at the start of March in support of the Queen of Charity, one of the queens in the Queen Carnival that would to be part of St Paul's parish bazaar in May. The bazaar was to raise funds for the school and the cost of renovations to the presbytery.

Aunty Mary and Kate arrived early to be sure of seats towards the front. The hall was decorated with green and gold streamers, and pot plants were arranged around the edge of the room. Both the Australian flag and the flag of Ireland hung on the wall at the front.

Aunty gazed at the backdrop on the stage, an Irish landscape with shamrocks and golden harps at the corners.

'Ah, Katie,' she sighed. ''Tis a beautiful country.' She squeezed Kate's hand. 'But Australia has given me those I love best.'

A small orchestra opened the concert, playing *Erins's Wreath*. Talented parishioners and professional singers, accompanied by a pianist, then sang their way through more than thirty songs, most of them old favourites. Dancers in national costume put on a display of Irish dancing and the evening ended with everyone singing *God Save Ireland* and *Auld Lang Syne*.

Mrs Ryan and Tom, who had been sitting further back, waited for them outside. They walked slowly away from the Public Hall, the crowd around them spreading out, some rushing away as tomorrow was a working day.

'I wish we had been sitting right at the front,' Kate said. 'I would have liked to see the way the dancers moved their feet.'

'I learnt step dancing as a child.' Tom stopped and, arms straight beside his body, began to dance, his steps fast and intricate as he tapped, lightly hopped and kicked.

'Ah, Tom.' Mrs Ryan smiled. 'There's no need to be showing off.' She came and stood beside Kate as Tom, illuminated by the street lamp, continued his performance. 'He was not a bad dancer but the dancing teacher, poor woman, banned him from her class.'

Tom brought his feet together and bowed to those who had stopped to watch him.

'Please, Mother. Not that story.'

Mrs Ryan ignored him. 'Tom was about ten. We'd had a concert, the children singing and showing off their dance steps. Then there was afternoon tea. The boys ate their fill of cream cake and scones and went outside. Now this one,' she tilted her head towards Tom, 'had firecrackers. He lit one and tossed it through the window and it landed under the teacher's chair. The cracker went off, a ha'penny bunger it was, and the poor woman fainted. She refused to teach him from then.'

'I'm not surprised,' Kate laughed.

They walked on and turned into Sydney Road.

Without thinking, Kate slid her right hand through the crook of Tom's elbow.

Tom changed his pace in time with Kate's and rested his hand on hers for a moment.

There was comfort in his touch.

At home, dressed in her nightgown, Kate sat on the side of her bed and took out the handkerchief case. She looked down at the ring on her finger.

She would keep seeing Tom—the old ones, as he called them, would continue their gentle matchmaking. And she didn't mind. She liked the idea of getting to know him better. Whatever the future was, it would happen slowly. But she was certain it would not be fair to Tom, and not respectful of Jack's memory, to walk arm in arm with Tom wearing Jack's ring.

She slid the ring off her left hand, kissed it and placed it in with

Jack's letters and photographs.

She looked toward the photograph of Jack on her bedside table. She couldn't put it away. Not yet.

28

Tom called in to the shop on his way home from work and, like most Friday nights, he stood back from the counter, waiting for the other shoppers to leave.

Kate gave the woman she was serving her change and smiled past her to Tom.

The door opened and Vera Brennan came in. She was a friend of Reenie's but didn't come to the knitting group. Reenie said she was the prettiest girl she knew—with her perfect skin and wavy dark blonde hair, she looked like the picture star, Mary Pickford. And now she was standing beside Tom gazing up at him as she spoke, as if he was the only man left on earth.

The shop was busy and customers kept coming. Every time Kate looked up, Vera was either smiling at Tom or fluttering her long dark eyelashes. She even rested her hand on Tom's forearm as she chattered on.

Finally, there was only one customer left, and Vera and Tom.

Aunty stepped back from the counter. 'If you don't mind Mrs Fowler, Kate will serve you next. Mr Ryan has been waiting for a while.' She looked over to Tom. 'Tom, if you would like to come out the back, I have your mother's groceries ready for you.'

Kate frowned. She hadn't seen Aunty making up a grocery order for Mrs Ryan—they didn't have a list for her.

Tom walked around the counter and followed Aunty into the house.

After Kate had finished with Mrs Fowler, she served Vera who only wanted a small bottle of vanilla essence. This was the third time Vera had come in on Friday night and made a small purchase, her shopping trips always coinciding with Tom's.

Vera took the bottle. 'Baking day tomorrow.'

In the background, they could hear the murmur of conversation

178

and a rumble of laughter from Tom.

Her vanilla in her hand, Vera stared down the passage. She smiled brightly at Kate. 'Well, I must be off.' She spoke as if it was Kate she had called in to see.

Kate watched her leave. Vera's jacket and skirt matched, a smart shade of navy blue trimmed with pink. Kate had to admit not only was Vera pretty but she always looked very smart.

Aunty poked her head out. 'All clear?' There was a twinkle in her eyes. She stepped into the shop, Tom behind her. 'Now Tom, if you'll give me that list, I'll get these bits and pieces together.'

Kate rang up the prices as Aunty handed her the groceries on the list: eggs, butter, tea, bacon and sago.

Tom's eyes flickered to Kate's hands as she gave him his change.

'Are you planning to go to the fete tomorrow at the recreation reserve?' he asked. 'I hear there will be a band competition. It's to raise money to buy uniforms for the Coburg Municipal Band.'

'We are saving out pennies for St Paul's garden fete at the end of the month,' Aunty answered for Kate. 'There are so many concerts and fetes and bazaars at the moment—a body can't be expected to go to them all, especially now a penny doesn't go as far as it once did.'

He looked around the empty shop, as if checking there was no one hiding in the corners. 'Kate.' He stopped and drew a quick breath. 'Would you like to come to the pictures tomorrow week.' Almost as an afterthought he added, 'You too Mrs Burke.'

Kate glanced at her aunt who nodded.

'Thank you, Tom. I would like that.' Although her heart didn't skip a beat, Kate was happy. Tom was asking *her* to the pictures— not Vera Brennan. They would be going together, not just accompanying the old ones even if they were coming too.

He beamed at her, looking as if a great burden had been lifted. 'It would be tomorrow but a few weeks back I arranged to meet a couple of mates to watch the last of the bicycle races at the reserve, then go off to the Coburg Hotel for a quick drink.'

'A quick drink?' A smile twitched at Aunty's mouth. 'And when the pub closes at six, the drinking may well continue elsewhere?'

'It may well, Mrs Burke.' Tom grinned back at her.

Aunty watched as he walked out the door. Once he was out of sight, she said, 'He was letting you know that his evening won't be spent chasing after the Vera Brennans of the world.'

'It never occurred to me that he would.'

Aunty raised her eyebrows. 'You have nothing to worry about with that one. He has eyes only for you.'

Heat rushed up Kate's face.

'I... I...' Aunty's words had made her heart skip a beat. 'I'll sweep the floor.'

'And I'll lock up.' Aunty walked over to the door, smiling as if she were the one Tom would be sitting beside at the pictures.

~

As they sat in the dark of the picture theatre, Tom reached over and held Kate's hand. And Kate was quietly happy. She would have liked to rest her head against his shoulder but she might end up getting the back of her seat kicked. There was none of the thrill she had with Jack. She doubted she would ever feel that way again. She stopped. She must not compare them. Anything she felt for Tom must be for himself, as he was.

Tom walked them home afterwards and accepted Aunty Mary's invitation to come in for a cup of cocoa.

Kate and Tom sat together on the sofa in the sitting room while Aunty stirred the stove to life and set the milk to boil.

'That serial, *The Stingaree*, was exciting,' Kate said.

'Who can resist a bushranger with a heart of gold? Would you like to go again next week?'

'I'd love to. Really, I would watch anything, even walking dogs.'

'How about monkeys driving motor cars?'

'Even better,' Kate laughed.

'Mother will come with us.'

Kate raised her eyebrows. 'As a chaperone?' Tom was so well-mannered she doubted they would ever need a chaperone.

'Seems so. Would you say that...' He paused then continued in a rush, '...this means we are walking out?'

Kate lowered her eyes. Was it too soon? She was sure Tom would not rush her towards anything she did not want. And she did like his company.

She looked up at him and smiled. 'I would say it does.'

Tom turned towards her. His lips were warm, his kiss gentle on her cheek.

She jumped as Aunty called from the doorway, 'Cocoa's ready.'

Aunty set the tray on the table and handed around the cups as if she hadn't noticed a thing.

She sat back in her armchair and took a sip of her cocoa. 'This fete of ours at the end of the month will be a grand one. There's to be a march along Sydney Road—with Irish pipers!'

'And an ocean wave in the reserve,' Tom said.

Kate frowned. 'The sea in the recreation reserve?'

'It's a fairground ride—a bit like a merry-go-round, it sways about and rocks from side to side.'

'Something to be enjoyed on an empty stomach,' Aunty said, a twinkle in her eyes. 'It is wise to stand a good distance away from it. I once saw a child spray the whole circle of onlookers.'

'I'll keep that in mind while I wait,' Tom laughed. 'I'll be going on it for sure.' Happiness seemed to be bubbling in him. 'You'll come on it with me, Kate?'

'Why not?' Kate laughed. His happiness was catching.

When time came for him to leave, Kate went with Tom out to the verandah. He stood away from the light spilling through the kitchen doorway and caught both of her hands in his. His eyes shining, he bent forward and kissed her, a dry brush of his lips against hers.

She smiled at him. 'Good night, Tom.'

'Good night, Kate.' He smiled back and walked into the darkness near the side gate, whistling.

She stood staring after him. Yes, she liked him a lot.

29

Kate handed the glass of lemonade to the boy who stood in front of the stall, his second. He guzzled it down, placed the glass back on the table, wiped his mouth on the cuff of his shirt and ran off towards the football ground where the children's sports were underway.

Kate watched him go. 'He was thirsty.'

'Yes,' Annie said, 'and has a sweet tooth considering the number of lollies he bought.'

'Perhaps he'll share them with his sisters.'

'I wonder.' She glanced at Kate. 'You have a soft spot for little boys.'

'Maybe. My younger brother is a little rascal. Not so little now, I suppose. He will be thirteen next month and, Mum says, he now insists they call him Bill, not Billy.'

Two girls, identically dressed in pale blue with flounces and bows, stood in front of the jars of sweets. Annie waited patiently while they took time over their selection, making sure they got value for their pennies.

Kate gazed around the reserve. The sun was shining and a band was playing near the sports ground. The reserve looked beautiful—the trees, and the plants in the rock-edged beds, had grown since it had been opened. There were people everywhere, young and old, parents with children; boys and girls running from stall to stall, to the hoopla and the ocean wave, or out to the donkey and the pony rides; couples arm in arm; groups of young men including a few soldiers on leave; young women, giggling and chatting, promenading in what might be their last chance to show off their summer frocks.

Tom stood over by the shamrock stall where small badges in the shape of a shamrock were sold to raise money that would be shared between local charities for children and the distressed children of Dublin. He was deep in conversation with a man in uniform. The soldier, a wry grin on his face, was talking quickly and Tom threw his head back and laughed. While he showed no active support of the war, it seemed he passed no judgement on those who wished to go.

'So. Tom Ryan,' Annie said, one eyebrow raised.

'What about him?' Kate tried to keep her face blank.

'I've heard a whisper that you have been keeping company with him.'

Kate's face flushed. 'I've been to the pictures with him a couple of times along with either Aunty Mary or his mother.'

'So why have you been so secretive?'

'It's only been a few weeks and there has always been something else to talk about.'

'Clearly Reenie doesn't know either.'

'No doubt she will have drawn her own conclusions by the end of the day.'

Annie laughed softly. 'If not sooner.'

Mrs Johnson came up and asked for a glass of raspberry cordial. As Kate passed her the glass, she said, 'It is good to see you lending a hand, Miss Burke.'

Kate ignored the veiled criticism. 'Are you enjoying yourself, Mrs Johnson?'

''Tis a grand day. Did you hear, they are having rides in a motor car. I am going on one with my grandson.'

'Be sure to hang on to your hat, Mrs Johnson,' Annie said. 'It can get quite windy in them.'

'I will, Miss Watkins.' She returned her glass, smiling at both the young women.

'She doesn't seem as annoying as she used to be.'

'Oh, she's a lovely old woman,' Annie said, 'just as long as she is getting her own way.'

'A dreadful stickybeak though.'

'Yes, there is that. Now...' Annie paused, as if gauging how Kate would react to what she was about to say. 'Next Sunday a few of us will be going to Keilor for a picnic—it is pretty out there. Harry is coming with a couple of friends. Why don't you and Tom come too?'

'That sounds lovely. I'll ask him.' It would be nice to be away from the watchful eye of aunts and mothers. 'I've been here two and a half years but have seen very little of Melbourne. I did go to Williamstown Beach on New Year's Day.'

'You didn't tell me that and we have seen each other since then.' She paused. 'And Tom was there too?'

Kate willed herself not to blush. 'Yes, but it was Aunty Mary and Mrs Ryan's idea. Aunty said that when Uncle Mick was alive, they often went there in summer.'

Mrs Egan, the manageress of the stall bustled up. 'You look like you've been doing a roaring trade by the state of these bottles. She picked up an empty bottle that had held lime cordial and a nearly empty raspberry and replaced them with full bottles from a box beneath the table. Will you make up some more lemonade, Annie? I'll take over now, Kate, and you can be on your way. Thank you for helping.'

'My pleasure, Mrs Egan. I'd be happy to help at other events if you need me.'

Mrs Egan's eyes lit up. 'I will hold you to that.'

Kate walked over to where Tom stood, still talking to the soldier about, of all things, a piece of machinery. It took both a minute to realise she was standing there.

'Kate!' Tom grinned, his happiness plain, and in it Kate could see all he felt for her.

'This is Dan Ryan. Not a relation.'

'If you go back far enough, Tom, I'm sure all of us Ryans are related, especially if you're from Tipperary.' He smiled at Kate.

185

'Pleased to meet you Miss ...'

'... Burke,' Tom finished for him. 'Dan worked with me at North Melbourne. He is off to France in a few weeks.'

Kate felt the lump settle in her stomach that always came when she thought of those she knew who were fighting in France or the Middle East. She prayed silently, *Lord protect you and bring you safely home.*

'I wish you all the best, Mr Ryan.'

'Thank you. I held off but with these rumours of German raiders in the Indian Ocean, it's time I did something to stop it before the war gets any closer. I tried to talk Tom into coming with me but he was having none of it.'

The weight in Kate's stomach grew heavier.

'I can see none of you have bought badges.' Reenie, wearing a tray displaying the small metal shamrocks, shook a tin with a big shamrock painted on it. 'And you standing here beside the stall.'

'We had better set that right.' Tom took a couple of coins from his pocket and bought two badges. He handed one to Kate.

Reenie smiled at Kate, a hundred questions in her eyes. And Kate knew she would get an extensive interrogation at the knitting circle next week.

Tom and Kate left Reenie happily chatting to Dan.

'Before we do anything else,' Tom drew her hand through his arm. 'I'm taking you over to the ocean wave.'

'I don't know. Surely, it's a children's ride.'

But Kate was wrong. There were as many adults as children on the ride. It was a large flat ring with thin metal poles extending from the ring up to a central pole. A metal hoop was set about a foot above the ring so those on the ride could either sit back or, facing outward, hold on to it. Many others stood, gripping onto the poles. The operator checked that the riders were spaced evenly around it to balance the weight.

Tom helped Kate onto the ring then clambered up beside her.

They stood holding on to the poles as the ride slowly began to sway. Kate held tight to her post, fearful she would fall. The ride gained speed, rocking first to one side then to the other. As it lurched backwards, she gasped. When it rocked forward, she screamed. All around her women and children were screaming. But it did not sound like fear. She glanced at Tom. He wasn't screaming but his face was alive, exhilarated. The ride sped up, faster and faster. She was flying, the wind buffeting her skirt and her hair. There was nothing she could do but hang on tight to the pole, laughing and screaming.

Too soon, far too soon, the ride slowed and, finally, came to a halt. Tom jumped off but Kate couldn't move.

'I'm stuck,' she laughed.

'Can you ease yourself down so you are sitting?'

Kate shook her head. 'I'm scared I'll fall.'

'Right. I'll lift you down.' He reached up, wrapped his arms tight around her legs, above the knees. 'Now close your eyes and let go.'

Kate froze.

'Trust me.'

Kate took a deep breath, closed her eyes, and let go.

Tom staggered and Kate slid down, startled by the unexpected thrill of being held so tight by him.

Her feet on the ground, he eased his hold and stepped away.

Kate straightened her skirt and grasped his arm. 'I can't walk.'

'Hang on to me and you'll be right.'

Hear heart still pounding, she didn't dare look at Tom yet.

She took another deep breath and found she could walk but she kept her arm linked through his.

'Once is enough?' Tom asked.

'Oh, for now.'

'What would you like to do? Go over and watch the children dance around the maypole and then get an ice cream?'

'Yes to both, and after that we can pretend we are adults.'

They watched the children dancing and wandered past the stalls. Kate was introduced over a dozen times to friends of Tom's, some local men, others visitors come to enjoy the fete.

Tom was pleased at the prospect of the picnic at Keilor with Annie and her friends. 'Perhaps we can do something over Easter.'

'I'll be away for Easter. I'm going back home on Tuesday week.'

'But you are coming back?'

She could hear the worry in his voice. Aunty Mary had been the same when she had told her.

'Yes. I'll be back by the day before Anzac Day at the latest.'

'Well,' he said brightly. 'When you get back, we can go dancing. Somewhere decent—some of the dance halls can be a bit rough.'

'I'd love that. I haven't danced for a long time.' Tomorrow she would take Mrs Sheehan's material to Miss Cooper to get a new dress made.

Towards evening, they found Aunty Mary and Mrs Ryan and sat beside them listening to the concert. The members of The Young Ireland Society, an organisation that encouraged both literary activities and political debate, sang the old Irish songs and some that were more modern. Occasionally, one or two in the audience, caught up by the music, sang along. The pipers who had led the parade on Sydney Road played as the men and women of the society danced reels, sets and steps.

They walked together only as far as Sydney Road. Mrs Ryan was tired and took the shorter route, along Bell Street. Aunty Mary and Kate turned down Sydney Road, humming tunes from the concert as they walked.

It had been a delightful day. With a jolt Kate realised she hadn't thought of Jack at all. She felt a whisper of sadness. But Jack had wanted her to find someone else. And Tom made her smile. He made her feel safe.

30

April 1917

Kate stood at the bench in the Briagolong Post Office, staring at the postcard with its tinted picture of cows standing in a shallow creek, gum trees in the background. She turned it over and wrote quickly.

> Dear Tom,
>   This is not our farm but our cows like to stand in their drinking water like this especially in summer. We have nearly caught up with the city here. Not only do two of our neighbours now have motor cars but my brother Jim has a motorcycle with a sidecar. And I have been for a ride in it. It is almost as thrilling as the ocean wave. Have you ridden one? Or is this one thing I have done that you have not?
>   I will be back by the 24th at the latest.

She paused. What should she write? *With love* or *Best wishes*? And should she add a kiss? Would *With love* and a kiss be too much?

> Best wishes,
> Kate X

She slid the card into an envelope, addressed and sealed it. She didn't want everyone reading what she had written, particularly that X.

'Who are you writing to?'

Kate started at the sound of her brother's voice. 'None of your business.'

Jim reached over and snatched it from her. '*Mr T Ryan*. Now who is this?'

'Give it back.'

'I'll post it for you.' He walked over to the counter.

The postmistress paused her conversation with a stout older woman and took the envelope from Jim. He paid the postage and went out into the street where Kate was waiting.

'I've done you a favour. No one can say, *Did you hear about Kate Burke? She is writing to a man in Coburg. What's going on there?*'

'Miss Cahill wouldn't do that.'

'But Mrs Wilkie in there talking to her might, and she is eagle-eyed and has the hearing of a bat.'

'Very well,' Kate said grudgingly. 'You have done me a favour.'

'Have you got everything Mum wanted?'

'Yes, all finished. And I have even bought a bag of lollies for the little ones.'

'You'll have to dole them out one at a time, or Bill will scoff the lot.' He gazed up at the sun, still high in the clear sky. 'We've plenty of time. Let's go over to Mrs Whaley's and you can tell me about Mr T Ryan over a cup of tea.'

'You'd be at home talking to Mrs Wilkie,' Kate laughed.

'Oh, I am.' Jim grinned. 'She thinks I'm a delightful young man.'

Kate looked around the room as they walked in. It was as smart as the city tea houses and coffee palaces with its white table cloths and specimen vases. The only other customers were a couple of women seated at a table on the other side of the room but, no doubt, it would be full when the cattle sales were on.

They took a table by the window. Jim sat down, leaving Kate to pull out her own chair. She thought of Tom and his good manners. Perhaps sisters didn't rate as ladies.

A young woman around Kate's age took their orders but Mrs Whaley brought over their tea and scones.

'Lovely to see you, Kate. Are you back for good?' She moved the vase to one side and placed the scones on a stand at the centre of the table.

'I'm home for a visit, Mrs Whaley. I'll be staying with my aunt until my cousin comes home from France.'

'The sooner we win this war the better,' Mrs Whaley said.

As soon as Mrs Whaley was out of earshot, Jim stretched back in his seat. 'Now who is this T Ryan?'

Jim would pester until he had it out of her. 'His name is Tom. His mother is a good friend of Aunty Mary's.'

'Is he your sweetheart?'

'He's a friend.' She poured the tea into both their cups, aware her face was reddening.

It wasn't a lie.

Jim looked up from the scone he was slathering with strawberry jam. 'Why all the secrecy?'

'I don't want fuss and teasing. You won't be carrying tales to Mum?'

'For heaven's sake, Kate, as if I would. Your secret's safe with me.' He took a sip of his tea. 'He hasn't enlisted?'

'No. He's the only one left at home with his mother.' Why was she making excuses? Tom would say it wasn't his war, or that he had no wish to fight the English king's war. But she had only heard him say that once, two years ago. Perhaps it had just been to niggle Mrs Miles.

'Have you thought about it?'

'I have.' Jim stared into his cup. He looked up, straight at Kate. 'I've thought hard about it but I can't go. Dad's over sixty now. He couldn't manage without me. If I joined up, he would have to pay someone, if he could find a man, and no labourer comes as cheap as a son.'

'I'm glad you are sensible.' Kate frowned deeply. 'So many are still enlisting, some still thinking it's an adventure. Not that the Prime Minister ever considers it enough.'

Jim looked past Kate, frowning, his eyes unfocussed. 'I will probably regret it for the rest of my life.' He brought his attention back to Kate. 'Dick Simmonds is talking of enlisting again.'

Kate's eyes prickled. 'He can't do that. His parents, his mother ... one son is more than enough.'

'I think he feels guilty.'

'He's got nothing to feel guilty—'

'Shhh, Kate. Everyone is watching.'

The two women had put their cups down and were staring towards Kate, as was Mrs Whaley.

Kate lowered her voice almost to a whisper. 'He's got nothing to feel guilty about. He did as much as he could.'

'You know Hannah is sweet on him?'

'Yes.' Kate groaned. 'I hope she never has to...' she couldn't say the words. It was too cruel to think of. 'I should talk to him. Maybe he doesn't understand what it will do to her, to his mother. But he must know, after Len.'

Jim shrugged. 'Mum's invited him for dinner on Sunday. Then he'll take Hannah for a spin up and down the drive.' He gave a dry laugh. 'It's as far as Dad will let her go on his motorcycle.'

'I hope he manages to stay in the saddle with that.'

Jim finished his scone and drained his teacup. 'It's a surprise but he does.'

'Right. I will talk to him.' She folded her napkin and placed it on the plate.

'We should be getting back.' Jim stood and pushed his chair in. 'Mum worries about me and this *infernal machine*.'

'You haven't taken her for a ride? You could bring her here to do some shopping.'

'I did offer but she was having none of it.'

Jim paid for their afternoon tea, Kate waving to Mrs Whaley as they walked to the door.

They crossed the road to where Jim's motorcycle was parked in front of the Briagolong Hotel.

Kate climbed, inelegantly, into the side car, settling her shopping on the floor around her feet.

Jim handed her a set of goggles.

'Kate! Kate Burke!'

Kate looked over her shoulder.

Mrs Wilkie, finished her gossip at the Post Office, was rushing down the street towards them.

'Oh Kate,' she puffed. 'I wanted to welcome you home.' She placed her hand on her broad bosom. 'I'm too old to be running about.' She took a couple of gasping breaths. 'I wanted to pass on my condolences at the death of your fiancé. So tragic, you barely engaged and him dead. A hero's death I'm told. And poor Mrs Sheehan...' She babbled on oblivious to the effect she was having on Kate.

Kate gripped her goggles. She put them on and tied her scarf tight. She interrupted Mrs Wilkie mid-sentence. 'We are running late, Mrs Wilkie. We have to leave now.'

Jim kicked the bike to life and they roared off, dust flying up, leaving Mrs Wilkie standing open-mouthed at the side of the road.

Kate stared ahead as they sped past the houses and out along the wide road, the tall gum trees flying past. For a long moment, anguish had threatened to overwhelm her at the old woman's prattle. But anger had pushed it away. She could never come back here to live. She would always be the girl who lost her sweetheart at Gallipoli, the object of gossip if she were walking out with another man as if she were besmirching Jack's memory. They would be trapped in the past with no peaceful rest for Jack, no future for her.

31

Kate sat on the verandah. The last of the roses were blooming in the flower garden, splashes of red, pink and white. Further off she could see the grazing cattle, and the paddocks of maize near ready for harvest. Despite its unpredictable seasons of flood and fire, she loved this place—the creek banks with ferns and wildflowers and, further on, the cliff faces dotted with hidden caves and swallows nesting in crevices. She had been born here, in this house, as had all her brothers and sisters. There were two tiny brothers, born far too early, buried under the crepe myrtles. Their beauty altered with the seasons from a riot of pink and mauve blossom in summer, a carpet of striking yellow and orange leaves in autumn, and smooth mottled bark in winter. Mum and Dad would never leave but Kate knew she had no future here. Her future here had been Jack and he was gone.

She could hear the laughter and the murmur of conversation from inside the house. Sunday dinner had been as festive as Easter with roast lamb, peas, carrots, parsnips and potatoes, cauliflower with cheese, followed by apple pudding and custard. Most of the food had been grown on the farm. Dick Simmonds had come over and Hannah had been on her best behaviour through dinner, offering no sharp comments at the antics of her younger brother and sisters. Mum and the younger girls were now in the sitting room, all knitting, even five-year-old Maggie. Bill was sitting at the large dining table with Jim and Hannah watching Dad and Dick play chess. Jim offered unhelpful advice to both and Hannah, glowing with happiness, watched only Dick. Kate had come out to the verandah to be with her thoughts.

Dick strolled out and sat in the wicker armchair along from Kate. He pulled a tin of tobacco from his pocket and began rolling a cigarette.

'Has your father ever lost a game of chess?'

'Not that I know.'

'Not even to Jack?' Dick sealed the cigarette paper and pushed the stray threads of tobacco in with a match.

'Especially not to Jack.'

Dick lit his cigarette, took a deep draw and slowly exhaled through his nose.

'Hannah says you are going back on Tuesday. Don't you like it here?'

'It's not that. Aunty Mary would be alone if I didn't go back.'

'Doesn't she have any other family?'

The question irritated her. What business was it of his whether she was here or not? 'No, she doesn't,' Kate said evenly. 'Vince, her younger son, was killed at Gallipoli and the other, Brendan, is in France.'

Dick said nothing. He smoked his cigarette and stared out across the paddocks.

'Jim said you were thinking of enlisting again.'

'It's time I did my bit.'

'You've already done your bit.'

'A trip to Egypt and a few marches in the desert is hardly doing my bit. There's nothing wrong with me now.'

'But what about your parents? They need you here.'

'They'll manage.'

'If anything happens to you, it will break Hannah's heart.'

He ground out his half-finished cigarette in the ashtray on the small table between their chairs and stood up.

'I have no intention of getting killed.' His hands jammed in his jacket pockets, he walked to the edge of the verandah, his back to Kate.

'Do you have any idea what it's like when you lose the person you love most, the one who is your entire world?'

Dick swung around, his face contorted with grief. 'I know what

195

it is to lose a brother. I know what it is to think, every single waking moment, that if I hadn't been such a weakling, I would have been there beside him, I could have saved him. If I'd been there, he wouldn't have died.'

Kate had no answer. She knew what it was to torment yourself with *if onlys*.

'Don't you think that I, like any decent man, would want to defend my country and pay back those who killed my brother?'

'You'll most likely be fighting Germans not Turks.'

'They are the same side, Kate.' He clenched his hands inside his pockets. 'I have heard of the One Woman, One Recruit League where each woman tries to get one man to enlist. It seems you have joined the One Woman, One Shirker League.' He stared at her, contempt clear in his dark eyes. 'Jack would be ashamed of you.'

His words were like a slap.

Dick stalked off down the path towards the garden gate.

Would Jack be ashamed of her? She jerked her head, fighting back hot tears. She would never know.

Hannah came out onto the verandah. 'I thought Dick was out here.'

Kate kept her voice steady. 'He's in the garden, near the roses.'

Hannah practically skipped down the path towards him.

Dick turned and smiled at her. She slid her arm through his and they walked over to the seat under the arch of climbing roses in the corner of the garden.

Kate got up and went back into the house, to the sitting room. She sat on the sofa beside her mother and took up her knitting.

Dad came in, the *Weekly Times* under his arm and settled into his armchair by the fire. He lit his pipe, opened the newspaper and began to read.

Kate finished her row of knitting. 'Dad, have you thought of getting yourself a motor car?'

Mum looked up. 'That would be nice.'

Her father scratched his beard, thoughtful. 'Would a motor car bring me safely home when I'm half asleep, like Robin does?'

Kate glanced at her mother. 'Mum would love to be driven about in one.'

'Oh, yes.' Mum's eyes lit up. 'And I could learn to drive it too.'

'Ah, you women and these modern fancies. If Jim's loving care of his motorcycle is anything to judge by, a motor car will need much more work than feeding and caring for a horse.' He lifted his newspaper and continued reading.

Mum smiled as she concentrated on her knitting.

Kate smiled too. She would not be surprised if, some time in the future, they did have a motorcar and Mum did the driving.

She was enjoying being back with her family and, especially, her mother's company. Mum, and all of them really, now treated her like an adult. And Mum had not once suggested Kate should come home for good.

As if reading her thoughts, Mum said, 'It has been wonderful having you back, Kate. I do wish this war would hurry up and end, and life could get back to normal.'

But, Kate knew, life would never be like the past had been.

A motorcycle roared to life at the front of the house.

'That will be Dick off home,' Mum said. 'That's odd, he usually comes in and says goodbye.'

Hannah stood in the doorway, hands on her hips, glaring at Kate. 'What did you say to Dick?'

'You know he is thinking of enlisting again?'

'Yes. He's keen to do his bit. What did you say to him? It upset him but he wouldn't tell me what it was.'

'I pointed out the effect it would have on you if anything happened to him.'

'And what business is that of yours?'

'Oh Hannah,' Kate groaned. 'I don't want you to go through...' She choked on her words.

'I am not stupid, Kate. I know the risks.' She lifted her chin. 'If Dick decides to enlist again, I'll wave him off and be proud of him and pray every moment until he comes home.'

'That's easy to say. You have no idea—'

Hannah cut Kate off, her eyes narrowed as she spoke. 'We are not all like you with your head in the clouds thinking your prince charming is invincible and everything will be happy ever after, then falling in a miserable heap when reality comes calling.'

'Enough! Hannah!' Mum raised her voice. 'You can have your disagreements but no nastiness.'

Hannah turned her back on them and walked out of the room. They heard the slap of the back door. Like Kate had often done, she would go down to the creek and stare at the running water until she was calm enough to face them all again.

Kate sat, her head bent, her eyes shut. Hannah was wrong. She had known the dangers from the start but that had not prepared her for the agony of Jack's death.

32

Aunty Mary was sitting, comfortable, in her armchair beside the fire, carefully winding a skein of wool into a ball.

Kate was on the sofa, staring across at the fire. The logs in the fire basket glowed, shining onto the glossy green tiles at the side of the fireplace. Kate sighed softly, a sigh of contentment. She was pleased to be back.

She threaded her needle in the light from the oil lamp on the table beside her and started on the buttonholes of a flannel shirt. 'What are you doing tomorrow? For Anzac Day?'

Aunty Mary completed her winding and picked up her knitting needles. 'I'm going to early Mass. Vincent is being remembered in the prayers for the faithful departed. I have arranged for Mass to be said for him every day for the next week.'

'Is there a memorial service at St Patrick's Cathedral?'

'It was held last Sunday afternoon. It was crowded but I managed to squeezed in at the back. The sermon was beautiful.' She blinked hard. 'Archbishop Mannix conducted Benediction of the Blessed Sacrament. The choir sang like angels and the service ended with the Last Post.'

Kate closed her eyes. She had no wish to summon back the grief of last year's Requiem for fallen soldiers.

'There's a big parade in the city tomorrow, it will be led by returned Gallipoli veterans who have re-enlisted. Afterwards a recruiting campaign ...'

Kate thought of Dick Simmonds. He was not the only one who felt compelled to re-enlist. If they were fit enough to fight, their war was not over. Women's grief was not weighed.

'I'll come with you to Mass tomorrow,' Kate said. This year her remembrance of Jack would be private.

They continued their knitting and sewing in companionable

silence, the only noise the settling of the logs in the grate.

'I'll make some cocoa. Then bed, I think.'

'Yes.' Kate covered a yawn with her hand. 'It's been a long day.'

In the kitchen, Aunty clattered around making the cocoa.

Kate paused her sewing at the sound of a light rapping at the back door.

The door creaked open and Aunty said, 'Come in, Tom.'

'Is she back?' Kate could hear the eagerness in his voice.

'She is indeed. Go into the sitting room and I'll bring you a cup of cocoa.'

Tom appeared in the doorway, a smile plastered to his face.

Kate couldn't help but smile back. 'Good evening, Tom.'

He came straight over and sat on the sofa beside her, leant in and kissed her cheek. His lips and nose were cold. His hand too, when she took it in hers.

'Go over and warm yourself by the fire.'

'I'll warm up here soon enough.' Happiness radiated from him.

Kate held her breath, a flutter in her stomach at the thought that he was so happy to see her. His eyes hadn't left her face since he came into the room.

She let her breath go.

'How was home?' he asked.

'Greener than I expected but there was heavy rain earlier in the year. Dad has a good crop of maize coming on, the cows are in calf and the hens are laying well.'

'Mine are too,' Aunty said as she carried a tray in with three large cups of cocoa.

'And your family are well?'

'They are. All growing up—even little Maggie is now an expert with the knitting needles.'

His questions, and her answers, were painfully polite, as if she were an aged aunt and he had been told to be on his best behaviour.

'What have you been up to while I've been away?'

'The usual—work, went for a bike ride with some mates. That's about it.'

'No fetes or visits to the beach?'

'Not this weather. Are you interested in going to the carnival on the recreation reserve next Saturday for the St John Ambulance? There's to be a procession down Sydney Road, as well as a military display with bands, soldiers and cadets, even a stage coach.'

Watching a military display was not Kate's idea of an enjoyable afternoon.

'They are talking as if it will be as good as St Patrick's day in the city,' Tom continued.

Aunty made a scoffing noise.

'I've never been to a St Patrick's Day march,' Kate said.

'We'll go next year.' He had said it without thinking and Kate realised his stilted questions were to fill up the silences of what couldn't be said with Aunty present.

'Ah, 'tis a grand day, Kate. After the procession there are sports and a concert at the Exhibition Building. Mick and I used to shut the shop and take the boys when they were young.'

'Something to look forward to.' Kate glanced towards Tom, her eyebrows raised. 'And did you go dancing?'

'I did not.'

He gave no reason but Kate read it in his eyes.

'But the Erin-Go-Bragh Dancing Club is running its Saturday night dances again, starting on the fifth of May.' He turned to Aunty. 'Do you have any objections to me taking Kate, Mrs Burke. It's at St Patrick's Hall in Bourke Street.'

'Not at all but make sure Kate is home by midnight.'

'You haven't asked me if I want to go. I might have other plans.'

He blinked and stuttered. 'I'm... I thought...'

Ah, Katie,' Aunty laughed. 'Don't tease the poor boy.'

Kate could see his happiness fading. She grabbed his hand and squeezed it. 'Of course I'd love to go.'

Tom let out a breath. 'That's a relief.'

He drained his cup. 'I had better be off, work tomorrow.'

Kate followed him out onto the verandah, the light from the kitchen spilling through the door.

He stood facing her. He reached out and gently lifted a whisp of hair from her face. 'I have missed you, Kate.'

'I've missed you too.' And she had, more than she had realised.

He wrapped her in his arms, closing his eyes as if he were storing up memory of her.

She slid her arms around him, slowly becoming aware of the warmth of his body, of the strength of his arms, of the man she was standing close against. Then his lips were on hers, gentle at first, building slowly. A sharp flame flickered through her and Kate wanted to lose herself, to forget everything but this man and what could be between them.

She drew an unsteady breath, and eased herself back from him.

Tom gasped and stepped away. He cleared his throat. 'Kate.'

She could not bear for him to apologise. She pressed two fingers to his lips. 'Shhh.'

He smiled slowly at her, his eyes warm, and walked away into the night, a spring in his step.

Kate's heart was beating fast. She wanted to dance, a swirl of colour under sparkling light.

~

Kate's handkerchief was a sodden mess. Tom passed his own to her, neatly ironed and unused.

She had never cried so much at the pictures before. And she wasn't alone, around her other women sniffled and rummaged in their bags for flimsy handkerchiefs. The picture was called *Faith* and Kate had been expecting a nice story of a mother and her daughter but this was a tale of a baby dumped in an orphanage by her heartless grandfather, who ended up working as a skivvy in his house, falsely accused of theft and put on trial. The ending brought tears of joy for those who deserved it but the road there had been heart-rending.

Walking home, she hoped the darkness hid the redness of her eyes.

They were alone tonight. Aunty Mary thought Mrs Ryan was going to the pictures with them but Mrs Ryan had gone out for the evening. Tom hadn't bothered to enlighten Aunty, and Kate did not mind at all.

'I imagine you preferred the serial to *Faith*?' Kate said.

'Yes, as you know, I can't resist a bushranger with a heart of gold.'

'And we will miss finding out whether he gets out of gaol.'

'We can come back next week if you'd prefer.'

'Absolutely not. I am looking forward to dancing.'

A tram rattled past, heading towards Moreland Road.

'We should have waited and caught that,' Tom said. 'It wouldn't be such a long walk for you.'

'I like the walk. If we took the tram the evening would be over too soon—these new electric trams do race along.'

Tom placed his free hand over hers for a moment, and she wished women didn't need to wear gloves.

'Did you go and watch the military display at the reserve this afternoon?'

'No. I wasn't interested. I spent yesterday afternoon walking up and down Sydney Road with Reenie rattling a collection tin and selling buttons. People were very willing to buy them. Some even gave more than the price. They were pretty too—a blue bugler on a yellow background.'

'I know, I bought two.'

'Were the girls you bought them from pretty?' She was surprised at the tiny flicker of jealousy.

'Ugly as sin. I bought them from an old feller at work. He has three sons in France. He brought a tin in and expected every one of us *stay-at-homes*, as he politely called us, to buy a button. The needs of the returned soldiers is a good cause.'

'People will give to a good cause but I think they are tired. They worry about the war but have moments when they want to put it from their minds. It seems like it will never end.'

'It will end but not soon enough.'

Kate looked up at the change in Tom's tone and was struck by the anguish in his face.

'I heard today that Martin Kelleher was killed in France.'

'Your cousin?' She felt the wash of misery that came whenever she heard of the death of a soldier she was connected to, no matter how slender the tie.

'Yes.' He sighed heavily.

'I'm so sorry, Tom.' She held his arm tighter. 'You could have called tonight off.'

'I needed to be with you.'

Kate pressed her head against his shoulder as they walked.

'Martin was more like a brother. He was the same age, same interests. We got into so much trouble together as children.' He paused and exhaled heavily. 'He wanted me to enlist with him.'

Kate heard the unspoken words, *Maybe if I'd been there...*

'And there will be many more like him. If Hughes and his so-called Win the War party win next Saturday's election, he'll take it as confirmation that people want conscription. He's saying the same things as before—that if the government truly believes it is needed, they will ask the people again. In other words, the last referendum counts for nothing. It's wrong to force men who know their families will barely survive without them. There has to be a way to end this war. And if it means more men have to go, so be it.'

Kate didn't understand what he was saying. It sounded like he was supporting conscription when a moment before he was against it.

'Martin said, in his last letter to me, that once they are out there in the thick of it, they fight for each other, for their mates—

empires, kings, prime ministers are forgotten. He told me of an instance where a sniper killed their captain and—' He stopped abruptly, as if remembering who he was speaking to.

They had arrived at the shop and stood facing each other.

'Oh, Kate.' Tom ran the back of his finger down her cheek. 'My beautiful girl. When we go dancing, we won't talk about the war, only sunny days to come.'

There in the street, he held her close and kissed her as if his life depended on her.

As he walked away, memories echoed of another man walking off into the night. Kate pushed the thought away.

33

Kate sat alone at the small table at the edge of the dance floor watching the couples of all ages swirl past her. Along the wall small knots of young women sat or stood, as well as groups of young men.

The hall was festooned in green and gold, potted palms and ferns were banked behind Allietti's Band playing on the stage. So far there had been a mixture of dances including waltzes, the fox-trot and a polka. She watched as an immaculately dressed older couple danced the two-step. Their movements were fluid, perfectly in step. Her gaze drifted to a group of three young men eyeing the young women before they made their choice. No doubt, they were positioned near the door so they could step outside for a drink from the flasks some would have in their pockets.

Tom had introduced Kate to several people he knew, but they were all dancing now. He had gone to get her a drink some time ago. She wished he would hurry up.

She looked around the room, trying to find him, lingering for half a second too long on the men by the door, catching the eye of a stocky blond man leaning against the wall. She turned her head and studied the band.

Out of the corner of her eye, she saw he was heading towards her. He had the swagger and confidence of young Joe Kelly.

He arrived at the table at the same time as Tom.

The young man lifted his hands in defeat and backed away. 'Sorry mate, I didn't know she was taken.' He disappeared into the crowd.

'Taken indeed! I am not a chair or a plate of sandwiches.'

Tom laughed. Kate liked his laugh. She could not remember him laughing since she had come back.

'I'm sorry I took so long. I ran into someone I knew. I did try to cut it short.'

'And his poor wife or girlfriend was left tapping her feet.'

'Fortunately, no. He's here in the hope of finding a nice Irish girl to marry.'

Kate sipped her lemonade. 'Which he won't manage if he spends the evening chatting to men.'

The band took a break. It was easier to talk now, although the noise of dozens of conversations swirled around them.

'Did you always want to work for the railways like your father?'

'No.' Tom gave a laugh that made it sound as if it was the last thing he wanted. 'I had no idea about the future but my parents had decided I was to be the priest. They had that old notion that a big family should have one son a priest and one daughter a nun. Josie, she's next after me, wanted to be a nun for as long as I can remember. She's in Adelaide with the Sisters of St Joseph. They had no luck with the older boys so I was their last hope. I was sent off down here to stay with a family they knew who had produced nothing but nuns and priests. Luckily for me, they got the dates wrong and I ended up sitting at Flinders Street station, my suitcase beside me, looking as brave as I could. A railway porter with the face of a Ryan came up to me. Turns out he was a cousin of my father of some sort. He took me in, showed me the town in the way suitable for a fifteen-year-old boy, and declared at the end of a week I was too good a sort to be a priest. He then set me up to sit the examination for an apprenticeship with the railways, signing the papers as if he were my father. And here I am.'

'Did your parents have something to say about that?'

'Mother was not happy but Father thought it would be the making of me. And I believe it has.'

'I can't imagine you as a priest.'

'Nor can I.'

The band started up again.

'Shall we dance?'

He held her hand in his, his other resting at her waist, a modest distance between them. So close, she could see the weave of his jacket, the brightness of his starched collar, the smooth skin of his recently shaven face, and she could breathe in the faint scent of his shaving soap. She looked across his shoulder as they moved around the dance floor through the swirling colours of the women's frocks. Tom seemed to sense whenever she glanced up at him. He looked down at her, light in his hazel eyes, the hint of a smile on his lips.

Kate was happy. Happy to be here. Happy to be dancing. Happy to be in Tom's arms.

And she was happy with her new dress. Aunty had clearly told Miss Cooper to do far more than simply make the dress up. There was embroidery on the bodice and the sleeves in thread the same colour as the material.

Earlier in the night, she had walked into the sitting room where Tom was waiting.

He had stood up and stared at her.

With no compliment forthcoming, Aunty had prompted him. 'Doesn't Kate look lovely?'

'She looks...' His smile lit his face as he said, '...lovely and fair as the rose of the summer.'

'She does indeed.' Aunty smiled.

All Kate could do was laugh. And blush.

Later, on the train home, Kate sat with her hand in Tom's, her head drifting toward his shoulder, her eyelids drooping. She jolted awake as the train rattled on.

Tom was staring out the window into darkness, his face set and serious. He appeared to be looking at nothing, not the lights of the streets and railway stations they passed through, not the reflections in the window.

Kate wondered if he was thinking about his cousin. It was hard. Nearly everyone carried a grief and everyone was burdened with fear.

'It has been a delightful evening,' she said as they walked through the dark streets, away from the station and towards Sydney Road.

'It has. We will do it again.'

There were so many things she wanted to do again—dancing, the pictures, fetes, outings with other people, like the picnic they had gone on with Annie and her friends. Kate had watched Tom as he played cricket with the other young men, fitting in as if he had known them for years. She wanted to know more about him, what his thoughts were on a hundred topics, to meet his friends, to meet the rest of his family.

He went with her around to the back of the house.

Kate opened the door. The light in the kitchen was turned low.

'I won't come in,' he said. He slid his arms around her and drew her close. His embrace was crushing, his kiss so hungry, it took her breath away.

He stepped back and, although it was too dark to see his face, she knew he smiled at her.

'Good night, Tom.'

She gently pressed her lips to his and went inside, his voice still whispering in her ear, *Goodnight my love.*

Kate turned off the light and walked towards her bedroom. A soft glow was showing under Aunty Mary's door, so she knocked lightly.

Aunty was sitting up in bed, knitting as she waited for Kate to come home.

Perched on the edge of the bed, Kate described the night—the dancing, the people who were there, the women's frocks, even the young man who thought she was a plate of sandwiches.

Today had been a day out of time, a day without the war, a day like life should be.

34

Kate expected to see Tom at Mass but neither he nor Mrs Ryan were there. Perhaps he would call in later and, even though the day was overcast, they could go for a walk to the lake.

After dinner, Aunty Mary lit the fire in the sitting room, put on a gramophone record, and began knitting.

Kate took up her own knitting but kept losing count of her stitches. She put her knitting aside and closed her eyes.

'You look tired, Kate.'

'I suppose I am. It was a late night.' She stared towards the fire remembering the swirl of the music and the women's skirts, the joy of dancing with Tom's arms around her. She looked towards her aunt. 'Tom and Mrs Ryan weren't at Mass this morning.'

'Maggie is in Ballarat with her daughter, Johanna. She'll be back early next week. I did invite Tom for dinner but he said he had arranged to spend the day with an old friend. He didn't mention it to you?'

Kate shook her head. 'No.' She wondered who the friend was. She didn't know enough of Tom's life beyond Coburg.

'Why don't you visit Annie or Reenie?'

'They are both at their monthly Children of Mary meeting.' She stood and went over to the gramophone. 'I'm happy here listening to these songs.' She placed another record on the turntable and cranked the gramophone, smiling as Aunty Mary softly joined in with John McCormack as he sang *When you and I were Young, Maggie*.

Perhaps Tom would call in on his way home from visiting his friend.

~

Monday brought the news that Archbishop Carr had died the night before. He was nearing eighty and had been Archbishop of

Melbourne for forty years. An affable old gentleman, his chief interest had been in the welfare of his flock, and in providing them with both churches and schools. Many of the older women were near to tears. When Mrs Johnson came in, she sat on the chair and wept as if her heart was breaking. Kate was ashamed of her thought that such tears were wasted on someone so old when so many young men, just beginning their lives, were being slaughtered.

The Hughes government had been returned in a landslide at Saturday's election. With better things on her mind these last few weeks, Kate had taken little notice of the election other than to attend the polling place and vote for James Fenton, the sitting Labor man who had campaigned strongly against conscription last year. Those who said Billy Hughes's victory would mean another push for conscription were probably right. Kate dreaded a campaign more vicious than the last one, with Catholics once again seen as traitors and shirkers. That was more likely with Dr Mannix now Archbishop of Melbourne. He had been forthright in his opposition to compulsion and, no doubt, would be again.

St Paul's bazaar, to be held the following Sunday, was postponed because of Archbishop Carr's death, and Kate was disappointed. She had volunteered to spend a couple of hours on the refreshment stall. She had been looking forward to spending the rest of the day with Tom. At least, it had been only put off for a month.

Then Reenie called in to say the knitting circle would not meet this week. She said it felt as if one of her grandfathers had died and she didn't think it right that they sit around enjoying themselves.

And Kate had not seen Tom since Saturday night. As he hadn't visited on Sunday, she had expected he would drop into the shop on his way home from work. She wondered what he was doing. It felt out of character or, at least, what she knew of Tom's character.

~

Kate was alone in the shop most of Wednesday. Aunty had risen before dawn to make sure she was at St Patrick's Cathedral for the eight o'clock Mass said by the Apostolic Delegate, Monsignor Cerretti, the Pope's representative in Australia. Archbishop Carr's remains had been removed from the Bishop's Palace to the Cathedral with great ceremony the night before. Until the day of the funeral, a vigil would be kept in the cathedral day and night, and Masses said on the half hour every morning.

Like thousands of others, her head bowed in prayer, Aunty Mary solemnly filed past the open coffin on its catafalque before the high altar.

When Aunty came back, Kate did her deliveries then took over in the shop so Aunty could rest. It was a busy afternoon with a number of customers who had been to the Cathedral catching up on their shopping. A flurry of last-minute shoppers meant she did not lock the door on time.

Kate sighed as the bell on the door jingled yet again. She handed the change to the person she had hoped was her last customer and glanced up. A soldier was standing patiently near the door. Once she had served him, she *would* lock up. It had been a long tiring day.

She stared at the soldier, not understanding what she was seeing. Her heart shuddered.

Tom stood there in khaki, the slouch hat shading his eyes. He wasn't smiling.

'No!'

He stepped towards her. 'Kate.'

'No. No!'

She ran into the house, twisting past Aunty who was standing in the doorway. Kate reached her room and slammed the door behind her.

The knot of anguish tightened in her chest. Her throat ached.

Not again.

She knew what was coming—the loneliness, the months of sick longing, the endless prayer, the guilt at the distracted moments when she forgot he was in danger, the bottomless pit of despair. The darkness.

Jack. She had loved him. She had prayed for him. And it was not enough.

She couldn't go through it all again.

Voices rumbled in the shop. The tread of feet along the passage. A light tapping on her door.

'Kate, come out and speak to Tom.'

'I will not.'

'He—'

Kate spoke over Aunty Mary. 'I will not speak to him.'

Aunty walked away.

Footsteps again, heavy boots.

Why had Aunty let him come to her bedroom door?

'Kate.'

She said nothing.

'Let me explain.'

'Go away.'

'Please, Kate.'

'Go away.'

She heard his sigh through the door, the slow tramp of his boots as he left.

She sat on the edge of the bed, dry-eyed, staring into the shadows that crowded the room. She would not give in to tears.

If he could do this without warning her, truly, what was she to him?

The house was silent now, except for Aunty moving around the kitchen.

Kate stood up, straightened her shoulders.

She glanced at the top of the bedside table where Jack's photo had stood. She had removed it after the first time she had kissed Tom properly.

The darkness of crushing grief hung over her once more.

Tom will die too.

Aunty turned from the stove as Kate came in. 'Kate...'

'I do not want to talk about it.'

'Kate,' she said gently. 'You should talk to Tom. He will be at his mother's until nine o'clock. He wants to explain.'

'He doesn't need to explain anything to me. It's his life—nothing to do with me.'

'You know that's not true.'

Kate took the cutlery from the dresser drawer and went into the dining room to set the table.

They ate their meal in silence. Kate pushed her food around the plate, eating little. She was aware, the whole time, of Aunty Mary watching her, a crease between her eyebrows.

The dishes done, Kate said, 'I'm going to bed.'

'But the rosary—'

'I'll say it in my room.'

But she didn't. She undressed and got into bed and lay staring into the darkness.

She should have realised it was coming. The hints were there with his talk of the war over recent weeks. Two years ago, he had said it was not his war. Too much had happened since to expect people wouldn't change the way they saw the war. But not Tom, she had not expected it of him. She thought she was safe with him.

There were no tears, only the ache in her throat, in her chest, spreading out through her body.

It didn't matter who it was, Tom or Jack, you loved them and they broke your heart, piece by piece.

Yes. She loved him. She had not acknowledged it but it was true—she wouldn't have kissed him if she hadn't loved him. It had happened by stealth, so quietly that she hadn't realised. And now, if this war were to claim him, she would be destroyed as surely too.

Anger swept through her. It didn't matter what she felt for him. He had thrown it away to go off with his mates and get himself blown to pieces.

She tossed and turned, unable to get comfortable, unable to set aside the crushing sense of dread.

Finally, she slept, fitful and unsettled. Images from the newsreels filled her dreams: ruined buildings, stark dead trees, the battered countryside of France. Injured and broken men, always with the same face—the dark straight eyebrows, the firm jawline, the gentle hazel eyes. She woke early from her troubled sleep and forced herself out of bed, trying, without success, to push Tom Ryan from her mind.

35

Archbishop Carr's funeral service was to be held on Saturday morning, followed in the afternoon by a procession in which every Catholic organisation in Melbourne would take part. The women's branch of the Confraternity of the Sacred Heart from St Paul's had the honour of leading the sodality in the march and Aunty Mary would be among them. Reenie and Annie would be marching with the Children of Mary. Aunty suggested that Kate ask Mrs Watkins if she could go into the city with Mr Watkins on Saturday. He wasn't a member of any of the organisations that were marching, he wasn't even a Catholic, but he was sure to watch the procession. The funeral of an Archbishop did not happen often.

'I could stay here and keep the shop open for you.'

'That would be disrespectful—Archbishop Carr has been like the head of our family. Go and see Mrs Watkins.'

Kate walked up Sydney Road, past Harding Street where the Watkinses lived. She was perfectly capable of getting herself to the funeral and back. She wandered aimlessly along the street, not even glancing at the displays in the windows, and found herself outside the church. As she neared the door, Mrs Ryan stepped out from the porch.

She caught Kate's hand and leant in, kissing her cheek. 'Ah, he didn't tell you either.'

Kate shook her head. 'How are you going to manage by yourself, Mrs Ryan?'

'Now then, do not worry yourself about me, Kate. My grandson, Edmund, is coming to stay. It was arranged a while back. He is such a clever boy, he is starting as a clerk at the big railway building in Spencer Street next month.'

'I am relieved. I didn't imagine Tom could be so heartless.'

'My boy is never heartless.' She grasped Kate's hands, her eyes glistening. 'He felt the death of his cousin Martin deeply. We all did. They were like brothers. He says it is his duty to go—not duty to the English king but duty to Australia and more than that, duty to protect his family and his friends. But I do not know...' Mrs Ryan's voice trailed off.

Kate could see the worry in her face.

'I dread to think what his father would have thought of this. And his brothers, they will have a word or two to say when they hear.' Mrs Ryan gave a sad smile. 'Now I must be on my way, but when Mary visits next, you should come too.'

Kate nodded and forced herself to smile.

She went into the church, dipped her fingers in the holy water stoup, and blessed herself. She walked halfway down the aisle, genuflected, and moved into a pew. The church was quiet and calm in the muted light from the stained-glass windows. At the front, an old woman knelt, head bowed in prayer. Kate stared up towards the wooden rafters and along to the altar where the sanctuary lamp burned. Its flickering red light should have brought comfort but Kate felt none. Prayer would not come. She was alone.

She would not visit Mrs Ryan. It would look like she cared for Tom. How could she claim she cared for him if she was incapable of recognising the depth of his grief for his cousin? But he must have known the anguish she would feel at his decision. He should have warned her.

She stood up, her genuflection little more than a bob, and walked out of the church, the door banging behind her. Fists clenched, she marched home in half the time it had taken her to get there. By the time she got to the shop, a dull headache had begun to niggle.

When Kate woke on Friday morning, the headache was like a cap pushed tight on her head. Her night had been restless, her sleep broken. The dreams she had were filled with nightmare images that faded with the light, leaving behind a bleak sense of foreboding.

Her face hurt, her jaw was clamped tight, her neck and shoulders stiff. She struggled through the morning in the shop, every muscle, every joint in her body aching.

Aunty packed her off to bed in the middle of the afternoon. Kate dozed fitfully, afraid to sleep, fearing the return of the scarred men and bombed buildings that haunted her nights. She woke properly when Aunty came up after closing the shop.

'I should stay home tomorrow. I can't leave you like this.'

Kate struggled up onto her elbows. 'Don't you dare. I'm not dying.' She lay back on her pillow. 'I'll be better in the morning.'

'Do you want anything to eat?'

Kate shook her head and winced as her head throbbed.

'I'll bring up a cup of milky tea with a nip of brandy in it. That will give you a good night's sleep.'

There was more than a nip of brandy in the tea and Kate slept like a log. She woke in the morning, her headache had faded, but her body still ached. She was exhausted.

When Aunty came in to check on her, she said, 'I feel almost well but I'll stay in bed until you come home.'

Kate dozed all morning, waking just before midday, as Aunty placed a cup of weak tea and a slice of dry toast on the bedside table.

'I'm leaving in quarter of an hour. A group of us are meeting at the railway station.'

'I want to see you dressed up before you go.'

Aunty was back in five minutes. Over her black dress she wore a red cloak and a medallion of the Sacred Heart on a red ribbon. She carried a transparent white veil which she draped over her head.

Kate gazed at her. 'You look striking.'

''Tis a pity you will miss this. They are saying it will be the longest funeral procession Melbourne has ever seen. The Children of Mary will be in their white dresses with black sashes and their blue cloaks and white veils, and us in our red capes. It will be something to behold. The women's group at St Paul's is the only branch of the

Confraternity of the Sacred Heart that dresses like this.'

Kate wished she felt fit enough to go too.

She dozed, not hearing Aunty leave, and slept fitfully through the afternoon.

When Aunty came home, well after dark, she was full of the procession. She sat by the bed as Kate ate the vegetable broth she had heated for her and, eyes shining, told her of the procession.

'Ah Kate, I will remember it all my days. The great long line of us, it took over two and a half hours from beginning to end. The head of it was back to the cathedral before the hearse had left. And the silence of those of us marching and of the crowds on the footpaths and watching from windows. All you could hear was the tramp of our feet and the muffled beat of the drums and, the closer you got to the Cathedral, the slow tolling of the bell. Troopers on horseback led the procession and soldiers not far behind them— from the camps as well as returned and discharged men, all in uniform. Tom Ryan would have been marching with them.'

Kate stared ahead, not acknowledging her aunt's comment.

'And behind them the cross bearer in scarlet robes and white vestments. Every Catholic organisation was marching, even men and women from the university in their black gowns and hats, some with bright satin across their shoulders. It was bitterly cold but, despite the black clouds, barely a drop fell. And every man and every boy in the procession was bareheaded. I think every single Catholic in Melbourne was there today.'

Every single Catholic except Kate. She had made herself sick with her anger and the fear that threatened to drown her.

~

Kate was much better by Monday but Aunty Mary insisted she not work in the shop until the following day.

The first customer through the door on Tuesday morning was Mrs Johnson, come more for a gossip than to buy.

'Good morning, Mrs Johnson, 'tis another cold day,' Aunty said brightly. 'You will want to get yourself back by the fire as soon as you can.'

'That I will.' She settled herself on the chair. 'Now wasn't that a beautiful procession? I only went for an hour. Not the best for someone of my age to be out there in the cold for too long.' She gave a weak cough as if to prove her point. 'Oh, the Irish pipers, they brought a tear to my eye. Did you hear them?'

'Faintly, I was further back in the procession.'

Mrs Johnson turned towards Kate who was at the other end of the counter checking the regular grocery orders against a list. 'I believe Tom Ryan has enlisted.'

Kate kept her head down, concentrating on her list.

Aunty glanced at Kate and said, 'Indeed, he has.'

Mrs Johnson raised her voice. 'And how do you feel about that, Miss Burke?'

Kate slowly lifted her head and stared at the old woman. 'I don't know that what I feel is of interest to anyone.'

'But you are keeping company with him, aren't you?'

Before Kate could answer, Aunty said, 'Now what can I be getting you today, Mrs Johnson?'

'Oh, a small bag of sweeties. Bullseyes would be nice.'

Kate walked towards the doorway. If she stayed, she would say something Aunty wouldn't like.

'He has kept that quiet. And he's already been in camp a month.'

'Only a week.' Aunty busied herself scooping Mrs Johnson's bullseyes into a small paper bag.

'They leave a lot sooner now and do some of their training in England,' Mrs Johnson said.

Kate paused in the doorway.

'He could be gone by the end of June or early July.'

Gone.

Kate's heart jolted.

Sailing off to his death.

Her breath was tight in her throat.

'The Archbishop's death was a shock,' Aunty said, changing the subject. 'I had imagined he would go on for years.'

'Ah, may he rest in peace.'

And now Mrs Johnson would be blessing herself, like the sweet old lady she wasn't.

Kate walked into the house and waited until the old woman left.

36

July 1917

June and July were cold and miserable. The newspapers, week after week, carried news of yet more slaughter in France and Belgium. The casualty lists kept growing. And Kate had not seen Tom for six weeks.

He had called to see her at least twice. The first time, one Sunday afternoon, she was in the sitting room and heard him talking to Aunty on the verandah. She grabbed her coat and hat and slipped out the side door. She walked the two miles down Sydney Road to Brunswick Road. By the time she got back, the light was fading and Tom was long gone. The second time she had been visiting Mrs Casey. Tom had left a letter for her. She had thrown it in the fire unopened once Aunty was out of the room, anger surging through her. Why would he not leave her alone? She knew the reason. It was the same reason she could not keep him out of her mind—he was there when she woke, there as she drifted to sleep. She thought of him more often throughout the day than she had before he had made his stupid decision.

But why had he enlisted? What had changed his mind? She would know if she read his letter or let him speak to her. She didn't want to know. If she let him explain, everything she felt for him would come surging back. She would not bear it when he was killed. The dread was there with every breath she took.

~

Aunty paused her knitting, and looked across at Kate. 'Tom will be home on leave next Saturday night.'

Kate kept her eyes on the button she was sewing onto a pyjama jacket.

'Maggie has arranged a farewell for him with family and a few friends.'

'I will not go.'

'You will go, Kate. You will shame me if you do not.' Her face softened. 'You cannot let him leave without saying goodbye.'

She didn't want to say goodbye to him. She didn't want him to go at all.

Kate went with Aunty Mary on Saturday night and Mrs Ryan welcomed her with a kiss. Tom stood beside his mother, smart in his uniform. Had he always stood so straight and tall? Beneath the uniform, was he still the man she had loved?

He smiled politely at her. The light that had been there whenever he looked at her was missing.

Did he hate her now? A rush of longing swept through her, for him, for what was lost.

She moved into the crowded sitting room and did not let herself look back.

Two men in their late thirties stood at the other side of the room deep in a forceful discussion, glasses of beer in their hands. Tom's brothers. Kate could see the family resemblance. The Watkinses and the Caseys were there. Harry was standing with Ned, Tom's nephew, and Reenie's younger brother, Nick. By Harry's hand movements, he was talking about cricket. Nick Casey stepped back and blocked Harry's ball with the swing of an equally invisible bat.

Tom's sister Agnes sat at the piano and began to play, songs they all knew. Together they sang popular Irish songs like *Mother Machree* and *The Dear Little Shamrock*. Some of the guests sang solo, others duets. Tom's brothers Frank and Pat did a comic turn with *Follow the Tram Tracks*. Annie, Reenie and Agnes sang *Three Little Maids from School*.

Then Tom sang *When You Were Sweet Sixteen*.

Mrs Ryan gazed at him, a faraway look in her eyes.

Annie whispered to Kate, 'Agnes said he would sing this. Their father used to sing it to Mrs Ryan and Tom sounds just like him when he sings.'

Kate held back tears. His voice was beautiful. She hadn't known.

There was so much about him she didn't know and now never would. She was not even sure of his birthdate other than it was in November. Why hadn't she asked? She had believed she had all the time in the world.

Now there is no time left.

Supper was served, toasts raised, speeches given by his brothers and friends. Some hinted they did not understand his decision to enlist, but they accepted it and stood beside him.

Kate waited by the sideboard, a cup and saucer in her hand, while Annie went off in search of more cake. She took a sip of her tea and stared into the fire.

'Kate.'

She closed her eyes at the sound of his voice. He was beside her, stooped so she could hear what he was saying despite the noise in the room.

'Come outside with me for a few moments.'

She put the cup and saucer on the sideboard carefully, her hands shaking. 'I will not.'

'I have things I need to say to you. I will say them here in front of everyone if you do not come with me.'

The noise of conversation around her dropped. She knew the eyes of the room were on her, some people watching openly, others more discreetly.

He caught her hand. The touch of his bare hand on hers and her longing for him, for his arms around her, flooded through her, a wash of pain.

'Please walk out as if we are not enemies.'

'I'm not your enemy, Tom.'

As they walked towards the door one of his brothers threw back his head and sang, full voiced.

Ah, now tell me Sean O'Farrell,
Tell me why you hurry so?

Tom glanced back, a flash of anger in his face.

He said nothing until they were out in the back porch.

'Nor am I your enemy, Kate. I thought once you accepted I was going, you would let me explain. And we could, at least, still be friends.'

'I can't accept it.' She stared out into the darkness.

Rain pounded down, splashing up across the floorboards of the porch.

'You said it wasn't your war.'

'I felt that once but not now. Too many good men have died, too many who mean something to me. I want this war to end but I can no longer sit waiting for someone else to make it end. It's my turn to go. And it is my own choice.'

'Yes, your choice. But don't expect me to happily wave you on your way, to cheer as you leave. I can't bear it.' She held herself rigid. 'Have you any idea what it's like to be here waiting and not knowing—the sickening worry, it's with you every minute. You hear of the battles and hold your breath. You get a letter and it's a relief, you think he's alive, but already he's been dead a month and you had no idea.'

She turned to him. In the light from the kitchen window, she could make out every feature, the hazel eyes, the straight brow, the line of his jaw. 'You love someone with your whole heart and it's shattered to pieces. I've been through it once. I can't do it again. I can't.'

The tears were running down her cheeks. If she could stop loving him, perhaps the pain would stop, perhaps then he would be safe.

His face was clear, as if he finally understood.

He stepped towards Kate.

She put up her hands. 'No. Please, no.'

Her tears would not stop.

'Oh, Kate,' he sighed. 'Stay here.'

He went back into the house.

She watched the rain beating down, pooling on the path in front of the porch.

As Aunty came through the door, Tom behind her, the singing followed them.

> *Death to every foe and traitor!*
> *Forward! strike the marching tune*

'They're in fine form tonight,' Aunty said, 'bringing out the old rebel songs.'

'They are. And all for my benefit. They think I'm a traitor.'

'Ah, not at all, Tom. Sure, isn't it always the way, when Irishmen are together with a few drinks in them, one of them will end up singing *The Rising of the Moon*.'

Tom nodded. 'I suppose so.'

'And they are here to bless you on your journey and they will keep you in their prayers the whole time you are away.'

Why can I not do that?

'We should go home, Kate,' Aunty said gently. 'I'll get our coats and umbrellas.'

Tom stood beside her, staring out into the dark garden, as they waited for Aunty to come back.

Kate longed for the comfort of his arms, to feel the warmth, the strength of him. But she could not give in. This was the only way she could endure what lay ahead.

She had stopped crying and was trying not to sniff.

'Here.' He handed her his neatly-pressed handkerchief.

She wiped her eyes. 'I still have your other handkerchief.'

'I'll collect them both when I come back.'

When?

The pain twisted.

If.

Aunty was taking her time. Kate supposed she was saying her goodbyes.

'I'll write to you,' he said. 'You don't have to answer.'

She nodded, not trusting her voice.

Then Aunty was back. They put on their coats and Aunty Mary kissed Tom's cheek. 'May God and Mary and St Joseph and all the saints be with you in your dangers. May He bring you safely home.'

'Thank you, Mrs Burke.'

Someone, inside, called his name.

He gazed at Kate before he left. She could read his eyes, even in the dark. She had hurt him yet he loved her still.

She took her umbrella from Aunty Mary.

Inside, Tom began to sing unaccompanied.

The pale moon was rising above the green mountain...

'Wait. Aunty rested her hand on Kate's arm.

It was the song he had hummed that night as he walked her home from the creek.

They stood together, listening. It was a beautiful song.

Tom began the third verse, the one he had told Kate he never sang.

In the far fields of France, 'mid war's dreadful thunders,
Her voice is a solace and comfort to me,

'Oh,' Aunty whispered. 'He has changed it.'

When this war ends that has rent us asunder,
Then I'll return to the Rose of Tralee.
She was lovely and fair as the rose of the summer,

Kate stepped off the verandah and opened her umbrella.

Yet 'twas not her beauty alone that won me;

She sensed what would come next and did not want to hear it.

Oh no, 'tis the truth in her eyes ever dawning,
That makes me love Katie, The Rose of Tralee.

Kate stared ahead, her lips clamped shut. She had given him nothing but pain since he enlisted. Why would he not let her go?

She tried to think only of the sound of their shoes on the gravel as they walked, and the patter of the rain, but words filled her mind, words she would repeat every day until the telegram came.

Christ be with him, Christ within him...

Christ in quiet, Christ in danger...

When they arrived home, Kate went straight to her bedroom and took out the handkerchief case with her memories of Jack. She slid her fingers in and drew out the small medal wallet she had made for him but never had the chance to send. She undid the press stud and opened out the cloth wallet, small enough to fit into the corner of a pocket. She had embroidered a cross on the front and, inside, had sewn a brown scapula on one panel. On the other, she had sewn three medals—a Miraculous medal so he would be under the protection of the Mother of God; a St Christopher to protect him on his journey; and one of St Michael the Archangel, the patron of soldiers, to guard him and keep him safe in battle. She hadn't thought to make it until after the landing at Gallipoli when Reenie had mentioned she had made one for Vince and her brother. And the day after Kate had finished it, the news came. Perhaps, if she had made it earlier... She shook the thought away. Perhaps, this time...

Why would this time be different?

Next morning, Kate knew as soon as she walked into the church that Tom was there. He was four seats in front of her, looking straight ahead. All through Mass she could barely concentrate on what was happening at the altar.

Afterwards, she went to where he was standing talking to two men who had been at Mrs Ryan's the night before.

Tom introduced them to her and said, 'Kate is the niece of Mrs Burke, the grocer.'

'Can I have a word, Tom?' She looked towards the other men. 'I won't keep him long.'

They moved over to the fence at the side of the small churchyard. 'Keep this with you.' She pushed the small wallet into his hand.

She hadn't wrapped it. He looked down, recognising what it was. 'Thank you, Kate, I will.'

There was a sheen on his eyes. She knew her own were the same.

'May the Lord protect you and keep you safe.'

Although she had murmured her prayer, he heard her.

Kate hurried away before he could reply. She could not bear his pain as well as her own.

~

Kate got up from setting the small fire in the sitting room, brushing her hands together to get rid of the wood dust.

Aunty Mary came to the door and pulled an envelope from her apron pocket. 'A letter for you.' She placed it on the table and left.

Whatever was in the envelope was stiff, more like a card than a letter. It was postmarked Broadmeadows Camp.

Kate was sure they had left a couple of days ago although there had been no whisper of it. Sometimes, but not always, there were marches. It was nothing like the fanfare and open secrets of three years ago.

She tore the envelope open. Inside was a single sheet of paper and a photograph—Tom standing in front of the painted backdrop of a tent. She didn't want a picture of him in uniform, but at least he wasn't wearing all his kit or posed like he was ready to use the bayonet attached to his rifle.

She unfolded the page.

> My dearest Kate,
>   I wish to thank you for your farewell gift. It means the world to me that it was made by your hand. I promise I will keep it with me at all times.

He thought she had made it just for him! Perhaps she should write back and tell him it was a dead man's wallet.

She gasped, wishing she could call the thought back.

Who was the dead man?

She squeezed her eyes shut.

Lord, watch over him and keep him safe.

>   I would be deeply grateful if you would send me a

photograph of yourself. I fear I will be away from home
for quite some time and do not want my memories of you
to fade.
Keep me in your prayers, my dear one, as you are in mine.
Tom.

She could hear his voice and in it all that was decent and good in
him. And she hated him. Hated herself.

She screwed the letter up and tossed it across the room towards
the now steadily burning fire. It landed on the hearth. She looked
at the photograph. Why couldn't he have sent one of himself in his
Sunday suit?

She tried to rip it up but the card was stiff. She tossed it toward
the fire too.

'Kate!' Aunty stood in the doorway, aghast. She swooped across
to the fireplace and picked both up. The photograph had landed
close to the grate. If left there much longer, the image would have
curled and melted.

She grabbed the envelope off the side table. 'That was a wicked
thing to do.'

Shaking her head, she walked out of the room.

It was wicked. Kate knew that, but she had to make herself stop
loving him.

37

August 1917

It was three weeks since Tom had left and Kate was angry, miserable and irritable by turns. She had little patience with customers like Mrs Johnson with her question, every second day, of whether she had heard from Tom. Kate's sharp answer, the last time Mrs Johnson asked, that the postman didn't collect mail from ships at sea didn't help. Aunty had frowned at her and Mrs Johnson, a glint of triumph in her eyes, had said some soldiers sent letters from the ports they called into.

Several times in the last week, she had looked up to catch Aunty watching her, her brow puckered with concern, or was it judgement. She was the only one who knew of Kate's rift with Tom. Everyone else assumed her sullenness was worry.

They sat by the fire, Kate in the chair opposite Aunty, the only noise the click of their knitting needles.

'Kate.'

She glanced up.

'Would you like to go back home?'

Kate gasped. It was the last thing she wanted. She nearly said, *But this is my home.*

'You want me to leave?'

'I do not.'

Kate was sure there was a touch of annoyance in Aunty's voice.

'I am asking if you would be happier back with your parents.'

Kate fought to keep misery from her voice. 'I like being here with you.'

'And I like you being here with me.'

Aunty smiled but Kate was sure she didn't mean it—she was simply being polite.

If Kate went back to her parents, she would be cut off from news of Tom. If anything happened to him, she wouldn't hear unless

Aunty sent her a letter. And she would only get to look through the casualty lists when her father bought the *Weekly Times*.

She scowled, angry with herself. Her first thought wasn't that if she left, Aunty would be alone with no one to help in the shop or to sit with her in the evening, even if Kate hadn't been good company lately. Yet Aunty was willing to face that loneliness if it made things better for Kate.

Aunty was busy knitting a thick woollen sock for a soldier she had never met.

Kate hated that, unlike her aunt whose thoughts were always of others, she had become someone who thought only of herself.

~

Kate locked the shop door behind the last customer and swept the floor. As she walked down the passage, she glanced into the dining room. Aunty Mary had set four boxes on the sideboard, one larger and three smaller. She was getting her Christmas packages ready. Once filled, the larger box would be sent by the Red Cross to a soldier at random. Aunty made a special effort with this each year, hoping it went to someone who had no family or friends to send him a personal Christmas parcel.

Kate wandered in and peered into the boxes. All there was at present was a tin of tobacco and papers, and two chocolate bars in each. As the days passed Aunty would add to them—socks, playing cards, biscuits, perhaps dried fruit, boiled lollies, handkerchiefs, tooth powder, shoelaces, tinned shaving soap. She tried to send a mixture of the practical as well as treats.

Four Christmas cards lay beside the boxes, three with pictures of holly and robins. The last showed a goose standing in the snow with the cheerfully printed greeting,

> *Just for a Christmas present*
> *This goose I send to you*
> *So, while you're cooking it, I hope*
> *You'll cook the Kaiser's too!*

Well, he deserved to have his goose cooked—he had started it and was the cause of all this death and destruction.

Aunty popped her head in. 'That one's for Brendan. I thought it would make him smile. You should start writing your letters. I'd like to get the boxes to the Post Office by the end of the month.'

'I've started one to Brendan. I'll begin Bert's on Sunday. Who is the third box for?'

'Tom. You could write a short note to him—just saying Merry Christmas.'

Kate scowled. It was none of her business if Aunty wanted to send him a Christmas box.

'I'm not writing to him.'

'Whyever not?' Aunty sounded exasperated.

Kate shrugged.

Aunty Mary glared at her. 'Catherine Burke, I do not understand you.' She crossed her arms across her bosom. 'He is a fine man and he cares for you, more than you care for him by the way you are behaving. He is heading into danger so, no matter what you feel about the war, he deserves all the comfort you can give him.' She drew a ragged breath. 'I would never forgive any girl who treated Brendan like this.'

Kate kept her mouth shut and went outside. She shivered. It was cold but she sat on the verandah anyway. She would hate any girl who did this to her brother.

She thought of Tom and anger flooded through her. She was angry with Tom for enlisting, angry with him for not warning her, angry with him for putting himself in danger, for making her love him, and she would be more than angry if he got himself killed. She was angry with herself for not being able to forget him. And for not being able to accept things like everyone else did. And she was angry with Jack who had done exactly what Tom was doing now, Jack who had got himself killed. And with politicians like Billy Hughes banging his drum about recruits and shirkers and all those like him, the women who went on and on about our brave soldiers, and the young women with their sweetheart badges with the Rising Sun on them, the men who had done their bit and thought they should do more, the little boys with snotty noses playing at soldiers with their wooden guns and digging trenches in the empty house blocks, Archbishop Mannix shouting out his views—not that he ever shouted and even if she did agree with some of them—and those people who said Catholics were traitors when they were enlisting like everyone else. And dying too!

Why couldn't she put aside her anger and misery and think how it would be for Tom out there in danger? Not like her, sitting safely at home.

But, at least, when she was angry, she wasn't afraid.

38

The rush of early customers over, Kate was halfway up the ladder stacking small tins of canned fruit. The smaller tins were popular now as they could fit into the comfort parcels people sent to their own men at the front.

The bell on the shop door jingled but she didn't turn as Aunty Mary was at the counter.

'You'll need to come down from there, Kate, we are going out for the day.'

Kate looked over her shoulder at Annie.

Annie looked very smart in her dark green costume. The tunic was calf-length, its bodice buttoned to the waist with large round buttons; the narrower skirt beneath the tunic ended just above her ankles. Her blouse was of a soft white linen, a jet brooch pinned below the high neckline. She wore a bucket style hat of a light green straw trimmed with ribbon of the same colour and a small spray of flowers at one side.

'I can't. Saturday morning is busy.'

'I've already asked Mrs Burke. She is happy for you to have the day off.'

'Go Kate,' Aunty said. 'I'll be fine by myself.'

So, they had been plotting together, again. 'It would have been nice to be asked if I wanted to go.'

'Of course you want to go. You've done nothing for weeks but work, sew and go to Mass. You haven't even been to the pictures.'

Kate opened her mouth to say she visited Reenie but Annie spoke first. 'Going to Reenie's on Tuesday evening and having a cup of tea with Mrs Casey doesn't count.'

'It will be a nice day out for you,' Aunty added.

'But what if it gets busy? What about your baking?'

'Go,' Aunty Mary said firmly.

Kate knew there was no point arguing further.

In her room, she looked down at her grey blouse and navy skirt. They were drab. Without realising it, she had gone back to the dull colours she had worn after Jack's death and hadn't worn anything she had made at the beginning of the year. But, whatever she wore, she would look dowdy beside Annie.

She changed into her best skirt, still navy, and put on the blue blouse that had been her favourite once, frowning at the thought that this was what she had been wearing on that day at the beach with Tom at the beginning of the year. Her coat on, she went back to the shop, pinning her hat as she walked.

Annie was sitting on the chair by the counter talking quietly to Aunty. They looked up as she came in and smiled as if there was something about Kate that pleased them. Surely, changing into a four-year-old blouse was not a cause for celebration.

'Ready?' Annie said.

'Yes.' Kate nodded. 'Where are we going?'

'We'll take the tram into the city and visit the art gallery and, after lunch at my favourite tea room, we will go for a walk in the fresh air in one of the nearby gardens.'

'Ah now, that sounds lovely.' Aunty said. 'And look, even the sun is shining for you.'

Aunty Mary followed them to the door and waved them off.

They caught the Brunswick cable tram at Moreland Road. It would take them within a block of the art gallery in the city.

Annie took her knitting out of her handbag, thick grey socks that some soldier in France or Belgium, Egypt or Palestine would be glad to receive.

Kate glanced around. Only one other woman on the tram wasn't knitting, an old woman with arthritic hands. It hadn't occurred to Kate to bring her knitting with her.

Today, she wasn't angry, just sad. Was this the way she would be until the worst happened?

She realized Annie was scowling, her lips a tight angry line.

Annie had been chatting away, Kate barely listening.

'I'm sorry, I didn't hear that—the tram is noisy.'

'A stupid young woman gave Harry a white feather the other day.'

Kate gasped. 'That is horrible. What did he do?'

'He offered to pull up his trouser leg to give her a good look at the memento he had brought back from Gallipoli. She turned pale and scurried off.'

What sort of woman would do her best to shame a man she knew nothing about, declaring him a coward simply because he was not in uniform? But what sort of a woman cut herself off from a man she cared for because he had enlisted?

When they got off the tram at the corner of La Trobe and Elizabeth Streets, Kate glimpsed the roof of St Francis's Church, a block further along. She thought of her first visit to the church. It seemed so long ago, as if that girl kneeling in the chapel praying fervently for her sweetheart was another person.

All those prayers made no difference.

They walked smartly up the hill, past a mixture of small factories, lodging houses, and a handful of shops. The street was busy with people coming and going, none lingering to stare at the window displays which were few.

They crossed Swanston Street and walked by the wrought-iron fence railings of an impressive two storey building with a large dome. Annie went in through the gateway but Kate stood staring. The portico looked like a temple with its row of towering columns holding up a stone gable, Melbourne Public Library carved across it. A manicured lawn stretched from the stone terrace in front of the library to the fence. A row of Moreton Bay fig trees crowded along the La Trobe Street boundary.

Annie called to her and Kate hurried to catch up. Together they climbed the steps, passing statues as they went. The first was the substantial figure of someone called Redmond Barry. Annie said he was the judge who had tried the bushranger, Ned Kelly. Kate had heard of Ned Kelly. Two bronze lions sat at the top of the steps. A statue of St George fighting his dragon stood at one end of the terrace, Joan of Arc in armour astride her horse at the other.

Kate stepped into the hushed lobby of the library. Marble shone on the floor and decorated the walls. Kate felt it was not the sort of building she had any place in but Annie knew where she was going, so she followed her.

They went around to the right, along a passage and into a gallery. Paintings of all sizes and shapes hung on the walls, a railing keeping viewers at a distance. Chairs were arranged down the middle of the gallery, men and women sitting on them, each staring towards a painting that had caught their fancy. The room was as quiet as a church, only the slightest rustle of conversation.

Annie whispered, 'Walk around and look at what's on the wall. If you find a painting you like, sit and look at it for a while.' She went to the end of the gallery and sat in front of a mother and child in a gold frame.

Kate moved along the rail, making sure each time she stopped she wasn't blocking someone's view. There were paintings of scenery, of women sitting on sofas, people in ancient times, men at their desks, boats floating on water, storms at sea. Some were pleasant to look at; others were not to her taste at all. She sat and viewed a large painting called *In Morocco*. A girl was seated on a white horse, a woman standing beside her held a bright blue parasol, and to the side was a young boy with a dog on a lead. The artist had captured the play of light on the figures and the wall behind them, yet all Kate could say of it was that it was pretty.

She got up and moved on. The quiet of the room was restful but there was not a single painting she would think about once she walked out of the room.

Annie came over and suggested they go into the next gallery. Like the previous room, the walls were covered with paintings, but for Kate there was only one. She went straight to the chair opposite it. From the blue of the river at the bottom of the painting to the hills in the hazy distance, the gumtrees on the riverbank, the cows drinking in the shallows, it was country she knew. She saw details the longer she looked—a windmill, houses, smoke rising from chimneys, the faint lines of the fencing. The colour of the sand on the riverbank and the light took her back to that January day at Williamstown Beach when hope had crept up on her.

Tom. How she missed him. At this moment, it was as if her anger had been washed away and all that was left was sadness. And fear. Always fear. She loved him. She couldn't stop loving him. She blinked back prickling tears. She would not think about it here. Not in public.

She didn't know how long she sat gazing at the painting. She felt completely calm. She rose and went to the rail and read the name. *The Purple Noon's Transparent Might*. She didn't know what it meant but she would remember it.

Annie came and stood beside her. 'What would you like to do when we have finished here?' she whispered. 'We could go to the sculpture gallery or we could have an early lunch. There are some beautiful statues in the gallery, but far too many muscly half-dressed men, either fighting animals or wrestling, for my taste.'

'An early lunch is a good idea.' Kate didn't want to look at men wrestling, even if they were frozen in stone.

The tea room was off the gallery. Tables were arranged around the room with white tablecloths and bentwood chairs. Indoor plants in brass pots stood in the corners of the room, smaller pot plants were on the windowsill and on the mantelpiece in front of a large mirror. The waitresses, dressed in white gowns and aprons, were prompt in their service. Customers were few as it was only just midday.

Kate and Annie ate the cold collation and afterwards had a slice of Victoria sponge and shared a pot of tea.

Annie gazed around the room and sighed, contented. 'I like it here. I sometimes come to read in the library and finish up with a cup of tea and a cake. It's so peaceful, away from the worry of the world.' She looked straight at Kate. 'Now.'

Kate stiffened.

She is going to do her best to talk me into joining the Children of Mary.

On their walks to the lake, Annie often spoke of the sodality and strength it gave members in times of trouble. Kate knew it was only a matter of time before Annie, once again, suggested she join it.

'Have you read *Pride and Prejudice*?'

Kate relaxed. 'No.' She hadn't read a book since she left school eight years ago. 'I don't read much.'

'It's a romantic story set in England a little over a hundred years ago. I'll lend it to you.'

'Thank you,' Kate said, as she knew was expected. When would she find time to read a book with all the sewing and knitting she had to do?

'I know your spare time is taken up with sewing but you should occasionally do other things that have nothing to do with the war—like reading for half an hour each night before you go to bed.'

Perhaps she should try.

They settled their bill and went out into the street.

'Let's go to the Carlton Gardens,' Annie said. 'It's the closest.'

It was no more than a ten-minute walk up La Trobe Street. An avenue of plane trees led up to the Exhibition Building. It was a vast cream-coloured building with a towering arched entrance and rows of narrow arched windows along the second floor. A central dome stood above the building with smaller domes at each corner. It was like a palace from an exotic fairy tale.

'This is where the St Patrick's Day celebrations are held. The sports are run on the track at the back of the building and, later, the concert is inside. You should go next year.'

Tom had said they would go next year.

It will not happen.

Not next year. Not ever.

They wandered along the winding paths, stopping to admire the flower beds, the fountains and the small lakes set around the gardens. Others were out enjoying the sunshine like Kate and Annie, men and women of all ages, friends in twos or threes, couples arm in arm, families with children skipping in front of their parents.

Pausing at the large fountain at the front of the building, they watched the water splashing down from three bowls of increasing size. It was a fantasy of merpeople and dancing boys, platypuses and small crocodiles squirting water, even a tortoise. At the very top a boy held up a shell from which water spurted. The water sparkled in the sunshine, dancing its way downward.

They turned away from the fountain and Annie went to a bench beside the path. She patted the seat beside her.

A male blackbird scratched in the grass on the other side of the path.

Kate came and sat beside her.

'Kate, what's wrong?'

Kate watched as the blackbird's mate joined him. She had heard they mate for life and grieve when their mate dies.

Annie spoke again. 'Kate. What is wrong?'

Kate looked up. 'Nothing's wrong.'

Annie made a scoffing noise. 'You have been silent except for the odd *Yes* and *Thank you* since we left Coburg. I've been chattering on the whole time and getting next to no answer. I doubt you've heard even half of what I've said today.'

Kate was about to deny it but realised Annie was right.

She looked up into the sky. A bird, wings spread, hovered high overhead. Kate imagined being carried by the wind, weightless, free of care.

'I want the war to end.' She let out a long breath. 'No, I wish it had never started.'

'You are missing Jack? I have wondered if it was wise to—'

Kate would not let her finish. She had followed her heart like Jack had wanted her to. 'I have long accepted that he is gone. I knew he was gone even before I had the news.' She remembered him sitting on the edge of her bed, the prickle of the stubble as her fingertips caressed his cheek. 'I know he is at peace.' She forced her eyes open, not blinking. She would not weep.

'Tom then?'

Kate shrugged, remembering the darkness that followed Jack's death.

'The fear is with me almost every minute of every day. I know what is coming and I will not be able to bear it when it does.'

'Oh, Kate.' Annie grasped Kate's hand, held it tight. 'You must stop thinking like this. You are making yourself ill. It might never happen.'

It might never happen.

'You are mourning Tom already. Would it not be preferable to brace yourself but cling to hope? You can't give into despair. It will destroy you.'

Already it had destroyed what had been between her and Tom.

'Have you talked to your aunt?'

Kate shook her head. 'She is very angry with me.'

'She is not angry with you. She is worried about you and doesn't know what to do.'

'She wants me to go back home.'

'She does not. If you left, she would be heartbroken.'

Kate often caught Aunty Mary staring at her, her brows drawn together, sadness in her eyes. Yes, it was sadness, not anger. They had been through the darkest times together. She would be lost without her aunt. Perhaps Aunty felt the same about Kate.

Kate blinked. Annie had been talking and she hadn't heard a word.

'Will we go home now? Annie asked.

'Yes.' She smiled at Annie. 'It has been a pleasant day.'

Annie looked at her, slightly bemused. 'I'm glad you enjoyed it. We will do it again.'

They walked along Queensbury Street to the Coburg Electric Tram terminus at Madeline Street, Kate wondering if she could take Aunty Mary to the art gallery and the tea rooms. She was sure Aunty would love the paintings. It would be good for Aunty, too, to have the chance to do things that had nothing to do with the war.

39

A s they prepared the evening meal, Kate told Aunty Mary of the day's outing, the art gallery, the paintings, the beauty of the gardens. Aunty told Kate of today's customers, Mrs Johnson's latest piece of made-up gossip and a visit by Joe Kelly.

'And how is Joe?'

'Sixteen and going on forty. Still not quite tall enough to enlist, thank heavens, but he has a plan. They are enlisting men as short as five foot as gunners and drivers so he's learning to drive. No doubt he'll talk his mother into signing the papers saying he's eighteen and giving permission for him to be sent overseas. He said Gus was injured but is back with his unit. Gus also wrote that the French Mam'selles are *a bit of all right* but not a patch on *Aussie sheilas*.'

'I know what you mean about going on forty,' Kate laughed.

After tea, the dishes done, they went to the sitting room and said the rosary.

Kate settled herself on the sofa, her sewing untouched in her lap—she was too tired even to thread her needle. She covered her mouth as she yawned.

'I'm visiting Maggie Ryan tomorrow afternoon. Would you like to come?'

'I thought I might drop in on Annie and collect a book she was telling me about.'

Aunty nodded. 'I'll make the cocoa. We could both do with an early night.'

Kate laid her head against the back of the sofa, her eyes closed as tears leaked out. She couldn't bear this much longer. Annie was right, she was mourning Tom. From the start she had believed it was only a matter of time before the inevitable telegram came. And when it came, there would be nothing but darkness.

It might never happen.

She thought of the woman she had argued with outside the

Public Hall. What had she said? Casualties were no more than one in three, and deaths half that. If that was true, there was no comfort in it. That would be every third person who came into the shop injured, every sixth killed. And each would have a family worrying or grieving. It was far too many.

She felt the movement of the cushions as Aunty sat beside her.

'What is the matter, my treasure.' Her voice was soft.

Kate opened her eyes. 'I am terrified Tom will die.'

Aunty took Kate's hand in hers. 'I know that fear. Every day I wake to it—the fear that the priest will walk through the door. I can't sleep some nights with the thought of it.'

Kate saw the kindness in Aunty's eyes and behind it a well of sorrow.

She looked up to the photograph hanging above the fireplace, taken nearly twenty years ago. Aunty sat with Vince on her knee, Brendan stood beside her, and Uncle Mick behind them all, one hand on Brendan's shoulder, one resting on Aunty Mary's—all looking towards a future promising happiness and good fortune. And below it, at the centre of the mantlepiece, stood a photograph in a dark frame of Vince in uniform, taken in October 1914.

Aunty Mary's burden was heavier than Kate's—why had Kate not recognised it? Aunty had lost so much, yet she never talked of her sorrows. She smiled and did what she could for those around her.

'Every single day, Brendan is in danger.' Aunty paused and took a slow heavy breath. 'And every single day I am safe. No matter what I feel, I must keep on because I am all he has left.'

'Tom has so many people waiting for him.'

'Ah, Kate, when this is over, you are the one he will be coming home to. You are the future he dreams of.'

'But if he doesn't come home. I don't know how I will keep going.'

Lord, keep him safe.

Aunty held tight to Kate's hand. 'If, God forfend, Tom were to die...' She blessed herself quickly and murmured a prayer. 'You would not be alone as you were when Jack was killed. You were away from the people who loved him and missed him, who you could laugh and cry and share your stories of him with. There are many people around you here who know and care for Tom, you would not be alone.'

It might never happen.

'We wait for this war to end and we pray for those we love to be among the lucky ones who come home. We do what we can to make their lives easier—write to them, and knit and sew for them, send them parcels.' She stared into Kate's eyes. 'We give them hope of a future.'

Kate nodded.

Twice Tom had been at her side when she needed help yet, when he needed her most, she had turned away.

~

Kate woke from the worst of dreams, her pillow wet with her tears. Not a dream of blackened buildings, churned mud, and dead and wounded men, but one woven from her memories of Tom's laughter as he spun on the ocean wave, his smile as he danced with her, the light in his eyes as he gazed into hers.

She could no longer endure what life had become.

After their Sunday dinner, Kate dried as Aunty washed the dishes.

'I might get a photograph taken.'

Aunty glanced at Kate. She didn't smile but her face softened.

'If you go first thing tomorrow morning Mr Fullwood, opposite the Brunswick Town Hall, might fit you in then and there.' She brought the serving dishes to the sink. 'And order four copies, two for yourself and one for me and one for your mother. And wear that pretty dancing dress.'

'I was thinking that,' Kate said.

She would write to Tom this afternoon when Aunty was visiting Mrs Ryan.

~

Alone in the house, Kate sat at the dining table and picked up her pen.

She stared at the page, not knowing what to say. Perhaps she should write and make a neat copy when she had it right. In the end it took three attempts before she was satisfied. She started with the greeting Tom had used.

17th August 1917

> My dearest Tom,
>
> I hope this finds you well and safe.
>
> Can you forgive me for the pain I have caused you? I did not mean to but I was so shocked to see you in uniform and terrified of what might happen to you. And to me. When Jack was killed, I felt there was no future. It was as if I had died too.

Was it bad luck to talk of death? But she must be honest with him.

> To this day I feel sick when I think of what might have happened if you had not been there at the lake that night. If I lost you, I would be as lost and without hope as I was then.
>
> From the day you told me you had enlisted, I have not stopped thinking about you and praying for you and missing you. I wanted you with me even when I would not see you and told you to go away. I think of all the days we could have had together and the memories we would have to comfort us while we are apart. It was cruel of me to ignore you and let you leave without a real goodbye or hope for the future but I was so very afraid. Life has been miserable without you.
>
> I will write to you every week if you want me to but I will understand if you do not. I am sending you a photograph like you asked. Thank you for yours. It is in a frame beside me now.

That wasn't really a lie. She would get the photograph back from Aunty and it would be in a frame by the time Tom got this letter.

> Please keep yourself safe Tom. You are constant in my
> prayers until you come home.
> With all my love,
> Kate

She ended the letter with a modest X.

He had said he would write. She prayed he had not changed his mind.

40

September 1917

The days dragged. At the earliest, Kate knew she wouldn't hear from Tom before the middle of November. She had written each week as she promised in her first letter and told him what she had been doing—the trip to the art gallery and the gardens, the book Annie had lent her, the moving pictures she had seen with Reenie and with Aunty Mary, her walks to the lake on Saturday afternoons with Annie or with Aunty Mary on Sundays, how pretty Lake Reserve looked and the countryside along Merri Creek. She didn't tell him she suspected these outing were arranged by Aunty, Reenie and Annie out of sheer kindness, that they had decided she would not be allowed to brood.

She also did not tell him she thought the whole country was falling apart. There were reports in the newspapers of dreadful things happening to ordinary people—an elderly woman had been attacked in her home in Brunswick, a baby abandoned in a laneway behind De Carle Street, a lad electrocuted while swinging on the wires of a flagpole at the rifle range behind Pentridge. Then there were the strikes, the inadequate wages and rising unemployment, food shortages, angry women marching in protest against rising prices. She did mention that recruiting was continuing with weekly Friday night meetings in Coburg, often in the open air despite the weather, with limited success. She told him that the calls for the introduction of conscription were growing louder once again.

Kate missed talking to Tom, hearing his thoughts on so many things. She had loved listening to his stories of his childhood, of his family and the people he had met.

She heard that sly whisper that had been her constant companion since Tom had enlisted, *You will never hear his stories again. You will never hear his voice.* She drowned it out with her murmured prayer, *Lord, watch over and keep him and bring him safely home.*

~

A gust of cold air blew into the shop as the door slammed open. Mrs Ryan rushed up to the counter, breathless, a slip of paper held tight in her gloved hand.

Kate swallowed the fear that had risen in her throat.

'I have this moment received a telegram from Tom.' The smile on her face was more of relief than happiness. She laid the paper on the counter, tried to smooth it, and pushed it towards Kate.

Kate picked it up, her hand shaking.

ARRIVED SAFELY. LETTERS FOLLOWING.

Aunty Mary peered over her shoulder. 'He doesn't say much.'

'It will all be in his letter. He writes a lovely letter.' Mrs Ryan looked at Aunty, blinking fast. 'How long do you think it will take to get here?'

'Five weeks at the earliest but you should certainly have it before Christmas.'

'And if I want to send him a parcel for Christmas?'

'It might be too late for Christmas—parcels take longer—but it will get to him. I sent mine at the end of last month. You have to pay your own postage so it can't be too big. Make sure what you send isn't perishable. You can send dried fruit and chocolate bars. Boxes of cocoa. Tins of condensed milk or fruit—they can find it difficult to get fresh fruit over there. Rolled oat biscuits are good too, sealed in a tin. And don't forget cigarettes or tobacco and papers.'

'Tom does not smoke.'

'Most learn to soon enough over there. Or else, he can trade it with another soldier for something else.'

'Thank you, Mary.' Mrs Ryan nodded. 'Now Kate, as soon as my letter arrives, I will bring it around. And when you get yours, let me know but I will not ask to read it.'

She smiled at Kate, her eyes glistening.

Kate thought of the pain Mrs Ryan must feel at a son taking part in a war Kate suspected she believed had nothing to do with him.

After Mrs Ryan had gone, Kate said, 'Perhaps, a couple of times a week, when I have finished my deliveries, I could call in at Mrs Ryan's and have a cup of tea with her.'

'That is a good idea. She has her grandson with her, but I think she is lonely. And so afraid for Tom.' Aunty put her arm around Kate's shoulder and hugged her to her side. 'You try not to worry for now. Tom's safe in England for the next few weeks.'

~

No one had come into the shop for nearly an hour. Kate had tidied and dusted the shelves and replenished the spices drawers and the lolly jars. With nothing else to do, she opened the newspaper Aunty had left folded on the counter, flicking past the columns of births, marriages and deaths, the wanted ads, the public notices. The articles on the war had the biggest headlines and shouted the loudest.

NEW OFFENSIVE NEAR YPRES

More names of places they would never forget—Ypres, Menin Road, Zonnebeke, Polygon Wood.

AUSTRALIANS GO INTO BATTLE

They went into battle as Australians generally do—not singing and laughing like many British regiments, but very grim and very silent with their officers marching quietly at the head of each small string of men...

They went into this great test, the same grand whole-hearted Australian boys who took Pozieres, and who stormed Gallipoli.

Kate lowered her head, her eyes closed. Today's Casualty List would not have included the names of those who had paid the price of this new offensive. She would not weep for those who had gone, their pain was over. The living needed prayers far more than tears, not that her prayers had done much good in the past. Tom would not be part of these battles. He would be safe in England, still training for a few weeks more.

Then it would all begin again—the fear, the dread, and endless the waiting.

41

Late October 1917

Kate leant her bicycle against the fence in front of the Caseys' house and carried Mrs Casey's order, her last for the morning, around to the back of the house. She knocked on the door frame and called to Mrs Casey.

A chair leg scraped on the floor but Mrs Casey didn't come to the door. Kate was sure she must be in there. Or, at least, somebody was.

There was a sound. A soft moaning?

Kate pulled the wire door open and went in. Mrs Casey was slumped at the end of the table, her head lying on her folded arms. A crumpled scrap of pink paper and an envelope lay in the middle of the table.

Kate placed the parcel of groceries on the table and laid her hand on Mrs Casey's shoulder.

'Mrs Casey?' Her mouth was dry but she forced the words out. 'What has happened?'

Mrs Casey looked up at Kate. Her face was wet, her breathing shallow and ragged.

'It's Pat. He...' She started sobbing again.

Kate picked up the paper and flattened it out. She whimpered as her eyes slid across the words.

REGRET TO ADVISE SON CORPORAL P CASEY WOUNDED.

WILL PROMPTLY ADVISE IF ANYTHING FURTHER RECEIVED.

She sat on the chair beside Mrs Casey and put her arms around her.

Mrs Casey clung onto Kate, her body shaking as she wept.

Poor Pat. With little information, she didn't know what to say. She couldn't say *Thank God he is alive* when he might be dead of his wounds already.

Mrs Casey's trembling subsided. She sat up and straightened her shoulders. 'Why do they tell us so little?'

Kate shrugged. 'You should get a letter in a week or two telling you more.' Or saying that he had died.

Mrs Casey nodded. 'I... I...' She fought back her tears. 'My beautiful boy. No mother should be put through this.' She pulled her handkerchief from her apron pocket, wiped her eyes, and blew her nose. I hate it. This damned war. I hate it so much.'

Kate got up and went to the stove, pulled the kettle forward and set the pot to warm on the hob.

'Do you think it has only just happened?' Mrs Casey asked.

'I don't know. They take their time telling us these things.' Kate spooned tea-leaves into the pot. 'Is Reenie here?'

'No, she's gone to Brunswick to find the perfect piece of ribbon for a hat she is making over.' She sighed. 'She always looks fetching. She's a beautiful girl. And Pat, such a handsome boy.

'What have they done to him?' she wailed.

The kettle began to hiss. Kate went to the stove and poured the water over the tea-leaves and waited. It helped having something to do, even if it only was making tea.

'I'll stay with you until Reenie comes home.'

'I will be fine now, Kate.' Mrs Casey sniffed and sat up straight. 'I'll keep busy and say a prayer or two.'

Kate placed a cup of tea on the table in front of Mrs Casey.

'Would you like me to call in at the smithy on my way back to the shop, ask Mr Casey to come home?'

'No.' Mrs Casey closed her eyes, took a deep breath and trembled as she exhaled. 'I'll tell him when he arrives home for dinner. Let him have a couple more hours without the heartache.'

'If you need anything at all, Aunty Mary and I are not far away.'

'Oh Kate. I know.' She squeezed Kate's hand. 'You two are almost family.'

As Kate rode away, she thought of Pat Casey and Bert Wilson.

They were the only men she knew in the 14th Battalion now. Bert would have been involved in the battle Pat had been wounded in. She prayed Bert was unharmed.

~

Kate told Aunty Mary when she returned from her deliveries. She saw in Aunty's eyes not just concern for Pat but fear for Brendan. He was the only one they knew who had not been injured. Except for Tom, Kate corrected herself. Except for Tom. Some men *must* come through this war unscathed.

Aunty went out the back to make herself a cup of tea and, most likely, to sit on the verandah and pray.

Not long after, Mrs Ryan hurried in. She looked almost happy, the ever-present worry faded. 'Now, Kate, what I have here is sure to bring a smile to your face.'

She took an envelope from her handbag and passed it to Kate.

'A letter from Tom?' Kate stared at it, her heart beating faster.

'Have you had one?'

'Not yet.'

'I shouldn't be asking.' Mrs Ryan's eyes sparkled. 'He told me I wasn't allowed to read anything he wrote to you.'

'Ah Maggie,' Aunty Mary stood in the doorway. 'I thought I heard your voice.' She glanced at the envelope in Kate's hand. 'And you are the postman today?'

'I am indeed—a letter from Tom.'

'Well, don't stand there staring at it, Kate. Take it out the back and read it.'

Kate hurried to the back verandah and slid the letter out of the envelope. It was six pages long.

23.9.17

Dearest Mother,

I hope this finds you in the best of health. I am fighting fit and they are making sure we keep that way.

The journey here took eight weeks and I was only seasick

for a few days at the beginning. Our first port of call was at Durban, a pretty place nestled among the hills on a small port. On the first day, after a march in the morning, we were granted leave until half past ten at night. While I was there, I visited the Art Gallery and Museum, and ate myself silly on fruit of all sorts, sandwiches, fish, cake, ice cream. The YMCA offers a fine spread served by lady volunteers. They were very pleasant and helpful women but do not hold a candle to our Australian girls.

I visited the zoo and had a ride in a rickshaw. Something I will not be doing again. It does not seem right to be carried around by another man's labour. At least most of our men paid the runners extra.

He described the fun and games they had when the ship crossed the equator, complete with King Neptune holding court and everyone on the deck ending up soaking wet.

The sunrises and sunsets at sea are a sight to behold. One day we even saw a waterspout. It was a swirling tube of water from the sea up into the clouds. Very eerie looking.

We landed at Liverpool and were brought by train down here.

He went on to talk of the countryside they travelled through and the camp, the huts they were in, thirty men to each, complete with a stove in the centre and an electric light. He talked of the drilling and the marches and musketry, bayonet and bombing practice.

The food is satisfactory but never quite enough. Sugar is in short supply and it is all brown bread, heavy like damper. I dream sometimes of a hunk of white bread toasted in front of the fire and slathered with butter and blackberry jam.

He was expecting some leave soon.

I wish it was long enough to take a trip to Ireland but I will visit your cousin, James, when I get to London and will pass on your best wishes to him.

I will not be with you this Christmas but here's hoping I will be home for the next.

Well, Mother, I will finish up. Keep me in your prayers.

From your loving son,

Tom

P.S. Make sure you show the letter to Kate. It will save me writing this all over again.

Kate read it once more before she went back to the shop.

She handed it back to Mrs Ryan. 'You can almost hear his voice in the letter.'

'Indeed. It is as if he is sitting in front of you.'

'The letter was sent five weeks ago.'

'It was but I think he is still safe in England. My neighbour's boy left at the beginning of the year and she said he stayed twelve weeks in England before he was sent to France.'

Kate wondered, after Mrs Ryan had left, if they should have told her about Pat Casey. It seemed cruel to spoil her happiness by reminding her of the danger Tom would soon be facing.

She would learn soon enough.

42

November 1917

The following Monday was washing day and Aunty Mary was out in the washhouse, boiling the sheets in the copper. Kate was busy in the shop. Three customers waited, chatting together, as Kate served another.

Mr McGregor, the postman, came up to the counter, a letter in his hand.

'A green envelope.' He raised one eyebrow. 'Intended for letters discussing personal matters, I'm told.'

Kate blushed, aware of the sudden interest of the women in the room. 'Perhaps it was the only envelope the writer had.'

'Perhaps it was.' He nodded. 'Tom Ryan must have used up his plain envelopes writing to his family—his mother got a letter last week.'

Kate held out her hand. 'May I have the letter, Mr McGregor?' She tried to hide her irritation.

He winked at Kate and handed it over, tipping his cap to the other ladies as he left the shop.

Kate glared after him and put the letter in her apron pocket.

'Don't mind him, dear,' the lady at the counter said. 'He's such an old woman at times but there is no harm in him—he doesn't spread gossip or makes it up, like some I could mention.'

Kate thought it best not to comment.

'When you answer that letter...' the woman continued.

Kate stiffened—they were such a flock of busybodies.

'...you should put in a couple of extra sheets of blank writing paper. They often don't have much paper over there.'

Kate relaxed. 'Thank you, I will.'

The customers all had long lists this morning. When, finally, they had all left the shop, she opened the letter and put the envelope back in her pocket.

It was written the same day as the letter to his mother.

> My dearest Kate,
>
> I am here in England. It was not a bad journey but I am glad to be on dry land. I have sent a letter describing my travels and life in camp to Mother and told her to show it to you. I expect she would have anyway. She has taken quite a shine to you.
>
> I have been thinking of you the whole time and I am deeply sorry for not telling you what I was planning to do. I was so wrapped up in my own concerns about enlisting that it did not occur to me what a great shock it would be to you. To my shame, I did not think of what you had already suffered. If I had, I would have tried to explain why I believe I had to go and you would have had the chance to tell me why I should not. I would, most likely, still be where I am today, but we would understand each other better and I believe there would not be this rift between us.

The door jingled open. Kate pushed the letter into her pocket and brushed away the tears she hadn't known were there.

It was a girl of about five years old with a note for a packet of Reckitt's blue. Before the child had even left, Kate was reading again.

> I did believe, when the war started, it was nothing to do with us. But too many good Australian men have been killed and maimed for it not to be about us and it is time I played my part. And then there is Martin. I should have gone with him. Now I need to take his place and settle the score. I think if I had explained myself, although you would not have wanted me to go, you would have accepted it. I have never given up hope that you still care for me. The night of my farewell, when we stood outside and you spoke of your anguish, I felt that you were saying that you loved me too. The medal wallet you gave me is the firmest proof of your wish for my safe return but,

selfishly, I wanted the memory of your arms around me and one final kiss to carry away with me.

Kate covered her mouth with her hand, stifling a sob.

I hope this rift can be healed and from now we can speak our minds completely to each other, no secrets, nothing held back. Kate, I love you. I have loved you from the moment I saw you, standing beside Mrs Burke, speaking of protecting the innocents of Belgium. But I knew your heart was given elsewhere. To walk with your hand in mine was a dream I had thought was impossible. Those brief months with you earlier in the year were close to heaven. I want what I wanted then—for our future to be together. I want you to be there when I come home. I want you to be my wife. And while there will be no dancing, or walks home from the pictures together, or sitting on the back verandah talking for quite some time, we can still talk through letters. I will write as often as I can until you tell me not to. If you say this is not what you want, I will stop. Keep me in your prayers my darling.
With all my love,
Tom X

'Those sheets will be dry in no time with this wind,' Aunty said as she walked in. She stopped. 'Oh Kate. What is the matter?'
Kate drew a deep shuddering breath. 'A letter from Tom.'
'What has happened?'
She heard the alarm in her aunt's voice.
'Nothing. Everything is fine.' She sniffed as she ratted around in her pocket. 'Why do I never have a handkerchief when I need one?'
Her aunt pulled a white folded handkerchief from her apron pocket and held it out. 'It is unused.'
Kate wiped her eyes. 'Nothing's wrong except Tom is over there.'
'Ah,' Aunty sighed. 'This damnable war.'

~

That night Kate opened the envelope containing her weekly letter to Tom. That morning, she had been in a rush and had forgotten to take it with her to post as she did her round of deliveries. She added a postscript on the back of the last page.

> Monday
>
> I received your letter today and was so relieved you had not thrown me over that I burst into tears. And I did not have a handkerchief and had to borrow one from Aunty Mary. It seems to be a habit of mine. And then I wanted to dance but I will not be dancing until you come home and I can dance with you. I am waiting for that day and hope it is not too far away. I will be here when you come home and I can think of nothing better than being your wife. And what you did not have when you left, I promise you when you return.
>
> Tom, I love you with my whole heart.
>
> X

43

That first week in November had brought almost daily casualty lists, as many men killed and almost twice as many injured as for the whole of September. The news from overseas told of air raids on London, the advance of the German army in Italy, the fighting at Beersheba in Palestine.

And Prime Minister Hughes announced that there would be another referendum on conscription in six weeks' time. It was no surprise as the newspapers had been full of speculation saying there was a growing public demand for it. The Prime Minister claimed he had been forced to it by the retreat of the Allied army in Italy.

The question was to be simpler than the last.

> Are you in favour of the proposal of the Commonwealth Government for reinforcing the Australian Imperial Force overseas?

After announcing the referendum, Mr Hughes had stated that half those who were against conscription were friends of Germany and enemies of the Allies. Kate groaned when she read that, sure that he included both Irish and Australian Catholics as friends of Germany. As the month went on, he made it clearer, pointing out that those who were campaigning against conscription were led by those same people who had inflicted the strikes on Australia over the last year, the International Workers of the World, and the supporters of the Irish nationalist Sinn Fein party. In that last group he seemed to number as unpatriotic and treacherous any Catholic who didn't support his views, no matter what their reasoning.

The casualty lists continued, each with more than one thousand names. On the last Monday of the month there were over eighteen hundred names. It was easier to bear if you called it a list of names,

Kate thought. But each name was a man, a man with women like Kate and Aunty Mary waiting and weeping.

Kate paused as she ran her finger down the list of the men killed in action. There at the end was a name.

WILSON, A., Hobart, 16/10/17

'Aunty Mary.' Kate's voice creaked as she spoke.

Aunty looked up, frowning. She came over and stared at the name Kate was pointing to.

'Is it Bert?'

'I would say so.' She blessed herself and murmured a prayer. 'I do wish they still printed the battalion with the soldier's name.' Her face was lined with worry. 'I will write to Base Records at Victoria Barracks. I'll say I'm his aunt so hopefully they will tell me. I have his sister's address. I'll write to her when I know for certain.'

'I'll write to her too. He was a good mate to Jack.'

Kate folded her arms tight across her bosom and walked through the house. She stood on the edge of the verandah and stared down the yard seeing Bert hard at work, splitting wood for Aunty Mary. She thought of his dream—a good sized vegetable garden with fruit trees and a few chooks. He deserved far better than a distant grave in foreign mud. Jack had had dreams too, of a thriving farm and a house full of laughing children. These were the modest dreams of good men.

Sorrow lodged, yet again, like a lump in Kate's throat, and her eyes stung but no tears came. She knew life was cruel.

And poor Pat Casey. The Caseys had received a letter, a week on from the telegram, telling them Pat had a gunshot wound to the face and had lost an eye. She had seen the faces of men with eye injuries. He had been such a handsome, smooth-faced young man when he left. He was in the King George Military Hospital in England. There was nothing in the letter to tell them how he was, whether he was recovering or struggling, only the routine words:

In the absence of further reports it is to be assumed
that satisfactory progress is being maintained.

And this government would not be satisfied until every eligible
man in the country was either dead or wounded in a war on the
other side of the world Australia had nothing to do with starting.

~

Late in the week, Kate sat down and wrote to Tom. She decided
she wouldn't tell him about Pat or Bert. He had enough to worry
about.

29th November 1917

My dearest Tom,

I pray you are safe and well as we are here. We have had
an early burst of summer. I would bottle some and send it
to you as I know you are heading into winter. Lately I have
been calling in on your mother a couple of times a week
and we have a cup of tea and a chat. She is keeping busy
knitting socks for the Red Cross. No doubt she will knit
you some too. She told me some stories about the mischief
you got into as a boy. I joined the lending library beside
the Police Station and have just finished a book from there
called Wuthering Heights. Have you read it? There were
parts I did not understand. They seemed to be written in
another language. And Heathcliff is an utterly horrible
creature. Imagine marrying someone out of spite so you
could mistreat her. His behaviour in the graveyard does
not bear thinking about. Tell me what your favourite
book is and I'll see if the library has it.

You will know of the reinforcements referendum. Mr
Hughes is doing everything he can to win this time. He
says it is only to make up the numbers to seven thousand
men a month and only single men. He says that is only one
person from every electorate a day. Only! That is a lot of
men. People know what the men are facing, not like at the
start when everyone thought it was a big adventure and it
would be over in six months. We were such fools.

So Mr Hughes is letting soldiers under twenty-one vote, but he called it so quickly that plenty of men aged twenty-one and over who could be conscripted did not have time to enrol. Australian born men and women with parents born in Germany are not allowed to vote unless they have a close family member in the army. Many of the Catholic bishops are speaking out this time because there is no exemption for seminarians and brothers. If enough are conscripted the Catholic boys schools will have to close. There are all the usual meetings and parades both for and against. You will be pleased to hear I have no intention of attending any meetings. As you would expect, plenty of nasty things are being said about us being traitors and shirkers and only ever looking after ourselves. But when the church collections were taken up for Hospital Sunday, the largest amounts in Coburg and Brunswick were from the Catholic churches, St Ambrose's and St Matthew's.

I will be voting No again. By the time this reaches you it will be over. I wish you were here to talk to about it. I just wish you were here.

Christmas will be over too. You will get to see snow—not like our hot Christmases. Even though this will reach you late

MERRY CHRISTMAS.

You are ever in my thoughts and my prayers my darling. I dream of when you come home and I can wrap my arms around you.

With all my love,

Kate.

XX

Kate reread the letter. It was the longest she had ever written. She wished it did not take so much time between letters. But more, she wished the war was over and they were sitting on the verandah side by side, shoulders touching, talking of things other than the war.

44

December 1917

The windows of the Caseys' sitting room were open to catch the breeze at the end of a long warm day. The only sounds in the room were the faint hiss of the gaslight and the click of needles as the young women concentrated on their knitting. A murmur of intermittent conversation carried from the kitchen where Mr and Mrs Casey were sitting, and the occasional rattle of paper as Mr Casey turned the pages of his newspaper.

Rita finished her row and paused her knitting. 'My father says Archbishop Mannix is leading us astray.'

There was a collective intake of breath.

'What does he mean by that?' Annie sat, her back straight, every inch the stern school teacher.

'Well.' Rita sat up too. 'He said holding that big meeting at the racecourse in Richmond last month about Ireland and its troubles was stupid at a time like this.'

Rita seemed unaware that every person in the room was staring at her.

'You would think being refused permission to hold it at the Exhibition Buildings would be enough to make him think again. Dad says he should know better and should keep his trap—' She stopped and stuttered, 'I... I... mean his mouth shut.'

Kate pressed her lips together to stop herself laughing. She had sometimes thought the same but in politer terms.

'Dr Mannix is perfectly entitled to voice his opinion,' Annie said coldly. 'And the thirty thousand people who attended that rally would disagree with your father.'

One of the other girls asked, 'Is your father a Protestant?'

'He is not.' Rita's face flushed red. 'He was baptized here at St Paul's. He's just sick of all this carry on about Ireland. Australia is not the place for this fight, not when there's a war on.'

As she spoke, a number of the other young women began to whisper.

'What happens in Ireland is of as much interest to people here as what happens in England,' Reenie said. 'But there are some people, like those in the Protestant Federation, that set up a branch here in Coburg last month, who believe only England matters and those of us who think differently are not loyal or patriotic. They would love to see Archbishop Mannix locked up. Probably the rest of us too even though many of us have soldiers over there.'

Suddenly everyone was talking at once, over the top of each other, barely listening to what anyone else said.

'My father says the government would be happy if the Catholic schools shut...' 'What about the tax on bachelors who haven't...' 'no one should be forced...' 'and the Brothers can't marry so they have to pay...' 'I wouldn't trust Billy Hughes's promises...' 'why should our brothers die for the English...' '...and why shouldn't he talk about Ireland?' '...conscripting women next...' '...fighting for the freedom of small nations...' 'Australia has done enough...' '...the casualty lists...no one will be left alive...' 'Ireland is a small nation...'

Even Annie was there in the middle of it, lecturing one of the girls on showing more respect when she spoke about bishops.

Rita was struggling on, but no one was listening. '...my brother Robbie. He left in 1914 and he's never been home on leave, not like the British soldiers who get to visit family. Mr Hughes says if conscription passes then men like Robbie can come home on furlough.'

Kate went over to Rita and took hold of her hand. 'My cousin Brendan is the same. He went with the first contingent in October 1914.'

Rita looked up, tears welling in her pale eyes. 'I'm so scared. The longer he's out there, the more chance he will die.'

Kate lowered her head. What could she say? That was Aunty

Mary's fear. Her own too, and not just for Brendan.

'Quiet! All of you.' Mrs Casey stood in the doorway, stiff, her fists clenched beside her, her face white. 'Sit. Down. And pick up your knitting. I will not have this uproar in my house. This is not a Town Hall meeting. You are here to knit. And have a pleasant evening. So do that.' She looked around the room at each young woman. 'There is to be no talk of conscription or Billy Hughes or Archbishop Mannix for that matter. Is that understood?'

The young women murmured and nodded, and went back to their seats. Heads bowed, they obediently took up their knitting.

'Reenie,' Mrs Casey said more calmly. 'Tell everyone about the picture show you saw last night. I'll prepare supper.'

She turned and walked back to the kitchen.

Kate got up and followed her.

'I'm sorry, Mrs Casey. I think everyone is so wound up the slightest thing sets them off.'

Mrs Casey nodded. 'But I don't want it here. I am sick of it. We are at each other's throats while men over there are being killed and maimed, their lives ruined. I am sick of this war and bloody politicians like Billy Hughes.'

'Nellie!' Mr Casey gaped, his eyes wide with shock. 'That's no way for a lady to speak.'

Mrs Casey glared at him and, for a moment, looked as if she would swear at Mr Casey next.

She was the picture of dignity, now, with her hands clasped at her waist, 'I am not a lady at present. I am an angry mother. I *do not* have to follow the rules. And who are you to talk? I have heard far, far worse from your mouth.'

Mr Casey went to speak but thought better of it. He lifted his paper up, as if making a barrier, but Kate could have sworn he had the hint of a smile, even though his mouth was hidden by his dark bushy moustache.

'I'll help you with the supper.'

'Thank you, Kate. You can make the tea, the big pot is at the back, on the hob. I'll slice the cake.'

'Have you heard any more about Pat?' Kate asked.

Mrs Casey exhaled loudly. 'Another letter came saying he is progressing well, whatever that means. Nothing from Pat himself. Maybe we will get a letter in the new year. Even a field postcard would do.'

Mrs Casey stared across at Mr Casey, hidden by the newspaper, and said, 'This bloody war.'

~

It was a relief when the referendum day arrived on the Thursday before Christmas. Kate hoped it would put an end to the anger and the shouting, the letters and speeches, the deluge of handbills, the meetings, the parades, the heckling, the stone throwing, and the fighting.

Aunty Mary went to vote once Kate was back from her morning deliveries. The polling place was only open from eight in the morning until eight at night and she was sure there would be a rush in the last couple of hours when working people had their only opportunity to vote.

Kate went in the early afternoon. Everywhere she looked there were posters and handbills shouting out Yes and No. Big Noes were painted in red on fences and footpaths and on the side walls of houses and shops. A Yes handbill had been changed to *Yes Spurts Blood*. There were a few other posters saying *For King and Country Vote No* and *To Save One's Honor Vote No*.

There weren't many people at the Public Hall so Kate didn't have to wait long to have her name struck through on the electoral roll and to cast her firm No vote.

As she turned into Sydney Road on her way home, Reenie waved to her from the other side of the street. She waited for a break in the traffic before walking smartly across to Kate.

'You've just been to vote?'

'Yes,' Kate said. 'For once, it wasn't a long wait.'

'I wish I could vote but I'm not twenty-one until October next year.'

Whenever anyone mentioned next year, Kate told herself the war would be over and tried to ignore the sly voice saying she was a fool.

'Will you have a party?' Peace was a time for parties.

'I certainly hope so. I'm already dropping hints to Mum and Dad.' She looked at Kate, puzzled. 'You never celebrate your birthday.'

'I haven't wanted to for a long time.'

'Well, next birthday I'll make sure you at least have cake.'

Reenie stopped and moved to the side of the busy footpath. 'Dad took Mum to vote at dinner time. He didn't trust her not to start speechifying outside the Public Hall if she went alone.'

Kate laughed. 'Your mother wouldn't do that.'

'You haven't heard?' Reenie sounded relieved. 'Mrs Johnson can't know, otherwise it would be all over Coburg.'

'Know what, Reenie?' What had Mrs Casey done?

They began walking again. Reenie glanced behind her, checking no one was close enough to hear. 'I don't know the whole story, only what I can piece together from Mum and Dad's arguments. It seems Mum went with another woman to a ladies' conscription meeting. It mustn't have been here in Coburg, or even Brunswick, or every single person would know about it. The pair of them were interjecting and shouting at the speakers, telling them if they were so keen to send young men at the start of their lives, why didn't worn-out old creatures like themselves volunteer. Mum called a rather rotund man a member of the Conscript the Other Fellow brigade and said he should get off his fat backside and get over there because if he stood as a shield between our boys and the Germans, he'd save at least three lives.'

Kate burst out laughing.

'It's not funny, Kate. Imagine if it was your mother, you'd be embarrassed.'

Reenie was right but Kate couldn't imagine her mother behaving like this. But neither could she imagine Mrs Casey.

'Anyway, the police marched them out of the meeting as Mum and the other woman sang *I Didn't Raise my Son to be a Soldier*. They weren't charged with anything otherwise it would have been in the papers. One of the constables, Ted McInerney, had been at school with Pat and he let her go.' Reenie glared at Kate. 'Will you stop laughing? This isn't funny.'

Kate tried to look serious. 'No harm has been done, though. And after today the meetings and the shouting will stop.'

'Not at our house.' Reenie rolled her eyes. 'Constable McInerney visited Dad at work and told him what had happened and said if it happens again, he will have to charge Mum with disturbing the peace.' She caught Kate by the wrist. 'Please, don't you tell anyone. Not even Mrs Burke.'

'I promise, Reenie. I won't.'

'I don't understand why she is behaving like this.'

'It's anger and fear.' Something Kate knew well. 'She will come back to herself, especially once she hears Pat is recovering and he's on his way home.'

And Kate hoped that, after today, people would go back to keeping their opinions to themselves.

When counting ended the next day, the Noes were ahead by just under one hundred and fifty thousand votes but many thought, or hoped, that a Yes victory was still possible. By Saturday it was clear the referendum had failed—there would be no conscription of men for overseas service.

Monday morning was Christmas Eve and Kate received what was the second-best Christmas present ever—two letters from Tom. One had been written before her first letter had arrived and was full of Tom's leave in London, the sights, the food and the weather. The other was a single page, written three weeks later.

My darling Kate,

A quick note as a mate is off on leave to London and this will get to you faster if posted from there.

Christmas came nearly two months early for me with today's post. I received THREE letters from you and that wonderful photograph. I have it here in front of me. You are wearing your dancing dress and look more beautiful than any moving picture star. I could have danced with happiness once I read them. The only thing stopping me was that I might be thought drunk and put on a charge.

All that matters, my love, is that the past is behind us. Merry Christmas my dearest girl. Here's hoping I am back with you for Christmas 1918.

I love you, Kate. Always and forever.

Tom.

Below it was an X that took up the rest of the page.

Kate couldn't think of a better present than Tom being home for Christmas.

1918

The joy of the mothers and fathers and wives of the Anzacs when they clasped to their breasts the men from whom they had been separated for so long was that felt only by those who have known the anguish of weary waiting and the constant, ever present dread of evil tidings ... Strong men broke down and wept, and were not ashamed. The habits and conventions of a lifetime were swept aside. Big, stalwart soldiers were kissed by their fathers as though they were little boys again. Mothers clung to their sons and would not let them go.

Return of the 'original Anzacs' on 23 November 1918
The Age 25 November 1918 p.7

45

February 1918

K ate woke exhausted. Pale early morning light filtered into the room through the gap in the curtains. The air was hot and still, as warm inside the house as out. It had been like this for days.

She lay, open-eyed, staring at the ceiling. Her first thoughts, as they always were now, were of Tom. Where was he? Was he safe? *Lord, protect him and keep him.*

He had been away six months and was sure to be somewhere in France. She had received a letter from him in the middle of January telling her about the camp and the English countryside and a visit to an ancient place made of massive stones called Stonehenge. There had been nothing since.

Kate sent a letter to Tom every week. On New Year's Day, she had written telling him of Christmas and the young soldiers who had come for dinner and left overloaded with Aunty's baking and knitting. One looked as if he was not old enough to shave and barely topped five foot. She told Tom of the quiet of Boxing Day when it seemed the whole town had gone to Altona Beach rather than Williamstown. How the angry red Yeses and Noes of the referendum still hadn't faded, making the celebratory 1918s chalked on the footpaths appear half-hearted.

In last Sunday's letter she had written of the unveiling of the Honour Board at the Coburg Town Hall. Aunty Mary had gone to the service and said it was pleasant there, under the trees in Elm Grove. The Mayor of Coburg, an army chaplain, the local Protestant ministers, and some members of parliament had been present. After prayers and a Bible reading, the Honour Board was unveiled and the names of one hundred and ten soldiers from Coburg were read out, including Vince's. Aunty said she shouldn't have gone because she had known it would be a Protestant service. But she wanted to go and thought it was better to take her medicine after than to ask the Parish Priest's permission and be refused. Kate had finished the letter by saying that, sometimes, the rules made no sense to her.

She would drift back to sleep if she didn't get up. She told herself today was a day no different to any other and she must get on with it. Once she was dressed, she lit the stove and put the kettle to boil while she set the kitchen table for breakfast.

She knocked lightly on Aunty Mary's door. 'Aunty Mary, it's half-past six.' She could hear the creak of the bedsprings and a groan.

'Come in, Kate.'

Aunty struggled up from her pillows, watching as Kate placed a jug of warm water onto the washstand.

'I don't know what I'd do without you, Kate.'

In the half-light, Aunty looked old and tired, dark circles under her eyes.

By the time she came into the kitchen, Kate had the tea made.

'Would you like some porridge?' Kate set the toast in front of the open firebox of the stove.

'Toast is enough in this weather, my treasure.' Aunty sat down and poured the tea. 'I couldn't sleep with the heat, tossing and turning. Then just before dawn, I fell into a dead sleep.'

'Do you want me to help in the shop?' She placed Aunty's toast in front of her. 'It's sure to be busy again this morning—people getting their shopping out of the way before the worst of the heat.'

'It might be an idea. I don't know that I can trust myself on the ladder today. I'll have something to say if Bridie Johnson comes in wanting to look at every single tin of jam we have.'

'I think she likes the labels. She's particularly taken with the apricot.'

They ate breakfast in silence. Kate glanced across at Aunty Mary. She had aged in the years Kate had been with her. When Kate had arrived, Aunty had seemed younger than Mum, despite being ten years older. Even dressed in widow's black, her clothes had been fashionable. Now she looked drab and worn down. Her hair was far greyer and the glow that had been in her face, and her easy laugh, were gone. It was not only the heat and tiredness; the weight of sorrow and more than three years of unremitting fear had left their mark.

Kate stood and collected together the breakfast things.

'Wait a moment,' Aunty said and disappeared into the dining room. She came back with a tissue wrapped parcel and an envelope.

'Happy Birthday, my dear.' She kissed Kate's cheek.

Kate smiled. 'Thank you, Aunty.' She had told herself it was a day like any other, but was quietly pleased she wouldn't be allowed to treat it that way.

Her hands quickly washed and dried, Kate carefully opened the envelope. Beside a bouquet of purple violets and maiden-hair fern on the card was the greeting *Wishing you a Happy Birthday*.

Aunty had written on the back,

To Kate my beautiful niece,
with all my love,
Aunty Mary X

'Oh, Aunty Mary,' she sighed, her eyes prickling. She hugged her aunt tight. 'Thank you so much.'

Aunty Mary's eyes lit up. Her smile made her look years younger. 'Now open your present.'

Kate parted the layers of tissue. Inside was a white blouse of fine cotton. The long collar had a pattern in drawn thread work at the edge that was repeated on the front panel of the blouse. As well, Aunty had included an opaque camisole to be worn beneath it.

'It is lovely,' Kate breathed.

'We will have to go somewhere special so you can wear it.'

'We should do that.' Kate kissed her aunt. 'Somewhere nice. Just the two of us. Perhaps the art gallery at the Melbourne Library where I went with Annie? It has a lovely tea room.'

'Or the Botanic Gardens—there's a tea house there too. For a few hours, we can forget all our worries.'

It was more than time, Kate thought, that she made an effort to lighten Aunty's spirits as Aunty so often did for her.

Later, as Kate came back in from shaking out the tablecloth, she noticed a small brown paper parcel sitting on the bench on the verandah. It had Kate written on the paper.

She took it inside and unwrapped it at the table. Inside was a small jeweller's box and a card.

> To my darling Kate
> Happy Birthday
> Tom X

For one wishful moment Kate imagined he had put it there himself.

The box contained a bar brooch with a rectangular peridot set at an angle, delicate gold wire scrolls curled at either side of the stone. The pale green stone was as clear as light through water.

She went into the shop where Aunty was checking the till and held out the open box. 'This is from Tom.'

'Ah, now, that is beautiful.' Aunty smiled, both eyebrows raised. 'And it would go well with your new blouse.'

'How did it get here?'

'Before he left, Tom asked me to take care of it.'

Kate closed her eyes. Despite her cruelty to him then, he had been thinking of her. And she still didn't know his birth date.

'I haven't had a letter from him for over a month.'

'There can be a long wait, then a whole bundle of them will arrive at once. Sometimes, they don't have time to write. It helps if you number your letters so they know if any are missing. They don't always get them in the order they are sent.'

'I'm worried.' Kate shut the jeweller's box. 'It feels like something is happening but they aren't telling us.'

In between the reports of bushfires in the west of the state, and a tornado in Brighton, the food shortages in England, and civil war in Russia, the newspapers reported on talk of a peace treaty but, and this terrified Kate, more and more there was talk that a German offensive was coming.

'We only know what they tell us.' Aunty sounded weary. 'There is always something happening, and we will not hear until it is over and the costs are being counted.'

Kate knew that too well.

A cool change swept through before midday and the temperature plummeted.

Her ironing done, Kate walked to the end of the yard, relishing the cool air on her face. Threatening clouds, black in places, massed in the sky. Yes, it was her birthday. She was now twenty-three and not living the life she had imagined she would by this age. Tonight, she would go as usual to Reenie's. Reenie had said there would be cake, as she had promised, and laughter and wishes of many happy returns. Kate dared not consider what those returns might bring. And happiness? That could not come until all their men were safely home.

46

March 1918

March arrived and the heat began to ease. The late afternoons were pleasant once the bite had gone out of the sun. The leaves were turning and Aunty Mary was busy making green tomato pickles.

The shop was full when Mr McGregor came in, red-faced and, lugging a heavy mailbag. 'I think almost every house in Coburg has received mail today.' He handed a bundle to Kate. 'Sorry, I can't stop for a chat.'

She placed them on the shelf behind her.

When the shop had finally emptied, Kate shuffled through the envelopes. She took them out to the kitchen and left them on the dresser, including a letter from her mother. The only other letter addressed to her she tore open as she walked back to the shop. It had been written at the end of January.

She had read no further than 'My darling Kate' when elderly Miss White came into the shop for a packet of cocoa and half a pound of butter. That was the beginning of a constant stream of customers. All afternoon, Kate was aware of the letter sitting in her apron pocket but it wasn't until the shop was closed that she finally had time to read it.

Tom had started writing before Christmas, adding to the letter every few days. He began by saying he had received Aunty Mary's Christmas package and was now wearing the socks she sent. He described Christmas at the training camp in England.

> We had a fine Christmas dinner and plenty of it—roast goose, turkey or chicken, roast pork and all the trimmings, followed by plum pudding. And for tea there was ham as well as jelly, fruit cake and custard tarts. I have never been so interested in food as I am now.

Then he spoke about the referendum.

> Opinions were as divided over here as at home. Some said they did not want a man beside them whose heart is not in the fight, as would be the case with a number of the conscripts. But there are men here who have been away from home for over three years, who have been through the worst of it like your cousin Brendan. They need and deserve a good rest but they cannot get it without more recruits. It is the only argument that might have swayed me. But I still consider it immoral for one man to force another who is unwilling to kill a third in cold blood. I am not a pacifist. I would feel differently if Australia were under direct attack. It is not as easy a decision as many at home seem to think.

And he answered her question from the letter she had sent in November.

> Now books. I like reading stories set in the future or about strange events, ghost stories too. Jules Verne, H. G. Wells, Sheridan Le Fanu are a few of the writers. I am not sure if they will be to your taste but take anything that appeals to you from the books I have at home.

Finally, he wrote of his journey to France and the camp there.

> I am now 'somewhere in France'. On the day we arrived here there was two inches of snow and for the next few days it was either snowing or raining and several times practice had to be cancelled because of the weather. It is better now, though I would not mind a decent Melbourne heatwave. A couple of days after we arrived, the Divisional Concert Party put on a show. It was very entertaining, one of the men looked quite fetching in a frock.
>
> We will be moving soon and I will have to face what we are here for. All I hope is that I do my duty and not let my mates down and come through to the other side. And like everyone else I look for the end of the war.

I miss you, Kate. I wish I were home sitting close to you,
my arm around you, your head on my shoulder. I pray it
will not be too long before I have that wish.
Keep me in your prayers my darling.
With all my love,
Tom XX
P.S. Thank you for the extra paper, it is a great help.

Kate checked the envelope. It was stamped on the twenty-eighth
of January. The familiar sick panic settled in her stomach. Tom
would have been in battle by now but he must have come through
unhurt. They would have heard otherwise. Most of the time the
news of deaths, injuries and sickness came through much quicker
than it had at the beginning.

~

Kate gazed around Mrs Ryan's sitting room while the old lady was
out in the kitchen arranging the tea tray. Kate had offered to help
but Mrs Ryan insisted Kate sit.

The room looked out onto the verandah and beyond to the
garden. The roses were in full bloom along the front fence. On the
walls were several pictures of scenery in dark carved frames; a large
oval framed photograph behind curved glass hung above the
fireplace. Kate hadn't looked at it closely on her previous visits. Mrs
Ryan stood, smiling gently, her hand resting on the shoulder of a
seated man, Mr Ryan no doubt. He was grey haired with a white
clipped beard. His eyes were darker than Mrs Ryan's, perhaps they
were hazel like Tom's. He appeared rather stern.

Mrs Ryan brought in the tea tray and set it on the table.

As she passed Kate a cup and saucer, Kate said, 'That is a lovely
photograph, Mrs Ryan.'

The older woman gazed up at it. 'Ah, it was taken only two years
before Mr Ryan died.' Her smile was wistful. 'With him up there,
I feel he is watching over us.'

She sat in the chair opposite Kate and offered her a lemon biscuit.

'These are my own recipe. I use lemon rind and a few drops of juice instead of essence.'

Kate took one and nibbled. 'It has a nice fresh taste.'

Mrs Ryan put the plate on the table. 'Have you heard anything from Tom? I have not had a letter for weeks.'

'One came yesterday.' She put her teacup on the table and took the letter from the pocket of her jacket. 'I'm sure he wouldn't mind you reading the first three pages.' There was nothing in the letter, other than the last paragraph, that she minded Mrs Ryan reading. She folded the last page over.

The old lady's hands trembled as she took the letter. She read quickly, gasping as she came to the end of the third page. 'He's in France.' She went straight back and read the letter again, more slowly this time.

Kate drank her tea in the silence.

Mrs Ryan's eyes were watery by the time she had finished.

'I will show you his books, but they are such strange stories. He always loved reading.' She gave a small laugh. 'When he was a lad, he used to read those awful penny dreadfuls, absolute rubbish his father called them. Once, when Tom was twelve or thirteen, his father grabbed his book and hurled it into the fire. Then he used the poker to push it further into the flames but a coal fell out of the grate and onto his slipper. He was jumping around, yelling, and Tom bolted out the door. There was no harm done to poor Patrick's foot, but Tom was very well behaved for the next couple of days.' She sighed. 'They were grand times despite the ups and downs.'

She looked across at Kate. 'I will show you these books now.'

It was a tidy room with a wardrobe, a chest of drawers, a wash-stand, and a single bed by the window. A crucifix hung on the wall above the bed. The books were lined up along the top of the chest of drawers.

Kate was aware of Mrs Ryan standing at the door, gazing around

283

the room, her eyes dull, her shoulders slumped.

'I will be in the sitting room.' She looked as if she was about to weep.

Kate picked up a book and flicked through the pages, stopping at an awful scene where a man transformed into a monster. She didn't like the sound of that. She put the book back.

She settled on a book of short ghost stories by Sheridan Le Fanu. Perhaps she could read them to Aunty Mary in the evening. Aunty did like a good ghost story.

Later, as Kate was leaving, Mrs Ryan said, 'It is a relief to me that you and Tom are writing to each other and...' She paused as if deciding what to say next. '...and there are parts of the letter you do not want me to read. I was worried you two had fallen out.'

'I was upset that he enlisted.' Kate thought she deserved part of the truth.

'We were too.' She nodded slowly. 'His brothers, Pat and Frank, were angry and said it was the last thing their father would have wanted, though less politely than that. They see it as Tom acting as he did as a boy, thoughtless and reckless. But my boy is no longer like that. He takes his time to make up his mind but once he is set upon something, he will not be swayed. All we can do is to pray for his safe return and do what we can for him from this distance.'

She grasped Kate's hand and leant towards her, kissing her cheek. She was a gentle white-haired woman, usually with an air of calm about her. But when she spoke of Tom, there was terror in her eyes.

47

It was difficult to work out what was happening. Always there was always talk of peace negotiations in the papers but nothing seemed to come of them. There were fewer names in the casualty lists this year, *only* one or two thousand for each month compared to fourteen and fifteen thousand last November and December. And there had only been two lists so far this month. Perhaps the war was truly ending.

Or perhaps it is the calm before the storm.

Kate shivered.

She put her worries about the war aside when she wrote to Tom and told him about her first St Patrick's Day parade. She said their day had begun with a packed Mass at St Paul's that had ended with everyone singing *Hail Glorious St Patrick* so loudly that she thought the roof beams shook. She described the parade itself— the crowds of people with their green ribbons and rosettes, and their Shamrock Day badges, cheering and waving flags; the Irish pipers and the returned servicemen marching; the long line of carriages carrying not only the new Apostolic Delegate and Archbishop Mannix but what seemed like hundreds and hundreds of priests; the schoolboys in their green sashes and the members of the Irish and Catholic organisations behind colourful banners with shamrocks, harps, saints and Irish heroes on them; the decorated wagons and drags with tableaus on the back; and the bands including both the Brunswick and the Coburg Municipal Band.

> It seemed as big as the farewell parades in 1914. We went afterwards to the Exhibition Building and watched the sports. Aunty and your mother ran into dozens of old friends. They had a great time laughing and talking about the old days. I wish you could have been here. We will go

next year. The sun will be shining and it will be a perfect day because you will be beside me.

It was such a pleasant day but there has been nothing but shouting and fist shaking since. It feels almost as bad as the conscription campaigns. The usual nasty whingers who blame Catholics for everything say that the ENEMY flags of Sinn Fein were flown amongst the other flags. And the Young Ireland Society's float was DISLOYAL because it had a tableau that included the names of the men who died during the Easter Week rising. Tomorrow a deputation is going to see the Lord Mayor of Melbourne who approved the march. There are already angry meetings and letters in the papers. I really think they will not be satisfied until Archbishop Mannix is either locked up or deported.

I am leaving to visit my parents tomorrow and I hope all this hullabaloo will be over by the time I get back. I probably will not be able to post any letters to you while I am away but I will send a very long letter when I come back. I am looking forward to the quiet of the farm. And seeing Mum and Dad and my brothers and sisters. I am hoping for another ride in the sidecar of Jim's motorcycle too.

I'll finish now my love and get on with my packing. No matter where I am or what I am doing you are always in my thoughts.

With every ounce of my love

Kate.

XXX

~

Kate sat in the sheltered corner at the back of the house, out of the wind, beside Mum's collection of pot plants. Rufus was asleep on the ground beside her. She closed her eyes against the sun, her book open on her lap, listening to the sounds of the farm: the distant lowing of cows, the cry of a crow overhead, the sleepy cooing of doves in the camellia at the corner of the house. Inside she could hear the chatter of her two youngest sisters as they played with their dolls, the rhythmic thud of the sewing machine as Hannah got on with a blouse Kate had helped her cut out yesterday.

Kate was glad to be home, to be away from stiff-necked opinions and nasty talk. Here people had their different ways and beliefs but they knew their neighbours and relied on each other. Life had its difficulties, not least that it was so cut off from the world, but that was a blessing when the world was in turmoil.

Kate looked up as the door creaked open and Mrs Sheehan came out.

She put her book on the seat of the chair and went to the older woman, kissing her on the cheek.

Mrs Sheehan smiled brightly but sadness lingered in her eyes. 'I've just dropped some Red Cross wool off for Hannah and wanted to say goodbye. You're going back early next week, aren't you?'

'I am. On Monday.'

'Your aunt is such a lovely lady. She writes to me now and again.' She exhaled heavily. 'She told me about poor Bert Wilson.'

Aunty had received a reply from Base Records confirming the name in the casualty list was that of Albert Wilson of the 14th Battalion. Kate felt the injustice of Bert's death—a man, to whom life had given so little, denied his simple dreams.

'And you are still enjoying life down there in Coburg?' Mrs Sheehan asked.

'I am. I love working in the shop and being with Aunty Mary. We went to the St Patrick's Day parade last month. It was good to see Aunty enjoying herself and meeting old friends.'

'Oh, it is a wonderful day. I went once as a girl when my parents took us to visit our grandparents in Melbourne.' She paused as if deciding what to say next. 'Hannah seems to be in good spirits.'

'I think she is. She has a very practical approach to life.'

Mrs Sheehan nodded. 'I could slap Dick Simmonds. Going off and enlisting again. All he's doing is Home Service at the Seymour Camp when he should be home here, helping on the farm. Then to throw Hannah over for a flibbertigibbet up there!'

'Hannah says there are plenty of better fish in the sea,' Kate said. 'She's sewing a new blouse to wear to the fundraising dance for the Red Cross next month. And, she says, she doubts she will have to sit a single dance out.'

'She is right.' Mrs Sheehan laughed. 'Hannah is a pretty girl with those flashing green eyes. And she is one of the best dancers in the district.' She rested her hand on Kate's arm. 'Now my dear, I must be on my way, but let us hope the next time I see you the world is at peace.'

Kate walked with Mrs Sheehan to the front of the house where her horse stood patiently.

They stopped at the corner. 'I saw that beautiful photograph you had taken last year. Is the dress made with the orange silk I gave you?'

'Yes, I finally had it made up.'

Mrs Sheehan cleared her throat. 'And have you been dancing?'

Kate nodded.

Mrs Sheehan did not look directly at Kate's hand, but she would have noticed that Jack's ring was not on her finger.

'Are you...' Mrs Sheehan paused. 'Are you walking out with someone?'

Kate took a quick breath. 'I am. But I haven't said anything to Mum yet. He enlisted last May and is now *somewhere in France*.'

'Oh, Kate.' Mrs Sheehan put her arm around her. 'What is your young man's name?'

'Tom Ryan. He's the son of one of Aunty's friends.'

'I am pleased, Kate. Truly pleased.' She grasped Kate's hands. 'Jack would want you to have a life as happy as you would have had with him.'

Mrs Sheehan's eyes were so like Jack's.

Kate looked past her and saw him as he was in 1914, standing there, leaning against the verandah post, a smile on his face, the smile that was only for her.

Mrs Sheehan gazed towards the verandah. She turned back to Kate, her eyelashes damp. 'I pray every joy comes your way.'

In that moment, with Mrs Sheehan's blessing—and Jack's too—Kate felt certain Tom would come safely home to her.

Mrs Sheehan leant forward and kissed Kate. 'Now, my dear girl, I must go.'

After Kate had waved her off, she went back to collect her book.

Mum was sitting on the chair in the sunshine, flicking through the pages.

Kate braced herself, waiting for her to ask who Thomas P Ryan was—the name Tom had written at the top of the front page.

She looked up at Kate, a line between her eyebrows. 'I don't like some of these stories.'

'It's mostly ghost stories, I'm not sure I'll finish it. I get the shivers thinking about some of them.'

Mum closed the book and stood. 'I'd rather listen to someone telling a story than reading it.' She passed the book to Kate.

'Next time I'm up here, I'll bring a book I can read to you all.'

As Kate held the door open for her, Mum said, 'That would be nice, a story with a happy ending.'

'Definitely with a happy ending.'

Everyone wanted a happy ending but, Kate knew, it was not wise to expect one.

48

April 1918

K ate sat in the armchair opposite Aunty Mary's and listened as she told Kate of all that had happened while she was away.

'I visited Maggie several times and we had an enjoyable dinner at Easter. Annie called around, and Nellie Casey and Reenie. And I had a letter from Brendan. He visited Ireland on his last leave and went to Castlecomer where I was born. There are only cousins left there now but they welcomed him home and he had the grandest of times.' Her smile held a hint of sadness. 'Perhaps the only good thing to come of this war.

'And Fr Divine came to Coburg for a visit. You would remember him—the young Irish priest—he was here when you first arrived. He was invalided home from France nearly a year ago but will be going back soon. The Belgians gave him a medal for bravery.'

Kate nodded. She had not understood it then, putting himself in the way of danger. Now she knew the comfort chaplains brought to the men, and understood how duty made people do things that seemed better avoided.

'Fr Devine will be saying the *De Profundis* for the fallen soldiers in the Anzac Requiem at St Patrick's on Thursday.'

'Will you be going?' Kate asked.

'I'm hoping to.'

'I'll go to early Mass here and keep the shop open for you. I'll get Jack's name included in the prayers for the faithful departed at St Paul's.'

'Oh, I had forgotten to arrange that,' Aunty said. 'When you go to the presbytery, ask them to include Vincent. I have placed an In Memoriam notice in the paper for him too.'

She sighed. 'He was a beautiful boy.'

He was. They all were. Time passed, tears dried, but the pain of their loss would never fade to nothing.

~

Kate was busy in the shop. In the brief silences between customers, she could hear the murmur of Aunty Mary and Annie chatting in the kitchen. It sounded like Annie was reading Aunty a letter.

The shop emptied and Kate opened the newspaper. She hadn't looked at one in the whole time she had been away and had resisted the urge in the four days she had been back. She turned the pages slowly until she reached the war news.

VICTORIOUS AUSTRALIANS

HOW ANZAC DAY WAS CELEBRATED

VILLERS-BRETONNEUX CAPTURED.

She read down the column, trying not to take in the grim detail, in the faint hope they might say which battalions were involved.

She looked up as the bell on the door jingled. Her heart thumped at the sight of the telegraph boy approaching the counter.

He held out an envelope. 'Telegram for Mrs Burke.'

'I'll take it to her.' Kate felt ill.

The boy tipped his cap and left.

Annie sat at the kitchen table, drinking tea, a folded letter on the table in front of her. Aunty stood, a mixing bowl in the crook of her elbow, beating furiously.

They both looked up as Kate came in.

Aunty gasped as she caught sight of the envelope in Kate's hand. Moving slowly, she carefully placed the bowl on the table, and sat heavily in the chair.

Annie froze, her eyes fixed on Kate.

'Read it.' Aunty's voice rasped.

Kate ripped open the envelope and pulled out the flimsy paper. 'It's Brendan.'

Aunty Mary's face drained of colour.

Annie whimpered and covered her mouth with her hand.

REGRET...

Kate's eyes slipped across the page. 'He's wounded.' She read on.

291

...TO ADVISE SON SERGEANT B BURKE WOUNDED.

WILL PROMPTLY ADVISE IF ANYTHING FURTHER RECEIVED.

She gave the telegram to Aunty Mary.

She stared at it, silent.

Annie placed her hand over Aunty's. 'If he was seriously injured, they would say. And you will be notified once he is in hospital.' She opened her eyes wide and blinked. 'And you might even receive a field postcard from Brendan himself.'

Aunty pressed her hands against the table and stood, her head bowed. Her lips moved but no sound came.

Kate and Annie watched her go, her footsteps fading along the passage.

The bell rang in the shop. Kate settled her shoulders, held her head up and walked out.

The rest of the morning was a constant stream of customers. She heard the clatter of baking dishes but didn't get a chance to go back and speak to Annie. At one o'clock, the door locked, the floor swept and the till emptied, she went to the kitchen.

Annie was by the sink, washing up, one of Aunty's aprons over her smart dress.

She turned and said, 'I've baked the cake Mrs Burke was making and I've made oatmeal biscuits and ginger too. I wasn't sure what else she would be baking.'

'That's kind of you, Annie.'

Annie pressed her hand over her mouth, tears running down her cheeks.

Kate wrapped her arms around her, surprised at the strength of Annie's distress. She had no inkling of anything between Annie and Brendan, other than they knew each other.

Annie clung to Kate for a moment, then pulled away, in control of herself again.

'I had no idea you and Brendan—'

'It is nothing like that.' Annie cut Kate off.

She pulled out her handkerchief, wiped her eyes.

'We simply write to each other. I first wrote after Vincent's death and Brendan wrote back and it has continued from there. We talk about things in general. I tell him what I think Mrs Burke might not and I suspect, occasionally, he tells me things he wouldn't say to his mother.'

'Sit down,' Kate said. 'I'll make you a cup of tea.'

'Thank you, but I should go. Mother will be wondering where I am.' Her face crumpled, tears welling again. 'Tell Mrs Burke I will ask the nuns at school to include him in their prayers. A whole convent of nuns praying for Brendan must do some good.'

Perhaps, this time, prayer would.

After Annie left, Kate pulled the kettle to the front of the stove and put the teapot on the hob.

She sat at the table, her head resting in her hands, her eyes shut, murmuring her own prayers for Brendan.

Tom was the only son uninjured of the families she knew well.

Lord, please keep him safe.

~

A week later, Annie slipped into the shop just as Kate was locking up.

'Any news of Brendan?' She looked from Kate to Aunty Mary who was standing behind the counter.

'Yes,' Kate said. 'Aunty Mary received the letter today.'

'I have it here.' Aunty closed the till and locked her cash box. 'It only took a week.' She took the letter out of her apron pocket and handed it to Annie. 'He has a gunshot wound in the left arm and is at the Base Hospital at Étaples.'

'Brendan may be sent to a convalescent hospital afterwards— that's more time out of harm's way.' Annie passed the letter back to Aunty. 'You will think me wicked but I had hoped Brendan's wound would be bad enough for him to be sent home, but not so bad it would make the rest of his life difficult.'

'Oh Annie.' Aunty came around the counter and embraced her. 'I had the same thought myself.'

~

Band music carried along Sydney Road. Kate stood at the edge of the footpath as a detachment of soldiers from the Broadmeadows Camp came into view, led by a brass band. They had marched through Essendon, Moonee Ponds and Brunswick and were now heading back to Broadmeadows. This route march, and many like it, was intended to promote recruiting.

Kate had stood where she was now when she saw her first march in Sydney Road of newly enlisted recruits on their way to the Broadmeadows Camp, young men marching with excitement and pride and no idea of what was ahead. There was that one high-spirited young fellow, handsome and tall, who had broken ranks and kissed as many girls as he could before being hauled back by his mates. Where was he now? Buried at Gallipoli, or in the waters beyond its shores? In the desert at Gaza or Beersheba? In the mud of France or Belgium? Had he come home broken and scarred? Or was he still fighting on?

She watched as they passed by, marching in perfect time, their uniforms neat, their faces stern, but they were not the exuberant innocents she had waved away in December 1914. They knew what awaited them on the other side of the world. Which of the many calls had drawn these men to enlist: duty, love of Empire, love of country, family, mateship, dreams of glory, or revenge? Did some, too, like Joe Kelly, the young fool, still see it as an adventure? He had finally managed to enlist last December but Kate knew, somehow, he would come through alive and grinning.

49

July 1918

Often there was a long wait for letters but, occasionally, Kate received a couple at once or in quick succession. There was the odd field postcard too, printed cards that told her not much more than that Tom was alive.

4th July 1918

My dearest Tom,

I was so pleased to receive your last two field postcards. They told me you were well and gave me your signature to look at.

I have just finished a book called The Scarlet Pimpernel by a Baroness. It was thrilling. I went with Reenie and Annie and the other girls from the knitting group to see the new picture The Hayseeds Come to Town. They are all asking me questions about whether farmers are really like that. I will admit when I first came to Melbourne I was amazed by the tall buildings and all the people and cars in the city like the Hayseed family were. Some parts of the picture were silly but it was fun.

The Our Boys fete at the Town Hall that I mentioned in my last letter raised £550 for the comforts fund. Aunty Mary closed the shop early on the last Friday night so we could go. The children from St Paul's gave a concert that night. Most of the local groups were involved in some way.

The Roll of Honour was on display with gum boughs and wattle-blossom around it. Vince's name is on it. There were all the usual stalls. The sideshows were outside including the ocean wave. I did not go on it. I am waiting for you to come home to do that again. The most popular was a big picture of the Kaiser that people could shoot at. I think that rather than going to war, problems between countries should be worked out by putting politicians in a ring and having them wrestle each other. Wily little Billy Hughes would be sure to tie the Kaiser in knots.

The best part of the whole fete was the coloured lights strung between the poles along Bell Street. It was like something out of a fairy story. And the fact that everyone was working together without the nastiness we have seen over the past couple of years.

Reenie's brother Pat is finally coming home and we are all so happy. He was wounded last October and lost an eye. He has written and said he is fit and well and that before he left he was just handsome but now he is ruggedly handsome and with his pirate's patch and crooked grin young ladies swoon into his arms. Reenie said her father roared laughing at that but Mrs Casey was not amused at all. Pat should be here by early October. Mrs Casey and Reenie are planning a big welcome home.

That is all for this week my love.
You are my first thought when I wake in the morning and my last thought at night. I pray without stopping for your safe return.
With every ounce of my love.
Kate

XXXX

Kate shuffled the sheets of paper covered with her mostly neat writing and folded them. Before the war, the most she had written outside school was a greeting on a card or a short note. And here she was, telling Tom everything she did and thought without embarrassment. She felt that, perhaps, they were coming to know each other better than if their courtship had been in person.

~

The year had begun with the British Prime Minister saying this year would bring victory, and many believed it was possible as the Americans with their vast resources of both money and men had joined the war last year. Newspapers reported the movements of armies, the battles and the long casualty lists, and the victories, but Kate no longer trusted what she read. They were told of victories at Gallipoli too, and what had that achieved except the deaths of thousands of good men?

Each time a letter arrived from Tom, she felt a rush of relief. For a few brief moments it was as if Tom was sitting with her. But the letters were at least five weeks old, if not longer. Who knew what had happened in that time?

26.5.18

My darling Kate,

I received mail yesterday with a whole bundle from you. I feel guilty that I answer with a single letter but often it is written over several days. I enjoy reading the Coburg news and hearing what you are doing. The letters remind me of all that is good and clean in life. They are a salve for the pain of missing you. I hope you received the field post-cards. At least they let you know I am alive. If I even add something as simple as 'With all my love' on the card it will not be sent. They are afraid you might be a German spy and I am writing in code to you. Know that any I send are covered with invisible messages like I am missing you, I love you, I long to hold you in my arms and a thousand other words I wish we had said to each other.

I am not surprised you did not think much of the Sheridan le Fanu stories, they are quite unsettling. You should ask Mother about ghosts, she says she saw one when she was young. Or you could ask her about poor Michael Connelly and the howling dog. Or maybe not, she would know I had put you up to it. Michael was a young boy who lived not far from us. He fell seriously ill with pneumonia and was thought to die. Late in the evening we heard a dog howl three times and Father said, 'Ah, that's poor Michael gone.' And Mother replied, 'God rest his soul'. Then they had us on our knees saying the rosary for the repose of his soul. The next morning Father went over to offer his condolences only to be told the crisis had passed and Michael was on the mend. Not all old beliefs are true.

Apart from being with you, my love, my biggest dream is to have a long hot bath, totally covered in soap with the water up to my neck. We get a bath when we come out of the line and at least a change of underclothes. If we are really lucky, we get a full change of clothing. Otherwise, we have to wait until the mud has dried, then we can knock it off. It is the itchy little passengers that are the greatest nuisance. Even after a bath and fresh clothing they are back in no time. But I promise I will be clean by the time I see you.

It is not all war and working parties though. We had a water carnival the other day. There were punt battles and wrestling, diving and swimming. Some men had proper bathing costumes, most made do with their drawers but a few had no shame and cavorted in the altogether. The officers too and they got dunked and splashed like any private—you cannot tell a man's rank once his uniform is off. A few of the men put on a performance dressed up in top hats and coats and, of course, some in ladies' frocks. A group of French gunners were there too and were splitting their sides at the antics of the 'ladies' like the rest of us.
Well, my love, I'll write again as soon as I can. Keep me in your prayers.
With all my love,
Tom X

50

Each day through August and September the newspapers reported on the Allies' advance, and of the Germans' retreat, the capture of thousands of enemy soldiers and guns. Amiens, Albert, the Somme, Mont St Quentin, Bellicourt—the list of places where they fought seemed endless. Whenever Kate saw mention of Australian troops, she stared at the newsprint as if to force it to tell her more, whether Tom and Brendan's battalions were involved. Brendan had recovered from his wound and was now back with his unit. There was mention too of stiff resistance by the Germans, fierce battles and heavy counter attacks. For Kate the only measure she had of the cost was the lists of casualties. The lists usually appeared twice a week but it was hard to compare them as they now only carried the names of those Victorians who had been killed and wounded. New South Wales would have at least as many and then there was the rest of the country. Whatever the real numbers were, they were bad.

The shop had emptied. Kate could hear the noise of plates and cutlery as Aunty prepared dinner. She flicked through the newspaper, scanning the headlines of the war articles.

HOME LEAVE FOR ANZACS

7000 MEN TO VISIT AUSTRALIA

She rushed out to the kitchen, the newspaper in her hand.

'Have you read this?'

Aunty dropped the breadknife onto the table and pressed her hand to her chest. 'I have not.'

'It's about leave, here in Australia, for the men who left in 1914. That's Brendan! He's coming home.'

Aunty pulled a chair out and sat. 'Thanks be to God.'

Home leave is to be given to Australians for the first time

since the beginning of the war. This magnificent piece of news was given to the Australian soldiers today by Mr. Hughes, who visited the Australian front.

She read quickly, picking out the most important information. 'It looks like, with the time it will take them to get here and back, they will be away from the war for six months.'

'Six months! It could be over in six months.'

'Oh, I hope so.' Kate read further. 'They will be leaving shortly. Three hundred men to begin with, then more will follow. They are leaving during the autumn. Isn't it autumn now over there? They might be home for Christmas!'

Kate stopped and stared out the door. *Home by Christmas.* She heard Jack's voice. That sunny day in September 1914, when he had told her he was enlisting, he had said it would be over quickly and he could be home by Christmas. That was never a possibility but what did they know then of war and its cruelties?

Jack. So strong, so tall, so beautiful and he was lost. All those fine men lost forever.

~

Kate received a letter from Tom written towards the end of July telling her of summer in France, of farms run solely by women and old men, of the wildflowers, and of the mangled wayside shrines, the figures on their crucifixes untouched by war. As she put the letter back in the envelope, she noticed a small wad of paper in the corner. She carefully unrolled it—a single sheet of crumpled paper. It was a letter, undated and unsigned. It was Tom's handwriting but as the letter progressed it became a scrawl.

Kate, the love of my life,
The weather is fine here somewhere in France. I have had a hot bath, a shave and a change of underclothing. And my boots have been fixed. It could almost be Paradise except you are not here. No, I would never want you here. It is only Paradise when compared to Hell. They tell us

Hell is a flaming pit but they are wrong. It is a filthy fog that scratches you raw, a flame filled sky, the air rent with the ear-splitting wailing of mechanical banshees, the earth trembling with the barking of the dogs of war. It is the never imagined sight of what man can do to man. Anyone who has been here has done his Purgatory and his Hell on earth, the ledger ruled off.

I dream of being home, of being clean, of the quiet. I dream of you, of the light in your eyes, of your smile, your scent, the silk of your hair, the softness of your skin. You are the light I am crawling through the darkness to—my life, my sweetness and my hope.

Pray for me, my love.

The words chilled her. *Pray for me.* He must have just come out of some sort of battle. They had days to rest and get cleaned up before they were sent back into something else. But this was more, she was sure of it. He had ended the letter with the words of a prayer, *my life, my sweetness and my hope*, words used to describe the Holy Mother not a mortal woman.

Kate was afraid.

She wrote back that evening. She wanted to say, *Tell me everything, don't keep anything from me*. But perhaps he didn't want to remember or to write of what he was suffering.

9th October 1918

My dearest Tom,

I have just received your letters written in July. I hope all is well with you my darling. Please know that you can tell me anything you want. Anything at all. I wish you were here with me. I wish I could hold you and keep you safe from everything that is wrong. I wish I could kiss away your worries. You are never out of my thoughts. Not for a single moment.

What more could she write? All she could think of was her ordinary days

301

Coburg is carrying on the same as ever. The St Paul's bazaar is on at present. It is running for a fortnight in the Town Hall. I have worked on the refreshment stall with Annie a couple of times. Archbishop Mannix opened it on Friday night and has donated land further up Sydney Road, past the Coburg Hotel, so the parish can build a bigger school.

The government is raising money for another war loan and to help with that they had a tank drive along Sydney Road. It was a monstrous thing like a beast from Hell. I hate to think of you having to face

She stopped. He wouldn't want to hear of that.

She took a new sheet of paper and copied what she had written, except for the last paragraph, and continued on.

Brendan is coming home as one of the 1914 men. Aunty Mary is delighted and happy and relieved. We hope he will be home for Christmas. He has been away such a long time. I wish you were coming home too. There is talk in the newspapers of peace negotiations. I know there has been talk like this from the beginning but this feels real. Peace cannot come soon enough.

I wish you were sitting here beside me and we could wrap our arms around each other and forget the world and all its troubles. I pray for you without ceasing. You are in my every thought, every dream, every breath. I long for the day you come home to me.

With all my love always,

Kate.

XXXXX

51

Much as she wanted to celebrate Reenie's birthday, Kate could not lift the unease that had settled on her with Tom's last letter. She couldn't even make simple decisions such as what to wear to Reenie's party. Aunty had suggested her dancing dress but that was waiting for when she could go dancing with Tom. He *would* come home. She *would* dance with him again.

In the end Kate wore the skirt she had just finished making. It was narrower than usual, in a soft green gabardine with a high wide waistband. She put on the blouse Aunty had given her for her birthday and pinned Tom's brooch above the first button.

When Kate went into the sitting room, Aunty was sitting waiting patiently. She was wearing a dress Kate had never seen before. The cloth was a dark burgundy, so dark it appeared almost black. When Aunty moved there was a slight shimmer of red.

'That dress is a beautiful colour.'

'I bought the material ages ago thinking it was black. I didn't realise until I had almost finished making it. Reenie's birthday and Pat's return are occasions to be celebrated.' She stood and twirled in front of Kate. 'So here it is.'

'You look a picture in it.'

'Ah Katie,' Aunty laughed. ''tis a pure flatterer you are.'

Kate grinned back at her aunt and wished the war was over. Then Aunty could be her old self more often.

Pat had arrived home a week ago and Reenie said it was the best birthday present she could possibly receive. The party, which was Pat's welcome home too, was well underway when Kate and Aunty Mary arrived.

The doors between the dining and the sitting rooms were wide open. The table had been moved into the sitting room and plates of cake, scones, jam tarts and other sweet and savoury treats were set out on it, covered with serviettes. The older ladies had arranged themselves around the room and were already drinking endless cups of tea. Reenie stood, blindfolded, in the middle of the dining room, a crowd of children and young women, and one or two young men, around her playing Squeak, Piggy, Squeak.

Kate and Aunty Mary found Mrs Casey in the kitchen with three young women who were cutting sandwiches. One took the plates of cheese biscuits and shortbread fancies Aunty had brought and said to Mrs Casey, 'You go and enjoy yourself. We can manage here.'

'If you are sure, Maureen.' Mrs Casey untied her apron and hung it behind the door.

She went out into the passage with Kate and Aunty Mary. 'They are such wonderful girls, friends of Reenie's from the Children of Mary. They help with the annual Communion Breakfasts so they know what they're doing.'

After Aunty went off to join the ladies in the sitting room, Mrs Casey looked Kate over. 'You look lovely tonight. That is such a pretty blouse.'

She frowned as a burst of raucous male laughter carried in from the back verandah. 'I don't know how this is going to work. We have Reenie and half the Children of Mary in the dining room playing children's games. And Jerry must have bought out a brewery with the crates of beer he has stacked in the washhouse. Two-thirds of the men in Coburg are out there drinking beer. That includes Clarrie Mitchell, the fiddler, and Ned Ryan who I am sure isn't meant to be drinking at all. And, if they get too drunk, we won't have any music.'

Kate caught her hands. 'But Pat is home, that's all that matters.'

'Oh, Kate. He looks well. He's got that scar but with the eyepatch and the twinkle in his other eye, and the roguish way he now has, he will break hearts. If I were half my age and not his mother, I'd fall in love with him too.' She stopped and stared straight at Kate.

'This war is going to end. Finally. I read in the papers today that Turkey is ready to surrender. And Austria. And we are pushing the Germans back. It *is* going to end.'

Kate nodded. It was true. But Tom and Brendan were still out there—it was not over yet.

Mrs Casey took herself off to sit with the other ladies and Kate went into the dining room and joined in playing Charades. That was followed by singing games and rounds sung unaccompanied. Some of the young men slowly drifted in and sang along.

Clarrie had come in and was tuning his fiddle, Ned waiting beside him, his flute in his hands. Finally, Reenie nodded at them, signalling it was time for the dancing to begin.

Taking a couple of the older girls with her, she went out the back and marched her father, as well as most of the younger men, into the room. Kate overheard the laughing comment that with a few Sergeants-Major like Reenie the war would have been over by the start of 1916.

Reenie looked stunning in a long-sleeved dress made of mulberry velveteen. A bright blue sash was tied at her waist over the floating panels of the loose tunic. Kate would have liked to stay and watch the dancing, the young women in pretty dresses, skirts swirling in a rainbow of blues, greens, pinks and pastels. But if she stayed, she would be asked to dance.

She hurried out of the room, almost colliding with Pat.

'Welcome home, Pat.' She reached up and kissed his unscarred cheek.

'Ah, Kate. It's grand to be home.'

She looked up at him. A scar ran from his forehead down his cheek and lifted the corner of his mouth. His left eye was covered with a dark eyepatch.

He smiled at Kate.

His mother was right. There was a twinkle in his eye as if he still saw much in the world to amuse him.

'Would you care to dance?' Pat asked.

'Thank you, but I'd rather not.'

She was surprised by the disappointment in his face.

'I'm sorry, Pat. I'm not dancing with anyone. I'm waiting for Tom to come home.'

'Tom Ryan is a lucky man.'

It struck her then. He was there with Bert. And, earlier, with Jack. Her eyes filled with tears.

He laid a hand on her shoulder. 'What's the matter?'

She shook her head slowly.

'Come here.' He led her along the passage, stopping by the back door where all that could be heard was the soft rumble of the old men's discussions and the light conversation of the young women in the kitchen.

'Tell me what's wrong.'

She blinked fast. 'You knew Bert Wilson?'

Pat nodded. 'He was a bonzer bloke, a character too. Smoked like a chimney but didn't touch a drop. He'd exchange his rum ration for tobacco or cigarettes.' He grinned. 'And the tongue on him, it sounded hot enough to make paint blister but if you listened to the words, they were made up. They just sounded filthy.' He stopped. 'He was one of the best.'

'How did he die?'

He laid his head back against the wall and groaned. 'You don't want to know any of this.'

'I do,' she said quietly.

'It was chaos, Kate. Utter chaos. And then I was knocked out of the fight.' He stared at the wall above her head. 'I don't know what happened to Bert.'

Kate shivered and crossed her arms across her bosom.

'What about Jack?'

Pat pressed his lips tight, still not meeting her eyes.

'Bert wrote to me. He said it was quick and clean. I'm afraid he only said that to make it easier for me.'

He looked at her, the roguishness gone from his face. He seemed older and harder than his twenty-four years.

'Bert was an honest man. If he said that happened, it happened.'

Kate wasn't sure, but she knew there was no point in pressing him.

'I'll tell you one thing, Kate.' His cheerful mask was back in place. 'Once this is all over, Tom Ryan should get himself home as soon as he can and take you out dancing.' He grinned, a twinkle in his eye. 'Nothing like dancing to help you forget the bloody war.'

He hadn't noticed he'd sworn.

Kate ignored it too. 'Annie Watkins is in there, why don't you dance with her. Reenie says she's very light on her feet.'

He let out a great bark of laughter. 'Oh no, that would be like dancing with Sr Ignatius, my Grade Four teacher.'

Kate frowned, not understanding what he meant.

Pat winked at her and sauntered off to the dining room.

Kate was sure the girls would be falling over themselves to dance with him.

When Tom came home, they *would* dance and dance, and forget the bloody war.

52

November 1918

The war was truly ending. The newspapers were full of the negotiations for peace and reports that ordinary Germans were demanding it. The terms had been drawn up and, it was said, the Kaiser was ready to abdicate. Bulgaria had surrendered a month ago and many thought peace would come quickly after that but, as a newspaper headlines warned, the moment had not yet come.

Despite the negotiations, war was still being fought and men were still dying. The first group of 1914 men was already on its way. Aunty Mary and Kate prayed Brendan was not far behind them. And when the war ended, then it would be Tom's turn to come home.

One fear eased, another replaced it. There was talk of a dangerous new influenza killing old and young, but especially those in their prime. Spreading from America, Europe, and Britain, it travelled from one country to another—to South Africa, India, and New Zealand. It was reported to be on steamers heading for Australia.

Worry never seemed to end.

Aunty came into the shop. 'Would you like to go out the back and have a cup...' She stopped, her eyes narrowed, as she peered towards the window. 'What's happening out there?'

An elderly man and two women stood together in front of the window. Two boys raced past them. Across the road from the shop, a group of women were talking excitedly.

Kate's heart jolted.

Is the war over?

She stepped out into the street.

One of the women smiled, her eyes shining. 'Oh, Miss Burke. The Turks have surrendered.'

'Isn't it wonderful?' the other woman said, her face bright with happiness. 'Austria and Germany will be next.'

The old man leaned heavily on his walking stick. 'My grandson is with the 4th Light Horse. He was in the charge at Beersheba.' His bottom lip quivered. 'He'll be coming home.'

Kate turned away. Why did she want to weep? This was good news.

Back in the shop, she said, 'The Turks have surrendered.'

'Thanks be to God,' Aunty murmured. 'It will be over soon.' She looked across at Kate, now standing behind the counter. 'You go and have a cup of tea. The pot's on the hob, not long made.'

Kate took her cup of tea and went out to the verandah. She stared down the yard at the chooks scratching around in the dirt. There was comfort in the sight of them, their gentle clucking, their calm busyness.

Her eyes were damp. Her throat ached with a helpless sadness. Jack. She remembered his face shining with happiness when he had first visited her here. She remembered him that morning when he had come to say goodbye. He had been her present and her future, the love of her life. An abyss of sorrow lay between that hopeful girl who had loved him and the woman she was now.

Kate placed her cup on the bench and walked over to the patch of grass near the fruit trees where she had danced with Jack under the stars. She could hear his singing, a whisper on the wind. He hadn't stolen her heart away with him. He had left it here, left it to love again.

Goodbye my love. Rest in peace.

The Turkish surrender was all people spoke of through the afternoon. While some people celebrated, for many there was little exuberance although they were quietly pleased. With the loss of those thousands of young men at the Dardanelles, in that first savage blow they had begun to pay the cost of war. It was a shock so profound it reverberated still and made the idea of celebration unthinkable. They were holding their breath, waiting for the final news that the Hun was finished. Then there would be no more unwanted telegrams, no more endless casualty lists.

The war to end war would be over.

~

The days dragged, Austria-Hungary surrendered, the terms for Germany's surrender discussed, and the German army retreated under pressure from the Allies. There was mention of the soldiers of the other countries involved but little about the Australians. Kate hoped that was a good thing.

On Friday, newspapers reported that a German delegation had arrived on the Western Front to meet with the Supreme Allied Commander, Marshal Foch, to conclude an armistice. But there would be no end to the fighting until the armistice was signed.

Rumours ran wild that the Armistice had been signed. Crowds streamed into the city to celebrate. In anticipation, all hotels were closed by military order under the War Precautions Act. Once the official denial was received, they were re-opened at four o'clock allowing the parched drinkers of Melbourne a mere two hours to slake their thirst.

On Monday morning Kate opened the paper to the headlines

THE KAISER ABDICATES
ALLIES' TERMS TO GERMANY
DELIVERED BY MARSHAL FOCH.
ENEMY'S DECISION AWAITED.

But the article beneath warned the Germans' answer would not come for several days.

Aunty walked in to check if the mail had come.

'How much longer can this go on?' Kate asked as Miss White came through the door.

'I'm going mad with the waiting,' Miss White said. 'And it isn't helped when there are rumours like on Friday. All those people in the city cheering, waving flags and singing. And they didn't stop even when they were told it wasn't true.' She rushed on, barely drawing breath. 'And the crowds in the city all weekend, hanging around the newspaper offices, waiting for news.'

'Can you blame them?' Aunty said. 'I'd join them if I didn't have so much to do.'

'You're waiting for your Brendan, aren't you?'

'I am.' Aunty Mary smiled. 'I suppose he won't be here until the New Year.'

'You never know, it might be sooner. If he was on a boat leaving today, he could be here by Christmas.'

'I hope so. Now, if you will excuse me Miss White, I need to get back to the washing.'

That night, as usual, they sat with their knitting and sewing.

'I suppose this won't be needed anymore,' Aunty said.

'What will we do in the evenings?'

'You can sew some pretty blouses or frocks for yourself.'

Kate nodded. She should at least make something new for when Tom arrived home.

Aunty finished her row and put the needles aside. 'Should I get a new outfit for Brendan's return?'

'Oh yes. You have worn black for such a long time.'

'It still doesn't feel right to be wearing bright colours. I was thinking of a smart new jacket and skirt.'

'If we closed early one day, I could come with you.'

'Perhaps not.' Aunty laughed. 'You would talk me into getting something in an outlandish colour or covered in spangles.'

'And it would suit you beautifully. But whatever you get, be sure to buy yourself a new hat too.'

Outside there was a roar of voices and, far off, the ringing of bells.

'This is it.' Aunty jumped up from her chair. 'Grab your coat, it will be cool out there.'

Sydney Road was filling with people shouting and cheering.

Fireworks were going off—crackers and bung-bungs exploding, rockets bursting into brilliant colours against the darkening sky. All the church bells were ringing. Whistles and squeakers sounded, horns blared. There were men playing squeeze-boxes, blowing trumpets, boys banging on tin cans.

Kate threw her arms around Aunty, hugged her tight. They were both bouncing up and down like exuberant schoolgirls, their eyes glistening with tears as they laughed. Around them, others were doing the same: men and women, young and old, children of all ages. Here and there a face showed relief but no great joy.

Annie wove her way through to them. 'Isn't it wonderful,' she shouted. It was almost impossible to hear. She hugged Aunty Mary and stood holding her hand.

Flags were everywhere, large and small—the Union Jack and the Australian flag, the occasional New Zealand, French, Canadian or American flag.

There were bursts of song: *God save the King, Rule Britannia.* The words were roared out. *Soldiers of the King, Keep the Home Fires Burning, God Save the King, Pack Up Your Troubles, Australia Will be There* and back to *God Save the King.* A song would end and a cheer would go up 'Three cheers for our brave boys', 'Three cheers for Foch', 'Three cheers for the Allies', 'Three cheers for Australia'. On and on it went.

Reenie found Kate and hugged her, tears running down her cheeks.

They were all there: Annie's parents, Mr and Mrs Casey, the girls holding Mrs Casey's hands. Nick stood with his brother Pat and Harry Watkins, their arms across each other's shoulders, cheering and roaring out the songs.

Kate caught sight of Ned Ryan and pushed through to him.

'Kate. Tom's coming back.'

'Yes!' Smiling, she shouted, 'Where's your grandmother?'

'She said it was too cold to be wandering in the dark.'

He saw a mate and with a wave disappeared into the crowd.

Just after eleven o'clock the Coburg Municipal Band marched along Sydney Road. Children ran beside the band as the crowd parted to let them through. At Bell Street, where some revellers danced to the music, it turned and marched back to Moreland Road, now led by George Bull, caretaker of the Town Hall, beating his drum.

It was almost one o'clock by the time it reached Moreland Road and the crowd began to drift away.

'I'm going to Mass tomorrow morning,' Aunty said when they got home.

'I'll come with you.' Kate covered her mouth as she yawned. 'But you might need to wake me.'

As Kate drifted towards sleep her cares floated away. The war was finished. Peace had arrived. The waiting was nearly done.

~

15th November 1918

My darling Tom,

It is over and you are coming home. I laugh and I cry at the same time whenever I think of it. Can you find a way to be on the first boat back?

We heard a bit before eight o'clock just on sunset and ran outside. Sydney Road was a mass of people singing and dancing and cheering. It was so noisy. The Band marched up and down the street. There were fireworks and crackers too.

Unfortunately, in the city there was a lot of hooliganism on Monday night and the next day which was made a Public Holiday. Trams were lifted off their tracks and crackers and bung-bungs thrown into the crowds and windows were broken too. Annie, Reenie and I thought of going in on Tuesday afternoon but Harry said it was not a good idea. It was packed by ten o'clock in the morning and although the hotels were closed, he said it might turn rowdy. The Melbourne Town Hall was decorated with red white and blue lights at night. I would have liked to see that. On Wednesday all the churches held thanksgiving services. Aunty Mary closed the shop so we could go to the Mass at St Paul's. We are planning to go to the Botanic Gardens on Sunday as out special celebration of the peace. Aunty and I have been thinking of going for months. She says it is beautiful there.

I will keep writing to you every week. The Red Cross had a raffle a while back of a cake a woman had sent to her son in France. It followed him through France and he only got it a fortnight after he got back to Coburg. I hope most of my letters will have to follow you home.

My darling I will close. It is over and every minute that ticks by is one minute less we have to wait. You are always in my thoughts and in my prayers.

Every breath every heartbeat is yours.

Kate

XXXXXX

53

December 1918

Kate could hear Aunty Mary singing. She was in the sitting room looping paper chains in red and green around the room from the picture rails. She had hung a banner along one wall saying *Welcome Home*, and beside it a collection of homemade cards and drawings from Kate's brothers and sisters. Kate had helped Aunty decorate the front of the shop with strings of colourful pennants and small flags of the Allies. Aunty had set aside another bright banner welcoming Brendan and two Australian flags to hang out the front on the day he arrived home.

Christmas was only a week away and Aunty Mary still had much to do. She had made the pudding in October and left it to hang, expecting to serve it to a couple of recruits who were to come from the Royal Park camp, but the camp was emptying fast and, like a dream come true, it would be Brendan who ate it.

As Kate scooped lemon drops and aniseed balls into separate paper bags for Mrs Johnson, the old lady asked, 'Are you going home now the war's over, Miss Burke?'

'No, Mrs Johnson, I'll be here a while longer giving my aunt a hand.'

Mum had sent a letter asking the same question. Kate had made the excuse that they didn't know when Brendan would be back and she didn't want to leave Aunty Mary by herself over Christmas. Truth was she didn't want to go home at all, but she didn't know how even Aunty would feel about her staying once Brendan was home.

Mr McGregor came through the open door, whistling.

'Lovely day, Miss Burke.' He touched his cap. 'Mrs Johnson.'

'Oh, it is Mr McGregor,' Mrs Johnson twittered. 'A perfect summer's day with that light breeze.'

'And, even better, a few more months and my bag will be half its weight.' He handed Kate three envelopes. 'I'll be skipping along the street as I do my deliveries.'

'Now that will be a sight indeed.' Aunty said from the doorway into the house. 'No mail for me, Mr McGregor?'

'I'm afraid not, Mrs Burke.' He smiled. 'Not long now.'

Aunty beamed. 'Next Monday they are saying.'

'I heard some of the ships have the influenza on them,' Mrs Johnson took her change from Kate.

Kate held her breath. To believe it was over, that the man you loved was almost home, then for him to die of influenza would be unbearable.

'We don't want to talk about that, Mrs Johnson,' Mr McGregor said quickly.

'There is one on the way from Fremantle that has forty cases on board,' Mrs Johnson said as if Mr McGregor had not spoken.

'It had forty cases a fortnight ago and not one of the men has died,' Aunty said. 'And that will be enough talk about influenza.' She turned to Kate. 'I'll stay out here for a while.'

'You are shutting the shop on Monday, I hear.' Mrs Johnson frowned.

'We are. Brendan is arriving home and we are going to meet him.'

'And Tuesday too? A lot of us might need last minute things for Christmas Day.'

'We will be open on Tuesday. And, you never know, Brendan might lend a hand.'

Kate smiled as she walked toward the kitchen. It was the happiest she had seen Aunty since before the war.

Kate sat outside and tore open the most recent of the letters.

28.10.18

My darling Kate,

The days here start with rain and fog but mostly it clears up in the afternoon. Today is fine but not a patch on the sunny Australian days you will be having by the time you get this.

They are keeping us busy. Some of us are working on the farms where we are billeted and I have discovered how hard farming is. The farmers appreciate our efforts and I thought it might help when I finally get to speak to your father.

The officers put on a dinner for us men a week back. A real decent feed with turkey, beef, potatoes, carrots, cabbage and turnips followed by boiled pudding, stewed apples and milk, and beer and tea. As you can see, food is now a major interest of mine. The villagers supplied the crockery for the feast. A football match was held in the afternoon. With the way some of us waddled out after the meal, it is a good thing we were not on the team. We have matches most afternoons with the regimental band providing extra entertainment.

From talk around the place the war is going well. Hoping it is not too long before I will be back with you, my love. Then we can start thinking of the future. I do not want to put the mozz on things by talking too soon. Let us just say I have plans.

Sweetheart, keep me in your prayers, as you are in mine.

Tom XXX

Kate quickly opened the earlier letters and skimmed them. In these, and all she had received in the last two months, Tom seemed to be his usual self. She wondered what had prompted him to write that undated letter. The way it was screwed up, she doubted he had meant to send it to her.

~

Kate stared around at the decorations in the room set aside for welcoming their Anzacs home. Flags and greenery hung on the walls, pot plants in corners, and on the wall facing the entrance a large shield was hung bearing the words, *Thanks, Anzacs*. The room was in the finalising depot in Dodds Street, at the rear of the St Kilda Road Base Hospital and was filled with the families of the soldiers returning on the same ship as Brendan.

The soldiers were to arrive at Port Melbourne at eleven o'clock and be taken by cars on a procession through the city. All along the route, posts were set up by a range of organisations with banners welcoming the men back. Because it was Christmas, instead of the reception and luncheon held by the Lord Mayor of Melbourne, they would be brought straight here and, after some military formalities, could go home with their families.

Aunty was talking to the woman beside her whose husband had left with the second contingent in December 1914. She told Aunty she had been expecting at the time, the little girl born in May 1915. She had called her Elizabeth Anzac. Kate had heard of a number of children called Anzac, and recently, Armistice.

She glanced across at Aunty Mary in her new outfit. She was wearing a skirt with a hemline that skimmed her ankles and a smart three-quarter jacket in charcoal grey, not black, beneath it a white blouse of fine linen, embroidered at the edge of the collar. Aunty had pinned a gold brooch with a red stone embedded in it below the neckline.

This morning, when Aunty came into the kitchen, Kate had said, 'You look beautiful.'

'Get away with you, Kate. At my age?'

'Yes, at your age.' Kate thought she looked ten years younger. And so happy.

Kate doubted this meant that Aunty would be wearing brighter clothing from now on. This outfit would only be worn for the weddings and baptisms that would come now the war was over.

Time dragged on and conversation flagged. Some sat still, staring into space; others huffed and wriggled in their chairs; those with children struggled to keep their offspring's behaviour and whining in check.

The noise in the room surged with the sound of engines, the slam of motor car doors and male voices outside.

The men came in, a pool of khaki spreading through the room. They were still tall fine-looking men. There was a hardness in their faces where there had been eager excitement in 1914. Now, their faces softened as they caught sight of those they had left to wait and pray.

Kate and Aunty Mary stood, staring across the room, watching every man who came through the door. Around them women were weeping, throwing their arms around their sons, their husbands, brothers, and sweethearts, holding them tight.

Then Kate saw him. He had stopped near the doorway and was slowly scanning each section of the crowd.

She raised her hand, waving, bouncing up and down on the balls of her feet, calling his name.

A great smile split his face as his eyes moved from Kate to his mother standing still and silent. A single tear slipped down Aunty's cheek.

He pushed through the crowd and folded his mother into his arms. When Brendan broke their embrace, Aunty stepped back and placed her hand against his cheek. 'My boy, my beautiful boy.'

And wound through their joy, Kate saw a whisper of the loss they would not speak of yet.

Brendan turned to Kate. She laid her hand on his forearm and, on tiptoes, reached up and kissed him on the cheek. 'It's wonderful to have you home, Brendan.'

He squeezed her hand. 'It's wonderful to be home at last.'

Young women in white uniforms with a red cross on the bib of their aprons moved through the crowd. They were members of the Red Cross Voluntary Aid Detachment, volunteers who worked at whatever was needed, often in convalescent and rest homes. Today the young women were handing out cups of tea or cordial and offering sandwiches and cake to the soldiers and their families.

Aunty sat with her cup of tea in her hand, intent on every word Brendan said.

He had taken off his hat and ran his fingers through his hair.

'There was a dust storm when we arrived. I was neat and tidy when I got off the ship—now I'm covered with grit.'

Kate watched, amused, as he took a slice of chocolate cake offered by a very pretty VAD. He already had a slice of the same cake on the saucer of his cup.

'Was there a crowd waiting?'

He nodded as he bit into the cake. It was gone in three bites.

'The whole placed was packed. There were women giving out gifts of all sorts, even tossing them into the cars. I've got sweets.' Holding his cup and saucer in his left hand, he opened one of the breast pockets on his tunic with the other and took out a small tin of caramel toffees. 'Here you go, Kate, a present for you.'

He passed her his teacup as well.

He lifted the flap on his haversack and carefully removed a small bunch of violets. 'These are for you, Mum.' He handed them to his mother and kissed her cheek.

She closed her eyes and breathed in the scent.

When Aunty looked at him, Kate could see in her eyes so many feelings entwined: relief and joy, disbelief and wonder, longing and sadness.

'And I even got a kiss with those,' he raised his eyebrows and grinned, 'and not on the cheek.'

From his other pocket he produced three packets of cigarettes. 'And these are for me.'

Kate laughed and handed back his cup of tea.

She had last seen Brendan six years ago, the year before his father died and they had come up to spend Christmas on the farm. He had been twenty-one, quiet and thoughtful but with the same twinkle of mischief Aunty Mary and Vince had. Now he was twenty-seven and seemed much older.

The sleeves of his uniform showed the story of his long years away. Below the Australia badge on the end of his shoulder straps was his brown over red 7th Battalion colour patch, a brass A in the centre showing that he was one of the original Anzacs who had served at Gallipoli. Beneath that were his three sergeant's stripes. On the lower right arm he wore his five overseas service chevrons, a red showing he had served in 1914 and four blue for each remaining year of service. He wore three good service chevrons on his lower left arm and below a single perpendicular strip of now tarnished gold braid showing he had been wounded once.

His service could be read like a book and anyone with an ounce of understanding could imagine what he had been through. Once he had put his uniform off, those who loved him would remember what he had done and what had been done to him, but who else would know his story?

'We wanted to make sure we were here when you arrived so we didn't watch the procession,' Kate said. 'Was it good?'

'There were hordes of people everywhere, waving and cheering. I even noticed a group from Coburg near the corner of Collins and Elizabeth Streets. They had a big banner with a picture of the new lake on it. Looks a lot flasher than when I was last there.'

He drained his tea cup. 'Mum, you're not saying much.'

'Oh, I have plenty to say. But I have no idea where to start.'

The soldiers were then called in for their medical examination and assessment.

The wait wasn't long before Brendan's name was called.

After he walked away, Kate said, 'Brendan looks well.'

'He does,' Aunty answered and lapsed back into silence.

Kate realised Aunty Mary was thinking of Vince. He should have come home too. Kate's heart twisted for her aunt. No joy would ever be simple again.

It seemed no time at all and Brendan was back.

'They say I'm fit as a fiddle. I'm officially on leave and once that's over, I'm a free man.' He slung his kitbag over his shoulder. 'And now I'm going home.'

Aunty stood and shook herself out of her reverie. 'We can try to catch a cab in St Kilda Road.'

'I'd rather walk to the station and catch the train,' he grinned at his mother, 'if you are up to it.'

'Up to it, indeed! I'm not in my dotage yet.'

He laughed and Kate could see the glint of mischief in his eyes.

'I want to see the way the city has changed while I've been away.'

'Once we're home, what will you do first?' Kate asked.

'Take a long hot bath and get out of these,' he tugged at the sleeve of his tunic, 'and become a normal man again—a simple grocer.'

When they got back Brendan had his bath and put on the clothes he hadn't worn for over four years. He took a walk around the backyard and stood staring at the vegetable garden, then went into the shop and made a similar inspection. He kept his thoughts to himself.

Aunty cooked the meal he said he had dreamt of while he was away—a large steak, mashed potatoes, cabbage and bacon made as only Aunty Mary could. Afterwards Brendan sat outside as the daylight faded, smoking his cigarettes. He didn't finish the bottle of beer Aunty had bought for him but took himself to bed early.

Kate and Aunty Mary said the rosary before they went to bed, the Joyful Mysteries in thanks for Brendan's safe return.

Kate sat upright, startled out of her sleep.

Brendan groaned and muttered, his bed creaking loudly as he tossed about.

Aunty, lying awake beside Kate, stared into the darkness.

'Should we do something?' Kate whispered.

'Not unless he starts screaming or stumbling round,' Aunty said quietly. 'He's having a nightmare.'

Kate, aware of the beads moving through Aunty's fingers, prayed that, in time, this too would pass.

54

K ate set the tea tray on the sideboard and began to pour the tea. After Mrs Casey had handed the cups to the women in the sitting room, Kate carried around a plate of shortbread biscuits, iced and topped with a glace cherry.

'Ooh, shortbread fancies.' Mrs Ryan, took one and placed it on her saucer. 'Did you make these, Kate?'

'Aunty Mary made them. She has been busy baking since Boxing Day.'

'And every minute of it a pleasure,' Aunty said.

'Ah, it would be, Mary.' Mrs Ryan sighed. 'I wonder how long until I can do this for Tom.' She patted the seat beside her. 'Will you sit with us, Kate, and have a cup of tea too?'

'I will a little later. I need to give Annie a hand in the kitchen.'

Annie was busy making sandwiches: cheese and pickle; cheese, tomato and lettuce; thinly sliced ham and tomato; even cucumber.

She glanced up at Kate. 'I've almost finished these.'

The music of a fiddle accompanied by a flute carried through the open window.

'Then you should go outside and dance with Brendan.'

'I'll do the dishes first.'

'Leave them, you've done enough tonight. I'll do them later.'

'No, I'll do them.'

Kate knew that tone. There would be no arguing with Annie over this.

Kate put the plates of sandwiches on the table in the dining room and placed a lightly damp serviette over each plate. There was a fine selection of food: sandwiches, cakes, pastries, fruit salad, jellies, cheese sticks and savoury scones. Not all of it was Aunty's work; many of the women had brought a plate. She closed the door behind her and went outside.

It puzzled her that Annie seemed to be avoiding Brendan. She and Harry had called in early in the afternoon of Christmas Eve. No one would think Brendan and Annie had been writing to each other for well over three years. Kate had seen the longing in Brendan's eyes when he looked at Annie. Other than a peck to his cheek, Annie had been strangely formal, as if they were strangers.

Reenie had shown no such restraint, almost throwing herself at Brendan, laughing and crying, a joyful welcome that acknowledged his immense loss. The welcome he needed.

She glanced along the verandah to where Ned Ryan was standing playing a flute, accompanying Clarrie Mitchell on the fiddle. The music made her want to dance but she would keep her promise that the next time she danced it would be with Tom.

It was a pity that the men, no matter how old or young, were more interested in each other's company. Talking animatedly and laughing, they sat on chairs, or stood along the path beside the washhouse where Brendan had placed the bottles of beer in cold water in the troughs.

Reenie and several other young women were standing together near the verandah, watching the musicians, and tapping their feet. Perhaps, if they danced together, it would shame the younger men into dancing with them. The children were dancing, skipping and twirling each other about; two little girls and a boy were step dancing in a line. The boy made her think of Tom. She wondered what his Christmas had been like. Had he written to her on Armistice Day or soon after? When would that letter arrive?

Brendan moved around the yard hanging lamps on hooks on the outhouses. He had hung Chinese lanterns along the clothes line. With the sun now setting, the yard looked magical.

He stepped on to the verandah and stood beside Kate, gazing down the yard. 'It's going well.'

'It is. We'll serve supper around nine o'clock. I know it's early but Aunty Mary said those over there,' she nodded towards the men near the washhouse, 'will need something to soak up the beer.'

Brendan laughed. 'She hasn't bought enough beer for it to need soaking up.'

'Oh! I doubt they will be too happy with cups of tea.'

'No need to worry. I had one or two extra crates delivered when Mum was around at Mrs Ryan's this afternoon.'

One or two probably meant four or five, if not more. 'How will you explain all the empty bottles?'

'I'll say it's a miracle, like the loaves and the fishes.'

Kate grinned. 'She's sure to believe you.'

'Kate, I want to thank you for being here with Mum. She said she wouldn't have got through it without you.'

Kate closed her eyes and exhaled slowly. 'I would never have got through it without her.'

Brendan put his arm around her shoulder and pulled her against him. 'I pray none of us ever have to go through that again.' There was a creak in his voice.

Kate looked up. He was staring into the deepening shadows. Did he see Vince there? Kate knew, for both Brendan and Aunty Mary, Vince's memory must linger in every corner of the house.

He cleared his throat. 'What do you want to do now? Go back home?'

Nothing would be gained by being cautious and polite. 'If I could do exactly what I want, I would stay here.'

'I've been thinking. I have plans for this place. Next week, I'm putting us down to be connected to the electricity. Busy times are coming but Mum would like things to go back to what they were before Dad died—her looking after the house and only coming out to the shop if it was very busy, or to talk to those customers who come in for a chat or who try the patience of a saint.'

'Mrs Johnson?'

'Mrs Johnson, just to begin with. But we need more than one person in the shop for that. If you stay, you could keep working in the shop and when it's quiet help Mum out the back.'

'Oh Brendan, I would love to stay.' She caught his hand and stretched up, kissing him on the cheek.

'Then,' he smiled. 'At the end of next year, we can think about what to do next.'

'The end of next year?' It wasn't for ever—she would have to go back home.

'Tom Ryan will be back so I imagine you will have other plans.'

She smiled at him. She hoped so. But now and again, that sly voice still whispered.

Don't think you know what the future holds.

Ned and Clarrie had taken a break and began to play again.

'Would you care to dance?' Brendan asked. 'It might encourage some of those slackers over there to lead the young ladies out.'

'It's not me you should be dancing with.'

He lifted an eyebrow.

'Go in and ask Annie.'

'I don't know...' his voice trailed off.

'Whyever not? I know you are sweet on her. Whenever she's in the same room, you can't keep your eyes off her.'

'But I doubt I'm what Mrs Watkins has in mind for Annie.'

'It's not Mrs Watkins you will be asking to dance.'

'I don't know.'

'Wait here. And don't you dare move.'

Annie was vigorously scrubbing the kitchen table and clearly had no plans of leaving the kitchen tonight.

Kate walked in. 'Take off your apron and come with me.'

Annie did not break her rhythm. 'I'm waiting to put the sausage rolls in.'

'They don't need to go in yet.' She untied Annie's apron.

Frowning, Annie stopped her scrubbing and went and washed her hands.

Kate led her out onto the verandah. To her relief, Brendan was still standing there.

Annie and Brendan stood, silent. Brendan was watching her, but Annie had lowered her eyes.

Brendan's longing was palpable. But with Annie, Kate had no idea what she felt.

Good heavens, what is wrong with them?

Someone needed to give both of them a jab with a cattle prod.

Kate grabbed both their hands and forced them together. 'Now go out there and dance and set an example for the rest.'

She watched them walk out, turn and finally look in to each other's face.

Well, that will be all over town by ten minutes past Mass tomorrow.

Ned and Clarrie sped up their playing.

Kate went to Reenie. 'You and the rest of the girls should go over there and drag a few of those loafers out for a dance while they can still stand up.'

'I'll be in that,' Reenie laughed.

'But a girl can't ask a man to dance,' Rita gasped. Rita was now eighteen, thin rather than willowy, and with her pale eyes and mousey hair, she seemed more a girl than a young woman.

'She can if she has a tongue in her head,' Kate said. 'If it makes it easier, pretend it's leap year day.'

The argument convinced her, or realising she would be left by herself, Rita rushed off after the rest.

Kate went into the kitchen, finished cleaning the table and made another pot of tea.

She looked out the kitchen window, watching the dancing for a few moments. She was surprised to see Rita dancing with Pat. She must have elbowed a number of other girls out of the way to claim him first. Pat looked to be enjoying himself.

Kate carried the teapot into the sitting room.

'Is there dancing out there now?' Mrs Casey asked.

'Yes, finally.'

She stood up. 'Come on, Dymphna,' she said to Mrs Watkins. 'We have to make the old men dance for their suppers too.'

Kate poured herself a cup of tea and sat beside Mrs Ryan.

'Don't you want to dance, Kate?' Aunty Mary asked.

'Not at the moment. I'm content here.' Where no young man would dare come and ask her to dance.

Later, when the dancing had given way to singing, Kate walked towards the back door. One of the men was singing *Danny Boy*.

Brendan was seated among the men, a glass of beer held on his thigh. His head was thrown back as he sang into the silence.

> *The summer's gone and all the roses falling*
> *It's you, it's you, must go and I must bide...*

The silence continued after he ended.

Brendan stood and drained his glass. He strode down the yard and was swallowed by the darkness.

Kate glanced at Annie. She was talking to Rita, unaware of anything else.

Reenie stared after Brendan, anguish in her face.

Kate walked into the house, into the bedroom. She stood in the shadows, wracked with sobs. Not for herself but for Brendan and his grief that asked for no comfort, that he could not let heal.

1919

In the brief hush that followed after the last clear notes of the bugles had died away could be heard a sound of quiet sobbing...

The Age 21 July 1919 p.10

55

They spent New Year's Day quietly at home. The day after, Brendan opened the shop to a steady stream of customers, some making small purchases, others buying nothing, all coming to welcome him back. He looked to be in his element standing behind the counter in his apron, exchanging lighthearted banter with the customers.

Aunty Mary spent little time in the shop. She busied herself with a belated and thorough 'spring' clean. Brendan arranged for a boy to do the deliveries twice a day and although Kate was in the shop, she had less to do. She feared a time would come when he realised she wasn't needed at all.

And customers like Mrs Johnson didn't help matters. She came in for her weekly bags of lemon drops and aniseed balls and, even if Kate was free, she waited until Brendan could serve her. She was all smiles with him, as good as fluttering her eyelashes.

'I think she's sweet on you,' Kate said.

Brendan rolled his eyes. 'She's old enough to be my grannie. She was worse with Dad and it used to make Mum so cranky.' He pulled a ledger from beneath the counter. 'I'm going out the back for a while to do some arithmetic.'

'I'll call you, if it gets busy.'

Mr McGregor came up to the counter with a bundle of letters.

'Good morning, Mr McGregor. It's a lovely day out there by the look of it.'

'It is indeed, Miss Burke. And your day will be made even lovelier by a nice green envelope in this lot.'

She smiled at him as she took the letters, hoping it would not be long before there would be no need for letters at all.

As the shop was now empty, Kate opened her letter as soon as he had gone. It had taken more than two months to get here but Kate supposed every single soldier had written a letter on the eleventh or the twelfth of November.

12.11.18

Well, my love,

The war is finally over and I will be coming home to you. We have not heard when but the old hands say it will probably depend on when we arrived. I suspect I will have to wait.

I suppose I can now tell you where we are but if there are great blocks blacked out you will know the censors are still reading our letters. We have been here at a place called Huppy for over a month, since we withdrew from the fighting around Bellicourt. It is a relief knowing we will not have to go through all that again. Huppy is in Picardy and is a farming area. It has a chateau, not the sort of place where we ordinary soldiers are billeted. There is a fine old church. The whole place must have been beautiful before the war.

Yesterday the usual football game was played in the afternoon and the band entertained us. When news of the Armistice was announced there was some cheering but not much excitement, most of us were simply relieved the war was over. Afterwards we were given free beer. No one complained about that. And a battalion concert in the YMCA hut which was a bit of fun.

We were hoping for a day off today but all we got was a bath, a change of clothing and time to write a letter. They have some nonsense organised this afternoon. I hope we are done with musketry and bomb throwing.

I have only just received your letter dated 9th October and by your comments you must have received a letter I never meant to send. I thought I had thrown it away. I am deeply sorry you had to read my ravings. I was pretty cut up at the time as a couple of mates had copped it in our last effort, one right beside me. Here there is little time for mourning.

Your letters are a balm to me. Now, with the madness of war over, I will be coming home and we can wrap our arms around each other and forget everything.

Summer is approaching for you but we will see another freezing winter. We have already been issued with our winter uniform and two new winter blankets. And to complete the luxury, fresh straw for our palliasses.

Apart from a hot bath in the privacy of the washhouse at home, I am looking forward to a soft bed. But I will have the chance to experience that when I go on leave. I might be getting some UK leave. If I do, I will send you a pretty postcard from there.

In the faint hope this arrives before the end of the year

MERRY CHRISTMAS

HAPPY NEW YEAR

I hate the waiting but, as you have said before, every minute that ticks by is one minute less we have to wait. See, I know your letters off by heart.

Keep safe my darling and pray for time to fly.

With all my love,

Tom XXX

'Good news?' Brendan asked as he walked back in.

Kate nodded. 'He is well and they were given free beer on the day the Armistice was signed. He says it might be a while before he comes home as they will probably be sent home in the order they arrived. I suppose that's fair.'

'Someone who arrived in 1915 or '16 would be pretty cut up to see someone who arrived six months ago leave before him.' He locked the till and pocketed the key. 'Mum has dinner ready.'

As he stood aside for Kate to go into the house, a lad raced in, red-faced and gasping. 'Miss Burke.'

'Yes, that's me.'

'Mrs Ryan says come quick.' He stood panting. 'Something's happened.'

'What?' Kate snapped.

'Don't know, Miss. But she looked bad.'

Kate gave a small whimper and glanced at Brendan.

'Go.'

Kate ran out the door and was halfway up the street before she realised she was still wearing her apron and had neither hat nor gloves on. It was too late to remedy now.

When she got to the house, the front door was open.

'Mrs Ryan,' she called from the doorway.

'Kate, I am in here.'

The old lady was half-lying on the sofa in the sitting room, her hand pressed to her chest.

Kate gulped. 'What's wrong?'

Mrs Ryan pointed to a slip of paper lying on the table beside the sofa.

Kate's stomach turned over.

But the war is over.

She snatched up the telegram. 'It says injured not wounded.' She was thinking aloud. 'It doesn't say serious. That's good.'

Mrs Ryan's breathing was loud and rapid.

Kate knelt beside her. 'Whatever has happened, I am sure he will recover.' She was saying it more from hope than conviction. 'In a week or two you will get a letter telling you where he is and what's wrong with him.'

Mrs Ryan grasped Kate's hand and looked up at her, fear in her eyes. 'My heart is racing.'

'You lie here quietly. I'll make you a strong cup of tea.'

When Kate came back, she put the cup on the side table. 'Would you like a nip of brandy in it?'

'I would, thank you. It is in the sideboard.'

Kate found it and poured two small splashes in. She returned the bottle to the sideboard and collected her own cup of tea from the kitchen.

Mrs Ryan was now sitting up, sipping her tea. Kate sat in the chair opposite her.

'Oh, Kate, I feel much better. I thought I was at death's door.' She pressed her hand against her breastbone. 'My heart has calmed down.' Her hands still shook.

'Perhaps you should visit the doctor.'

Mrs Ryan nodded. 'I might, but the doctors are very busy.'

Kate knew she wouldn't go unless someone took her there. She would talk to Aunty Mary about it.

'This influenza is a worry,' Mrs Ryan pressed her fingers against her forehead as if she had a headache. 'So many people are dying overseas. I heard it is very bad in New Zealand. And it is even on the ships bringing soldiers home to Australia.'

The newspaper reports of the numbers dying overseas brought back the casualty lists of the war. Kate pushed the thought away.

'But the men are quarantined when they arrive and they are given good medical care. I read that it is waning in England and the government is confident they have everything under control here and we have escaped it.' But Kate knew governments didn't always tell the truth.

She jumped at a sudden knock at the door. 'Kate? Maggie?'

'We're in here, Aunty Mary.'

Kate made a fresh pot of tea and left Aunty talking with Mrs Ryan. Despite her reassurances to Mrs Ryan, Kate was uneasy. She hoped whatever was wrong with Tom, it could be easily mended.

Pray for time to fly.

And she needed to pray its flight was smooth.

The letter, eight days later, told them Tom was in the Southwark Hospital in London and that he had broken his leg a few days after the New Year—he must have been on leave. Kate wished she knew more. She hoped the reports of the influenza waning in England were correct and Tom was in no danger of it.

The belief Australia had avoided it seemed misplaced. There

were troubling reports of soldiers dying in quarantine. There was talk too of a Coburg lad who worked in the city having caught it and passed it on to his family. But still the government said this was ordinary influenza not the dangerous pneumonic type some were calling Spanish influenza. If they were wrong...? Kate shivered.

~

By late in the month, it was obvious that the Spanish influenza had arrived. There were seven confirmed cases in Coburg and more in other suburbs and towns. Free inoculations were offered at the Town Hall and they all went at different times. Kate talked Mrs Ryan into coming with her. The doctor explained to them that an inoculation wouldn't stop a person getting influenza but it should make the disease less severe.

Finally, the State Government declared the Spanish influenza was present in Melbourne. All theatres, picture theatres, music and concert halls were closed as well as the schools. People were advised to get inoculated, to wear masks and to avoid crowds whether they were in the streets or on trains or trams. Parties were to be avoided and meetings limited.

That night, Aunty Mary, Brendan and Kate sat around the table in the dining room with the evening paper trying to work out how the newly announced emergency measures would affect them and the shop.

'Should we wear masks in the shop?' Aunty asked.

'I've seen a couple of people wearing them,' Kate said. 'They look thick and unpleasant to wear.'

'Rather that than being dead.' Brendan's voice was harsh. 'We should all wear them.'

'Ready-to-wear masks are available at Myer's and Craig's in the city,' Aunty Mary said. 'I'll go in tomorrow morning, after the rush of everyone getting to work, and buy a few. I'll try Craig's first as they are closest to the railway station.'

'When we go in and come out of the shop,' Kate said, 'should we gargle with that mixture they say we should use before leaving home and after coming back? Boric acid, salt and bicarbonate of soda in warm water.'

'Yes, that is a good idea.' Brendan nodded. 'There's sure to be a run on disinfectant—I'll see if we can get in more of that.' He paused, his forehead furrowed. 'Eucalyptus too. I doubt we'll be treading on the Dispensary's toes.' He looked from Aunty to Kate. 'If you think of anything else that might be of use, let me know.'

'Camphor,' Aunty said. 'People will want to make up camphor bags. They've always been used to keep infection at bay.'

'You could sew some little bags for the camphor, Mum, for those who don't want the trouble of doing it themselves.'

He really was a businessman. Kate could imagine him one day, middle-aged and prosperous, owner of a string of shops. He would find a way to make his shops places everyone felt they should go.

When Aunty returned from her shopping trip the next day, she was wearing a mask. She placed two parcels on the kitchen table and went out the back to scrub her hands.

'There were people wearing them everywhere in the city,' she said when she came back in, her mask now removed. 'Even in the shops and on the train. Plenty not wearing them, too,' She unwrapped the paper on one of the parcels and took out a mask. 'The young lady who served me in Craig's said they recommend changing them three times a day.'

'Do you then throw them out?' Kate asked.

Aunty passed a mask to Kate. 'You disinfect and wash them and hang them in the sunshine to dry.'

Kate tied it on. The mask was bulky, six layers of muslin. She gasped, felt as if she was suffocating. She closed her eyes and forced herself to take a slow deep breath. It wasn't so much the difficulty in breathing—it was fear of what would come next.

'Kate! Are you all right?'

She opened her eyes. 'They will take some getting used to.'

'The lass in the shop said to sprinkle eucalyptus on it. Some people add creosote or phenyl but that might make them very unpleasant.'

Aunty unwrapped the second parcel. 'I bought some butter muslin and tape to make more myself. I'll start on it straight away.'

Kate picked up another mask. 'I'll take one out to Brendan.'

As he tied it on, a man came in that Kate hadn't seen before.

He took one look at Brendan and laughed. 'You look like one of those Gippo sheilas in Cairo.'

'Better than dead of the influenza, Stan.' There was no warmth in Brendan's eyes. 'Now what can I get you?'

'The missus wants six eggs and half a pound of tea.'

While Brendan was getting the eggs and the packet of tea, Stan turned to Kate. 'If your brother is wearing these mask things, I suppose I should too. He knows what he is doing. He was the best man to have beside you in a stoush. There was this time on the Peninsula—'

'Edwards!' Brendan spoke over him. 'Enough!'

He snapped to attention and saluted. 'Yes, Sergeant Burke.'

In the silence that followed, the rhythmic whirr and thud of Aunty's sewing machine carried out from the house.

Brendan handed Stan his shopping. 'If you want masks, I'll have a few for sale tomorrow.'

When he had gone, Brendan said, 'The man always was a fool. It's a miracle he made it back at all, let alone without a scratch.' He frowned. 'We were at school together. He knows I don't have a sister.'

'I don't mind if people think you're my brother.'

'And I can't think of a better sister.' He smiled at her, something Kate noticed he now rarely did.

56

February 1919

Over the next few days even more emergency measures were announced. Libraries and art galleries were closed and indoor public meetings of greater than twenty people were prohibited. And, although it was not an order from the government, railway authorities decided there was to be no waiting under the clocks at Flinders Street Station.

Day by day, the number of those with influenza grew. Only the most serious cases were now admitted to the large public hospitals. The Exhibition Building was set up as an emergency hospital and local councils were encouraged to establish their own. Coburg's hospital was to be in the High School beside the recreation reserve. The Australian Comforts Fund and the Red Cross were helping to equip it. Local residents were asked for donations of furniture and of money.

Kate saw a notice in the local newspaper saying that helpers were needed for these hospitals, not only nurses and members of the Red Cross Voluntary Aid Detachment but anyone who was willing to help. She felt she hadn't done enough during the war unlike Aunty Mary with her knitting and letter writing to soldiers and their families, especially to anyone who had lost a son. Or like Reenie and Annie with their knitting and fundraising. All she had done was a bit of sewing and knitting but mostly she had wallowed in misery and worried about her own concerns. Perhaps this was her chance to make up for it.

At the end of their evening meal, as they chatted about the day, Kate said, 'They are looking for people to help with the nursing at the emergency hospital at the High School. I might offer to work there.'

'What?' Aunty Mary gasped.

'No!' Brendan slammed his hand on the table.

Kate started back in her chair, stunned by his anger.

'You are not a nurse.'

'They give you some training and I have a First Aid certificate.'

He crossed his arms and glared at her, his mouth a stern line.

'Oh Kate, why?' Aunty groaned.

'I need to do something. Everyone has worked so hard and I've drifted along. I've knitted socks and made shirts and that barely counts at all.'

Brendan stood. 'It bloody well does count.' He walked out into the yard. A moment later the side gate slammed loudly behind him.

'You have done as much as anyone,' Aunty said.

'I haven't. Look at Reenie and Annie, they have done so much more than I have. I haven't helped anyone.'

'You've helped me.' Aunty's voice wavered. 'I would never have survived these last years without you. Is that not enough?'

'I would always have done that.'

'Please don't do it, Kate. I couldn't bear to lose you too.'

'You won't lose me. Nothing is going to happen to me.'

Aunty closed her eyes and slowly shook her head.

Kate stood and began collecting their plates.

'Leave that. I'll do the dishes by myself tonight.'

It was like a slap. They had been doing the dishes together each night for four and a half years.

Kate went out and sat on the verandah. It had not occurred to her that they would be upset. But she wasn't going to die—she was inoculated and she would do all the right things, wear her mask, gargle, wash her hands. Even wear a horrible-smelling camphor bag around her neck.

She walked down the yard. Above her the vivid orange, pink and mauve gently faded as the light disappeared.

'Kate.'

She turned. She hadn't heard Brendan come back. In the fading light, his face looked as hard as granite.

'Do you have any idea what you are risking? You could die.' He spat the word, a harsh bitter thing. 'You think you won't—we all thought that, but we died all the same. In our tens of thousands.'

He pressed his mouth tight shut as if holding back more than anger.

Jack had not thought he would die.

'This flu is vicious. Hundreds of thousands are dead overseas. It is just beginning here. We might only have one, maybe two dozen cases here in Coburg but Brunswick has over a hundred, thirty-nine of them yesterday. And people are dying, even doctors and nurses. Why would you deliberately put yourself in the middle of it all?

'And do you have any idea what this will do to my mother? She loves you like a daughter. If you died, it would break her heart. Hasn't she suffered enough?' He turned away but swung back. 'All those socks, scarves and shirts didn't mean nothing to us. They kept us warm and it was good to have something new and clean occasionally. People put notes in them wishing us well—women, and men, people of all ages, even little boys knitted them for us. It showed us that although we were in Hell, we weren't forgotten.'

He groaned and looked up into the night sky. 'Any version of Hell a pulpit thumping Redemptorist missioner could dream up is a children's picnic by comparison. We did what we must but in the quiet moments we dared to dream of home, thinking of what we had left behind, hoping we would have it back.' He stared straight at Kate. 'So you imagine what it will be like for Tom Ryan. He is waiting, dreaming of coming home, dreaming of you. And he arrives home only to be told you are lying up at Fawkner, three months dead, because you deliberate put yourself in harm's way. That you cared more for playing at nurses than for him.'

He went back to the house, slamming the wire door behind him.

Kate let go of the sob she had held back as he spoke. Her arms wrapped tight around herself, she walked slowly to the verandah. Her sobs, now silent, shuddered through her.

She stared down the yard. Was the idea of nursing at the hospital just a whim? She was no nurse despite her First Aid certificate. She would be helping rather than nursing—emptying chamber pots and basins of vomit and doing laundry for all she knew. Was doing that worth adding to what Aunty Mary already had to bear?

Brendan was right. It would be the cruelest thing she had done to Tom.

Kate shivered and hugged herself tighter. The heat of the day was gone, the stars glittered, the world quiet but for the rattle of a tram along Sydney Road.

The house was silent, not a light on. Kate closed the back door and went to bed.

She lay beside her aunt. 'Aunty Mary,' she whispered.

Aunty did not answer.

Kate sighed. Why had she not considered how this would affect those around her? Even Mrs Ryan. Ned was with her, but he was at work all day and often out at the weekend. She had come to rely on Kate and Aunty Mary. Kate visited every second day, Aunty every other. That would be another burden laid on Aunty if Kate went to work at the hospital.

She tried again. Aunty did not stir. Kate was sure her aunt was awake. She rested her hand on Aunty's back. 'It was only an idea. I hadn't thought about it properly. I promise I won't do it.'

She heard her aunt's sigh but still she said nothing.

Kate drifted towards sleep.

A blood-curdling yell jerked her awake.

She lay still, her heart thumping.

Across the passage, Brendan groaned and called out, his words incoherent, panicked, the bedsprings creaking as he threw himself around the bed.

Kate had no doubt she was the cause of his distress. He had slept quietly this last week.

What memories had she churned up for him? She thought he had come back uninjured. She was wrong. His wounds were hidden in the daylight.

~

When Kate walked out to the verandah next morning, Brendan was sitting cleaning his shoes, a cup of tea on the bench beside him. Aunty's best shoes were set neatly on the ground to one side.

She stopped beside him. 'I'm sorry Brendan, I wasn't thinking clearly. I won't be doing it.'

He looked up at her. His face was haggard. He nodded and began polishing his shoes with a soft cloth.

Kate came out of the honeysuckle-screened lavatory in the far corner of the yard and stopped to watch the chooks scratching in the dirt, unconcerned by the troubles of the world. It might be a nice life. The neighbour's cat leapt from the fence with a thud and came and rubbed himself around her legs. A cat's life might be better, lying behind a window in the sunshine, thinking of nothing at all.

Brendan was now brushing Kiwi polish over Aunty's shoes. He nodded towards Kate's feet. 'Take them off—I'll shine them for you.'

'Thank you.' She undid the buckles and slid her feet out, placing the shoes beside the bench.

She tiptoed on stockinged feet into the kitchen. Aunty was setting the table for their breakfast when they came back from Mass.

Kate wound her arm around Aunty Mary's waist, resting her head against her shoulder.

'I'm sorry, Aunty Mary. It was an idea, not a plan.'

'Kate, my treasure, I could not bear it if anything happened to you.' She stepped back from the table and turned to Kate, kissing her cheek. 'This is wrong of me, but I want you to stay here with me, not go home to your parents.'

'I want to stay here with you.'

Aunty sniffed back her tears and glanced up at the clock on the mantelpiece above the stove. 'We should get our hats and gloves or we'll be late.'

'Maybe our shoes too?' Kate laughed.

'Definitely our shoes.'

~

St Paul's Church was not as full as usual but all who were there were wearing masks, including Fr McGee, the parish priest. Archbishop Mannix's instructions regarding Mass had emphasised the government's requirement that masks must be worn. Mass went for just under twenty-five minutes, much shorter than usual, as no hymns were sung and there was no sermon. Kate thought the last a vast improvement. Sermons were fine if they weren't too long and started with interesting stories about ordinary people— everyone loved a good story. Prayers were said that God might arrest the progress of this disease. Fr McGee said confession would now be heard at the sanctuary rails, and Communion was available at the end of the service. Kate and Aunty Mary went forward to receive it but Brendan walked straight out to the churchyard.

Once they were outside, people could not help themselves. They stood and talked, then moved slowly out into the street, heading towards home and their Sunday dinner, some taking their masks off as they went. Brendan and Annie stood outside the gate, well apart, as they spoke. There was such a careful respect in the way they were with each other. Kate wished they were more impulsive but this was not the time for rash behaviour.

She walked Mrs Ryan home.

'Do you think I could take this off?' the old lady asked. 'I feel I can't breathe when I'm walking.'

'Some doctors say there is no need for them in the open air.' Kate took hers off. 'One doctor has even said that we would do better drinking Bovril than wearing masks.' She grinned. 'When Brendan heard that, he ordered an extra box.'

Mrs Ryan untied her mask and took a deep breath. 'Perhaps I should get some Bovril. I quite like the taste.' She told Kate about the letter she had from Johanna, and how the influenza was in Ballarat. Then she spoke of her worries about Tom.

Kate tried to reassure Mrs Ryan, and herself, that the fact they had no news of him was a good thing. The last letter had said he had broken his leg. No mention of damage to his hands or arms. Surely, he could manage a few lines to his mother, if not to Kate.

'Is Ned at home today?'

'He went to early Mass and has gone off on his bicycle.'

'What will you be having for dinner?'

'I might boil myself an egg.'

'That's not enough. Aunty is making rice pudding for dinner. I'll tell her to bring you some when she calls in this afternoon.'

And she would probably bring some leftover cold lamb and potatoes as well. Kate wondered if Mrs Ryan could come regularly for Sunday dinner. It was not the same as having a party which was to be avoided at present.

'I love rice pudding, especially with the skin on the top.'

'And a good dollop of jam?'

Her eyes lit up. 'Oh, indeed.'

Mrs Ryan was thinner than when Kate first met her and seemed to have aged in the last six months. There had been the worry of the war but now it was as if she was pining. It must be hard to go from being at the centre of a family with nine children to being almost alone. Kate had to make sure Mrs Ryan was well and happy when Tom came home.

57

Halfway through the month, Mrs Ryan received another letter from Base Records. Tom was in hospital with influenza but was in a satisfactory condition. The old lady was beside herself and again Kate had to reassure her with words Kate had no faith in.

'He's strong and healthy. He will pull through.'

'Are you sure?'

Who can be sure of anything?

'He might already be over it. Most people spend no more than a couple of weeks in hospital and that letter said he caught it three weeks ago.'

Kate wished she could believe her own words.

The number of cases rose as February progressed, as did those hospitalised and dying. Funerals were conducted promptly, some even the same day as the patient died. More regulations were put in place. Billiard rooms were closed, racecourses too. Hotels could only sell alcohol at meal times to those staying in the hotels. But tea houses and restaurants were allowed to operate. There seemed to be no sense to it.

At the emergency hospital at the Exhibition Building in Carlton, there were only enough nurses to care for two or three hundred beds although there was space for many more. When Archbishop Mannix heard people were lying sick at home, neglected, dying unattended, he approached the State Government suggesting that the Rectress of St Vincent's Hospital in Fitzroy be placed in charge of the Exhibition Hospital, across the road from St Vincent's. He could, at no cost to the government, provide the services of enough nursing nuns to care for one thousand patients, freeing the nurses at the hospital to work elsewhere. The Government accepted his offer willingly but this raised the ire of one Reverend Henry Worrall, a Methodist minister, and his followers. He delivered a rancorous sermon at Wesley Church in Lonsdale Street. He said it was wrong to place the care of Protestant patients into the hands of *anti-Protestants*. How could the ill recover when they were forced to look at nuns in their strange garb?

Aunty Mary threw the newspaper down after reading the report of Worrall's sermons. 'Bigoted old creature. Doesn't he know that the Sisters of Mercy are, at this moment, nursing those ill with influenza at the Richmond temporary hospital? And what about all the Protestants over the years who have been nursed at St Vincent's Hospital by the Sisters of Charity? I've never heard of anyone dropping dead at the sight of a nun in her habit.'

'I suppose the old bastard was banging the drum for conscription and blamed the Catholics alone for its defeat.'

'Brendan! Your language!'

He sat back in his chair. 'Is it an inaccurate description?'

Aunty crossed her arms. 'It is not,' she snapped.

'You voted against conscription?' Kate asked. She was interested to know how the soldiers had voted.

'Did you?'

'I did. I think it is immoral for one man to force another, who is unwilling, to kill a third in cold blood.'

'Is that your own opinion or Tom Ryan's?'

She saw the glint of humour in his eyes and glared at him. 'It is my own.' He didn't need to know it was Tom's too. 'I can think for myself.'

He grinned. 'I do know that.'

'You haven't answered my question.'

'Kate, the voting booth is every bit as sacred as the confessional and what passes in there is as bound by secrecy. And that is a very good thing. Imagine if the likes of old Worrall knew what each person in his parish wrote on his or her ballot paper.'

'There's one or two priests I know who would be delighted with that too,' Aunty said dryly.

The Government declined Archbishop Mannix's offer following a petition from the staff of the Exhibition Hospital saying that if they were replaced by the nuns, they would refuse to offer their services elsewhere.

Brendan shook his head when he heard. 'Under fire we saw no difference between Catholic and Protestant but it seems nothing has changed here.'

'Here, there has been no let-up since 1916,' Kate said.

'1916,' Aunty scoffed. 'It has been going on for near to four hundred years.'

~

It was clear, as February drew to a close, that the number of cases of influenza was declining. The government gradually relaxed its regulations. Of paramount importance, hotels and wine bars were opened at the end of the first week in March, and racecourses too. Normal church services resumed. Theatres, music and concert halls threw open their doors and, if ventilation was adequate, picture theatres could hold two sessions a day. Schools opened. Excursion trains and steamers ran. Life was almost back to normal. Though, for many devout Catholics, like Mrs Ryan, Aunty Mary and Annie Watkins, the world was still not right. Lent began but because of the influenza epidemic, Archbishop Mannix granted a general dispensation from the Lenten fast. Catholics were only required to abstain from eating meat on Fridays.

Admissions to Coburg's emergency hospital decreased and, by the middle of March, the last nine patients, now convalescent, were discharged home and the hospital was closed. The high school, thoroughly cleaned and fumigated, was ready to open to students four days later. The Council announced, with a degree of satisfaction at the hard work of council officers and medical and nursing staff, that there had been only two deaths among the total of sixty-six cases reported in Coburg.

The whole world was out and about, going to dances, concerts and carnivals and parties, visits to the beach, to the gardens and the countryside to stroll and enjoy the scenery and have picnics.

Mrs Ryan seemed happier. She and Ned came most Sundays for dinner. Aunty told Kate she had given Ned a talking to about not leaving his grandmother by herself in the evenings too often and to tell her of the funny things that happened in his day, even if he had to embellish them a bit.

In Coburg, the month ended on a hot bright day with a Brass Band carnival. Watched by cheerful crowds, six bands led by their drum-majors marched from Moreland Road to the recreation reserve. Flags fluttered along Sydney Road and Bell Street and decorated the trams. The bands marched and played. There were tugs of war and flag races. Stalls selling refreshments did a roaring business through the afternoon and into the evening when the bands entertained the many who had come with a concert.

The only shadow that fell across the day was the withdrawal of the cornet player from the Hopetoun Band. He had felt unwell when boarding the train at Bendigo that morning and by evening he had been admitted to the Exhibition Hospital suffering from influenza.

58

April 1919

A letter came from Tom and it had barely taken five weeks to reach Kate. She ripped the envelope open.

7.3.19

Kate my love,

As you will know, I got my leave and ruined it. I had a grand few days seeing the sights, staying in a hotel, even having a bath three days in a row. They thought I was mad. I then stayed with Mother's cousin. One of his sons has a motorcycle. We drove out into the countryside and he was showing me how to ride it. I skidded and fell off and ended up with a broken leg. It was a clean break and they say it has healed well. And, fortunately, there was no harm done to the machine. When the hospital was ready to send me off, I came down with influenza. I felt horrible but they say that was not a bad case either. I should not be much longer here. I am not sure what will happen next. Most likely, I will be sent back in France to wait my turn.

Mother said she had a most delightful time at Brendan's welcome home. I hope she left you some time to sing and dance with the rest of them. It will be good to get home and live a normal life. I should be able to get my job at the railway workshops back. I cannot imagine anything better than tinkering with an engine in a dirty noisy shed. Well, I can but that and everything else will have to wait. We have eighteen months' worth of dancing and picturegoing to catch up on and so much else.

Let us hope the day I set foot on Australian soil is not far away.

With all my love,

Tom XXX

~

Aunty Mary set the teapot on the kitchen table and pulled out her chair.

'They have reopened the hospital at the High School. And Brunswick has set up a new hospital out at the Broadmeadows Camp. It must be getting bad again.'

Brendan placed his knife and fork on his plate with a clatter. 'I do not understand why they haven't reintroduced the restrictions. All they have now is vague rules about theatres and a limit of twenty people in bars, the rest are mere recommendations. They are even saying this is no worse than the usual flu, just there's more of it.' He picked up his knife and fork and angrily stabbed one of the sausages on his plate.

'They say to avoid crowds and keep away—' Aunty stopped, her head cocked at the sound of the side gate creaking.

'Mrs Burke?'

Kate looked up from her plate. 'That's Ned Ryan.'

Aunty opened the door. 'Ned, come in.'

'I should stay out here. Grannie is ill. She is still in bed and says she has pains in the head, a sore throat and aches everywhere.'

Kate stared across the table at Brendan, her rising panic mirrored in his eyes.

'You go back home, Ned.' Aunty said. 'One of us will be around in a few minutes.'

Kate stood up. 'I'll go.'

'Finish your breakfast first.' Aunty came back to the table. 'Five more minutes won't make a difference.' She picked up her tea cup and put it down again. 'I'll come with you.'

'If Mrs Ryan does have the flu, I will stay with her. Ned can't possibly nurse her.' Kate looked across at Brendan. 'Do you have any objections to that?' She would go no matter what he said.

'Of course not.' Fear flickered in his eyes. 'There is a world of difference between duty and a whim.'

Kate finished the last of her tea, and stood, her mind running through what she should take with her: the disinfectant gargle, aprons and masks. If she needed to stay, Brendan or Aunty would have to bring anything else around later.

When they arrived at Mrs Ryan's house, Kate said, 'You should wait outside, Aunty Mary. I'll see what's wrong.'

Kate called to Ned and went straight in.

He was in the sitting room, hunched on the edge of the sofa, his elbows on his knees. He stared up at Kate. 'She's not going to die, is she?' His voice was unsteady.

Kate wanted to say, *Of course she isn't*, but how could she know?

'Where is your grandmother's bedroom?'

He nodded towards the doorway. 'Across the passage.'

Mrs Ryan lay tangled in the bedclothes, her face flushed. Kate touched her hand to the old woman's forehead. She was as hot as she looked.

She murmured, 'Agnes, is that you?'

Kate crouched beside the bed. 'It's Kate Burke, Mrs Ryan.'

'I'm thirsty, Kate.'

There was no more than a dribble of water in the glass on the bedside table. Kate went to the kitchen and filled a jug she found in the dresser with water.

Back in the bedroom, she straightened the pillows and eased Mrs Ryan up the bed. She slid her hand beneath the old lady's neck, lifting her head, and held the glass to her lips.

Mrs Ryan took a few sips and started coughing.

Kate waited, helpless, for the spasm to pass.

Mrs Ryan's coughing finally stopped and she drank a few more mouthfuls. Her eyelids drooped and she dozed off.

Ned was at the front door talking to Aunty Mary.

'Ned wants to go to work but I don't think it is a good idea,' Aunty said as Kate arrived.

Kate rested her hand on his arm. 'If it is the Spanish influenza, they'll consider you a contact so you'll have to stay here until it's over.'

'But I need to let them know.'

'Are you all right, Ned?'

'Yes, yes.' She could feel him trembling. 'I'm worried, that's all. And I don't know how to look after her.'

'I'll stay here as long as I'm needed.'

Really, he was little more than a boy. He needed to be hugged and told that all would be well.

'Tell Aunty Mary who she needs to tell at your work and she or Brendan will get the message to them.'

Once he had given Aunty the details, Kate said, 'If you put the kettle on, I'll make you a cup of tea in a minute.'

Kate looked at Aunty standing on the path beyond the verandah. She longed for her aunt's arms around her, holding her tight. She wanted Aunty to tell her everything would be all right.

'Can you get the doctor to come?'

'I will.' Aunty walked away down the path.

Kate felt like a child standing, forlorn, on a railway platform, watching as a train carried her family away.

Aunty turned at the gate. 'One of us will come around this afternoon to see what you need.'

Even at a distance, the worry in Aunty Mary's face was plain.

'Oh Kate, do take care of yourself.'

~

The doctor was a tall, tired-looking man. He had put on a gown and a mask before entering the house and went straight into the bedroom.

He raised the blinds fully and opened the windows. 'The patient needs fresh air and light.'

Mrs Ryan lay against the pillows, her eyes shut. Her breathing was laboured.

The doctor went over to the washstand and scrubbed his hands thoroughly with soap and the hot water Kate had brought in for him.

Kate touched Mrs Ryan's shoulder. 'The doctor's here.'

The old lady's eyes fluttered open. She reached for Kate's hand, her voice rasping as she said, 'Stay with me, Kate.'

The doctor came to the bed. 'How long has Mrs Ryan been unwell?'

'Only today. She woke up with a headache, a sore throat and pains everywhere.'

Mrs Ryan clung tight to Kate's hand as the doctor examined her, feeling beneath her jaw, peering into her mouth. He spent a long time listening to her chest.

'Mrs Ryan has mild pneumonic symptoms at present,' he said as he straightened up. 'But you must keep a very close eye on your mother. If her skin develops a bluish hue, even the slightest, or she has difficulty breathing, send for us immediately.'

Kate nodded. 'I'm not Mrs Ryan's daughter—I'm a family friend, Kate Burke, but I am staying here as long as she needs me.'

'Good. Good. Make sure she drinks—water, weak tea, broth. Any other light food she fancies. Aspirin for her pains. Plenty of fresh air and light.' Back at the washstand, he scrubbed his hands again. 'How long have you been here?'

'Only a couple of hours.'

'Does anyone else live here?'

'Mrs Ryan's seventeen-year-old grandson.'

'I'll examine him too.'

Before he left, the doctor spoke again to Kate. 'Young Mr Ryan is showing no symptoms at present. He should not go into the sickroom and you should keep your distance from him as much as possible. Wear a mask when you are in with Mrs Ryan, keep an apron aside for use only in there. Wash your hands before and after attending the patient.

'And no going out at all—you are both here until Mrs Ryan is declared recovered. I will arrange for an inhalant mixture to be sent, you and young Mr Ryan are to use it four times a day. I will call in tomorrow. I am hopeful Mrs Ryan's case will be relatively mild.'

He hung his gown on the hallstand in case he returned.

Mrs Ryan was sleeping so Kate went out to Ned.

He was sitting on a chair in the backyard playing a flute, a slow melancholy tune. He paused as soon as he saw her.

'It's influenza but her symptoms are mild.'

His shoulders slumped. 'I hope she doesn't get any worse.'

'I hope so too.' Kate rubbed her fingers against her forehead. She didn't know how she would manage if Mrs Ryan took a turn for the worse, especially at night. Always, there had been someone nearby to take charge—her mother, Aunty Mary.

She was on her own.

'What's the tune you were playing?'

'*She Lived Beside the Anner*. It is a song about emigration—those who go and those who are left behind. Dad says it was one of Grandad Ryan's favourites.'

Ned stretched back in the chair. 'I suppose I should treat this as some sort of holiday but it's not much of one if I can't go out.'

'What would you rather be doing?'

'Out riding the bike. I hate being cooped up.'

They both jumped as a loud banging started up at the front of the house.

Kate left Ned to his music and went to investigate.

Brendan was squatting by the fence, hammering a wooden box into place. He stood as Kate came out and dropped his hammer into a tool bag on the ground beside him.

'It's for any deliveries you might need.' He passed Kate a square sheet of plywood with a SOS painted on it. 'You can hang this either on the box or the front door if you need the doctor or anything else urgently. It's a suggestion of the Coburg Council.'

He stared past Kate, towards the house, his eyebrows drawn together, almost a single line. 'How is Mrs Ryan?'

'It is influenza but the pneumonic symptoms are mild. Ned doesn't have it, thank heavens, but I will have to stay here.'

'What do you need?'

'More aspirin, disinfectant, carbolic soap. As for clothing, tell Aunty Mary everything I'll need for a few days. She'll know.' She looked at him. 'You're not angry with me?'

'Why would I be?'

Kate opened her mouth to speak but Brendan spoke over her.

'I meant everything I said. Especially about you being like a daughter to Mum.' He paused. 'And a sister to me.' Scowling, he crossed his arms. 'We've lost enough. But this is different. The Ryans are as good as family—we can't leave them to fend for themselves.' He picked up his tool bag from the footpath. 'One of us will be along later. And Mum said not to worry about meals— she'll send over some of whatever we're having.'

Kate watched him go. Brendan was as goodhearted, and as annoying, as any brother.

59

The next few days passed in a haze of tiredness. When Kate was not nursing Mrs Ryan, she was busy in the washhouse boiling handkerchiefs and sheets, or in the kitchen washing, in a lather of soap, every plate, cup and glass they used. In the afternoons, when the old lady was at her most restful, she managed to take a long dreamless nap lying, fully clothed, on Tom's bed.

Mrs Ryan's coughing and aches worsened towards evening. Kate sat with her through the night as she tossed and turned, wiping the perspiration from her forehead and her hands when she threw off the bedclothes, covering her up when she began shivering. By the time the night sky started to lighten, Mrs Ryan slept quietly. Kate dozed curled up in the armchair by the bed, her facemask slipping down to her chin.

~

Kate woke, stretched, and took off her mask. She went out to the verandah, breathing in the fresh early morning air.

She blinked, surprised to see Ned ride up to the gate on his bicycle and went out to speak to him.

'I will go mad if I have to stay locked in the whole time.' He had such a pleasant, believable face. 'Don't worry—I didn't go near a living soul.'

Kate wasn't sure she believed him. 'If the council finds out you'll be fined.'

'I'll tell them my name is Billy Hughes.'

'Why not Henry Worrall?'

He gave a whoop of laughter. 'I just might do that.'

Kate smiled. Ned seemed like a younger version of Tom. He had the same deep brown hair and straight eyebrows, though Ned's eyes were darker. He was more exuberant too. Kate wondered if Tom had been the same when he was Ned's age.

'If they find out it will be because someone who knows who you are reported you,' she warned. 'The fine is twenty-five pounds.'

'Good luck to them, I don't have twenty-five pounds.'

'As you are under twenty-one, your father might have to pay.'

He grinned. 'Now, that might be a problem.'

Ned wheeled his bicycle along the side of the house, whistling as if he had not a care in the world.

That night Mrs Ryan took a turn for the worse. She was hot to touch, her skin flushed. She coughed and coughed, tossing from side to side, groaning. She thought Kate was her daughter Agnes.

She refused to drink the water Kate offered, wouldn't swallow the aspirin. There seemed to be no bluish tinge to her skin but Kate couldn't be certain in the lamplight. Her toes were warm—Kate hoped it was a good sign.

She prepared a mustard footbath. It was a recipe Aunty Mary had sent, saying it was a good way to bring down fever if nothing else was working.

It was a struggled to get Mrs Ryan into the chair beside the bed. Once there, the old lady sat slumped against the side of the chair, her feet in the basin, a blanket draped over her knees. Her face flushed, she huffed and coughed. Sweat filmed her forehead and soaked through her nightgown.

Kate was near to tears. She didn't know what she was doing. Mrs Ryan—Tom's mother—couldn't die. She clenched her jaw and held her head up. Weeping would achieve nothing.

She changed the sheets on the bed and, apologising to Mrs Ryan, stripped off her nightgown and quickly sponged her over with a cool flannel.

Mrs Ryan groaned and whimpered, her eyes closed. She began to shiver.

Kate dressed her in a clean nightgown and wrestled her back into bed—although thin, the old lady was a dead weight. Finally, lying back in bed, blankets tucked around her, Mrs Ryan fell into a calm sleep.

Kate pulled off her mask and went to Tom's room and collapsed onto the bed.

~

Kate woke with a start, sunlight streaming through the window.

Ned poked his head around the door. 'Kate. Grannie is asking for you.'

She jumped off the bed. 'What time is it?'

'Half-past eight.'

She had slept for six unbroken hours. With her shoes on!

'How is she?'

'Much better, I think.'

Mrs Ryan was lying back against the pillows. She opened her eyes as Kate came in.

'You do look better today.' Kate went to the window and raised the blinds. 'Would you like something to eat?'

'I'd love a cup of tea.' The old lady coughed. 'Weak though. And maybe...' she coughed again, '...a slice of dry toast.'

She might be on the mend, but she was a long way from well.

After Kate had helped Mrs Ryan with her breakfast, she left the old lady dozing. If Mrs Ryan didn't slip backwards later in the day, Kate dared to imagine she might spend a whole night in bed herself, in a nightgown. With her shoes off!

The doctor called in that afternoon and said that provided Mrs Ryan's temperature stayed down and the cough disappeared, she would be considered convalescent. But until then, she had to remain in her room and have meals brought to her.

Kate spent some of each afternoon keeping Mrs Ryan company. She took a chair to the door of the bedroom and sat talking about her family and hearing a great deal about Tom and his brothers and sisters. Ned often joined them and told jokes and tales of the characters he worked with, and the occasions when he and his brothers and sisters got the better of their rather strict father.

Finally, well over a week on, Mrs Ryan was declared convalescent and could move around the house but not leave it.

Annie came to the gate that afternoon. Kate sat on the verandah and Annie on a chair, on the footpath, that Kate had brought out for her.

'Did you know,' Annie said, 'Reenie is working at the influenza hospital out at the Broadmeadows Camp?'

Kate shook her head. 'I haven't seen any of the Caseys for weeks.'

'Apparently, when Reenie told her parents, she said that as she was twenty-one, she could do as she liked, no matter what they thought.'

Kate grinned. 'For certain, Reenie has a mind of her own these days.'

'Too much of a mind of her own.' Annie pressed her lips tight as if in judgement. 'She should show respect for her parents.'

Kate thought it best not to comment. 'As the schools are shut, have you thought of helping in the hospitals too?'

'I made the mistake of thinking aloud about it. My parents were unimpressed. Mother even spoke to Brendan—as if he has any say over what I do! I have never seen him so angry.'

Kate nodded. 'If he's truly upset, he is quite forceful.'

'It surprised me, he has always been a perfect gentleman.'

'Have you two admitted you are walking out together?'

'We are not.' Annie scowled at Kate. 'Yet everybody, including my parents and Mrs Burke, assumes it.'

'He hasn't asked—'

'Now is not the time with this influenza about.' Annie jerked her head. 'Brendan won't go to the pictures or to a dance, or anything else indoors. He keeps saying the rules from February should be reinstated.'

Kate had seen the way Brendan looked at Annie and couldn't believe he would allow the flu to come between them. Walking out with someone was more than going to the pictures or a dance. They could sit and talk, a distance apart, and learn each other's thoughts on everything from the superiority of cats over dogs to what their dreams for the future were.

And...' Annie glanced up and down the street, as if making sure no one was near enough to overhear her. '...he refuses to go to Mass until it's over. He had a roaring argument with Mrs Burke. He told her not to go either.'

'Who won that argument?'

'Mrs Burke, of course.'

'Did he tell you to stay home?'

'He did.' Colour spread up her cheeks. 'I told him that I would not compromise my faith for anyone. We are wearing masks, that should be enough for him.'

Kate sighed. 'He is afraid he will lose the rest of us.'

Annie looked away, her mouth a tight line, as if saying, *That is no excuse.*

Poor Brendan.

He, most likely, was beside Vince when he was shot. He would be terrified by the thought that any of them—Aunty Mary, Annie, Kate—would be taken by this awful disease. Could Annie not understand that?

60

May 1919

Kate opened Mrs Ryan's bedroom windows and gazed out into the pearly early morning light. Mrs Ryan's convalescence ended tomorrow. Ned had to stay within the yard for three days more. Kate had to spend the time in isolation in her room.

Then they would be free.

Kate wanted to go home, to sleep in her own bed beside Aunty Mary; to stand in the shop and chat with customers, even Mrs Johnson; to sit by the fire in the evening talking with Aunty and Brendan.

Ned limped through the front gate and wheeled his bike around the side of the house. He moved as if his legs were dead weights.

Kate rushed out into the backyard. 'What's happened?'

He leant the bike against the back wall of the house. 'I fell off.' His hands were grazed and the right leg of his trousers torn. 'At the end of the street. Felt dizzy.'

'You still look unsteady.'

'I'm fine.' He winced. 'Need to clean myself up.'

Kate followed him inside and put the kettle on for breakfast.

By the time the kettle was boiling and the porridge cooked, Ned still hadn't come out.

Kate moved the saucepan to the side of the stove and went to his door. As she lifted her hand to knock, he gave a dry drawn-out cough.

'Ned?' She pushed the door open.

He was sprawled across the bed, still fully dressed, his eyes shut. She rushed over.

He moaned as she rested her hand on his forehead.

'You're burning. Ned. Put your pyjamas on and get into bed.'

He hauled himself upright. 'My head hurts when I move it.' He slowly unbuttoned his shirt.

Kate pulled his pyjamas from beneath the pillow and laid them beside him. 'Do you want me to help?'

His eyes still shut, he whimpered. 'No.'

She hurried to Mrs Ryan's room. 'It's Ned. He's not well.'

The old lady blessed herself. 'Holy Mother of God, pray for us.'

'I'm going to send for the doctor.'

There was no one in the street. Kate waited for a few minutes but no one came. She went back inside and wrote a note asking for a doctor to come to Edmund Ryan who was showing symptoms of influenza, and their address. She put it in the box and hung the SOS sign on it.

She took water and aspirin in to the bedroom, remembering to put on her mask. She placed the water jug and a glass on Ned's bedside table, plumped up his pillows, and helped him sit up.

He swallowed the aspirin and lay back. 'Kate, I'm scared. Don't leave me.' He looked like a little boy in need of his mother.

'I have to check on your grandmother but I will come straight back.'

Kate checked the box on the fence too. The note was gone so she brought the sign inside.

Mrs Ryan was kneeling at the side of her bed, her head bowed, rosary beads in her hands.

Kate called to her. 'I've sent for the doctor. I'll sit with Ned until he arrives.'

The old woman nodded, her lips still moving.

'Please don't wear yourself out. You can pray just as well sitting in the chair.'

She brought a basin of cold water to the bedroom and, using a flannel dipped in the water, wiped Ned's hands and laid the flannel across his forehead. He was too sick to do any of the things she had tried with his grandmother.

He swallowed as if his throat hurt. 'Water.' His voice was husky.

She held the glass to his mouth and he drank thirstily.

Kate picked up the book lying on the bedside table beside his rosary beads. 'Would you like me to read to you?'

Ned nodded his head slightly and coughed.

When he had his breath back, she opened the book and glanced down the page. 'Oh, it's about Melbourne.' She began to read.

> At the same time, he felt by no means easy in his mind, and as he stepped out on to the platform at the Melbourne station he looked round apprehensively ...

She read a couple of pages and glanced at Ned.

He had fallen asleep. His face was flushed, his breathing shallow. He was sick, far sicker than his grandmother had been.

She was certain this was Spanish influenza. It had come on him so quickly. She fought a surge of panic. Young healthy people died of it.

The clock in the sitting room chimed twelve. The note had been taken hours ago and the doctor had not come.

She went out to the gate.

A boy of eight or so with grubby knees and his shirt tail hanging out dawdled along on the other side of the street, rattling a stick against fence palings.

Kate waved to him. 'Excuse me! Can you come here?'

He sauntered over, whistling tunelessly.

'Will you deliver a message for me? There's thruppence in it for you.'

His eyes lit up. 'Sure, Missus.'

'Do you know Burke's, the grocer shop in Sydney Road?'

'The place run by that big Anzac bloke?'

'That's the one. Now go as fast as you can and tell him to send for a doctor and a priest for Ned. Then tell him that Kate said to give you thruppence.'

The boy whistled between his teeth. 'That's bad.'

'Now repeat the message to me.'

'Doctor and priest for Ned. Kate says give me thruppence.'

'Very good.'

He raced off, his stick discarded on the footpath.

When Kate came back in, Mrs Ryan had set a steaming bowl of Aunty Mary's soup on the kitchen table for her. A slice of buttered bread was on a plate beside it.

'You eat that now. I looked in at Ned from the doorway. He is slightly restless but still asleep.'

Kate went to the washhouse and scrubbed her hands.

She sat at the table, her head lowered. She prayed, not just grace but for Ned.

As she picked up her spoon, she said, 'I've sent for the priest.'

The old lady whimpered. 'The Sacrament can give a body the strength to recover.' She quivered, as if forcing courage into herself to face what lay ahead. 'You eat up. I'll get together what Father will need and explain what you have to do.'

Her lips moved in silent prayer as she left the room.

Kate sipped a spoonful of the soup and was suddenly ravenous. She ate her soup and took a second slice of bread. She hadn't realised she was hungry.

61

Ned opened his eyes as Kate put the tray down on the bedside table, now moved to the foot of the bed. There he could see the crucifix set at the centre of the tray between two candles. The tray was covered with a pristine tray cloth and held everything the priest would need for the Last Rites, from a glass of water and a small bowl of Holy Water to a bell and a folded piece of fine linen.

Ned beckoned Kate to him.

'I lied.' He coughed, his breath catching. Finally, he gasped out the words. 'Met mates ... one ... in hospital ... yester ... day.'

Where is that doctor?

She looked up. Fr McGee stood at the door, wearing a mask and gown. Beneath the gown, she glimpsed the purple of the stole he wore around his neck, the symbol of his authority as a priest. He was a man in his fifties, yet he seemed so much older, as if at this moment he knew the sorrows of the world.

Kate covered her hair with the fine net veil Mrs Ryan had given her.

The priest went straight to the bedside. 'Ned, can you hear me?

Ned nodded, a slight movement of his head.

'Can you speak?'

He opened his mouth but only a whisper came out.

The priest turned to Kate. 'I'll hear Ned's confession.'

Kate went out and stood in the passage, away from the closed door. She could hear the drone of the priest but no sound from Ned. It was little time before the bell rang for Kate to go back in.

She lit the candles on the tray.

Kate genuflected, as Mrs Ryan had told her she should, when Father placed the pyx, the small golden container for carrying the Blessed Sacrament, on the tray. He put a small silver topped jar of oil beside it.

'*Pax huic domui.*'

Kate didn't know the Latin responses but Mrs Ryan knelt at the door, a veil on her head, her prayer book open, and answered, '*Et omnibus habitantibus in ea.*'

The priest took up the bowl of holy water and continuing his prayers in Latin, he blessed Ned then Kate and Mrs Ryan. He genuflected and took the Blessed Sacrament from the pyx, holding it in front of Ned saying, '*Ecce Agnus Dei.*'

Ned opened his eyes.

Father placed the consecrated wafer in Ned's mouth.

Ned closed his eyes and, with some effort, swallowed this *Viaticum*, provision for the journey that lay ahead of him.

Father's prayers, in both Latin and English, flowed through the room bringing to Kate a sense of calm.

He moved closer to the bed and began the anointing of the sick. Praying softly, he first anointed Ned's eyelids with holy oil, wiped his fingers with the fine linen, then moved on.

Finally, he anointed Ned's feet.

Kate glanced at his feet as she drew the blanket back over him. They looked cold, a bluish tinge to the toenails.

The room was dim. The sun had withdrawn.

Time stopped.

In the shadows, Kate sensed those who had come before Ned, waiting to welcome him home.

She stopped listening to the prayers thinking only of him, what she knew of him, the love he had for both his grandmother and for Tom, his good humour, his jokes, the beauty of his music, the joy he took in it, the glory of life within him only just begun. And all that was fading.

This disease was moving fast.

Ned was dying.

~

Kate held Ned, her arm around his shoulder as he coughed. His cough was prolonged. He struggled to breathe, tried to cough up the mucus she could hear in his throat but little came.

Exhausted, he collapsed back against the pillows Kate had piled behind him.

She wiped his face and hands with a damp cloth and offered him water.

He took a few sips and closed his eyes.

He was flushed, his skin darker. Gone was the fresh complexion with its bloom of health. Kate noticed the patches of light stubble and wanted to weep. He did not yet need to fully shave.

She took off her mask. She would not have Ned's last sight be of a face covered like someone ashamed. She sat down again and took his hand in hers.

He turned his head towards her and said, a faint gleam in his eyes, 'Tom ... lucky.'

Kate smiled at him, her eyes filmed.

He reached out, his hand brushing hers. 'Rosary.'

She picked the beads up from the bedside table and tried to place them in his hands.

He pushed them away. 'You.' Each breath an effort, he gasped, 'Josie.'

She told herself she would give them back to him when he was well.

His cough rumbled deeper in his chest.

Kate jumped at the sharp knock at the door.

The doctor. Thank God.

She re-tied her mask.

The doctor came straight in, looking as if he hadn't slept for a week. He stood beside the bed, did not even examine Ned. 'I'll arrange for an ambulance.'

Then he was gone.

Kate pulled off her mask. 'They will be able to help you better in hospital.'

He looked at her, unbelieving. 'Sing ... happy...'

Only miserable songs came to mind. 'I know, *I Do Like to be Beside the Seaside.*' A happy song for happier times.

Ned lay with his eyes shut as she sang.

Kate thought he gave the slightest of smiles.

He groaned, muttered as if he was having a conversation.

Kate sat beside him, helpless. She had no idea what to do. She was not a nurse, had no training. Good intentions were not enough.

He coughed and coughed, whimpering between. 'Hurts.'

Kate rubbed her hand against his chest, hoping it brought some comfort.

He coughed again.

She could hear his mouth filling and grabbed the basin, sliding her arm behind his shoulders, holding him as he spat up glistening mouthfuls of greeny-yellow phlegm.

It took over half an hour for the ambulance to arrive. When she heard it pull up, she bent over the bed and kissed Ned's clammy forehead.

His eyes flickered behind his closed eyelids.

His grandmother, waiting in the passage, rested her hand on his chest and, despite the ambulance attendants' scowls, pressed her lips to Ned's forehead as they carried him out.

Kate followed the stretcher to the gate and stood watching as the ambulance drove away.

God go with you, Ned.

She was sobbing by the time she reached the verandah.

Mrs Ryan stood at the door, her eyes dull and empty, her hand covering her mouth.

No words could express Kate's misery and fear.

Instead, she said, 'I'll clean Ned's room tomorrow. Right now, I am going to have a thorough wash and go to bed.'

She had broken so many rules sitting with Ned and she did not care. No one suffering and near to death should be left without a warm hand to hold, a loving face to look upon.

~

Kate woke late, her pillow damp, the memory of a flute playing *She Lived Beside the Anner* lingering in her ears.

Mrs Ryan was up and dressed, kneeling by her bed praying. Kate got her own rosary and knelt at the door. The repetition, the slip of the smooth glass beads through her fingers was consoling.

Their prayers finished, Mrs Ryan eased herself up from her knees. Her cheeks wet with tears, she said, 'My grandson died early this morning.' Her face was collapsed in grief. 'Why would He take Edmund and leave me?'

Kate sobbed, open mouthed, and walked slowly out into the back garden.

Why would He take either of them at all?

She knew the common reasoning but it was cruel. It was unfair.

She stared at the chair Ned had sat on when he played. She heard, softly, the lilt of his music.

Kate turned and went back into the house. She put on her mask and her apron and explained to Mrs Ryan that it would be safest if she kept her distance in case she had caught the influenza too. She began cleaning Ned's room. She hung the blankets on the line and went back to collect the sheets. She would leave washing them until tomorrow.

Mrs Ryan was in the sitting room, by the window, staring out unseeing. She turned when Kate came to the door.

Kate took Ned's rosary beads from her apron pocket. 'Ned asked for his rosary. When I tried to put them in his hand, he pushed them back at me. He said, *You* and then he said *Josie*.'

Mrs Ryan stared at the beads in Kate's hand. 'He wanted you to have them.' She sighed. 'Josie is Josephine, my second youngest daughter. She's two years younger than Tom. A Sister of St Joseph in South Australia, Sister Perpetua. She sent the rosary to Edmund for his Confirmation.'

She closed her eyes. 'I knew he had gone long before the nurse came and told me. I woke to a dog howling. Three times it was.'

Sometimes the old beliefs are true.

The next morning, as Kate pushed a sheet through the wringer, Mrs Ryan came to the washhouse door.

'Frank is outside. He would like to speak to you.'

Frank Ryan stood at the gate. He cleared his throat. 'I have come from burying my boy.' He stopped. Drew a ragged breath. 'Mother has told me how much you did for Ned. I wanted to thank you.'

'I'm sorry I could not do more.' Kate blinked, she would not cry. 'He was a wonderful young man.'

'He was.' The man's face was stiff, his jaw clenched. He nodded to Kate and marched over to the buggy standing on the other side of the street.

Ned must have been buried at the Fawkner cemetery. She would visit his grave when this was over.

Kate went back to her washing. Using the pot stick, she hauled the next sheet from the copper into the trough of cold water and pushed it through the wringer, turning the handle. She stepped back and rolled her shoulders. They were stiff with the effort and she had pain in her back.

Because Ned had caught the flu, they both had three more days of isolation. Kate hoped one of Mrs Ryan's children or many grandchildren would come and stay with her—she couldn't be left on her own. Then Kate could go back to the shop and work beside Brendan, or sit with Aunty Mary listening to her stories.

She wanted to go home.

62

The air around her is full of light—the sky a pale washed blue, clouds mere streaks of white. A gentle wind quivers through the gum leaves. Behind, the creek rushes over rocks. Rufus, lying by the kitchen door, does not stir as she passes by.

She walks through the house. All is still, the ticking of the clock soft and slow.

She looks out from the front verandah, across the reds, pinks and whites of the roses to the crepe myrtles in glorious pink bloom.

A cloud moves across the sun, throwing shadows.

Someone, somewhere, is keening. Raw and piercing. Grief tearing a heart apart.

She moves out from the garden, down into the paddocks of golden maize. Here it is warmer, here she can see more clearly.

She won't find him here.

Him?

Sun beats down, warmth spreading through her.

Blazing. Scorching.

Hot thick air, clogging her lungs, searing, every breath burning.

Fire screaming through air.

Explosions of pain, lacerating, mutilating.

Scrubby bushes on yellow cliffs, men crying out.

Women mourning and weeping in this valley of tears.

The pale sea glistens, beckoning her.

Sliding down, down.

Dark icy water. Freezing.

Cold as the grave.

She opens her mouth. Cries out.

She has no voice.

Her mouth is full of fog.

Coughing, and coughing, and coughing.

Darkness wraps around her.

Trees loom, stark and lifeless.

The sky shrieks—a never-ending scream.

The earth heaves and breaks open.

Silence.

A lantern sways.

The candle barely flickers.

Fog muffled, a flute plays. A song of separation. A song of loss.

She wants to dance. A slow dance, held close, held safe.

Who is she to dance with?

He is not here.

He?

She will know when she finds him.

Fog drifts away.

Ahead, so many. Standing. Waiting.

Some she knows, some not at all.

All know her. All belong to her.

Untroubled faces full of joy.

She cannot move forward.

Voices weave around her.

Turn back.

He is waiting.

Turn back.

Her eyes flutter open.

63

The air around her was full of light. She lay still, motes dancing above her. She felt no pain, nothing, nothing at all. She did not know how, but she knew it was the afternoon.

A woman leant over the bed—a nurse, her eyes a kind soft grey above her white mask. The corners of her eyes crinkled as if she was smiling. 'You're awake.'

Kate nodded. She wasn't sure that her voice would work.

'Would you like a sip of water?' The nurse slid her arm behind Kate and lifted her shoulders, holding the cup up to Kate's mouth.

The water was cool, soothing. She drank quickly.

'Careful, not too much at once.'

Kate lay back against the pillows. She tried her voice. 'I'm in hospital?'

'Yes, Coburg's emergency hospital in the High School.'

Kate closed her eyes.

She woke later, the sunlight was gone, shadows filled the corners of the room. It was an ordinary room now. There was a screen on the right of Kate's bed. To her left and on the opposite side of the room, there was a row of beds with women lying in them. At the far end of the room a nursing sister sat at a table, busily writing.

A younger nurse came in. She wore a cap, one of the Voluntary Aid Detachment not a trained nurse.

'Would you like some broth?' she asked. She had brown eyes, a twinkle of mischief in them, and a cheery manner so like Reenie's.

'I would.' Kate coughed against her hand.

The nurse watched, a crease between her eyebrows.

The cough was shallow. It didn't hurt, didn't reach inside Kate and try to rip out her soul.

The nurse turned away but was quickly back with a small stack of handkerchiefs. She handed one to Kate and placed the rest on the small table beside the bed. 'Cough into these. There's a bin at the other side of the bed you can drop them in so they can be boiled up.'

After washing Kate's hands and helping her to sit up against the pillows, she brought her a cup of clear soup.

Kate's mouth watered. Yes, she was hungry.

The nurse spread a towel across the bedding and gave Kate the cup.

Kate held it tight, her hands trembling. She doubted she could drink it without spilling.

The nurse took back the cup and picked up a spoon from the bedside table. 'You'll get your strength back in no time.' She fed Kate, a spoonful at a time, wiping her chin with a napkin to catch any spills.

Kate felt as helpless as a small child.

Halfway through, the nurse asked, 'Do you want to try again?'

Kate nodded. This time, it was easier, already her hands were steadier.

Between mouthfuls, Kate asked, 'How long have I been here?'

'Five, six days. We thought we'd lose you. But the night nurse said you wouldn't die. She's Irish, you know, one of those Roman Catholics and they believe all—' She stopped. 'Oops, your one of them, aren't you?'

'Yes, I'm a Catholic but I was born here.' The girl didn't need her family's history. 'Why did the nurse say that?'

'She said you were being watched over, guarded—three men standing in the shadows, maybe soldiers. She says she heard a flute playing but, really, that could have been out in the street.'

Kate sat motionless.

They had kept Death at bay.

A sense of safety washed through her.

The nurse chattered on. 'One of the other nurses said that night nurses see all sorts of things. She used to see cats walking down the middle of the ward. Sometimes they hear voices too, loud in their ear, but usually it's when they're drifting off. That's not a bad thing because it wakes them up. Oh, have you finished?'

'Almost.' Kate drained the cup.

The soup had made her warm and sleepy. She lay back against the pillows and closed her eyes.

She woke in the darkness before sunrise. The woman to the right of her, behind the screen, was sobbing softly. As she drifted back to sleep, Kate wondered what burden the woman carried other than her illness.

The next morning, the nurse washed her in the bed. It was mortifying even though she was covered with a towel.

'I can manage this myself.'

'Sorry, I have to do it. Maybe in a day or two, if Sister thinks you are up to it.'

Despite the embarrassment, Kate was pleased to feel clean and fresh in a new nightgown. She lay against the pillows imagining the hot bath she would take when she got home. It would be scented with bath salts and the water would be up to her neck. She laughed softly. It was a dream of Tom's too. She hoped it wouldn't be too much longer and she would see him. He was waiting for her.

~

One day seemed much like the next but there were little changes. Gradually Kate's coughing eased and slowly her strength came back. The food became more interesting, changing from broths, boiled custards and poached eggs to steamed fish, stewed mutton, mashed potatoes, and stewed apples, and sago pudding.

She was allowed to sit out of bed during the day, then to walk the length of the ward, the nurse beside her. The nurse said her name was Violet Hodges, but she would be in trouble if Kate called her anything but Miss Hodges, or just plain Nurse, because she wasn't trained.

'Miss Hodges.' Kate lowered her voice. 'I keep hearing someone crying at night. What's wrong?'

'That's Mrs Wright,' she whispered. 'She's in the bed next to yours. She lost her baby. She was five months gone. And she's one of the lucky ones—pregnant women often die with this flu.'

Kate gasped. Another of life's cruelties.

'She's about your age. She married a month before her husband left with the first lot of Anzacs. He came home late last year. Now this. It's a shocking disease.' She cocked her head. 'I can hear Sister coming. Better be off.'

Sister came to the door with Fr Daly, the young Irish assistant priest. He walked to the end of the room, speaking softly to whoever was in the bed there.

Kate gazed at the light falling from the window, her mind empty of everything but the sounds, the stir of movement in the room at this moment.

It was restful knowing nothing of what was going on in the world. But she wanted to see Aunty Mary and Brendan. And Mrs Ryan. And, most of all, Tom. She was too tired for it to be more than a wish she could wait for.

'Miss Burke.' Fr Daly was at the foot of her bed, his voice barely muffled by his mask. 'It is a pleasure to see you out of bed and looking so well.'

'Thank you, Father. I do feel quite well.'

'God willing, it won't be long before you can go home. Mrs Burke is counting the days.'

'You have spoken to Aunty Mary?'

'I have. She is certainly missing you.'

'And how is Mrs Ryan?'

For a brief moment, Ned stood there. He was smiling, his eyes shining. Then he was gone, his duty done.

'She is staying with her son at Warburton.'

Kate nodded slowly. It was comforting to know Mrs Ryan was not alone.

'Is there anything I can do for you at present?'

She moved in her chair, sitting straighter.

'I have no rosary beads with me and I lose count when I use my fingers.'

'Now, I never come unprepared.' He tugged his gown up and reached into his jacket pocket, pulling a purse out. He took out a rosary of small white beads and placed them in Kate's hand.

'I will give them back to you when I am out of here.'

'Please keep them. Remember me in your prayers when you use them.' He sketched a sign of the cross and was gone.

That night, once the lights were out, Kate started the rosary, relaxing into the comfort of its repetitions. Foremost in her prayers was Mrs Wright in the bed beside her. If life had been different, that could have been her and Jack. Poor woman. After all those years of worry and fear, a baby was a gift of hope. To have it snatched away would be almost beyond bearing. Even worse that she was here alone with no one to hold her tight, to make her feel safe, to whisper that there would be a future.

~

Kate walked across the ward and settled herself on the chair beside her bed. She had been strolling along the balcony at the rear of the building. A couple of times, on days when the weather was mild, she had sat out there and read, or chatted with one or two of the other convalescent women. In the fresh air, with the breeze on her face, she felt completely well. Well enough to go home.

She picked up the magazine Fr Daly had left for her to read on his last visit and flicked through the pages. *The Madonna* was the quarterly magazine of the Children of Mary. She wished it was something more exciting—every story had a moral. She preferred magazines with pictures of frocks and hats, and love stories that didn't involve discussions of faith.

'Good afternoon, Miss Burke.'

Dr Mathew stood at the end of the bed. He was around Kate's

age, yet responsible for the medical care of the patients in the emergency hospital. Nurse Hodges said he was only a fifth-year medical student but was already a good and conscientious doctor. The son of the local Presbyterian minister too.

'I wish to check your breathing, Miss Burke. If you would loosen your dressing gown, please.'

Kate dropped the dressing gown from her shoulders and leant forward.

He pressed the stethoscope against her back, listening through the cloth of her nightgown.

'Sister tells me, you are doing well. All things considered, you can go home tomorrow.'

'Oh,' Kate gasped. 'Thank you, Doctor.'

'A few rules though. No gadding about, no visitors for another week. Sit out in the sunshine as much as you can, well rugged up. Take things easy.'

Kate was so happy she wanted to twirl around the room. But he might consider that gadding about and delay her discharge.

~

Kate sat waiting, impatient, in her hospital dressing gown, hoping she didn't have to wear it home.

Just before dinnertime, Miss Hodges carried in a bag, looking as happy as Kate felt. 'Your aunty dropped your clothes off. She's waiting outside but you're not allowed to leave until one of the Sisters discharges you.'

Kate dressed carefully. Aunty had sent the skirt Kate had worn to Reenie and Pat Casey's party, and the blouse Aunty had given her for her birthday, and her coat and her best shoes. Dressed, with her hair pinned up, she was ready to face the world whatever state it was in.

Miss Hodges poked her head around the screen and gave a soft whistle. 'You look all right, Kate.'

'Thank you,' Kate lowered her voice, 'Violet. Thank you for

everything.'

Violet winked at her. 'Good luck out there. I hope there's a nice fellow waiting for you.'

Sister Seymour, the matron, discharged Kate, accompanying her down the stairs. As they walked to the entrance, Kate glimpsed a man in pyjamas through the opened door to the men's ward—the place where Ned had died.

Did they hear his flute too?

One day, she would tell Mrs Ryan what the night nurse had seen and heard. It might bring her some comfort.

64

June 1919

The door closed behind Kate. She stood in the porch at the front of the school, looking out on a typical June day—the sky blue and cloudless, the breeze sharp and cold.

She drew a deep breath and waited. She had no urge to cough.

Annie's car was parked in front of the school.

They caught sight of each other at the same moment and waved. Aunty leapt out of the car and raced up the path.

'Kate.' She threw her arms around Kate, squeezing her tight.

'Aunty.' Kate closed her eyes.

'Now.' Aunty wrapped a scarf around Kate's neck and pulled a knitted hat down on her head. 'I'm not having you catch a chill.'

Annie's smile was as wide as Aunty's. She watched as Kate made herself comfortable in the back of the car. 'Welcome back.'

Welcome back?

Yes. She had been a journey—a long dark journey.

Aunty cranked the car and climbed in beside Annie, and they were off.

Kate gazed at the shops, the people on the footpaths, the other traffic along Sydney Road. It was just as it had been when she arrived. No, not the same—there were more motor cars on the road, more people too, but no one in khaki that she could see. The excitement, the enthusiasm was gone, many faces were blank and stoic, perhaps glimpsing amongst the crowds the shades of those who were never coming back.

Annie pulled up in the side street and Aunty helped Kate from the car.

As the backdoor slapped shut behind them, Brendan appeared in the passage. He came into the kitchen and opened his arms. He crushed Kate to him then stepped back, his hands resting lightly on her shoulders.

'Kate. Thank God.' He smiled, relief in his face. He went to speak but the shop bell jingled. He paused before he reached the doorway to the shop and blew his nose.

Kate took off her coat and hung it on the back of the chair and sat down. She had done nothing but sit in a car for a few minutes and she was worn out.

'What would you like to do first?' Aunty asked.

'A cup of tea and a long hot bath.'

Aunty went out and lit the copper while Annie made the tea. She pulled out the chair opposite Kate at the table and passed her a small package wrapped in coloured tissue paper and tied with a bow.

Kate undid the ribbon and tore off the paper. 'Lily of the valley bath tablets! I'll use them straight away.'

Annie reached over and squeezed her hand.

Kate closed her eyes. She had been granted life—a life to be lived to the full, not to fade in the shadows of the past.

~

Under Aunty's instruction, Brendan had brought Vince's old bed into the sitting room and moved the sofa and one armchair out. Aunty said the doctor had wanted Kate to go to a convalescent hospital but she had convinced him Kate would recover faster in familiar surroundings. He had said Kate should have her own room where, if she needed rest, she would be undisturbed.

Kate lay in the bed, pillows mounded behind her. Aunty was in the armchair, knitting, finishing a long cardigan jacket in emerald green wool. She said she had started it when Kate was admitted to hospital—each stitch carried a prayer for Kate's recovery.

'I can't remember falling ill.'

'Mrs Ryan said you were scrubbing the floor in the kitchen and just collapsed. She ran out into the street calling for help. There was a doctor visiting across the road and he took one look at you and arranged for an ambulance.'

A tear trickled down Kate's cheek. 'I wish I could have done that for Ned. I put a message in the box early in the morning. It was taken but no one came. Then I sent that message to Brendan. The priest came straight away but the doctor was over an hour after.'

'They do their best,' Aunty said gently. 'They have had hundreds of people to deal with.'

'I keep thinking, if he'd been in hospital sooner, he might have survived.'

'Who can say?' Aunty stared ahead, her eyes unfocussed. 'Life is full of *if onlys*. Nothing will be gained by tormenting yourself. He is at peace.'

'And how is Mrs Ryan?'

'She's staying with Frank until Tom gets home.'

'Whenever that will be.'

'She received a letter saying around the twentieth of this month.'

Kate sat upright, a thrill shivering through her. Two more weeks and life would truly begin again!

'You didn't say!'

'Oh Kate, I was so overjoyed at having you home, it slipped my mind.' She gripped the arms of her chair and stood up. 'And there's something else.'

Kate heard her rummaging in a drawer in the kitchen.

Brendan came to the doorway. 'I'm off to bed. Sleep well, Kate.'

He turned away but Kate called him back.

'I meant to ask, the boy who brought you the message about Ned, did you give him the thruppence I told him he could have.'

'Thruppence! He said you had promised him a shilling. I didn't believe that but I gave him sixpence.'

Kate laughed, 'The cheeky little rascal.'

Aunty was now standing next to Brendan.

'Speaking of rascals,' Kate said, 'have you seen anything of the Kelly boys?'

'Gus is back and he came around with a bottle of porter like he promised. We shared a small glass or two and toasted the future. Himself,' Aunty nodded toward Brendan, 'was not impressed. Joe is still waiting to be sent home.'

'It's a long wait for some of them,' Brendan said. 'Hopefully, they'll all be home by the end of the year.'

Aunty came over to Kate and kissed her on the forehead. 'I forgot to give you this too.' She laid an envelope in Kate's lap.' As she pulled the door to, she said, 'Sweet dreams, my treasure.'

Kate didn't hear Aunty. She had torn the envelope open and was already reading.

> Well, my darling,
>
> I am coming home. With my latest run of luck, I was sure that I would be sent back to France to wait until the final ship left. They clearly want to be rid of me. Perhaps they were worried I would catch some other nasty disease and take up even more of their time. Or else they have mixed me up with some other poor Tom Ryan who has been here longer.
>
> The leg has mended and I am now at Salisbury where they are preparing us for freedom. There are a variety of classes on offer with the aim of helping us find jobs once we are demobilised. I suppose it keeps us out of trouble.
>
> I do not have an exact date but I hope to be home by July at the latest. When I get home there is so much we have to do to make up for all the pictures and dances we have missed. And all the things we have not done before. Perhaps a trip on a paddle steamer to Sorrento for a picnic to the accompaniment of a band?
>
> And I will have to meet your family. I want to see where you grew up. I want so much, Kate, but most of all, I want you. I want you with me for the rest of my life.
> Each second that ticks by brings that closer, my love.

Kate's heart was racing. The waiting was nearly over.

65

Kate stood on the verandah staring down the yard as the dusk settled. Inside she could hear Aunty Mary moving about in the kitchen, further off, Brendan emptying the till.

Tom would be home by now. Mrs Ryan had sent a brief letter saying she expected it would be dark by the time they got back from the finalising depot, but they would both visit tomorrow.

Kate knew, in his place, she would have run straight to him, no matter how late, how dark the night was. She did her best to push away the disappointment—he would be tired, he would need a bath, perhaps he no longer liked going out after dark.

She walked along the path towards the back of the yard. In the corner of their yard, the chooks were sleeping, heads settled on their breasts, snuggled together along the roosts.

Kate.

His voice was clear in her head. Perhaps he did want to come but he needed to stay with his mother.

Kate.

Louder now.

She turned.

He was standing at the start of the path.

It was not leaping joy she felt but a longing so deep it hurt, just to be with him, to lay the palm of her hand against his cheek, to slide her fingers between his, to hold on to him and never let go.

They moved towards each other, ocean swimmers in sight of the shore.

He reached out, brushed a whisp of hair from her face, and kissed her, a gentle kiss, as if he didn't believe this was real. Then his arms were around her, or was it hers around him? She kissed him back and there was only him in the whole world.

They broke away laughing. 'I thought I would never get back to you.' He said it first but it was her thought too.

They walked back towards the house and sat on the verandah, Kate pressed close against his side.

'Mother said you almost died of the flu.' There was a tremor in his voice.

'I couldn't die—I said I would be here when you came home.'

His arm tightened around her. 'And you are truly well?'

'I am. I tire easily but with you here it won't be long before I'm fit to go out dancing every night of the week.'

'I don't know that I'm fit enough for that.' He kissed her again, a slow gentle kiss. 'I can't stay long. Mother thinks I am in the bath. Which I do sorely need.' He tried to move away but she held him fast. 'I am a bit whiffy.'

She pressed her nose against his neck, breathing in the scent of his skin. 'I haven't noticed.' He stretched his neck away but she moved closer, sniffing again, her lips on his neck now.

No.' He groaned. 'Not a good idea.' He stood up, laughing. 'Not yet.'

She jumped up, laughing too. There was a familiarity between them that had been absent before. She felt she knew him through and through.

Aunty opened the door. 'I heard— Tom! You're back.'

'I am, Mrs Burke.' He went over and kissed her cheek.

'Your mother said you would be around tomorrow afternoon.'

'I'd come in the morning but I have some business to attend to first. Now I must get back. Mother will be wondering what has happened to me.'

'I'll walk with you to the corner,' Kate said.

They stopped in the street, near the door to the house and moved into the porch, kissing again. She wanted the kissing never to stop.

But it did and she went with him to the corner and watched as he crossed Sydney Road and headed up towards Munro Street.

She wondered how soon they could be married.

~

Mrs Ryan threw her arms around Kate and burst into tears.

'Please don't cry, Mrs Ryan or I'll start too.'

The old lady sniffed. 'I am so happy to see you.' She kept hold of Kate's hand as they went into the sitting room which had now been returned to normal. Kate sat on the sofa, Mrs Ryan beside her, tightly clasping her hand as if she was afraid Kate would run away.

Kate had never known Mrs Ryan to be so talkative, chatting on about her time with Frank and his family, how well the Council had fumigated and cleaned her house once she was over the influenza, what an angel Kate had been looking after her. No one, not even Aunty, could get a word in.

She didn't speak of Ned.

Kate stared down at her hand, still held firmly in Mrs Ryan's grip. She glanced up, across to Tom, exiled to the armchair opposite. She would rather be holding his hand.

Tom was staring at her, that crinkle of amusement at the corners of his eyes, the merest hint of a smile.

Kate felt a flush rising up her neck and forced herself to look away.

Aunty brought in the tea tray and, finally, Mrs Ryan released her hold on Kate.

Brendan was behind Aunty with a plate of ginger biscuits. He lowered himself into the other armchair and began talking with Tom about, of all things, how hard it was to get used to wearing ties again.

Kate hadn't realised how loud Brendan's voice was. They went on to discuss the churches and cathedrals they each had visited in England and France—both Westminster Cathedral and Abbey, Notre Dame in Paris, the Leaning Virgin of Albert Cathedral, and the survival of Amiens Cathedral—like a pair of good little altar boys.

Mrs Ryan stopped and listened with interest, Aunty Mary too.

'It's a miracle it survived,' Mrs Ryan said.

'It is.' Brendan nodded slowly. 'The sort of miracle that comes of men using their God-given forethought and intelligence.'

Mrs Ryan's brow wrinkled as if she didn't quite understand what Brendan was saying. She looked over at the clock on the sideboard. 'I'm sorry, Mary, we must be going. Brian Kelleher and his boys are calling in at four o'clock.'

Tom raised his eyebrows as he stood. 'Mother has arranged a roster of visitors for me.'

'Now Tom, I have not. People want to welcome you back. You have been sorely missed.'

Aunty Mary murmured her agreement.

He stood back to let his mother and Aunty Mary leave. Brendan followed them.

Tom lowered his voice. 'You haven't joined the Sacred Heart sodality, have you? Mother will be going to their meeting with Mrs Burke tomorrow afternoon.'

'I am planning to be too tired to do anything but stay at home and read a book.'

'That's a grand idea. I've already told Mother I'm going for a ride after dinner tomorrow. I'll call in here if you don't mind.'

'Why would I mind? In fact, I can't wait.'

'Tom, are you coming?' Mrs Ryan called.

He took her hand and kissed her lightly. 'Better go.' He had a gleam in his eyes when he looked at her.

Kate wanted to laugh but she barely had the breath.

~

Kate sat with her book in the sitting room. She had read the same paragraph three times and still did not know what it said.

Brendan, seated in the armchair opposite, was reading yesterday's newspaper. He folded it and placed it on the side table. 'Will you be all right by yourself if I go around to Annie's'?'

'I have my book to keep me company.'

'She is teaching me to drive.'

'Don't crash the car, it belongs to Harry.'

'I'm not that bad,' he laughed. 'And I'd say it's Annie's if possession is nine parts of the law.'

After Brendan left, Kate gave up trying to read. She laid her head against the back of the sofa and listened to the sounds of the traffic in the street, trams, motor cars, a lone motorcycle.

She jumped at the knock on the back door.

'Come in,' she called.

Tom walked in to the sitting room. He was hatless, his hair ruffled by the wind. He took off his heavy jacket and placed in on the empty chair. Underneath he was wearing the vest and trousers of his second-best suit. When he smiled at her, he looked to be exactly the man who had come into Aunty's shop and needled Mrs Miles over four years ago, but she knew that he wasn't.

He came straight over and sat close beside her, and kissed her.

Her heart racing, Kate drew back to catch her breath. She pressed her nose against his neck. 'Yes, you smell like you should. Though I must admit, your uniform was slightly stale.'

'Sorry about that. But I needed to see you.'

Kate couldn't think what to say next. All she wanted was to sit here, to feel the warmth of him along her side, to press her palms against his, to be with him. There was no need for words.

'All this time apart,' he said. 'And we have lost our tongues.'

'I'll read to you until we get them back.' She picked up her book.

Tom loosened his tie and undid his top button. He lay his head on her shoulder. 'I have dreamt of this for so long.'

Kate read three pages and stopped. Tom had fallen asleep. She gazed at him, the dark lashes resting on his weather-tanned cheeks; the lines at the corner of his eyes that had only meant laughter; his neck, strong, vulnerable, disappearing into his shirt; his lips curved in sleep, the laughter still there. She thought of the touch of his lips against hers and, without conscious thought, closed the book and dropped it gently to the floor. She eased herself along the sofa beside him and pressed her lips to his. He wound his arms around her, answering her kisses, and she gave herself into it, willingly. Later, there was a moment when she froze, the last chance to turn back. It was a heartbeat only. She looked deep into his eyes and saw the shadows and the light, saw that he knew as clearly as she did what this was. If either had spoken, the world and its mundane judgements would have entered in, but she held him tighter and for better or for worse lost herself in all that he was.

In the moments after, hearts still racing, he breathed, 'Oh Kate. My Kate, the breath of my heart, the love of my life.'

'I love you, Tom.' Yes. Heart, soul, and body. She loved him.

He kissed her once more.

She closed her eyes. She was where she was meant to be—wherever Tom was.

A car backfired in the street.

Startled, she opened her eyes and saw a flash of pure terror in his.

He clung to her, his face buried against her neck, trembling.

This war, it had marked them all.

His voice was muffled. 'I thought I'd never make it home to you.'

'All that matters now is that we are together.'

She felt his silent sigh, as if he were expelling the horror and the fear of the last two years.

Slowly, he let go of her and sat up.

Kate stood, letting her skirt fall back into modesty. She glanced around the room. One of her shoes was missing. How had that happened?

Tom rearranged his clothing and stood, tucking in his shirt, doing up all his buttons.

He reached under the side table. 'Missing this?' He grinned as he passed her the shoe.

Oh yes, he had changed. He made Kate's heart beat faster than it ever had.

She smiled back at him. 'Perhaps, now you are decent, you can put the kettle on.'

'I'm told I brew a fine pot of tea these days.'

Kate tidied the sitting room and went into her room to make sure she too was neat and decent, murmuring, 'The breath of my heart, the love of my life.'

~

Kate came out onto the verandah where Tom was sitting drinking his tea. She sat on the bench beside him and took up the cup he had set there for her.

She sipped her tea in silence, afraid to look straight at him. The rush of exultation had faded. What would he think of her now? There had been a compulsion, as if it was what life had demanded. But she had been taught that she was meant to resist it even if he could not.

'Kate.' He took the cup from her and set it aside. 'Look at me.'

He lifted her chin and stared into her eyes. 'Don't let shame sit in your heart. All we have done is borrowed time from the future, from after we are married.'

She frowned, not understanding.

'It's like borrowing against your next pay. Not something to be recommended, but necessary in an emergency.'

She raised her eyebrows. 'That was an emergency?'

There was a twitch of laughter on his lips. 'Most certainly.'

Kate covered her mouth with her hand, fighting back her own laughter. This was serious.

He drew her hand away. 'Laugh, if you want to. Laugh when you are happy. Laugh when you want to weep. It is what keeps us going through the worst and the best of times—a God-given gift.'

'You still believe in God?'

He leant back against the wall and stared up into the sky.

'I don't think Brendan does any more. Not that he has said.'

'That doesn't surprise me. Whatever I've been through, for him it's a thousand times worse. It's easy to believe in God here. But out there...' His mouth twisted. '...it was worse than Hell. Yet there were times...' He continued staring into the empty sky. 'You call on him, on Christ, and his mother, in the cold heat of it all. There are times when you see Christ in the faces of your mates, and in the stretcher bearers, the doctors and the nurses, and in the chaplains in the casualty clearing stations, in those who crawl out under fire to bring comfort to the dying. But the big feller with the white beard, I'm not so sure. If I had employed Him to create a world and take care of it, I'd sack him without pay.'

Kate held her breath. She didn't know how to answer him, didn't know that she wanted to.

He was staring down the yard, his face stiff, scowling. He jerked his head and stood up. 'Enough of this. We have far better things to talk about.'

Kate stood and took his hand in hers. He was trembling again. She wrapped her arms around him and held him fast, her head against his chest, hearing the hammer of his heart.

'Kate.' He sighed, long and drawn out.

She looked up at him.

He smiled at her, his eyes clear of trouble.

She let go and Tom bent and picked up the tea cups.

'I have a fortnight's leave before I am discharged and there's a few things I need to get done before I talk the Railways into giving me a job. Would you be free tomorrow morning to come to the city with me?'

Kate followed him into the kitchen. 'I'll make sure I am.'

'Tomorrow, we'll buy a ring. And, after, go somewhere nice for dinner.'

There would be time, too, to go to confession at St Francis's. It had not felt like sin but Kate accepted what her faith and the world around her said. And, with contrition and the resolve not to give in to temptation again, she would be forgiven in the privacy of the confessional. If the world knew, it would be far less forgiving—whispers would always follow her.

She would go to the church first, so there would be no shadows on her conscience when Tom placed the ring on her finger.

She slid her arm around his waist.

He kissed her lightly and said, 'Let's go and find my mother and your aunty and give them something to celebrate. But first come out and see what I bought yesterday morning.'

Kate's eyes lit up. 'You've bought a motorcycle?'

'How do you...?

'I heard a motorcycle but it didn't occur to me that it could be you. And a sidecar I hope.'

'I thought I'd be in trouble if I didn't.'

'I'll get my hat and coat.' She almost skipped along the passage to her room.

66

July 1919

The treaty ending the war, the Treaty of Versailles, was signed on the twenty-eighth of June. Eight days later, on the first Sunday of July, every city, town and village throughout the British Empire celebrated the Proclamation of Peace.

The proclamation was read at a service held at the Coburg Town Hall. A massed choir sang and the Coburg Municipal Band played. The bandmaster blew his trumpet to the four corners of the hall. Kate heard that it was spine tingling. Prayers were said by a number of the local Protestant ministers so Catholics could not go. That morning, though, every church no matter what its faith held a special service.

High Mass sung at St Paul's. Some of the returned soldiers came in uniform, Brendan included, and sat in the front pews. Tom sat further back, wearing his Sunday suit, Kate sat on one side of him, his mother on the other. The church was packed to overflowing, many showing open relief that peace had come, and that the plague was abating. Silent tears were shed for the dead, buried so far away. All fervently hoped they had seen the end of war.

The *Te Deum* was sung by the choir at the end.

Aeterna fac cum sanctis tuis in gloria numerari.

Make them to be numbered with Thy Saints in glory everlasting.

~

9th July 1919

Dear Kate

I hope this finds all of you well.

The flurry of letters late last month gave us quite a surprise but it prepared us for Tom Ryan's arrival. He is a pleasant young man. He will have told you that your father is happy for him to marry you. He is sober and hardworking and well-mannered and it is clear he cares for you. I know appearances can be deceiving so it was good to have Mary's views on him. I was touched by Mrs Ryan's letter and what she said about you and your care for her and her grandson when they both were ill with influenza. We have been fortunate that there have been few cases here. It is one of the benefits of living in the bush.

Otherwise, I am lost for words. While I knew of your friendship with Tom, I had no idea he was more than someone who had lent you a book. You could have given me a hint. One thing I will not agree to is a rushed marriage. This engagement must be at least six months. I will not have people thinking you have to marry quickly. You should both think about that and the way it affects your reputation. Early January next year seems a good time to me. If you are satisfied with that let me know and I will begin arranging it. I will write to Mrs Ryan and invite her to stay with us for as long as she likes after the wedding. Another thing I insist on is that you come back home by September at the very latest. I want to spend some time with my eldest daughter before she marries and leaves me forever. I have missed you, Kate.

I truly am happy for you both. We would be delighted if you would visit us now and then once you are married. Tom got on well with Jim. He seems to be every bit as silly about these motorcycles.

I will close for now my dear daughter wishing you every happiness in the years ahead.

I look forward to having you home.

Your loving mother. X

Kate laughed. 'I am lost for words'—then Mum had gone on to write nearly another page.

It had taken Mum nearly two weeks to write despite Tom saying he had received a warm welcome from her parents. Kate had wondered if the silence meant her mother was cross with her for not going up with Tom. The journey would have exhausted her and, most probably, Mum would have insisted she was not strong enough to come back to Melbourne.

They would have to accept the six month wait—for everything. It was such a relief that she didn't have to write back and tell Mum that the wedding simply had to be sooner. The gossips, both at home and in Coburg, would have had a field day. But she couldn't go back home in September—she would have to endure over three months without seeing Tom. She would find excuses to delay it as long as she could.

~

In true Melbourne style, Peace Day arrived with a cold, biting wind and the threat of rain. A public holiday had been proclaimed so Kate, Annie, and Reenie and their families went into the city to watch the parade of returned soldiers. The city was crowded but they managed to squeeze in behind the barriers at the top of Collins Street, around the corner from the Federal Parliament House.

Despite the louring sky, the city was brightly decorated. Flags, the Australian and the Union Jack and those of the Allied nations, flew from upper windows of buildings or were displayed at the front of shops. Bunting in red, white and blue was strung from verandahs. Along the route of the march, banners stretched across the street, each with the name of a battle from Gallipoli and Pozières near the beginning to Villers-Bretonneux and Palestine towards the end. Brightly coloured streamers fluttered everywhere, many unfurled by those sitting at first and second storey windows. Above, five aeroplanes performed stunts to the gasps and amazement of the crowd.

At a quarter past ten the march set off from Princes Bridge into Swanston Street to the pealing of bells from St Paul's Cathedral and a roar of welcome. It did a circuit of the city before reaching the top of Collins Street where Kate, Aunty Mary and the others waited. First came a stream of cars carrying wounded and invalided men from the military hospitals and with them the nurses in their grey uniforms, scarlet capes and white veils. They took up position near the saluting base at Federal Parliament House to watch the rest of the procession. Thirteen platoons of sailors were cheered as they marched by. The cheering increased in volume at the sight of the Light Horse. After them came the Camel, Cyclist and Flying Corps. At eleven o'clock the head of the parade halted at the saluting base where the dignitaries stood.

A bugler sounded the Last Post. As the notes carried, the soldiers stood to attention and the crowd fell silent, men removed their hats and all heads were bowed, all thinking of those tens of thousands— soldiers, sailors and airmen, and twenty-five nurses—lying dead so far from home. Except for muffled sobs, the hush spread through the streets. Then, as if shaken from a solemn reverie, the parade moved on.

The battalions were divided into groups, each group led by a Brigadier General on foot. They marched with precision, in the same steady rhythm as they had when Kate had watched the farewell parade in December nearly five years ago. Then they had held themselves straight and tall, their faces tanned and grim, marching in ranks of four, rifles with fixed bayonets on their shoulders, a solid mass of men moving as one. Now they were spread across the road in ranks of twelve, in uniform but without their rifles. Not all looked straight ahead, some glanced towards the crowd, grinning at a family member or a friend glimpsed beyond the barriers. No longer a solid mass but men bound forever by what they had endured.

Amid the tramp of feet, the pealing bells, the bands and the cheering, the 14th Battalion came into view. Reenie was jumping up and down and waving. She cupped her hands around her mouth and sounded a loud coo-ee. Pat Casey turned his head and grinned. He was the only man Kate now knew from the 14th. She hoped that among the ranks of those marching past were some of the men she had met when she was with Jack at Broadmeadows

Camp or in Royal Park, or the men who had delivered messages for him when he couldn't get leave. At the thought of Jack, and of Bert, her throat tightened. She glanced at a young woman beside her, dressed in black. She wore, pinned to her coat, a sweetheart brooch enamelled in blue and yellow, the colours of the 14th Battalion. She stared as the Battalion marched by, her face empty of everything but grief, a grief that in that moment stabbed Kate too. Kate took hold of the young woman's hand. She held on to Kate until the 14th had passed them. She turned and, with a nod of acknowledgement, faded into the crowd.

Kate gazed after the woman as if watching the ghost of herself from another life. Around her, not everyone was cheering and waving flags. Some stood silent, stiff with self-control, others wept openly. Today's celebration of peace and of victory was for many a day of remembrance of the lost.

Annie grabbed her arm. 'The 7th is coming.'

Kate did not have to look hard to find Brendan. He was marching beside Harry, both a half head taller than the men beside them. Aunty Mary stood, her shining eyes fixed on her son as he marched past, now the pride of her life. She wore her Mothers' Badge pinned to her coat, a black ribbon hanging between two white metal bars with the Rising Sun badge and two sprigs of wattle embroidered on it in gold. A single star was set in the middle of the bottom bar, a star for Vincent, the son she had lost.

At intervals between the marching battalions the war trophies captured from the Turks and the Germans were paraded: machine guns, field guns on infantry wagons, a massive grey tank lumbering slowly along.

The 59th Battalion marched past and Kate caught sight of Tom. She stretched up and waved her flag furiously, calling his name. He looked across at her, smiling, but maintained discipline and did not wave back.

When the last battalion had passed the dignitaries at the saluting base, they marched to the Carlton Gardens where light refreshments and cigarettes were available for them. And, the parade over, the day was theirs. They could go to the races at Caulfield, or to the football, where they would be admitted free of charge. Or spend their day in whatever way took their fancy. A day to be spent as they pleased before they faced the reality of the peace.

67

The rain that had held off through the parade started falling as they arrived at the Caseys' house.

Mrs Ryan was in the sitting room with Teresa, the youngest of the Casey girls, who was reading a story book to the old lady. Mrs Ryan looked happier than she had for the last two years, more like the woman who, on the night Tom had shown off his step dancing in Bell Street, had told Kate mothers' tales of him.

She had not come with them to watch Tom march but had taken nine-year old Teresa to Coburg's main celebration of the peace, a carnival for the children of the town at the recreation reserve. Kate wondered if, while she had worried for her son, she still had reservations about his service, partly in loyalty to what she knew would have been her late husband's views.

'Teresa and I had a wonderful time at the carnival. We even had a ride on the merry-go-round.'

'We?' Kate asked.

'Indeed, I had a ride too.' Her eyes lit up. 'There were all sorts of sideshows and Teresa won a tin of sweeties at the hoopla stall. She has a very good aim for such a little girl.'

Mrs Ryan stood up. 'I'll check the sausage rolls and put the kettle on.'

Kate, Annie and Reenie handed around the sandwiches while Mrs Casey took care of the tea. Nick swallowed five sandwiches and two sausage rolls and disappeared out the door, now the rain had stopped, to find a mate to kick a ball around with.

After everyone had eaten, the young women took their cups of tea with them and sat on the front verandah.

'Are you glad to be back home, Reenie?' Annie asked.

'I am. And it has cured me of any dream of being a nurse.' She sipped her tea. 'When the boys first left for overseas, I imagined myself a nurse in the grey uniform with the scarlet cape, in France, wiping fevered brows. I now know how hard nursing is and I wasn't dealing with wounded men. Don't tell Mum but it was mainly skivvying, washing out bedpans and vomit basins. But it needed to be done and I'm glad I could help.'

'You managed to avoid getting sick?'

'Luckily, but when I came home Mum put me in the sleepout for a week. She is terrified of any of us getting it but it is truly on the wane.' She drained her cup. 'I've talked Mum and Dad into letting me train as a teacher next year. I think I might be good at that.'

'Yes!' Annie clapped her hands. 'I can imagine you at the front of a class. You wouldn't need to use the cane—you would enthrall the children.'

'And what about you, Annie?' Reenie asked. 'Any plans?'

'I'll continue teaching. I love it—helping boisterous girls grow into fine young ladies.'

'Nothing else?' Reenie persisted, an eyebrow arched.

'No,' she said firmly. 'Nothing else.'

Reenie turned to Kate. 'You're quiet.'

'It's been a long day.'

It wasn't that Kate was up early and had spent hours standing watching the parade. When Reenie had started talking about influenza and nursing, she had thought of Ned. It was little more than two months since his death. Tom had wanted no party because, if they had held one, there would have been singing and dancing. They would feel Ned's absence and glimpse him beside the fiddler, hear him in the silence after the music stopped.

'I don't have to ask what your plans are, Kate. Now, show me that ring.'

Kate held out her hand, light glittering across the row of modest diamonds in an elegant filagree setting.

'Oooh, sparkly.' Reenie held Kate's hand examining the ring.

'Can I try it on?'

'Absolutely not!'

'Spoilsport.' Reenie laughed. 'Some girls don't mind at all.' She smiled and tossed her head. 'Now. One thing I can't wait to do is to go back to the pictures. Would you two be interested in going one night this week?'

'Oh, yes,' Kate said.

'Do you know what's on?' Annie asked.

'I don't think it matters at all.' Kate laughed. 'Monkeys driving motor cars would be good enough for me.'

~

Kate and Aunty Mary walked Mrs Ryan home and later, in the evening, went to the recreation reserve. Although the rain had stopped, the planned campfire concert had been cancelled, but the fireworks display went ahead.

They stood with the Caseys and the Watkinses as the sky lit up, rockets bursting into brilliant colours and spreading out across the now clear sky. A massive bonfire had been built of brushwood, timber, and anything else that would burn. An effigy of the Kaiser had been hoisted to the top and the wood below well doused with kerosene. At half past eight, on the dot, the Mayor of Coburg set fire to the wood. The flames rose steadily through the pile, licking upwards to the effigy, burning off the clothing. When the head tumbled downward into the bonfire, a massive cheer rang around the reserve.

'Will you listen to that?' Aunty Mary laughed and looked behind her.

Two soldiers came out of the darkness, the taller with his arm across the other's shoulder, singing their own version of *Tipperary*.

> *It's a long way to Coburg Tow-oun,*
> *It's a long way to go.*

'Brendan! You're drunk!'

'Mother, I am stone cold sober.' He lifted his arm from Tom's shoulder. 'And my arm was around my cobber here to ensure he was walking straight.'

Tom stood to his full height, his hat at a rakish angle. 'And I'm not all that drunk either.'

'But,' Kate couldn't help smiling, 'you do admit you are a little bit drunk.'

He held up his finger and thumb, half an inch apart. 'Just a tiny bit.' He came over and slid his arm around her but, thankfully, didn't kiss her with everyone watching.

'Well,' said Mrs Casey, 'It's late, we should be getting home.' She called the girls and Nick over to her.

'Mrs Casey,' Brendan said. 'We took Pat home and put him to bed. More put him on top of the bed. He's well and truly shicker. I pulled his boots off and he did have enough sense to do what he had to with his eye.'

'Oh, that is good. Thank you, Brendan.'

'Did Pat have a good time though?' Mr Casey asked.

'He did indeed. The young ladies were...' He stopped, aware of the women listening. 'They were very impressed with him. Pat's a fine story teller when he gets going.'

Kate could well imagine the young ladies, whoever they were, being impressed with Pat.

'I wouldn't get him up for Mass tomorrow.' Brendan grinned. 'I'd say his head will be penance enough for missing one Sunday.'

'I thought the hotels were shut today,' Mrs Watkins said primly.

'They were, but there are ways and means.'

Both Mr Casey and Mr Watkins laughed.

'Any idea where Harry is?' Mr Watkins asked.

'He's home too. Happy but fully in charge of himself.'

Annie looked up at Brendan. 'If you are stone cold sober, your head will be clear enough for Mass.'

'It could well be.' He smiled at her.

Kate watched them, certain it was not Brendan who needed the cattle prod.

Each family went its own way in the misty rain that glistened on every surface. As they walked along Sydney Road, Brendan said, 'It's pretty wild in the city at the moment, close to riot in places from what we last heard. It's a pity—it started out a good day.'

'Is that why you left?' Kate asked Tom.

'We left because the pubs were closed. A mate knew of a place in Fitzroy where we could get a quiet drink after hours. That's where I ran into Brendan and company. Men who came in later said there was a lot of hooliganism in the city, trams commandeered, their windows broken, one even lifted off the rails. Cars *borrowed*, shop windows smashed. The police were out with horses and batons. We were well out of it.'

As they neared the shop, Tom asked, 'Do you think, before I go home, I could have a cup of tea?'

'Of course. Would a cheese sandwich help?'

'Oh God, Kate, you're an angel.'

'You are drunk.'

'Mother doesn't touch a drop and she says you're an angel too. She wants us to live with her when we are married.'

Kate stopped on the footpath. She hadn't thought about what would happen to Mrs Ryan after they were married. She did like the old lady and, in some way, she was now tied to her. It would be cruel to leave her by herself.

'I would like that.'

'Frank used to say I was the white-haired boy but I've lost the title. As far as Mother is concerned you are the white-haired girl and can do no wrong. If we ever have a disagreement, she will take your side even if I'm in the right.'

'That is a very good reason to live with her.' She brushed her lips against his.

Brendan stood holding the gate open. 'Will you two come inside and do your courting in private?'

They hurried towards him and, as Kate walked through, she asked, 'Would you like a cup of tea and a cheese sandwich too?'

'I certainly would, Kate. We haven't eaten much today.'

Tom and Brendan sat together on the seat out the back, talking and smoking, while Aunty Mary made the tea and Kate the sandwiches.

Kate carried out Tom's tea and sandwich, as Brendan said, '...and one wit from within the ranks called out, *Twist his ear, sergeant.*'

Both men roared with laughter.

Brendan glanced across at Kate and stood. 'Tea's made then?' He looked embarrassed.

She handed Tom his tea and set the plate on the seat.

'Funny story?' she asked as she sat beside him.

Tom nodded his head. 'Mmmmm.'

He wasn't going to explain—it was probably something rude.

He finished his mouthful. 'This is the best thing I've ever eaten.'

'You haven't eaten one of Aunty Mary's Sunday dinners. I've seen boys leave the table barely able to walk.'

He washed the rest of the sandwich down with the tea and laid his head back against the wall. 'Kate, you have no idea how happy I am.'

'I might. I'm happy too.

'I wish we didn't have to wait so long but your mother is right.'

'Five months isn't too long, not if we keep busy.'

'Working?' He screwed up his face. 'I don't know about that.'

'No, the pictures, dancing, outings with the old ones.'

'The chaperones,' he laughed. 'Well, all this waiting will give us time for the courtship we have missed.'

'It will.' Kate did want the courtship they would have had if Tom had not enlisted—happy, free of care, no shadows or worries over it.

'A dance next Saturday, then? We can drag Brendan and Annie, or Reenie, along with us.' He put the teacup down and got up from the seat. 'I can't imagine the old ones wanting to do the two-step.'

'Oh, you never know,' Kate laughed. She stood and looked into his face. 'I haven't danced with anyone since you left so Saturday can't come fast enough.'

She clung to him, lost for a moment as they kissed. She was the one to step away this time, thinking she was wrong, five months was a long time.

68

August 1919

The Coburg emergency hospital closed in the middle of the month. The second wave of influenza had now waned but it had gone on far longer than the first and the cost was so much higher—three hundred and six cases had been admitted to the hospital and many more had suffered at home. There had been nineteen deaths of influenza and three prematurely-born infants who did not survive.

Peace Day had left Kate with the feeling that all was done, the war was over, and life would begin again. But the past could not be left behind so easily. So many of those they knew were gone, bright lives cut short. As long as they drew breath, those who had loved them would never forget.

On the last Saturday in August, a beautiful afternoon with clear skies, a memorial service was held at Lake Reserve to honour those men from Coburg who had returned and to pay respect to those who had fallen. A memorial avenue of trees was to be planted—Monterey cypresses, Dutch elms, and plane trees—each with a metal plaque dedicated to the memory of a Coburg serviceman who had given his life for family, country and King. It would be a place they could visit and remember those not buried in family graves.

The returned soldiers marched to the reserve led by the Coburg Municipal Band. Those who had watched and waited and prayed at home came in their hundreds, families and friends, and others who simply wished to show their respect. Kate stood with Mrs Ryan and Aunty Mary who wore her mother's medal pinned to her jacket. The Watkinses and the Caseys were nearby. Mrs Johnson was at the very front of the crowd, of course. Kate recognised many of those who regularly made their way through the doors of the shop, even Mrs Miles, her substantial chest puffed out as if she had personally provided an entire section of soldiers.

The memorial service was to be addressed by Brigadier-General Elliott. Many Coburg men had been under his command—those who had served in the 7th Battalion at Gallipoli like Brendan, Vince, Pat and Harry or later, in France, in the 15th Brigade like Tom. The soldiers called him by the nickname given to him early in the war, Pompey. Kate had heard the returned men speak of him not just with immense respect but with what could only be described as love.

The Brigadier-General was late. There were murmurs among the men that Pompey was never late. A message arrived that his car had broken down so the Mayor, dressed in his ceremonial robes and chain, began the service.

The National Anthem was played by the band, followed by *All People that on Earth Do Dwell*. The Mayor presented illuminated certificates to the returned soldiers present or to their relatives, and to the relatives of those who had fallen. When Brendan's turn came, he went forward to receive not only his own certificate but Vince's too.

Finally, the Brigadier-General arrived. He was a tall, solid, ruddy-faced man. There was silence as he addressed those gathered there. Kate swallowed the ache in her throat, forced back the tears she thought she had finished with, as he spoke of Gallipoli and of the hand of providence in the strong currents that had taken them beyond the planned landing place where the Turkish soldiers had been ready for them, not just with guns, but with a hundred yards of barbed wire hidden in the sea beyond the shore. 'Not a man would have got ashore.' Not only Jack and Vince who were lost, but those who had made it home, Brendan, Pat and Harry. Tangled in barbed wire, all would have drowned or been killed by Turkish bullets. And those at home would have drowned in the grief.

She looked across at Brendan, standing straight-backed, staring ahead. Had she been beside him, she would have taken his hand in hers.

Brigadier-General Elliott ended his address by saying that the Coburg men under his command had proved themselves second to none. He then planted the first tree in honour of Private J Hopkins, and Mrs Elliott planted the next in honour of Lieutenant Catron. They were followed by the mayor and mayoress who each planted a tree. When Aunty Mary's turn came, with Brendan's help, she placed the small cypress in the ground, pressing the dirt down around it—a memorial to Vince they could visit. Altogether one hundred and sixty-two trees were planted by relatives and friends. The final piece of music was played, 'Dead March' from *Saul*.

Buglers sounded the Last Post.

It was over.

Kate walked away to the lake's edge, leaving Tom with the group of returned men surrounding Pompey Elliott. The blue sky was reflected in the lake, the water sparkling in the sunshine. An ibis, in a flurry of wings, took flight and soared up from the water's edge into the sky.

She thought of a day that was another life away when an ibis had flown down and landed high in a tree opposite. She had stood here with Jack. Then she had been young and full of hope and Jack was the love of her life. The war had changed everything. It had changed her—she was no longer that young innocent incapable of imagining life's cruelties. She was older now, more clear-eyed and aware of her own frailties. And she had been granted another love, a good man she loved entirely, who she would walk beside into the unknowable future. Yet, always, there would be a tender corner of her heart that was Jack's alone.

She drew a deep breath and, letting it out slowly, turned and walked up the slope to Tom.

Epilogue

Kate stared down at her feet, pale and smooth in the clear water, a light froth of bubbles touching her ankles. Tom's feet, beside hers, were as pale in the water but larger and bonier.

He was staring out at the horizon where sea and sky merged into one. His boots were laced together and hanging over his shoulder.

'Mum arrives on Monday. She says she has to make sure I have all sorts of linen and other bits and pieces that a girl from a respectable family brings with her when she is married. I thought I could come up with some excuse to stay until the end of the month but Mum insists I am to go home with her when she leaves.'

Tom continued to look out across the glistening water. 'When will that be?'

'Next Saturday, I imagine.'

'That will leave seven weeks.'

'I suppose seven weeks isn't so long.'

'Forty-nine days exactly.'

'I prefer counting in days—they go faster.'

They both laughed.

'So where do you want to go after, for the honeymoon?'

Kate smiled into the sunlight. 'Anywhere. No, somewhere I have never been. But there has to be a beach.'

'Can you swim?'

'Not really. I can paddle.'

'I can teach you but you'll need a swimming costume.'

Kate blinked. 'I couldn't wear one of those. When they are wet, they don't hide anything.'

'I'd find somewhere quiet.'

Kate glanced up at him. He was grinning.

'One thing I've learnt is that it doesn't matter whether you are dressed in the height of fashion or are stark naked, if you carry yourself as if you are the best dressed person in the room, people will take you at your own estimation.'

Kate gasped and hit his forearm with the back of her hand. 'It was you!'

'What was me?'

'You were one of those men cavorting in the altogether in that canal in France.'

Tom laughed. 'I admit nothing.'

'You don't need to admit anything.' Kate laughed too. 'I will always know.'

She slid her hand into his, his fingers winding through hers. They stood side by side, their faces raised to the sun, the breeze eddying around them warming even the shadows.

~~~

A Soliloquy

A bluish haze in the far astern
And galloping seas between,
The last-long look at one's native land,
Where boyhood days we've seen.
For our bows are dipped in smothering spray,
Our course to the setting sun.
We're bound for the front, with foot and horse,
And a-clanking steel and gun.

The transport reels in the battering seas,
All her decks with troops asprawl,
A foamy wake from her churning screw,
Where the billows rise and fall;
The wind in the shrouds moans constant plaint.
Does it mourn a grim fate sealed?
Does it tell of the blood-red clash of war,
And graves in a frozen field?

The troopers lie on the deck asprawl
(Who cares if the wild seas rave?)
A pleasing sense is a pipe aglow
(Who spoke of a frozen grave?)
Then pass the pouch with the fragrant weed,
And shuffle the cards anew;
There's room for the lad with quip and jest;
No room for a whining crew.

While the clamouring gulls in wheeling flight,
Swoop down in our bubbling wake,
There are those at home, with cheerful smiles
Yet whose hearts are like to break,
For a woman's lot is to watch and wait

And stifle the grief that stirs,
While the man strides forth in careless strength,
A-swagger in boots and spurs.

Those lips now clasping the smoking stem,
Or curling in gruff grimace,
Have whispered fond vows and pressed a kiss
On a clinging tear-stained face.
Will they clasp in death on a foreign field
On a couch of earth-soaked red?
Or curl in a torturing fever-grip
On a medical service bed?

The transport reels in the battering seas,
In the smothering, flying spray,
And the ones at home, with straining hearts,
They watch and wait and pray,
For the cards are dealt with careless flip
As the round of the game begins;
But the clutching hand of sombre Fate,
Aye, will hold the card that wins.

William O'Brien
(1882-1936)

I came across this poem while researching possible titles for the novel. It was first published in Australia in the Queensland Labor newspaper *The Worker* of 17 December 1914. It may have been written aboard the troopship *Omrah* and posted at one of the ports enroute as the 1st Light Horse Brigade travelled to Egypt. The poem was reprinted in Australian newspapers three more times in February and March 1915. I have been unable to find mention of it elsewhere since. The poem shows great depth of understanding of what lay ahead for the members of the Australian Imperial Force as well as the effect on those at home.

When he enlisted on 20 August 1914, William O'Brien was a clerk with the Queensland Railway Service from Fig Tree Pocket, on the Brisbane River, near Indooroopilly. He gave his age as thirty but he was actually thirty-three years old. He was 5' 11¾" tall with a fresh complexion, blue eyes and black hair. He embarked on the transport *Omrah* from Brisbane on 24 September 1914.

Initially William served with the 1st Light Horse Brigade Train, 5th Company Army Service Corps, arriving at Gallipoli in early May 1915. In October 1915, he contracted dysentery and enteritis. He was hospitalised at Mudros, on Lemnos, and then sent to St Patrick's Hospital, Malta. He was discharged to Heliopolis, Egypt on 13 December 1915, just before the withdrawal from Gallipoli.

With the reorganisation of units in Egypt due to the great loss of men at Gallipoli, William was transferred to the 2nd Light Horse Regiment in January 1916. The following July, he was transferred to the 1st Light Horse Machine Gun Squadron and took part in the Battle of Romani. The Squadron was involved in the Egypt and Palestine campaigns in 1916 to 1918.

In February 1917 William was promoted a 2nd Lieutenant and, in July, a full Lieutenant. At Beersheba on 3 November, he suffered a gunshot wound to the left arm. He embarked for Australia on 28 December 1917 on the NZT *Tofua*, arriving on 30 January 1918. William was discharged from service on 17 April 1918.

Back in Australia, he returned to work as a clerk with the Queensland Railways and in 1926 married Honora O'Sullivan; they had one son. William was actively involved in the Returned Soldiers and Sailor's League and the local progress association. He contributed pieces to the *Bulletin*, the *Queensland Digger* and other publications. He was also described as an eloquent speaker.

William O'Brien died aged fifty-four on 13 October 1936 after an illness of six weeks. His obituary in the Brisbane *Telegraph* (17 Oct 1936, p.11) described his life as one of 'service to his country in war time and to his fellow soldiers in peace-time'.

Historical Note

World War 1 is a vast topic even when considering the involvement of a country as small as Australia was between 1914 and 1919. From a population of around five million people, 416,809 men enlisted in the First Australian Imperial Force (AIF). This was 38.7% of the male population aged between eighteen and forty-five years of age. Of these men, 331,781 served overseas and suffered 215,585 casualties (64.98%) including 60,284 deaths. Of the 2,861 Australian trained nurses, single and aged between twenty-five and forty, who served overseas in the Australian Army Nursing Service, twenty-five died.

The personal nature of the war is lost when it is described using cold statistics. To understand the reality of these statistics, we need to recognise each number as a person, someone who had family and friends waiting anxiously for news of them, or mourning them. I first encountered the weight of grief experienced as a result of this war when I took over my mother's genealogical research. In the newspapers, I read the In Memoriam notices placed year after year, even into the 1950s, for the mainly young men who had died overseas. And beyond the grief for the war dead was the grief and distress experienced in the decades that followed the war at the premature deaths of those who had returned. Then there were the struggles of those returned men who carried life altering injuries, both physical and psychic, and the effect this had on them and those around them.

The reality of the war was not hidden from those at home. They saw the effect of war on France and Belgium in the newsreels at local picture theatres. They read of the war in the letters written home, some of which were published in the newspapers, quite often in surprising detail. The scenes of the Gallipoli landing in the film *The Hero of the Dardanelles*, released within three months of the landing, were mistaken as real footage by those viewing it. In later decades, this footage was included in documentaries as such.

They knew the cost of war, not only through the lengthy casualty list but through what was happening to those around them. They knew families who had received the dreaded visit by the minister, and feared the same for themselves. They saw the maimed and scarred men who came home. And they were denied the usual rituals of mourning; they had no bodies to bury or graves to visit. And through those years of unremitting fear and anxiety, society demanded stoicism. They truly were required to 'stifle the grief that stirs'.

And the Women Watch and Wait is a work of imagination which attempts to depict the struggles of those women in Australia who watched, waited and prayed during those four long years. It is not based on any one person's life. The characters are fictional but I have drawn on family stories to build their lives. Kate and Tom's families have similar structures and something of the histories of my maternal grandparents but they are nothing like them in either appearance, personality or course of life. Like most ordinary people, the characters follow the conventional morality and mores of their time, as did the respectable of all classes and religious denominations.

The general settings are real places except for Kate's parents' farm at Smith's Creek. Smith's Creek is fictional but the farm is loosely based on my great-grandparents' farm in Gippsland. Mrs Whaley's Coffee Palace at Briagolong was real but there is some question whether it was operating in the late 1910s. Mrs Whaley would have been nearing seventy in 1917 but she was listed as proprietor in the Sands & McDougall *Directory of Victoria* up to 1925. I could find no description of the interior so have presented it as similar to most coffee palaces and tea houses of the period.

Coburg, by comparison, is very real. In 1914, it was on the northern edge of Melbourne with dairy farms and a large poultry farm within its bounds. At various times livestock wandered the streets much to the chagrin of the council ranger. It was home to a steadily increasing number of workers and their families and was a proudly self-reliant community. In later decades, Coburg gained the reputation of being the suburb with the highest level of working-class home ownership.

I have done my best to ensure that the historical timeline and my representation of Coburg is realistic and accurate. But *And the Women Watch and Wait* is not a history of Coburg so only those elements that I believe would have affected my characters are mentioned. Some events are left out because they had no direct bearing on my story's timeline. The visit on 28 May 1918 of the new Apostolic Delegate, Cardinal Cattaneo to administer the sacrament of Confirmation at St Paul's church is one such event. And, unfortunately, I could find no way to naturally include the Coburg Cowboys. They were a group of local young men who performed feats of horsemanship including trick-riding, buck-jumping and whip and lasso tricks at carnivals.

Contemporary newspapers accessed via the National Library of Australia's Trove portal have been invaluable in gaining an understanding of Coburg at this time but events were not always reported in great detail and this has meant that I have had to be creative. One instance is the public reaction to the signing of the Armistice. News came through around sunset. The *Brunswick & Coburg Leader* reported that people filled the streets and that the Coburg Municipal Band marched from Moreland Road to Bell Street, where there was some celebratory dancing underway, and back again. To bring the scene to life, I have drawn on the more descriptive reports from the surrounding suburbs of fireworks, singing and the playing of all manner of musical instruments. Kate's altercation with the pro-conscription supporter outside the Public Hall is entirely fictional. Meetings were often loud and angry—in Footscray in December 1917 a constable 'had to come between two enthusiastic ladies who seemed inclined to come to blows'. (*The Advertiser* 15 Dec 1917 p.3)

There are other areas within the novel where I have woven in stories I found in my research. There was a man at Broadmeadows Camp who 'attired in a resplendent dressing gown making all haste to the bath ... who receives a "hoy" from numerous lines'. (*Maffra Spectator* 28 Jan 1915 p.3) The Coburg Red Cross did raffle a cake sent to a soldier by his mother. 'It followed him through France and reached him only a fortnight after he had returned to Coburg.' The raffle raised two pounds. (*Brunswick & Coburg Leader* 2 Aug 1918 p.3). Towards the end of Chapter 65, Kate overhears the end of an anecdote. The complete anecdote is found in Ross McMullin's *Pompey Elliott* and was a favourite of Brigadier-General H E Elliott. Anyone who wants the complete anecdote, will need to read this excellent biography.

There are other stories reported in the newspapers that I have taken at face value as readers did at the time. *The Advocate* of 3 Jul 1915 (p.15) reported that the Catholic chaplain, Fr John Fahey 'attached to the 3rd Infantry Brigade, worked like a hero in the fighting line. When no officers were left, he took a rifle and shouted, "Come on, boys; at 'em!"' I suspect similar stories may have been told about the chaplains of other denominations. The stories of chaplains leading charges are apocryphal and always second hand—the chaplain was forbidden by the rules of war to take part in the fighting and these men took their duties seriously. *Padre, Australian Chaplains in Gallipoli and France* (Allen & Unwin, 1986) by Michael McKernan provides an excellent understanding of the role and personalities of the chaplains who accompanied the AIF, and the absolute horror of this war.

The proportion of casualties mentioned by the woman Kate argues with on page 156 comes from a letter published in the *Brunswick & Coburg Leader* (20 Oct 1916 p.2) from Brunswick councillor, F. T. Hickford, a supporter of conscription. The letter includes the statement that 'a very small percentage suffers actual death'. I have taken this as being the contemporary understanding of the level of casualties.

While Catholics enlisted at less than their proportion of the population, it was not so low that they could truly be considered to be shirking. Catholic men made up roughly 21% of the male population. The Department of Defence released figures for 1917 and 1918 which showed that Catholics made up 18.57% and 18.9% of the AIF for those two years respectively. At the time, it was suggested in *The Advocate* that the disparity was partly due to the greater number of children in the Catholic population. It is also possible that the number of male religious brothers, who were not free to enlist, might have reduced the pool from which Catholic enlistments were drawn. Interestingly, in the early part of the war, 27% of volunteers in Brunswick were Catholic. And in April 1915, the Coburg branch of the St Patrick's Society (a benefit society) made an unequivocal statement in support of enlistment: 'all members of this branch who have no ties to prevent them from so doing should offer their services to the Empire'. (*Herald* 14 Apr 1915, p.8). Those Catholics who had husbands, sons, brothers and other family fighting overseas continued in their support for their men through the war. But support for those fighting, and for the war itself, did not automatically mean support for conscription.

The form of everyday Catholicism presented in the novel is based on research as well as observations and conversations with a range of people of my grandparents' generation over the years. Most observant Catholics of the period had a deep personal piety, attended Sunday Mass and fulfilled their other religious obligations. They held nuns and priests with the utmost respect, although that respect was not infinite. A fair number, including some members of my family, considered that priests and bishops had no business telling them who to vote for at elections. They did not argue—just quietly went their own way.

All denominations had social networks centred around their

churches. These provided both social and devotional activities and encouraged younger parishioners to socialise within their faith. Catholic parishes had a number of organisations including benefit societies such as the Hibernian Catholic Benefit Society and the St Patrick Society, as well as the more political Catholic Federation. The Catholic Young Men's Society was present in most parishes and was the only parish organisation for young men. It was not strictly spiritual; its emphasis instead was on social, sporting, and educational activities and it developed debating skills in members. The sodalities were pious associations for lay people intended to foster the faith through devotional activities, prayer and spiritual talks. Close friendships often developed between members. Each sodality had a monthly communion and a meeting which members were expected to attend. The sodalities also took an active role in parish social and fundraising events. At a minimum, most parishes had branches of the Sacred Heart Sodality for adult men and for married women, and the Children of Mary for young unmarried women. Not all Catholics joined sodalities, only the more devout. Information about the operation of the sodalities comes mainly from research and interviews I conducted in the 1980s with former members as part of research for my Master of Arts.

The Requiems held for soldiers killed in action were, most likely, not routinely held. In Victoria, they seemed to be more common in the Sale Diocese, where the fictional Smith's Creek is located, though there was occasional mention of them elsewhere.

I have tried to avoid anachronisms in direct speech by checking the date of first use of words and phrases in the Oxford English Dictionary. In some instances, through my use of contemporary newspapers, I have found modern words in use decades earlier than the OED states The OED lists the first use of *a bundle of nerves* (being in a state of extreme nervousness) as 1940 but I have found the phrase used this way in Australian newspapers as early as the 1890s. I was surprised at the relative antiquity of a number of phrases too. People have been having their *work cut out for them* since 1574 and have used *to a T* to describe something exactly since 1693. They have been *cut up* by events since 1840 and Australians have been *having a fit* when situations are not to their liking since 1910. Also, I have used the term *war to end war* to describe the Great War rather than the currently more usual *war to end wars* because up to the end of 1919, this was the term most commonly used in contemporary newspapers.

Australia's involvement in the Great War is a massive topic and an almost overwhelming number of books have been written on it. I have posted on my website a partial list of works consulted while researching this novel. The following works are those I consider to be a good starting point for anyone wanting to gain an initial understanding of the war.

Beaumont, Joan *Broken Nation: Australia in the Great War.* (Allen & Unwin, 2014.)

Gammage, Bill *The Broken Years; Australian Soldiers in the Great War.* (Penguin, 1990. c.1974.)

McMullin, Ross *Pompey Elliott* (Scribe, 2008. c.2002.)

I would also recommend two novels by Australian men who served during World War 1.

Mann, Leonard *Flesh in Armour.* (Penguin. 2014. c.1932.)

Manning, Frederick *The Middle Parts of Fortune.* (Text. 2000. c.1929.)

Finally, thank you for reading this novel. I hope you have found it as worthwhile as I have found researching and writing it. And I hope, through it, I have honoured that stoic generation of women who watched and waited and the men who, at great cost, did what they saw as their duty.

Melbourne
October 2025

Quotations

Map of Coburg – adapted by Catherine Meyrick and based on a section of the map, *Municipality of Coburg* by Anderson Gowan c.1921(out of copyright) Courtesy State Library Victoria.

p.72 – 'Dardanelles Attack' *The Age* 26 Apr 1915 p.7

p.73 – 'The Dardanelles' *The Age* 28 Apr 1915 p.9

p.74 – Editorial 'It was neither kind nor fair in Britain...' *The Age* 30 Apr 1915 p.8

p.77 – 'Careers of Killed and Wounded' *The Age* 3 May 1915 p.9

p.87 – 'Australians Excel in Bayonet Attack' *The Herald* 22 May 1915 p.12

p.94 – 'the pain of earth for the joy of heaven' from 'The Sermon' *The Advocate* 6 May 1916 p.14

pp.97 – 'A terrible landing' *Brunswick & Coburg Star* 25 Jun 1915 p.1

p.116 – 'Australians leave Anzac' *The Argus* 22 Dec 1915 p.9

p.160 – 'a fine affirmative vote' *The Brunswick & Coburg Leader* 3 Nov 1916 p.2

p.232 – 'Just for a Christmas present' – rhyme on postcard by Inter-Art Co., Xmas Gift Series No. 1148, c.1914-c.1918. Held by State Library Victoria.

p.251 – 'New Offensive near Ypres' *The Age* 22 Sept 1917 p.13

p.291 – 'Victorious Australians' *The Age* 27 Apr 1918 p.13

p.299 – 'Men Cheer the News' *The Age* 17 Sept 1918 p.5

p.301 – 'my life, my sweetness and my hope' from the prayer, *Salve Regina*.

p.310 – 'The Kaiser Abdicates' *The Age* 11 Nov 1918 p.7

p.364 – *The Mystery of the Handsome Cab* by Fergus Hume, Text Publishing, c1886, 2012 edn.

p.372 – 'women mourning and weeping in this valley of tears' from the prayer, *Salve Regina*.

p.408 – 'not a man would have got ashore' *The Brunswick & Coburg Leader* 5 Sep 1919 p.1

All songs quoted are in the Public Domain as either the creator's death date is prior to 1955 or more than ninety-five years have elapsed since the date of registration of copyright.

Acknowledgements

I would like to thank everyone who has helped me with the development and publication of *And the Women Watch and Wait*.

I am particularly grateful to all who read and commented on the novel at various stages: Janine Smith, Gabrielle Higgins, Heather Lyndsey and Sarah Kirby. Most especially I would like to thank Vivienne Brereton, author of the wonderful Tudor series *The House of the Red Duke*. Vivienne's friendship, and her support through the process, has been critical, particularly through those times when I thought the whole project was beyond me. Thanks also to the Coburg Historical Society for their assistance with information about Lake Reserve.

Many thanks go to Jenny Quinlan of Historical Editorial for her detailed editorial help. Jenny has now edited three of my books and her insights and advice have helped in adding depth to the stories. Thanks also to Dee Dee of Dee Dee Book Covers for designing the beautiful cover.

Last, but by no means least, I would like to thank my family for their support over many years. I am indebted to my husband for his cheerful tolerance of domestic chaos and my random and quite strange questions. Finally, thanks to Dusty for her companionship late into many a dark night—there is nothing more conducive to writing than the gentle snoring of a cat.

About the Author

Catherine Meyrick is an Australian writer of romantic historical fiction. She lives in Melbourne, Australia, but grew up in Ballarat, a large regional city steeped in history. She has a Master of Arts in history and is a retired librarian. She is also an obsessive family historian.

Find out more about Catherine, her books and the background to her stories at

www.catherinemeyrick.com

If you have any questions about *And the Women Watch and Wait* or the history upon which it is based or, heaven forfend, you find typographic or other errors in the novel, please do not hesitate to get in touch with Catherine through the contact page on her website.

Also by Catherine Meyrick

Cold Blows the Wind

The past is never far away, never truly forgotten.

Hobart Town 1878 – a vibrant town drawing people from every corner of the earth where, with confidence and a flair for story-telling, a person can be whoever he or she wants. Almost.

Ellen Thompson is young, vivacious and unmarried, with a six-month-old baby. Despite her fierce attachment to her family, boisterous and unashamed of their convict origins, Ellen dreams of marriage and disappearing into the ranks of the respectable. Then she meets Harry Woods.

Harry, newly arrived in Hobart Town from Western Australia, has come to help his aging father, 'the Old Man of the Mountain' who for more than twenty years has guided climbers on Mount Wellington. Harry sees in Ellen a chance to remake his life.

But, in Hobart Town, the past is never far away, never truly forgotten. When the past collides with Ellen's dreams, she is forced to confront everything in life a woman fears most.

Based on a period in the lives of the author's great-great-grandparents, Sarah Ellen Thompson and Henry Watkins Woods, *Cold Blows the Wind* is not a romance but it is a story of love – a mother's love for her children, a woman's love for her family and, those most troublesome loves of all, for the men in her life. It is a story of the enduring strength of the human spirit.

www.ingramcontent.com/pod-product-compliance
Lightning Source LLC
Chambersburg PA
CBHW031946130726
47904CB00012B/86